BAMBI

Bambi saw two fawns standing side by side.

BAMBI

A Life in the Woods

By

Felix Salten

Foreword by
John Galsworthy

SIMON AND SCHUSTER

NEW YORK

1928

ISBN- 978-1-61793-016-4

TRANSLATED BY WHITTAKER CHAMBERS

ILLUSTRATIONS BY KURT WIESE

F O R E W O R D

B *AMBI* is a delicious book. For delicacy of perception and essential truth I hardly know any story of animals that can stand beside this life study of a forest deer. Felix Salten is a poet. He feels nature deeply, and he loves animals. I do not, as a rule, like the method which places human words in the mouths of dumb creatures, and it is the triumph of this book that, behind the conversation, one feels the real sensations of the creatures who speak. Clear and illuminating, and in places very moving, it is a little masterpiece.

I read it in galley proof on the way from Paris to Calais, before a channel crossing. As I finished each sheet I handed it to my wife, who read, and handed it to my nephew's wife, who read, and handed it to my nephew. For three hours the four of us read thus in silent absorption. Those who know what it is to read books in galley proof, and have experienced channel crossings, will realize that few books will stand such a test. Bambi is one of them. I particularly recommend it to sportsmen.

March 16th, 1928   JOHN GALSWORTHY

ILLUSTRATIONS

ILLUSTRATIONS—*Continued*

CHAPTER I

HE CAME INTO THE WORLD in the middle of the thicket, in one of those little, hidden forest glades which seem to be entirely open, but are really screened in on all sides. There was very little room in it, scarcely enough for him and his mother.

He stood there, swaying unsteadily on his thin legs and staring vaguely in front of him with clouded eyes which saw nothing. He hung his head, trembled a great deal, and was still completely stunned.

"What a beautiful child," cried the magpie.

She had flown past, attracted by the deep groans the mother uttered in her labor. The magpie perched on a neighboring branch. "What a beautiful child," she kept repeating. Receiving no answer, she went on talkatively, "How amazing to think that he should be able to get right up and walk! How interesting! I've never seen the like of it before in all my born days. Of course, I'm still young, only a year out of the nest, you might say. But I think it's wonderful. A child like that,

[13]

hardly a minute in this world, and beginning to walk already! I call that remarkable. Really, I find that everything you deer do is remarkable. Can he run, too?"

"Of course," replied the mother softly. "But you must pardon me if I don't talk with you now. I have so much to do, and I still feel a little faint."

"Don't put yourself out on my account," said the magpie. "I have very little time myself. But you don't see a sight like this every day. Think what a care and bother such things mean to us. The children can't stir once they are out of the egg but lie helpless in the nest and require an attention, an attention, I repeat, of which you simply can't have any comprehension. What a labor it is to feed them, what a trouble to watch them. Just think for a moment what a strain it is to hunt food for the children and to have to be eternally on guard lest something happen to them. They are helpless if you are not with them. Isn't it the truth? And how long it is before they can move, how long it is before they get their feathers and look like anything at all."

"Pardon," replied the mother, "I wasn't listening."

He stood there, swaying unsteadily on his thin legs.

The magpie flew off. "A stupid soul," she thought to herself, "very nice, but stupid."

The mother scarcely noticed that she was gone. She continued zealously washing her newly-born. She washed him with her tongue, fondling and caressing his body in a sort of warm massage.

The slight thing staggered a little. Under the strokes of her tongue, which softly touched him here and there, he drew himself together and stood still. His little red coat, that was still somewhat tousled, bore fine white spots, and on his vague baby face there was still a deep, sleepy expression.

Round about grew hazel bushes, dogwoods, black-thorns and young elders. Tall maples, beeches and oaks wove a green roof over the thicket and from the firm, dark-brown earth sprang fern fronds, wood-vetch and sage. Underneath, the leaves of the violets, which had already bloomed, and of the strawberries, which were just beginning, clung to the ground. Through the thick foliage, the early sunlight filtered in a golden web. The whole forest resounded with myriad voices, was penetrated by them in a joyous agitation. The wood-thrush rejoiced incessantly, the doves cooed without stopping, the blackbirds whistled, finches warbled, the tit-mice chirped. Through the midst of these songs the jay flew, uttering its quarrelsome cry, the magpie mocked them, and the pheasants cackled loud and high. At times the shrill exulting of a woodpecker rose above all the other voices. The call of the falcon shrilled, light and piercing, over the tree-tops, and the hoarse crow chorus was heard continuously.

The little fawn understood not one of the many songs and calls, not a word of the conversations. He did not even listen to them. Nor did he heed any of the odors which blew through the woods. He only heard the soft licking against his coat that washed him and warmed him and kissed him. And he smelled nothing but his mother's body near him. She smelled good to him and, snuggling closer to her, he hunted eagerly around and found nourishment for his life.

While he suckled, the mother continued to caress her little one. "Bambi," she whispered. Every little while she raised her head and, listening, snuffed the wind. Then she kissed her fawn again, reassured and happy.

"Bambi," she repeated. "My little Bambi."

[18]

CHAPTER II

IN EARLY SUMMER the trees stood still under the blue sky, held their limbs outstretched and received the direct rays of the sun. On the shrubs and bushes in the undergrowth, the flowers unfolded their red, white and yellow stars. On some the seed pods had begun to appear again. They perched innumerable on the fine tips of the branches, tender and firm and resolute, and seemed like small, clenched fists. Out of the earth came whole troops of flowers, like motley stars, so that the soil of the twilit forest floor shone with a silent, ardent, colorful gladness. Everything smelled of fresh leaves, of blossoms, of moist clods and green wood. When morning broke, or when the sun went down, the whole woods resounded with a thousand voices, and from morning till night, the bees hummed, the wasps droned, and filled the fragrant stillness with their murmur.

These were the earliest days of Bambi's life. He walked behind his mother on a narrow track that ran through the midst of the bushes. How pleasant it was to walk there. The thick foliage stroked his flanks softly and bent supply aside. The track appeared to be barred and obstructed in a dozen places and yet they advanced with the greatest ease. There were tracks like this everywhere, running criss-cross through the whole woods. His mother knew them all, and if Bambi sometimes stopped before a bush as if it were an impenetrable green wall, she always found where the path went through, without hesitation or searching.

Bambi questioned her. He loved to ask his mother questions. It was the pleasantest thing for him to ask a question and then to hear what answer his mother would give. Bambi was never surprised that question after question should come into his mind continually and without effort. He found it perfectly natural, and it delighted him very much. It was very delightful, too, to wait expectantly till the answer came. If it turned out the way he wanted, he was satisfied. Sometimes, of course, he did not understand, but that was pleasant also because he was kept busy picturing what he had not understood, in his own way. Sometimes he felt very sure that his mother was not giving him a complete answer, was intentionally not telling him all she knew. And, at first, that was very pleasant, too. For then there would remain in him such a lively curiosity, such suspicion, mysteriously and joyously flashing through him, such anticipation, that he would become anxious and happy at the same time, and grow silent.

Once he asked, "Whom does this trail belong to, Mother?"

His mother answered, "To us."

Bambi asked again, "To you and me?"

"Yes."

"To us two?"

"Yes."

"Only to us two?"

"No," said his mother, "to us deer."

"What are deer?" Bambi asked, and laughed.

His mother looked at him from head to foot and laughed too. "You are a deer and I am a deer. We're both deer," she said. "Do you understand?"

Bambi sprang into the air for joy. "Yes, I understand," he said. "I'm a little deer and you're a big deer, aren't you?"

His mother nodded and said, "Now you see."

But Bambi grew serious again. "Are there other deer besides you and me?" he asked.

"Certainly," his mother said. "Many of them."

"Where are they?" cried Bambi.

"Here, everywhere."

"But I don't see them."

"You will soon," she said.

"When?" Bambi stood still, wild with curiosity.

"Soon." The mother walked on quietly. Bambi followed her. He kept silent for he was wondering what "soon" might mean. He came to the conclusion that "soon" was certainly not "now." But he wasn't sure at what time "soon" stopped being "soon" and began to be a "long while." Suddenly he asked, "Who made this trail?"

"We," his mother answered.

Bambi was astonished. "We? You and I?"

The mother said, "We, we . . . we deer."

Bambi asked, "Which deer?"

"All of us," his mother said sharply.

They walked on. Bambi was in high spirits and

felt like leaping off the path, but he stayed close to his mother. Something rustled in front of them, close to the ground. The fern fronds and wood-lettuce concealed something that advanced in violent motion. A threadlike, little cry shrilled out piteously; then all was still. Only the leaves and the blades of grass shivered back into place. A ferret had caught a mouse. He came slinking by, slid sideways, and prepared to enjoy his meal.

"What was that?" asked Bambi excitedly.

"Nothing," his mother soothed him.

"But," Bambi trembled, "but I saw it."

"Yes, yes," said his mother. "Don't be frightened. The ferret has killed a mouse." But Bambi was dreadfully frightened. A vast, unknown horror clutched at his heart. It was long before he could speak again. Then he asked, "Why did he kill the mouse?"

"Because," his mother hesitated. "Let us walk faster," she said as though something had just occurred to her and as though she had forgotten the question. She began to hurry. Bambi sprang after her.

A long pause ensued. They walked on quietly again. Finally Bambi asked anxiously, "Shall we

[23]

kill a mouse, too, sometime?"

"No," replied his mother.

"Never?" asked Bambi.

"Never," came the answer.

"Why not?" asked Bambi, relieved.

"Because we never kill anything," said his mother simply.

Bambi grew happy again.

Loud cries were coming from a young ash tree which stood near their path. The mother went along without noticing them, but Bambi stopped inquisitively. Overhead two jays were quarreling about a nest they had plundered.

"Get away, you murderer!" cried one.

"Keep cool, you fool," the other answered, "I'm not afraid of you."

"Look for your own nests," the first one shouted, "or I'll break your head for you." He was beside himself with rage. "What vulgarity!" he chattered, "what vulgarity!"

The other jay had spied Bambi and fluttered down a few branches to shout at him. "What are you gawking at, you freak?" he screamed.

Bambi sprang away terrified. He reached his mother and walked behind her again, frightened

Overhead two jays were quarreling. "What vulgarity!" he chattered, "what vulgarity!"

and obedient, thinking she had not noticed his absence.

After a pause he asked, "Mother, what is vulgarity?"

"I don't know," said his mother.

Bambi thought a while; then he began again. "Why were they both so angry with each other, Mother?" he asked.

"They were fighting over food," his mother answered.

"Will we fight over food, too, sometime?" Bambi asked.

"No," said his mother.

Bambi asked, "Why not?"

"Because there is enough for all of us," his mother replied.

Bambi wanted to know something else. "Mother," he began.

"What is it?"

"Will we be angry with each other sometime?" he asked.

"No, child," said his mother, "we don't do such things."

They walked along again. Presently it grew light ahead of them. It grew very bright. The trail ended with the tangle of vines and bushes. A few steps more and they would be in the bright open space that spread out before them. Bambi wanted to bound forward, but his mother had stopped.

"What is it?" he asked impatiently, already delighted.

"It's the meadow," his mother answered.

"What is a meadow?" asked Bambi insistently.

His mother cut him short. "You'll soon find out for yourself," she said. She had become very serious and watchful. She stood motionless, holding her head high and listening intently. She sucked in deep breathfuls of air and looked very severe.

"It's all right," she said at last, "we can go out."

Bambi leaped forward, but his mother barred the way.

"Wait till I call you," she said. Bambi obeyed at once and stood still. "That's right," said his mother, to encourage him, "and now listen to what I am saying to you." Bambi heard how seriously his mother spoke and felt terribly excited.

"Walking on the meadow is not so simple," his

mother went on. "It's a difficult and dangerous business. Don't ask me why. You'll find that out later on. Now do exactly as I tell you to. Will you?"

"Yes," Bambi promised.

"Good," said his mother, "I'm going out alone first. Stay here and wait. And don't take your eyes off me for a minute. If you see me run back here, then turn round and run as fast as you can. I'll catch up with you soon." She grew silent and seemed to be thinking. Then she went on earnestly, "Run anyway as fast as your legs will carry you. Run even if something should happen . . . even if you should see me fall to the ground. . . . Don't think of me, do you understand? No matter what you see or hear, start running right away and just as fast as you possibly can. Do you promise me to do that?"

"Yes," said Bambi softly. His mother spoke so seriously.

She went on speaking. "Out there if I should call you," she said, "there must be no looking around and no questions, but you must get behind me instantly. Understand that. Run without pausing or stopping to think. If I begin to run, that means for you to run too, and no stopping until we are back here again. You won't forget, will you?"

"No," said Bambi in a troubled voice.

"Now I'm going ahead," said his mother, and seemed to become calmer.

She walked out. Bambi, who never took his eyes off her, saw how she moved forward with slow, cautious steps. He stood there full of expectancy, full of fear and curiosity. He saw how his mother listened in all directions, saw her shrink together, and shrank together himself, ready to leap back into the thickets. Then his mother grew calm again. She stretched herself. Then she looked around satisfied and called, "Come!"

Bambi bounded out. Joy seized him with such tremendous force that he forgot his worries in a flash. Through the thicket he could see only the green tree-tops overhead. Once in a while he caught a glimpse of the blue sky.

Now he saw the whole heaven stretching far and wide and he rejoiced without knowing why. In the forest he had seen only a stray sunbeam now and then, or the tender, dappled light that

played through the branches.   Suddenly he was
standing in the blinding hot sunlight whose boundless power was beaming upon him.   He stood in
the splendid warmth that made him shut his eyes
but which opened his heart.

Bambi was as though bewitched.   He was completely beside himself with pleasure.   He was
simply wild.   He leaped into the air three, four,
five times.   He had to do it.   He felt a terrible
desire to leap and jump.   He stretched his young
limbs joyfully.   His breath came deeply and easily.   He drank in the air.   The sweet smell of the
meadow made him so wildly happy that he had to
leap into the air.

Bambi was a child.   If he had been a human
child he would have shouted.   But he was a young
deer, and deer cannot shout, at least not the way
human children do.   So he rejoiced with his legs
and with his whole body as he flung himself into
the air.   His mother stood by and was glad.   She
saw that Bambi was wild.   She watched how he
bounded into the air and fell again awkwardly,
in one spot.   She saw how he stared around him,
dazed and bewildered, only to leap up over and
over again.   She understood that Bambi knew

only the narrow deer tracks in the forest and how his brief life was used to the limits of the thicket. He did not move from one place because he did not understand how to run freely around the open meadow.

So she stretched out her forefeet and bent laughingly towards Bambi for a moment. Then she was off with one bound, racing around in a circle so that the tall grass stems swished.

Bambi was frightened and stood motionless. Was that a sign for him to run back to the thicket? His mother had said to him, "Don't worry about me no matter what you see or hear. Just run as fast as you can." He was going to turn around and run as she had commanded him to, but his mother came galloping up suddenly. She came up with a wonderful swishing sound and stopped two steps from him. She bent towards him, laughing as she had at first and cried, "Catch me." And in a flash she was gone.

Bambi was puzzled. What did she mean? Then she came back again running so fast that it made him giddy. She pushed his flank with her nose and said quickly, "Try to catch me," and fled away.

[32]

Bambi started after her. He took a few steps. Then his steps became short bounds. He felt as if he were flying without any effort on his part. There was a space under his hoofs, space under his bounding feet, space and still more space. Bambi was beside himself with joy.

The swishing grass sounded wonderful to his ears. It was marvelously soft and as fine as silk where it brushed against him. He ran round in a circle. He turned and flew off in a new circle, turned around again and kept running.

His mother was standing still, getting her breath again. She kept following Bambi with her eyes. He was wild.

Suddenly the race was over. He stopped and came up to his mother, lifting his hoofs elegantly. He looked joyfully at her. Then they strolled contentedly side by side.

Since he had been in the open, Bambi had felt the sky and the sun and the green meadow with his whole body. He took one blinding, giddy glance at the sun, and he felt its rays as they lay warmly on his back.

Presently he began to enjoy the meadow with his eyes also. Its wonders amazed him at every step he took. You could not see the tiniest speck of earth the way you could in the forest. Blade after blade of grass covered every inch of the ground. It tossed and waved luxuriantly. It bent softly aside under every footstep, only to rise up unharmed again. The broad green meadow was starred with white daisies, with the thick, round red and purple clover blossoms and bright, golden dandelion heads.

"Look, look, Mother!" Bambi exclaimed. "There's a flower flying."

"That's not a flower," said his mother, "that's a butterfly."

Bambi stared at the butterfly, entranced. It had darted lightly from a blade of grass and was fluttering about in its giddy way. Then Bambi saw that there were many butterflies flying in the air above the meadow. They seemed to be in a hurry and yet moved slowly, fluttering up and down in a sort of game that delighted him. They really did look like gay flying flowers that would not stay on their stems but had unfastened themselves in order to dance a little. They looked, too, like flowers that come to rest at sundown but have no fixed places and have to hunt for them, dropping down and vanishing as if they really had settled somewhere, yet always flying up again, a little way at first, then higher and higher, and always searching farther and farther because all the good places have already been taken.

Bambi gazed at them all. He would have loved to see one close by. He wanted to see one face to face but he was not able to. They sailed in and out continually. The air was aflutter with them.

When he looked down at the ground again he was delighted with the thousands of living things he saw stirring under his hoofs. They ran and jumped in all directions. He would see a wild swarm of them, and the next moment they had disappeared in the grass again.

"Who are they, Mother?" he asked.

"Those are ants," his mother answered.

"Look," cried Bambi, "see that piece of grass jumping. Look how high it can jump!"

"That's not grass," his mother explained, "that's a nice grasshopper."

"Why does he jump that way?" asked Bambi.

"Because we're walking here," his mother answered, "he's afraid we'll step on him."

"O," said Bambi, turning to the grasshopper

[35]

who was sitting on a daisy; "O," he said again politely, "you don't have to be afraid; we won't hurt you."

"I'm not afraid," the grasshopper replied in a quavering voice; "I was only frightened for a moment when I was talking to my wife."

"Excuse us for disturbing you," said Bambi shyly.

"Not at all," the grasshopper quavered. "Since it's you, it's perfectly all right. But you never know who's coming and you have to be careful."

"This is the first time in my life that I've ever been on the meadow," Bambi explained; "my mother brought me. . . ."

The grasshopper was sitting with his head lowered as though he were going to butt. He put on a serious face and murmured, "That doesn't interest me at all. I haven't time to stand here gossipping with you. I have to be looking for my wife. Hopp!" And he gave a jump.

"Hopp!" said Bambi in surprise at the high jump with which the grasshopper vanished.

Bambi ran to his mother. "Mother, I spoke to him," he cried.

"To whom?" his mother asked.

"To the grasshopper," Bambi said, "I spoke to

him. He was very nice to me. And I like him so much. He's so wonderful and green and you can see through his sides. They look like leaves, but you can't see through a leaf."

"Those are his wings," said his mother.

"O," Bambi went on, "and his face is so serious and wise. But he was very nice to me anyhow. And how he can jump! 'Hopp!' he said, and he jumped so high I couldn't see him any more."

They walked on. The conversation with the grasshopper had excited Bambi and tired him a little, for it was the first time he had ever spoken to a stranger. He felt hungry and pressed close to his mother to be nursed.

Then he stood quietly and gazed dreamily into space for a little while with a sort of joyous ecstasy that came over him every time he was nursed by his mother. He noticed a bright flower moving in the tangled grasses. Bambi looked more closely at it. No, it wasn't a flower, but a butterfly. Bambi crept closer.

The butterfly hung heavily to a grass stem and fanned its wings slowly.

"Please sit still," Bambi said.

[37]

"Why should I sit still? I'm a butterfly," the insect answered in astonishment.

"O, please sit still, just for a minute," Bambi pleaded, "I've wanted so much to see you close to. Please."

"Well," said the butterfly, "for your sake I will, but not for long."

Bambi stood in front of him. "How beautiful you are!" he cried fascinated; "how wonderfully beautiful, like a flower!"

"What?" cried the butterfly, fanning his wings, "did you say like a flower? In my circle it's generally supposed that we're handsomer than flowers."

Bambi was embarrassed. "O, yes," he stammered, "much handsomer, excuse me, I only meant. . . ."

"Whatever you meant is all one to me," the butterfly replied. He arched his thin body affectedly and played with his delicate feelers.

Bambi looked at him enchanted. "How elegant you are!" he said. "How elegant and fine! And how splendid and white your wings are!"

The butterfly spread his wings wide apart, then raised them till they folded together like an upright sail.

"O," cried Bambi, "I know that you are handsomer than the flowers. Besides, you can fly and the flowers can't because they grow on stems, that's why."

The butterfly spread his wings. "It's enough," he said, "that I can fly." He soared so lightly that Bambi could hardly see him or follow his flight. His wings moved gently and gracefully. Then he fluttered into the sunny air.

"I only sat still that long on your account," he said balancing in the air in front of Bambi. "Now I'm going."

That was how Bambi found the meadow.

CHAPTER III

IN THE HEART of the forest was a little
glade that belonged to Bambi's mother. It lay
only a few steps from the narrow trail where the
deer went bounding through the woods. But no
one could ever have found it who did not know
the little passage leading to it through the thick
bushes.

The glade was very narrow, so narrow that
there was only room for Bambi and his mother,
and so low that when Bambi's mother stood up
her head was hidden among the branches. Sprays
of hazel, furze, and dogwood, woven about each
other, intercepted the little bit of sunlight that
came through the tree-tops, so that it never
reached the ground. Bambi had come into the
world in this glade. It was his mother's and his.

His mother was lying asleep on the ground.
Bambi had dozed a little, too. But suddenly he

[40]

had become wide awake. He got up and looked around.

The shadows were so deep where he was that it was almost dark. From the woods came soft rustlings. Now and again the tit-mice chirped. Now and again came the clear hammering of the woodpecker or the joyless call of a crow. Everything else was still, far and wide. But the air was sizzling in the midday heat so that you could hear it if you listened closely. And it was stiflingly sweet.

Bambi looked down at his mother and said, "Are you asleep?"

No, his mother was not asleep. She had awakened the moment Bambi got up.

"What are we going to do now?" Bambi asked.

"Nothing," his mother answered. "We're going to stay right where we are. Lie down, like a good boy, and go to sleep."

But Bambi had no desire to go to sleep. "Come on," he begged, "let's go to the meadow."

His mother lifted her head. "Go to the meadow," she said, "go to the meadow now?" Her voice was so full of astonishment and terror that Bambi became quite frightened.

[41]

"Can't we go to the meadow?" he asked timidly.

"No," his mother answered, and it sounded very final. "No, you can't go now."

"Why?" Bambi perceived that something mysterious was involved. He grew still more frightened, but at the same time he was terribly anxious to know everything. "Why can't we go to the meadow?" he asked.

"You'll find out all about it later when you're bigger," his mother replied.

"But," Bambi insisted, "I'd rather know now."

"Later," his mother repeated, "you're nothing but a baby yet," she went on tenderly, "and we don't talk about such things to children." She had grown quite serious. "Fancy going to the meadow at this time of day. I don't even like to think of it. Why, it's broad daylight."

"But it was broad daylight when we went to the meadow before," Bambi objected.

"That's different," his mother explained, "it was early in the morning."

"Can we only go there early in the morning?" Bambi was very curious.

His mother was patient. "Only in the early

morning or late evening," she said, "or at night."

"And never in the daytime, never?"

His mother hesitated. "Well," she said at last, "sometimes a few of us do go there in the daytime. . . . But those are special occasions. . . . I can't just explain it to you, you are too young yet. . . . Some of us do go there. . . . But we are exposed to the greatest danger."

"What kind of danger?" asked Bambi all attention.

But his mother did not want to go on with the conversation. "We're in danger, and that's enough for you, my son. You can't understand such things yet."

Bambi thought that he could understand everything except why his mother did not want to tell him the truth. But he kept silent.

"That's what life means for us," his mother went on, "though we all love the daylight, especially when we're young, we have to lie quiet all day long. We can only roam around from evening till morning. Do you understand?"

"Yes," said Bambi.

"So, my son, we'll have to stay where we are. We're safe here. Now lie down again and go to sleep."

[43]

But Bambi didn't want to lie down. "Why are we safe here?" he asked.

"Because all the bushes shield us," his mother answered, "and the twigs snap on the shrubs and the dry twigs crackle and give us warning. And last year's dead leaves lie on the ground and rustle to warn us, and the jays and magpies keep watch so we can tell from a distance if anybody is coming."

"What are last year's leaves?" Bambi asked.

"Come and sit beside me," said his mother, "and I will tell you." Bambi sat down contentedly, nestling close to his mother. And she told him how the trees are not always green, how the sunshine and the pleasant warmth disappear. Then it grows cold, the frost turns the leaves yellow, brown and red, and they fall slowly so that the trees and bushes stretch their bare branches to the sky and look perfectly naked. But the dry leaves lie on the ground, and when a foot stirs them they rustle. Then someone is coming. O, how kind last year's dead leaves are! They do their duty so well and are so alert and watchful. Even in mid-summer there are a lot of them hidden beneath the undergrowth. And

The leaves fall slowly.

they give warning in advance of every danger.

Bambi pressed close against his mother. It was so cozy to sit there and listen while his mother talked.

When she grew silent he began to think. He thought it was very kind of the good old leaves to keep watch, though they were all dead and frozen and had suffered so much. He wondered just what that danger could be that his mother was always talking about. But too much thought tired him. Round about him it was still. Only the air sizzling in the heat was audible. Then he fell asleep.

CHAPTER IV

ONE EVENING Bambi was roaming about the meadow again with his mother. He thought that he knew everything there was to see or hear there. But in reality it appeared that he did not know as much as he thought.

This time was just like the first. Bambi played tag with his mother. He ran around in circles, and the open space, the deep sky, the fresh air intoxicated him so that he grew perfectly wild. After a while he noticed that his mother was standing still. He stopped short in the middle of a leap so suddenly that his four legs spread far apart. To get his balance he bounded high into the air and then stood erect. His mother seemed to be talking to someone he couldn't make out through the tall grasses. Bambi toddled up inquisitively.

Two long ears were moving in the tangled

grass stems close to his mother. They were gray-ish-brown and prettily marked with black stripes. Bambi stopped, but his mother said, "Come here. This is our friend, the Hare. Come here like a nice boy and let him see you."

Bambi went over. There sat the Hare looking like a very honest creature. At times his long spoon-like ears stood bolt upright. At others they fell back limply as though they had suddenly grown weak. Bambi became somewhat critical as he looked at the whiskers that stood out so stiff and straight on both sides of the Hare's mouth. But he noticed that the Hare had a very mild face and extremely good-natured features, and that he cast timid glances at the world from out of his big round eyes. The Hare really did look friendly. Bambi's passing doubts vanished immediately. But oddly enough, he had lost all the respect he originally felt for the Hare.

"Good evening, young man," the Hare greeted him, with studied politeness.

Bambi merely nodded good evening. He didn't understand why, but he simply nodded. He was very friendly and civil, but a little condescending.

[49]

He could not help it himself. Perhaps he was born that way.

"What a charming young prince," said the Hare to Bambi's mother. He looked at Bambi attentively, raising first one spoon-like ear, then the other, and then both of them, and letting them fall again, suddenly and limply, which didn't please Bambi. The motion of the Hare's ears seemed to say, "He isn't worth bothering with."

Meanwhile the Hare continued to study Bambi with his big round eyes. His nose and his mouth with the handsome whiskers moved incessantly in the same way a man who is trying not to sneeze twitches his nose and lips. Bambi had to laugh.

The Hare laughed quickly, too, but his eyes grew more thoughtful. "I congratulate you," he said to Bambi's mother. "I sincerely congratulate you on your son. Yes, indeed, he'll make a splendid prince in time. Anyone can see that."

To Bambi's boundless surprise he suddenly sat straight on his hind legs. After he had spied all around with his ears stiffened and his nose constantly twitching, he sat down decently on all fours again. "Now if you good people will ex-

There sat the Hare looking like a very honest creature.

cuse me," he said at last, "I have all kinds of things to do to-night. If you'll be so good as to excuse me. . . ." He turned away and hopped off with his ears back so that they touched his shoulders.

"Good evening," Bambi called after him.

His mother smiled. "The good Hare," she said; "he is so suave and prudent. He doesn't have an easy time of it in this world." There was sympathy in her voice.

Bambi strolled about a little and left his mother to her meal. He wanted to meet his friend again and he wanted to make new acquaintances, besides. For without being very clear himself what it was he wanted, he felt a certain expectancy. Suddenly, at a distance, he heard a soft rustling on the meadow, and felt a quick, gentle step tapping the ground. He peered ahead of him. Over on the edge of the woods something was gliding through the grasses. Was it alive? No, there were two things. Bambi cast a quick glance at his mother but she wasn't paying attention to anything and had her head deep in the grass. But the game was going on on the other side of the meadow in a shifting circle exactly as Bambi himself had

[53]

raced around before. Bambi was so excited that he sprang back as if he wanted to run away. Then his mother noticed him and raised her head.

"What's the matter?" she called.

But Bambi was speechless. He could not find his tongue and only stammered, "Look over there."

His mother looked over. "I see," she said, "that's my cousin, and sure enough she has a baby too, now. No, she has two of them." His mother spoke at first out of pure happiness, but she had grown serious. "To think that Ena has two babies," she said, "two of them."

Bambi stood gazing across the meadow. He saw a creature that looked just like his mother. He hadn't even noticed her before. He saw that the grasses were being shaken in a double circle, but only a pair of reddish backs were visible like thin red streaks.

"Come," his mother said, "we'll go over. They'll be company for you."

Bambi would have run, but as his mother walked slowly, peering to right and to left at every step, he held himself back. Still, he was

[54]

bursting with excitement and very impatient.

"I thought we would meet Ena sometime," his mother went on to say. "Where can she have been keeping herself? I thought I knew she had one child, that wasn't hard to guess. But two of them! . . ."

At last the others saw them and came to meet them. Bambi had to greet his aunt, but his mind was entirely on the children.

His aunt was very friendly. "Well," she said to him, "this is Gobo and that is Faline. Now you run along and play together."

The children stood stock-still and stared at each other, Gobo close beside Faline and Bambi in front of him. None of them stirred. They stood and gaped.

"Run along," said Bambi's mother, "you'll soon be friends."

"What a lovely child," Aunt Ena replied. "He is really lovely. So strong, and he stands so well."

"O well," said his mother modestly, "we have to be content. But to have two of them, Ena! . . ."

"O yes, that's all very well," Ena declared; "you know, dear, I've had children before."

"Bambi is my first," his mother said.

[55]

"We'll see," Ena comforted her, "perhaps it will be different with you next time, too."

The children were still standing and staring at each other. No one said a word. Suddenly Faline gave a leap and rushed away. It had become too much for her.

In a moment Bambi darted after her. Gobo followed him. They flew around in a semi-circle, they turned tail and fell over each other. Then they chased each other up and down. It was glorious. When they stopped, all topsy-turvy and somewhat breathless, they were already good friends. They began to chatter.

Bambi told them how he talked to the nice grasshopper and the butterfly.

"Did you ever talk to the gold bug?" asked Faline.

No, Bambi had never talked to the gold bug. He did not even know who he was.

"I've talked to him often," Faline declared, a little pertly.

"The jay insulted me," said Bambi.

"Really," said Gobo astonished, "did the jay treat you like that?" Gobo was very easily astonished and was extremely timid.

"Well," he observed, "the hedgehog stuck me in the nose." But he only mentioned it in passing.

"Who is the hedgehog?" Bambi asked eagerly. It seemed wonderful to him to be there with friends, listening to so many exciting things.

"The hedgehog is a terrible creature," cried Faline, "full of long spines all over his body and very wicked!"

"Do you really think he's wicked?" asked Gobo. "He never hurts anybody."

"Is that so?" answered Faline quickly. "Didn't he stick you?"

"O that was only because I wanted to speak to him," Gobo replied, "and only a little anyhow. It didn't hurt me much."

Bambi turned to Gobo. "Why didn't he want you to talk to him?" he asked.

"He doesn't talk to anybody," Faline interrupted, "even if you just come where he is he rolls himself up so he's nothing but prickles all over. Our mother says he's one of those people who don't want to have anything to do with the world."

"Maybe he's only afraid," Gobo said.

But Faline knew better. "Mother says you

[57]

shouldn't meddle with such people," she said.

Presently Bambi began to ask Gobo softly. "Do you know what 'danger' means?"

Then they both grew serious and all three heads drew together. Gobo thought a while. He made a special effort to remember for he saw how curious Bambi was for the answer. "Danger," he whispered, "is something very bad."

"Yes," Bambi declared excitedly, "I know it's something very bad, but what?" All three trembled with fear.

Suddenly Faline cried out loudly and joyfully, "I know what danger is—it's what you run away from." She sprang away. She couldn't bear to stay there any longer and be frightened. In an instant, Bambi and Gobo had bounded after her. They began to play again. They tumbled in the rustling, silky green meadow grass, and in a twinkling had forgotten all about the absorbing question. After a while they stopped and stood chattering together as before. They looked towards their mothers. They were standing close together, eating a little and carrying on a quiet conversation.

Aunt Ena raised her head and called the children. "Come, Gobo. Come, Faline. We have to go now."

And Bambi's mother said to him, "Come, it's time to go."

"Wait just a little longer," Faline pleaded eagerly, "just a little while."

"Let's stay a little longer, please," Bambi pleaded, "it's so nice." And Gobo repeated timidly, "It's so nice, just a little longer." All three spoke at once.

Ena looked at Bambi's mother. "What did I tell you," she said, "they won't want to separate now."

Then something happened that was much more exciting than everything else that happened to Bambi that day. Out of the woods came the sound of hoofs beating the earth. Branches snapped, the boughs rustled, and before Bambi had time to listen, something burst out of the thicket. Someone came crashing and rustling with someone else rushing after him. They tore by like the wind, described a wide circle on the meadow and vanished into the woods again, where they could be heard galloping. Then they came bursting out of the thicket again and suddenly stood still, about twenty paces apart.

Bambi looked at them and did not stir. They looked like his mother and Aunt Ena. But their heads were crowned with gleaming antlers covered with brown beads and bright white prongs. Bambi was completely overcome. He looked from one to the other. One was smaller and his antlers narrower. But the other one was stately and beautiful. He carried his head up and his antlers rose high above it. They flashed from dark to light, adorned with the splendor of many black and brown prongs.

"O," cried Faline in admiration. "O," Gobo repeated softly. But Bambi said nothing. He was entranced and silent. Then they both moved and, turning away from each other, walked slowly back into the woods in opposite directions. The stately stag passed close to the children and Bambi's mother and Aunt Ena. He passed by in silent splendor, holding his noble head royally high and honoring no one with so much as a glance.

The children did not dare to breathe till he had disappeared into the thicket. They turned to look after the other one, but at that very moment the green door of the forest closed on him.

[60]

Faline was the first to break silence. "Who were they?" she cried. But her pert little voice trembled.

"Who were they?" Gobo repeated in a hardly audible voice. Bambi kept silent.

Aunt Ena said solemnly, "Those were your fathers."

Nothing more was said, and they parted. Aunt Ena led her children into the nearest thicket. It was her trail. Bambi and his mother had to cross the whole meadow to the oak in order to reach their own path. He was silent for a long time before he finally asked, "Didn't they see us?"

His mother understood what he meant and replied, "Of course, they saw all of us."

Bambi was troubled. He felt shy about asking questions, but it was too much for him. "Then why. . . ." he began, and stopped.

His mother helped him along. "What is it you want to know, son?" she asked.

"Why didn't they stay with us?"

"They don't ever stay with us," his mother answered, "only at times."

Bambi continued, "But why didn't they speak to us?"

[61]

His mother said, "They don't speak to us now; only at times. We have to wait till they come to us. And we have to wait for them to speak to us. They do it whenever they like."

With a troubled heart, Bambi asked, "Will my father speak to me?"

"Of course he will," his mother promised. "When you're grown up he'll speak to you, and you'll have to stay with him sometimes."

Bambi walked silently beside his mother, his whole mind filled with his father's appearance. "How handsome he is!" he thought over and over again. "How handsome he is!"

As though his mother could read his thoughts, she said, "If you live, my son, if you are cunning and don't run into danger, you'll be as strong and handsome as your father is sometime, and you'll have antlers like his, too."

Bambi breathed deeply. His heart swelled with joy and expectancy.

CHAPTER V

TIME PASSED, and Bambi had many adventures and went through many experiences. Every day brought something new. Sometimes he felt quite giddy. He had so incredibly much to learn.

He could listen now, not merely hear, when things happened so close that they struck the ear of their own accord. No, there was really no art in that. He could really listen intelligently now to everything that stirred, no matter how softly. He heard even the tiniest whisper that the wind brought by. For instance, he knew that a pheasant was running through the next bushes. He recognized clearly the soft quick tread that was always stopping. He knew by ear the sound the field mice make when they run to and fro on their little paths. And the patter of the moles when they are in a good humor and chase one another around the elder bushes so that there is just the

[63]

slightest rustling. He heard the shrill clear call of the falcon, and he knew from its altered, angry tones when a hawk or an eagle approached. The falcon was angry because she was afraid her field would be taken from her. He knew the beat of the wood-doves' wings, the beautiful, distant, soaring cries of ducks, and many other things besides.

He knew how to snuff the air now, too. Soon he would do it as well as his mother. He could breathe in the air and at the same time analyze it with his senses. "That's clover and meadow grass," he would think when the wind blew off the fields. "And Friend Hare is out there, too. I can smell him plainly."

Again he would notice through the smell of leaves and earth, wild leek and wood mustard, that the ferret was passing by. He could tell by putting his nose to the ground and snuffing deeply that the fox was afoot. Or he would know that one of his family was somewhere nearby. It might be Aunt Ena and the children.

By now he was good friends with the night and no longer wanted to run about so much in broad daylight. He was quite willing to lie all day long in the shade of the leafy glade with his mother.

[64]

He would listen to the air sizzling in the heat and then fall asleep.

From time to time, he would wake up, listen and snuff the air to find out how things stood. Everything was as it should be. Only the tit-mice were chattering a little to each other, the midges who were hardly ever still, hummed, while the wood-doves never ceased declaiming their ecstatic tenderness. What concern was it of his? He would drop off to sleep again.

He liked the night very much now. Everything was alive, everything was in motion. Of course, he had to be cautious at night too, but still he could be less careful. And he could go wherever he wanted to. And everywhere he went he met acquaintances. They too were always less nervous than in the daytime.

At night the woods were solemn and still. There were only a few voices. They sounded loud in the stillness, and they had a different ring from daytime voices, and left a deeper impression.

Bambi liked to see the owl. She had such a wonderful flight, perfectly light and perfectly noiseless. She made as little sound as a butterfly,

and yet she was so dreadfully big. She had such
striking features, too, so pronounced and so deeply
thoughtful. And such wonderful eyes! Bambi
admired her firm, quietly courageous glance. He
liked to listen when she talked to his mother or to
anybody else. He would stand a little to one side,
for he was somewhat afraid of the masterful
glance that he admired so much. He did not understand most of the clever things she said, but
he knew they were clever, and they pleased him
and filled him with respect for the owl.

Then the owl would begin to hoot. "Hoaah!—
Ha!—Ha!—Haa!—ah!" she would cry. It
sounded different from the thrushes' song, or the
yellow-birds', different from the friendly notes of
the cuckoo, but Bambi loved the owl's cry, for he
felt its mysterious earnestness, its unutterable
wisdom and strange melancholy.

Then there was the screech-owl, a charming
little fellow, lively and gay with no end to his
inquisitiveness. He was bent on attracting attention. "Oi, yeek! oi, yeek!" he would call in a terrible, high-pitched, piercing voice. It sounded as
if he were on the point of death. But he was
really in a beaming good humor and was hilari-

ously happy whenever he frightened anybody. "Oi, yeek!" he would cry so dreadfully loud that the forests heard it for a mile around. But afterwards he would laugh with a soft chuckle, though you could only hear it if you stood close by.

Bambi discovered that the screech-owl was delighted whenever he frightened anyone, or when anybody thought that something dreadful had happened to him. After that, whenever Bambi met him, he never failed to rush up and ask, "What has happened to you?" or to say with a sigh, "O, how you frightened me just now!" Then the owl would be delighted.

"O, yes," he would say, laughing, "it sounds pretty gruesome." He would puff up his feathers into a grayish-white ball and look extremely handsome.

There were storms, too, once or twice, both in the daytime and at night. The first was in the daytime and Bambi felt himself grow terrified as it became darker and darker in his glade. It seemed to him as if night had covered the sky at mid-day. When the raging storm broke through the woods so that the trees began to groan aloud, Bambi trembled with terror. And when the lightning flashed and the thunder growled, Bambi was numb with fear and thought the end of the world had come. He ran behind his mother, who had sprung up somewhat disturbed and was walking back and forth in the thicket. He could not think about nor understand anything. The rain fell in raging torrents. Everyone had run to shelter. The woods were empty. But there was no escaping the rain. The pouring water penetrated even the thickest parts of the bushes. Presently the lightning stopped, and the fiery rays ceased to flicker through the tree-tops. The thunder rolled away. Bambi could hear it in the distance, and soon it stopped altogether. The rain beat more gently. It pattered evenly and steadily around him for another hour. The forest stood breathing deeply in the calm and let the water drain off. No one was afraid to come out any more. That feeling had passed. The rain had washed it away.

Never before had Bambi and his mother gone to the meadow as early as on that evening. It was not even dusk yet. The sun was still high in the sky, the air was extremely fresh, and smelt sweeter than usual, and the woods rang with a thousand voices, for everyone had crept out of his shelter and was running excitedly, telling what had just happened.

Before they went on to the meadow, they passed the great oak that stood near the forest's edge, close to their trail. They always had to pass that beautiful big tree when they went to the meadow.

This time the squirrel was sitting on a branch and greeted them. Bambi was good friends with the squirrel. The first time he met him he took him for a very small deer because of the squirrel's red coat and stared at him in surprise. But Bambi had been very childish at that time and had known nothing at all.

The squirrel pleased him greatly from the first. He was so thoroughly civil, and talkative. And Bambi loved to see how wonderfully he could turn, and climb, and leap, and balance himself. In the middle of a conversation the squirrel would run up and down the smooth tree trunk as though there were nothing to it. Or he would sit upright on a swaying branch, balance himself comfortably with his bushy tail, that stuck up so gracefully behind him, display his white chest, hold his little forepaws elegantly in front of him, nod his head this way and that, laugh with his jolly eyes, and, in a twinkling, say a lot of comical and interesting things. Then he would come down again, so swiftly and with such leaps, that you expected him to tumble on his head.

He twitched his long tail violently and called to them from overhead, "Good day! Good day! It's so nice of you to come over." Bambi and his mother stopped.

The squirrel ran down the smooth trunk. "Well," he chattered, "did you get through it all right? Of course, I see that everything is first rate. That's the main thing."

He ran up the trunk again like lightning and said, "It's too wet for me down there. Wait, I'm going to look for a better place. I hope you don't mind. Thanks, I knew you wouldn't. And we can talk just as well from here."

He ran back and forth along a straight limb. "It was a bad business," he said, "a monstrous uproar! You wouldn't believe how scared I was. I hunched myself up as still as a mouse in the corner and hardly dared move. That's the worst of it, having to sit there and not move. And all

The squirrel sat up, balancing himself with his handsome upright tail.

the time you're hoping nothing will happen. But my tree is wonderful in such cases. There's no denying it, my tree is wonderful. I'll say that for it. I'm satisfied with it. As long as I've had it, I've never wanted any other. But when it cuts loose the way it did to-day you're sure to get frightened no matter where you are."

The squirrel sat up, balancing himself with his handsome upright tail. He displayed his white chest and pressed both forepaws protestingly against his heart. You believed without his adding anything that he had been excited.

"We're going to the meadow now to dry ourselves off in the sun," Bambi's mother said.

"That's a good idea," cried the squirrel, "you're really so clever. I'm always saying how clever you are." With a bound he sprang onto a higher branch. "You couldn't do anything better than go to the meadow now," he called down. Then he swung with light bounds back and forth through the tree-top. "I'm going up where I can get the sunlight," he chattered merrily, "I'm all soaked through. I'm going all the way up." He didn't care whether they were still listening to him or not.

[73]

The meadow was full of life. Friend Hare was there and had brought along his family. Aunt Ena was there with her children and a few acquaintances. That day Bambi saw the fathers again. They came slowly out of the forest from opposite directions. There was a third stag too. Each walked slowly in his track, back and forth, along the meadow. They paid no attention to anyone and did not even talk to one another. Bambi looked at them frequently. He was respectful, but full of curiosity.

Then he talked to Faline and Gobo and a few other children. He wanted to play a while. All agreed and they began running around in a circle. Faline was the gayest of all. She was so fresh and nimble and brimming over with bright ideas. But Gobo was soon tired. He had been terribly frightened by the storm. His heart had hammered loudly and was still pounding. There was something very weak about Gobo, but Bambi liked him because he was so good and willing and always a little sad without letting you know it.

Time passed and Bambi was learning how good the meadow grass tasted, how tender and sweet the leaf buds and the clover were. When he nestled against his mother for comfort it often happened that she pushed him away.

"You aren't a little baby any more," she would say. Sometimes she even said abruptly, "Go away and let me be." It even happened sometimes that his mother got up in the little forest glade, got up in the middle of the day, and went off without noticing whether Bambi was following her or not. At times it seemed, when they were wandering down the familiar paths, as if his mother did not want to notice whether Bambi was behind her or was trailing after.

One day his mother was gone. Bambi did not know how such a thing could be possible, he could not figure it out. But his mother was gone and for the first time Bambi was left alone.

He wandered about, he was troubled, he grew worried and anxious and began to want her terribly. He stood quite sadly, calling her. Nobody answered and nobody came.

He listened and snuffed the air. He could not smell anything. He called again. Softly, pathetically, tearfully, he called "Mother, Mother!" In vain.

Then despair seized him, he could not stand it and started to walk.

He wandered down the trails he knew, stopping and calling. He wandered farther and farther with hesitating steps, frightened and helpless. He was very downcast.

He went on and on and came to trails where he had never been before. He came to places that were strange to him. He no longer knew where he was going.

Then he heard two childish voices like his own, calling, "Mother! Mother!" He stood still and listened. Surely that was Gobo and Faline. It must be they.

He ran quickly towards the voices and soon he saw their little red jackets showing through the leaves. Gobo and Faline were standing side by side under a dog-wood tree and calling mournfully, "Mother, Mother!"

They were overjoyed when they heard the rustling in the bushes. But they were disappointed when they saw Bambi. They were a little consoled that he was there, however. And Bambi was glad not to be all alone any more.

"My mother is gone," Bambi said.

[76]

"Ours is gone too," Gobo answered plaintively.

They looked at one another and were quite despondent.

"Where can they be?" asked Bambi. He was almost sobbing.

"I don't know," sighed Gobo. His heart was pounding and he felt miserable.

Suddenly Faline said, "I think they may be with our fathers."

Gobo and Bambi looked at her surprised. They were filled with awe. "You mean that they're visiting our fathers?" asked Bambi and trembled. Faline trembled too, but she made a wise face. She acted like a person who knows more than she will let on. Of course she knew nothing, she could not even guess where her idea came from. But when Gobo repeated, "Do you really think so?" she put on a meaningful air and answered mysteriously, "Yes, I think so."

Anyway it was a suggestion that needed to be thought about. But in spite of that Bambi felt no easier. He couldn't even think about it, he was too troubled and too sad.

He went off. He wouldn't stay in one place. Faline and Gobo went along with him for a little

[77]

way. All three were calling, "Mother, Mother!" Then Gobo and Faline stopped, they did not dare go any farther. Faline said, "Why should we? Mother knows where we are. Let's stay here so she can find us when she comes back."

Bambi went on alone. He wandered through a thicket to a little clearing. In the middle of the clearing Bambi stopped short. He suddenly felt as if he were rooted to the ground and could not move.

On the edge of the clearing, by a tall hazel bush, a creature was standing. Bambi had never seen such a creature before. At the same time the air brought him a scent such as he had never smelled in his life. It was a strange smell, heavy and acrid. It excited him to the point of madness.

Bambi stared at the creature. It stood remarkably erect. It was extremely thin and had a pale face, entirely bare around the nose and the eyes. A kind of dread emanated from that face, a cold terror. That face had a tremendous power over him. It was unbearably painful to look at that face and yet Bambi stood staring fixedly at it.

For a long time the creature stood without moving. Then it stretched out a leg from high

[78]

up near its face. Bambi had not even noticed that there was one there. But as that terrible leg was reaching out into the air Bambi was swept away by the mere gesture. In a flash he was back into the thicket he came from, and was running away.

In a twinkling his mother was with him again, too. She bounded beside him over shrubs and bushes. They ran side by side as fast as they could. His mother was in the lead. She knew the way and Bambi followed. They ran till they came to their glade.

"Did you see Him?" asked the mother softly.

Bambi could not answer, he had no breath left. He only nodded.

"That was He," said the mother.

And they both shuddered.

CHAPTER VI

BAMBI WAS OFTEN ALONE NOW. But he
was not so troubled about it as he had been the
first time. His mother would disappear, and no
matter how much he called her she wouldn't
come back. Later she would appear unexpectedly
and stay with him as before.

One night he was roaming around quite forlorn
again. He could not even find Gobo and Faline.
The sky had become pale gray and it began to
darken so that the tree-tops seemed like a vault
over the bushy undergrowth. There was a swishing in the bushes, a loud rustling came through
the leaves and Bambi's mother dashed out. Some
one else raced close behind her. Bambi did
not know whether it was Aunt Ena or his father
or someone else. But he recognized his mother
at once. Though she rushed past him so quickly,
he had recognized her voice. She screamed,

[80]

and it seemed to Bambi as if it were in play, though he thought it sounded a little frightened too.

One day Bambi wandered for hours through the thicket. At last he began to call. He simply couldn't bear to be so utterly lonely any more. He felt that pretty soon he'd be perfectly miserable. So he began to call for his mother.

Suddenly one of the fathers was standing in front of him looking sternly down at him. Bambi hadn't heard him coming and was terrified. This stag looked more powerful than the others, taller and prouder. His coat shone with a deeper richer red, but his face shimmered, silvery gray. And tall, black, beaded antlers rose high above his nervous ears.

"What are you crying about?" the old stag asked severely. Bambi trembled in awe and did not dare answer. "Your mother has no time for you now," the old stag went on. Bambi was completely dominated by his masterful voice and at the same time, he admired it. "Can't you stay by yourself? Shame on you!"

Bambi wanted to say that he was perfectly able to stay by himself, that he had often been

[81]

left alone already, but he could not get it out. He was obedient and he felt terribly ashamed. The stag turned around and was gone. Bambi didn't know where or how, or whether the stag had gone slow or fast. He had simply gone as suddenly as he had come. Bambi strained his ears to listen but he could not catch the sound of a departing footstep or a leaf stirring. So he thought the old stag must be somewhere close by and snuffed the air in all directions. It brought him no scent. Bambi sighed with relief to think he was alone. But he felt a lively desire to see the old stag again and win his approval.

When his mother came back he did not tell her anything of his encounter. He did not call her any more either the next time she disappeared. He thought of the old stag while he wandered around. He wanted very much to meet him. He wanted to say to him, "See, I don't call my mother any more," so the old stag would praise him.

But he told Gobo and Faline the next time they were together on the meadow. They listened attentively and had nothing to relate that could compare with this.

[82]

"Weren't you frightened?" asked Gobo excitedly.

O well—Bambi confessed he had been frightened. But only a little.

"I should have been terribly frightened," Gobo declared.

Bambi replied, no, he hadn't been very much afraid, because the stag was so handsome.

"That wouldn't have helped me much," Gobo added, "I'd have been too afraid to look at him. When I'm frightened I have streaks before my eyes so that I can't see at all, and my heart beats so fast that I can't breathe."

Faline became very thoughtful after Bambi's story and did not say anything.

But the next time they met, Gobo and Faline bounded up in great haste. They were alone again and so was Bambi. "We have been hunting for you all this time," cried Gobo. "Yes," Faline said importantly, "because now we know who it was you saw." Bambi bounded into the air for curiosity and asked, "Who?"

Faline said solemnly, "It was the old Prince."

"Who told you that?" Bambi demanded.

"Mother," Faline replied.

[83]

Bambi was amazed. "Did you tell her the whole story?" They both nodded. "But it was a secret," Bambi cried angrily.

Gobo tried to shield himself at once. "I didn't do it, it was Faline," he said. But Faline cried excitedly, "What do you mean, a secret? I wanted to know who it was. Now we all know and it's much more exciting."

Bambi was burning up with desire to hear all about it and let himself be mollified. Faline told him everything. "The old Prince is the biggest stag in the whole forest. There isn't anybody else that compares with him. Nobody knows how old he is. Nobody can find out where he lives. No one knows his family. Very few have seen him even once. At times he was thought to be dead because he hadn't been seen for so long. Then someone would see him again for a second and so they knew he was still alive. Nobody had ever dared ask him where he had been. He speaks to nobody and no one dares speak to him. He uses trails none of the others ever use. He knows the very depths of the forest. And he does not know such a thing as danger. Other Princes fight one another at times, sometimes in fun or to try each other out, sometimes in earnest. For many years no one has fought with the old stag. And of those who fought with him long ago not one is living. He is the great Prince."

Bambi forgave Gobo and Faline for babbling his secret to their mother. He was even glad to have found out all these important things, but he was glad that Gobo and Faline did not know all about it. They did not know that the great Prince had said, "Can't you stay by yourself? Shame on you!" Now Bambi was very glad that he had not told them about these things. For then Gobo and Faline would have told that along with the rest, and the whole forest would have gossipped about it.

That night when the moon rose Bambi's mother came back again. He suddenly saw her standing under the great oak at the edge of the meadow looking around for him. He saw her right away and ran to her.

That night Bambi learned something new. His mother was tired and hungry. They did not walk as far as usual. The mother quieted her hunger on the meadow where Bambi too was used to eating most of his meals. Side by side they nibbled

at the bushes and pleasantly ruminating, went
farther and farther into the woods.

Presently there was a loud rustling in the
bushes. Before Bambi could guess what it was
his mother began to cry aloud as she did when
she was very terrified or when she was beside herself. "Aoh!" she cried and, giving a bound,
stopped and cried, "Aoh, baoh!" Bambi tried to
make out the mighty forms which were drawing
near as the rustling grew louder. They were
right near now. They resembled Bambi and
Bambi's mother, Aunt Ena and all the rest of his
family, but they were gigantic and so powerfully
built that he stared up at them overcome.

Suddenly Bambi began to bleat, "Aoh baoh-
baoh!" He hardly knew he was bleating. He
couldn't help himself. The procession tramped
slowly by. Three, four giant apparitions, one after
the other. The last of them was bigger than any
of the others. He had a wild mane on his neck
and his antlers were tree-like. It took Bambi's
breath away to see them. He stood and bleated
from a heart full of wonder, for he was more
weirdly affected than ever before in his life. He
was afraid, but in a peculiar way. He felt how

It took Bambi's breath away to see them.

pitifully small he was, and even his mother seemed to him to have shrunk. He felt ashamed without understanding why, and at the same time terror shook him. He bleated, "Baoh! b-a-o-h!" He felt better when he bleated that way.

The procession had gone by. There was nothing more to be seen or heard. Even his mother was silent. Only Bambi kept giving short bleats now and then. He still felt the shock.

"Be still," his mother said, "they have gone now."

"O, Mother," Bambi whispered, "who was it?"

"Well," said his mother, "they are not so dangerous when all is said and done. Those are your big cousins, the elk—they are strong and they are important, far stronger than we are."

"And aren't they dangerous?" Bambi asked.

"Not as a rule," his mother explained. "Of course, a good many things are said to have happened. This and that is told about them, but I don't know if there is any truth in such gossip or not. They've never done any harm to me or to any one of my acquaintances."

"Why should they do anything to us?" asked Bambi, "if they are cousins of ours?" He wanted to feel calm but he kept trembling.

"O, they never do anything to us," his mother answered, "but I don't know why, I'm frightened whenever I see them. I don't understand it myself. But it happens that way every time."

Bambi was gradually reassured by her words but he remained thoughtful. Right above him in the branches of an alder, the screech-owl was hooting in his blood-curdling way. Bambi was distracted and forgot to act as if he had been frightened. But the screech-owl flew by anyhow and asked, "Didn't I frighten you?"

"Of course," Bambi replied, "you always frighten me."

The screech-owl chuckled softly. He was pleased. "I hope you don't hold it against me," he said, "it's just my way." He fluffed himself up so that he resembled a ball, sank his bill in his foamy white feathers and put on a terribly wise and serious face. He was satisfied with himself.

Bambi poured out his heart to him. "Do you know?" he began slyly, "I've just had a much worse fright."

"Indeed!" said the owl displeased. Bambi told him about his encounter with his giant relations.

"Don't talk to me about relations," the owl exclaimed, "I've got relations too. But I only fly around in the daytime so they are all down on me now. No, there isn't much use in relations. If they're bigger than you are, they're no good to you, and if they're smaller they're worth still less. If they're bigger than you, you can't bear them because they're proud, and if they're smaller they can't bear you because you're proud. No, I prefer to have nothing to do with the whole crowd."

"But, I don't even know my relations," Bambi said, laughing shyly, "I never heard of them, I never saw them before to-day."

"Don't bother about such people," the screech-owl advised. "Believe me," and he rolled his eyes significantly, "believe me, it's the best way. Relatives are never as good as friends. Look at us, we're not related in any way but we're good friends and that's much better."

Bambi wanted to say something else but the screech-owl went on, "I've had experience with such things. You are still too young but, believe me, I know better. Besides, I don't like to get mixed up in family affairs." He rolled his eyes thoughtfully and looked so impressive with his serious face that Bambi kept a discreet silence.

CHAPTER VII

ANOTHER NIGHT PASSED and morning brought an event.

It was a cloudless morning, dewy and fresh. All the leaves on the trees and the bushes seemed suddenly to smell sweeter. The meadows sent up great clouds of perfume to the tree-tops.

"Peep!" said the tit-mice when they awoke. They said it very softly. But since it was still gray dawn they said nothing else for a while. For a time it was perfectly still. Then a crow's hoarse, rasping caw sounded far above in the sky. The crows had awakened and were visiting one another in the tree-tops. The magpie answered at once, "Shackarakshak! Did you think I was still asleep?" Then a hundred small voices started in very softly here and there. "Peep! peep! tiu!" Sleep and the dark were still in these sounds. And they came from far apart.

Suddenly a blackbird flew to the top of a beech. She perched way up on the topmost twig that stuck up thin against the sky and sat there watching how, far away over the trees, the night-weary, pale-gray heavens were glowing in the distant east and coming to life. Then she commenced to sing.

Her little black body seemed only a tiny dark speck at that distance. She looked like a dead leaf. But she poured out her song in a great flood of rejoicing through the whole forest. And everything began to stir. The finches warbled, the little red-throat and the gold finch were heard. The doves rushed from place to place with a loud clapping and rustling of wings. The pheasants cackled as though their throats would burst. The noise of their wings, as they flew from their roosts to the ground, was soft but powerful. They kept uttering their metallic, splintering call with its soft ensuing chuckle. Far above the falcons cried sharply and joyously, "Yayaya!"

The sun rose.

"Diu diyu!" the yellow-bird rejoiced. He flew to and fro among the branches, and his round, yellow body flashed in the morning light like a winged ball of gold.

[93]

Bambi walked under the great oak on the meadow. It sparkled with dew. It smelled of grass and flowers and moist earth, and whispered of a thousand living things. Friend Hare was there and seemed to be thinking over something important. A haughty pheasant strutted slowly by, nibbling at the grass seeds and peering cautiously in all directions. The dark, metallic blue on his neck gleamed in the sun.

One of the Princes was standing close to Bambi. Bambi had never seen any of the fathers so close before. The stag was standing right in front of him next to the hazel bush and was somewhat hidden by the branches. Bambi did not move. He wanted the Prince to come out completely, and was wondering whether he dared speak to him. He wanted to ask his mother and looked around for her. But his mother had already gone away and was standing some distance off, beside Aunt Ena. At the same time Gobo and Faline came running out of the woods. Bambi was still thinking it over without stirring. If he went up to his mother and the others now he would have to pass by the Prince. He felt as if he couldn't do it.

"O well," he thought, "I don't have to ask my mother first. The old Prince spoke to me and I didn't tell mother anything about it. I'll say, 'Good morning, Prince.' He can't be offended at that. But if he does get angry, I'll run away fast." Bambi struggled with his resolve which began to waver again.

Presently the Prince walked out from behind the hazel bush onto the meadow.

"Now," thought Bambi.

Then there was a crash like thunder.

Bambi shrank together and didn't know what had happened. He saw the Prince leap into the air under his very nose and watched him rush past him into the forest with one great bound.

Bambi looked around in a daze. The thunder still vibrated. He saw how his mother and Aunt Ena, Gobo and Faline fled into the woods. He saw how Friend Hare scurried away like mad. He saw the pheasant running with his neck outstretched. He noticed that the forest grew suddenly still. He started and sprang into the thicket. He had made only a few bounds when he saw the Prince lying on the ground in front of him, motionless. Bambi stopped horrified, not understanding what it meant. The Prince lay bleeding from a great wound in his shoulder. He was dead.

"Don't stop!" a voice beside commanded. It was his mother who rushed past at full gallop. "Run," she cried. "Run as fast as you can!" She did not slow up, but raced ahead, and her command brought Bambi after her. He ran with all his might.

"What is it, Mother?" he asked. "What is it, Mother?"

His mother answered between gasps, "It—was —He!"

Bambi shuddered and they ran on. At last they stopped for lack of breath.

"What did you say? Tell me, what it was you said," a soft voice called down from overhead. Bambi looked up. The squirrel came chattering through the branches.

"I ran the whole way with you," he cried. "It was dreadful."

"Were you there?" asked the mother.

"Of course I was there," the squirrel replied. "I am still trembling in every limb." He sat erect, balancing with his splendid tail, displaying his

[96]

small white chest, and holding his forepaws protestingly against his body. "I'm beside myself
with excitement," he said.

"I'm quite weak from fright myself," said the
mother. "I don't understand it. Not one of us
saw a thing."

"Is that so?" the squirrel said pettishly. "I saw
Him long before."

"So did I," another voice cried. It was the
magpie. She flew past and settled on a branch.

"So did I," came a croak from above. It was
the jay who was sitting on an ash.

A couple of crows in the tree-tops cawed
harshly, "We saw Him, too."

They all sat around talking importantly. They
were unusually excited and seemed to be full of
anger and fear.

"Whom?" Bambi thought. "Whom did they
see?"

"I tried my best," the squirrel was saying,
pressing his forepaws protestingly against his
heart. "I tried my best to warn the poor Prince."

"And I," the jay rasped. "How often did I
scream? But he didn't care to hear me."

"He didn't hear me either," the magpie

croaked. "I called him at least ten times. I wanted to fly right past him, for, thought I, he hasn't heard me yet; I'll fly to the hazel bush where he's standing. He can't help hearing me there. But at that minute it happened."

"My voice is probably louder than yours, and I warned him as well as I could," the crow said in an impudent tone. "But gentlemen of that stamp pay little attention to the likes of us."

"Much too little, really," the squirrel agreed.

"Well, we did what we could," said the magpie. "We're certainly not to blame when an accident happens."

"Such a handsome Prince," the squirrel lamented. "And in the very prime of life."

"Akh!" croaked the jay. "It would have been better for him if he hadn't been so proud and had paid more attention to us."

"He certainly wasn't proud."

"No more so than the other Princes of his family," the magpie put in.

"Just plain stupid," sneered the jay.

"You're stupid yourself," the crow cried down from overhead. "Don't you talk about stupidity. The whole forest knows how stupid you are."

[98]

"I!" replied the jay, stiff with astonishment. "Nobody can accuse me of being stupid. I may be forgetful but I'm certainly not stupid."

"O just as you please," said the crow solemnly. "Forget what I said to you, but remember that the Prince did not die because he was proud or stupid, but because no one can escape Him."

"Akh!" croaked the jay. "I don't like that kind of talk." He flew away.

The crow went on, "He has already outwitted many of my family. He kills what He wants. Nothing can help us."

"You have to be on your guard against Him," the magpie broke in.

"You certainly do," said the crow sadly. "Good-by." He flew off, his family accompanying him.

Bambi looked around. His mother was no longer there.

"What are they talking about now?" thought Bambi. "I can't understand what they are talking about. Who is this 'He' they talk about? That was He, too, that I saw in the bushes, but He didn't kill me."

Bambi thought of the Prince lying in front of him with his bloody, mangled shoulder. He was

[99]

dead now. Bambi walked along. The forest sang again with a thousand voices, the sun pierced the tree-tops with its broad rays. There was light everywhere. The leaves began to smell. Far above the falcons called, close at hand a woodpecker hammered as if nothing had happened. Bambi was not happy. He felt himself threatened by something dark. He did not understand how the others could be so carefree and happy while life was so difficult and dangerous. Then the desire seized him to go deeper and deeper into the woods. They lured him into their depths. He wanted to find some hiding place where, shielded on all sides by impenetrable thickets, he could never be seen. He never wanted to go to the meadow again.

Something moved very softly in the bushes. Bambi drew back violently. The old stag was standing in front of him.

Bambi trembled. He wanted to run away, but he controlled himself and remained. The old stag looked at him with his great deep eyes and asked, "Were you out there before?"

"Yes," Bambi said softly. His heart was pounding in his throat.

The old stag kept gazing at him.

"Where is your mother?" asked the stag.

Bambi answered still very softly, "I don't know."

The old stag kept gazing at him. "And still you're not calling for her?" he said.

Bambi looked into the noble, iron-gray face, looked at the stag's antlers and suddenly felt full of courage. "I can stay by myself, too," he said.

The old stag considered him for a while; then he asked gently, "Aren't you the little one that was crying for his mother not long ago?"

Bambi was somewhat embarrassed, but his courage held. "Yes I am," he confessed.

The old stag looked at him in silence and it seemed to Bambi as if those deep eyes gazed still more mildly. "You scolded me then, Prince," he cried excitedly, "because I was afraid of being left alone. Since then I haven't been."

The stag looked at Bambi appraisingly and smiled a very slight, hardly noticeable smile. Bambi noticed it however. "Noble Prince," he asked confidently, "what has happened? I don't understand it. Who is this 'He' they are all talking about?" He stopped, terrified by the dark glance that bade him be silent.

[103]

Another pause ensued. The old stag was gazing past Bambi into the distance. Then he said slowly, "Listen, smell and see for yourself. Find out for yourself." He lifted his antlered head still higher. "Farewell," he said, nothing else. Then he vanished.

Bambi stood transfixed and wanted to cry. But that farewell still rang in his ears and sustained him. Farewell, the old stag had said, so he couldn't have been angry.

Bambi felt himself thrill with pride, felt inspired with a deep earnestness. Yes, life was difficult and full of danger. But come what might he would learn to bear it all.

He walked slowly deeper into the forest.

CHAPTER VIII

THE LEAVES WERE FALLING from the great oak at the meadow's edge. They were falling from all the trees.

One branch of the oak reached high above the others and stretched far out over the meadow. Two leaves clung to its very tip.

"It isn't the way it used to be," said one leaf to the other.

"No," the other leaf answered. "So many of us have fallen off to-night we're almost the only ones left on our branch."

"You never know who's going to go next," said the first leaf. "Even when it was warm and the sun shone, a storm or a cloudburst would come sometimes, and many leaves were torn off, though they were still young. You never know who's going to go next."

"The sun seldom shines now," sighed the second leaf, "and when it does it gives no warmth. We must have warmth again."

"Can it be true," said the first leaf, "can it really be true, that others come to take our places when we're gone and after them still others, and more and more?"

"It is really true," whispered the second leaf. "We can't even begin to imagine it, it's beyond our powers."

"It makes me very sad," added the first leaf.

They were silent a while. Then the first leaf said quietly to herself, "Why must we fall? . . ."

The second leaf asked, "What happens to us when we have fallen?"

"We sink down. . . ."

"What is under us?"

The first leaf answered, "I don't know, some say one thing, some another, but nobody knows."

The second leaf asked, "Do we feel anything, do we know anything about ourselves when we're down there?"

The first leaf answered, "Who knows? Not one of all those down there has ever come back to tell us about it."

They were silent again. Then the first leaf said

[106]

"Have I changed much?" asked the second leaf, shyly but
determinedly.

tenderly to the other, "Don't worry so much about it, you're trembling."

"That's nothing," the second leaf answered, "I tremble at the least thing now. I don't feel so sure of my hold as I used to."

"Let's not talk any more about such things," said the first leaf.

The other replied, "No, we'll let be. But— what else shall we talk about?" She was silent, but went on after a little while, "Which of us will go first?"

"There's still plenty of time to worry about that," the other leaf assured her. "Let's remember how beautiful it was, how wonderful, when the sun came out and shone so warmly that we thought we'd burst with life. Do you remember? And the morning dew, and the mild and splendid nights. . . ."

"Now the nights are dreadful," the second leaf complained, "and there is no end to them."

"We shouldn't complain," said the first leaf gently. "We've outlived many, many others."

"Have I changed much?" asked the second leaf shyly but determinedly.

"Not in the least," the first leaf assured her.

"You only think so because I've got to be so yellow and ugly. But it's different in your case."

"You're fooling me," the second leaf said.

"No, really," the first leaf exclaimed eagerly, "believe me, you're as lovely as the day you were born. Here and there may be a little yellow spot but it's hardly noticeable and only makes you handsomer, believe me."

"Thanks," whispered the second leaf, quite touched. "I don't believe you, not altogether, but I thank you because you're so kind, you've always been so kind to me. I'm just beginning to understand how kind you are."

"Hush," said the other leaf, and kept silent herself for she was too troubled to talk any more.

Then they were both silent. Hours passed.

A moist wind blew, cold and hostile, through the tree-tops.

"Ah, now," said the second leaf, "I. . . ." Then her voice broke off. She was torn from her place and spun down.

Winter had come.

CHAPTER IX

BAMBI NOTICED that the world was changed. It was hard for him to get used to this altered world. They had all lived like rich folk and now had fallen upon hard times. For Bambi knew nothing but abundance. He took it for granted that he would always have plenty to eat. He thought he would never need to trouble about food. He believed he would always sleep in the lovely green-leafed glade where no one could see him, and would always go about in his smooth, handsome, glossy red coat.

Now everything was changed without his having noticed the change take place. The process that was ending had seemed only a series of episodes to him. It pleased him to see the milk-white veils of mist steam from the meadow in the morning, or drop suddenly from the gray sky at dawn. They vanished so beautifully in the sunshine. The hoar frost that covered the meadow with such dazzling whiteness delighted him too. Sometimes he liked to listen to his big cousins the elks. The whole forest would tremble with their kingly voices. Bambi used to listen and be very much frightened, but his heart would beat high with admiration when he heard them calling. He remembered that the kings had antlers branching like tall, strong trees. And it seemed to him that their voices were as powerful as their antlers. Whenever he heard the deep tones of those voices he would stand motionless. Their deep voices rolled towards him like the mighty moaning of noble, maddened blood whose primal power was giving utterance to longing, rage and pride. Bambi struggled in vain against his fears. They over-powered him whenever he heard those voices, but he was proud to have such noble relatives. At the same time he felt a strange sense of annoyance because they were so unapproachable. It offended and humiliated him without his knowing exactly how or why, even without his being particularly conscious of it.

It was only after the mating season had passed and the thunder of the stags' mighty voices had grown still, that Bambi began to notice other things once more. At night when he roamed through the forest or by day as he lay in the glade, he heard the falling leaves whisper among the trees. They fluttered and rustled ceaselessly through the air from all the tree-tops and branches. A delicate silvery sound was falling constantly to earth. It was wonderful to awaken amidst it, wonderful to fall asleep to this mysterious and melancholy whispering. Soon the leaves lay thick and loose on the ground and when you walked through them they flew about, softly rustling. It was jolly to push them aside with every step, they were piled so high. It made a sound like "Sh! sh!"—soft and very clear and silvery. Besides, it was very useful, for Bambi had to be particularly careful these days to hear and smell everything. And with the leaves you could hear everything far off. They rustled at the slightest touch and cried, "Sh! sh!" Nobody could steal through them.

But then the rain came. It poured down from early morning till late at night. Sometimes it rained all night long and into the following day. It would stop for a while and begin again with

[113]

fresh strength. The air was damp and cold, the whole world seemed full of rain. If you tried to nibble a little meadow grass you got your mouth full of water, or if you tugged the least little bit at a bough a whole torrent of water poured into your eyes and nose. The leaves no longer rustled. They lay pale and soggy on the ground, flattened by the rain and made no sounds. Bambi discovered for the first time how unpleasant it is to be rained on all day and all night until you are soaked to the skin. There had not even been a frost yet, but he longed for the warm weather and felt it was a sad business to have to run around soaked through.

But when the north wind blew, Bambi found out what cold is. It wasn't much help to nestle close to his mother. Of course at first he thought it was wonderful to lie there and keep one side warm at least. But the north wind raged through the forest all day and all night long. It seemed to be driven to madness by some incomprehensible ice-cold fury, as though it wanted to tear up the forest by its roots or annihilate it somehow. The trees groaned in stubborn resistance, they struggled mightily against the wind's fierce onslaught.

[114]

You could hear their long-drawn moans, their sigh-like creakings, the loud snap when their strong limbs split, the angry cracking when now and again a trunk broke and the vanquished tree seemed to shriek from every wound in its rent and dying body. Nothing else could be heard, for the storm swooped down still more fiercely on the forest, and its roaring drowned all lesser noises.

Then Bambi knew that want and hardship had come. He saw how much the rain and wind had changed the world. There was no longer a leaf on tree or shrub. But all stood there as though violated, their bodies naked for all to see. And they lifted their bare brown limbs to the sky for pity. The grass on the meadow was withered and shortened, as if it had sunk into the earth. Even the glade seemed wretched and bare. Since the leaves had fallen it was no longer possible to lie so well hidden as before. The glade was open on all sides.

One day, as a young magpie flew over the meadow, something cold and white fell in her eye. Then it fell again and again. She felt as if a little veil were drawn across her eye while the small, pale, blinding white flakes danced around

[115]

her. The magpie hesitated in her flight, fluttered a little, and then soared straight up into the air. In vain. The cold white flakes were everywhere and got into her eyes again. She kept flying straight up, soaring higher.

"Don't put yourself out so much, dearie," a crow who was flying above her in the same direction called down, "don't put yourself out so much. You can't fly high enough to get outside these flakes. This is snow."

"Snow!" cried the magpie in surprise, struggling against the drizzle.

"That's about the size of it," said the crow, "it's winter, and this is snow."

"Excuse me," the magpie replied, "but I only left the nest in May. I don't know anything about winter."

"There are plenty in the same boat," the crow remarked, "but you'll soon find out."

"Well," said the magpie, "if this is snow I guess I'll sit down for a while." She perched on an elder and shook herself. The crow flew awkwardly away.

At first Bambi was delighted with the snow. The air was calm and mild while the white snow-

*Bambi had to paw the snow away with endless labor before he
could find one withered little blade of grass.*

stars whirled down and the world looked completely different. It had grown lighter, gayer, Bambi thought, and whenever the sun came out for a little while everything shone and the white covering flashed and sparkled so brightly that it blinded you.

But Bambi soon stopped being pleased with the snow. For it grew harder and harder to find food. He had to paw the snow away with endless labor before he could find one withered little blade of grass. The snow crust cut his legs and he was afraid of cutting his feet. Gobo had already cut his. Of course Gobo was the kind who couldn't stand anything and was a constant source of trouble to his mother.

The deer were always together now and were much more friendly than before. Ena brought her children constantly. Lately Marena, a half-grown doe, had joined the circle. But old Nettla really contributed most to their entertainment. She was quite a self-sufficient person and had her own ideas about everything. "No," she would say, "I don't bother with children any more. I've had enough of that particular joke."

Faline asked, "What difference does it make,

if they're a joke?" And Nettla would act as if she were angry, and say, "They're a bad joke, though, and I've had enough of them."

They got along perfectly together. They would sit side by side gossiping. The young ones had never had a chance to hear so much.

Even one or another of the Princes would join them now. At first things went somewhat stiffly, especially since the children were a little shy. But that soon changed, and they got along very well together. Bambi admired Prince Ronno, who was a stately lord, and he passionately loved the handsome young Karus. They had dropped their horns and Bambi often looked at the two slate-gray round spots that showed smooth and shimmering with many delicate points on the Princes' heads. They looked very noble.

It was terribly interesting whenever one of the Princes talked about Him. Ronno had a thick hide-covered swelling on his left fore-foot. He limped on that foot and used to ask sometimes, "Can you really see that I limp?" Everyone would hasten to assure him that there was not the trace of a limp. That was what Ronno wanted. And it really was hardly noticeable.

"Yes," he would go on. "I saved myself from a tight corner that time." And then Ronno would tell how He had surprised him and hurled His fire at him. But it had only struck his leg. It had driven him nearly mad with pain, and no wonder, since the bone was shattered. But Ronno did not lose his head. He was up and away on three legs. He pressed on in spite of his weakness for he saw that he was being pursued. He ran without stopping until night came. Then he gave himself a rest. But he went on the next morning until he felt he was in safety. Then he took care of himself, living alone in hiding, waiting for his wound to heal. At last he came out again and was a hero. He limped, but he thought no one noticed it.

They were often together now for long periods and told many stories. Bambi heard more about Him than ever before. They told how terrible He was to look at. No one could bear to look at His pale face. Bambi knew that already from his own experience. They spoke too about His smell, and again Bambi could have spoken if he had not been too well brought up to mix in his elders' conversation. They said that His smell differed each time in a hundred subtle ways and yet you could

[121]

tell it in an instant, for it was always exciting, unfathomable, mysterious and terrible.

They told how He used only two legs to walk with and they spoke of the amazing strength of His two hands. Some of them did not know what hands were. But when it was explained, old Nettla said, "I don't see anything so surprising in that. A squirrel can do everything you tell about just as well, and every little mouse can perform the same wonders." She turned away her head disdainfully.

"O no," cried the others, and they gave her to understand that those were *not* the same things at all. But old Nettla was not to be cowed. "What about the falcon?" she exclaimed. "And the buzzard? And the owl? They've got only two legs and when they want to catch something they simply stand on one leg and grab with the other. That's much harder and He certainly can't do that."

Old Nettla was not at all inclined to admire anything connected with Him. She hated Him with all her heart. "He is loathsome!" she said, and she stuck to that. Besides, nobody contradicted her, since nobody liked Him.

But the talk grew more complicated when they

[122]

told how He had a third hand, not two hands merely, but a third hand.

"That's an old story," Nettla said curtly, "I don't believe it."

"Is that so?" Ronno broke in. "Then what did he shatter my leg with? Can you tell me that?"

Old Nettla answered carelessly, "That's your affair, my dear, He's never shattered any of mine."

Aunt Ena said, "I've seen a good deal in my time, and I think there's something in the story that He has a third hand."

"I agree with you," young Karus said politely. "I have a friend, a crow. . . ." He paused, embarrassed for a moment, and looked around at them, one after the other, as though he were afraid of being laughed at. But when he saw that they were listening attentively to him he went on. "This crow is unusually well informed, I must say that. Surprisingly well informed. And she says that He really has three hands, but not always. The third hand is the bad one, the crow says. It isn't attached like the other two, but he carries it hanging over His shoulder. The crow says that she can always tell exactly when He, or anyone

[123]

like Him, is going to be dangerous. If He comes
without the third hand He isn't dangerous."

Old Nettla laughed. "Your crow's a blockhead,
my dear Karus," she said. "Tell her so for me. If
she were as clever as she thinks she is, she'd know
that He's always dangerous, always." But the
others had different objections.

Bambi's mother said, "Some of Them aren't
dangerous; you can see that at a glance."

"Is that so?" old Nettla asked. "I suppose you
stand still till They come up to you and wish you
a good day?"

Bambi's mother answered gently. "Of course
I don't stand still; I run away."

And Faline broke in with, "You should always
run away." Everybody laughed.

But when they talked about the third hand they
became serious and fear grew on them gradually.
For whatever it might be, a third hand or something else, it was terrible and they did not understand it. They only knew of it from others' stories,
few of them had ever seen it for themselves. He
would stand still, far off, and never move. You
couldn't explain what He did or how it happened,
but suddenly there would be a crash like thunder,

[124]

fire would shoot out and far away from Him you would drop down dying with your breast torn open. They all sat bowed while they talked about Him, as though they felt the presence of some dark, unknown power controlling them.

They listened curiously to the many stories that were always horrible, full of blood and suffering. They listened tirelessly to everything that was said about Him, tales that were certainly invented, all the stories and sayings that had come down from their fathers and great-grandfathers. In each one of them they were unconsciously seeking for some way to propitiate this dark power, or some way to escape it.

"What difference does it make," young Karus asked quite despondently, "how far away He is when He kills you?"

"Didn't your clever crow explain that to you?" old Nettla mocked.

"No," said Karus with a smile. "She says that she's often seen Him but no one can explain Him."

"Yes, he knocks the crows out of the trees, too, when he wants to," Ronno observed.

"And he brings down the pheasant on the wing," Aunt Ena added.

[125]

Bambi's **mother** said, "He throws his hand at you, my grandmother told me so."

"Is that so?" asked old Nettla. "What is it that bangs so terribly then?"

"That's when he tears his hand off," Bambi's mother explained. "Then the fire flashes and the thunder cracks. He's all fire inside."

"Excuse me," said Ronno. "It's true that He's all fire inside. But that about His hand is wrong. A hand couldn't make such wounds. You can see that for yourself. It's much more likely that it's a tooth He throws at us. A tooth would explain a great many things, you know. You really die from his bite."

"Will he never stop hunting us?" young Karus sighed.

Then Marena spoke, the young half-grown doe. "They say that sometime He'll come to live with us and be as gentle as we are. He'll play with us then and the whole forest will be happy, and we'll be friends with Him."

Old Nettla burst out laughing. "Let Him stay where He is and leave us in peace," she said.

Aunt Ena said reprovingly, "You shouldn't talk that way."

[126]

"And why not?" old Nettla replied hotly, "I really don't see why not. Friends with Him! He's murdered us ever since we can remember, everyone of us, our sisters, our mothers, our brothers! Ever since we came into the world He's given us no peace, but has killed us wherever we showed our heads. And now we're going to be friends with Him! What nonsense!"

Marena looked at all of them out of her big, calm, shining eyes. "Love is no nonsense," she said. "It has to come."

Old Nettla turned away. "I'm going to look for something to eat," she said, and trotted off.

CHAPTER X

WINTER DRAGGED ON. Sometimes it was warmer, but then the snow would fall again and lie deeper and deeper, so that it became impossible to scrape it away. It was worst when the thaws came and the melted snow water froze again in the night. Then there was a thin slippery film of ice. Often it broke in pieces and the sharp splinters cut the deers' tender fetlocks till they bled.

A heavy frost had set in several days before. The air was purer and rarer than it had ever been, and full of energy. It began to hum in a very fine high tone. It hummed with the cold.

It was silent in the woods, but something horrible happened every day. Once the crows fell upon Friend Hare's small son who was lying sick, and killed him in a cruel way. He could be heard moaning pitifully for a long while. Friend Hare was not at home, and when he heard the sad news he was beside himself with grief.

Another time the squirrel raced about with a great wound in his neck where the ferret had caught him. By a miracle the squirrel had escaped. He could not talk because of the pain, but he ran up and down the branches. Everyone could see him. He ran like mad. From time to time he stopped, sat down, raised his forepaws desperately and clutched his head in terror and agony while the red blood oozed on his white chest. He ran about for an hour, then suddenly crumpled up, fell across a branch, and dropped dead in the snow. A couple of magpies flew down at once to begin their meal.

Another day a fox tore to pieces the strong and handsome pheasant who had enjoyed such general respect and popularity. His death aroused the sympathies of a wide circle who tried to comfort his disconsolate widow.

The fox had dragged the pheasant out of the snow, where he was buried, thinking himself well hidden. No one could have felt safer than the pheasant for it all happened in broad daylight. The terrible hardship that seemed to have no end spread bitterness and brutality. It destroyed all their memories of the past, their faith in each other, and ruined every good custom they had. There was no longer either peace or mercy in the forest.

"It's hard to believe that it will ever be better," Bambi's mother sighed.

Aunt Ena sighed too. "It's hard to believe that it was ever any better," she said.

"And yet," Marena said, looking in front of her, "I always think how beautiful it was before."

"Look," old Nettla said to Aunt Ena, "your little one is trembling." She pointed to Gobo. "Does he always tremble like that?"

"Yes," Aunt Ena answered gravely, "he's shivered that way for the last few days."

"Well," said old Nettla in her frank way, "I'm glad that I have no more children. If that little one were mine I'd wonder if he'd last out the winter."

The future really didn't look very bright for Gobo. He was weak. He had always been much more delicate than Bambi or Faline and remained smaller than either of them. He was growing worse from day to day. He could not eat even the little food there was. It made his stomach ache. And he was quite exhausted by the cold, and by the horrors around him. He shivered more and more and could hardly stand up. Everyone looked at him sympathetically.

Old Nettla went up to him and nudged him good-naturedly. "Don't be so sad," she said encouragingly, "that's no way for a little prince to act, and besides it's unhealthy." She turned away so that no one should see how moved she was.

Ronno who had settled himself a little to one side in the snow suddenly sprang up. "I don't know what it is," he mumbled and gazed around.

Everyone grew watchful. "What is it?" they asked.

"I don't know," Ronno repeated. "But I'm restless. I suddenly felt restless as if something were wrong."

Karus was snuffing the air. "I don't smell anything strange," he declared.

They all stood still, listening and snuffing the air. "It's nothing, there's absolutely nothing to smell," they agreed one after another.

"Nevertheless," Ronno insisted, "you can say what you like, something is wrong."

Marena said, "The crows are calling."

"There they go calling again," Faline added quickly, but the others had already heard them.

"They are flying," said Karus and the others.

Everybody looked up. High above the tree-tops a flock of crows flapped by. They came from the farthest edge of the forest, the direction from which danger always came, and they were complaining to one another. Apparently something unusual had happened.

"Wasn't I right?" asked Ronno. "You can see that something is happening."

"What shall we do?" Bambi's mother whispered anxiously.

"Let's get away," Aunt Ena urged in alarm.

"Wait," Ronno commanded.

"But the children," Aunt Ena replied, "the children. Gobo can't run."

"Go ahead," Ronno agreed, "go off with your children. I don't think there's any need for it, but I don't blame you for going." He was alert and serious.

"Come, Gobo. Come, Faline. Softly now, go slowly. And keep behind me," Aunt Ena warned them. She slipped away with the children.

Time passed. They stood still, listening and trembling.

[132]

"As if we hadn't suffered enough already," old Nettla began. "We still have this to go through. . . ." She was very angry. Bambi looked at her, and he felt that she was thinking of something horrible.

Three or four magpies had already begun to chatter on the side of the thicket from which the crows had come. "Look out! Look out, out, out!" they cried. The deer could not see them, but could hear them calling and warning each other. Sometimes one of them, and sometimes all of them together, would cry, "Look out, out, out!" Then they came nearer. They fluttered in terror from tree to tree, peered back and fluttered away again in fear and alarm.

"Akh!" cried the jays. They screamed their warning loudly.

Suddenly all the deer shrank together at once as though a blow had struck them. Then they stood still snuffing the air.

It was He.

A heavy wave of scent blew past. There was nothing they could do. The scent filled their nostrils, it numbed their senses and made their hearts stop beating.

[133]

The magpies were still chattering. The jays were still screaming overhead. In the woods around them everything had sprung to life. The tit-mice flitted through the branches, like tiny feathered balls, chirping, "Run! run!"

The blackbirds fled swiftly and darkly above them with long-drawn twittering cries. Through the dark tangle of bare bushes, they saw on the white snow a wild aimless scurrying of smaller, shadowy creatures. These were the pheasants. Then a flash of red streaked by. That was the fox. But no one was afraid of him now. For that fearful scent kept streaming on in a wider wave, sending terror into their hearts and uniting them all in one mad fear, in a single feverish impulse to flee, to save themselves.

That mysterious overpowering scent filled the woods with such strength that they knew that this time He was not alone, but had come with many others, and there would be no end to the killing.

They did not move. They looked at the tit-mice, whisking away in a sudden flutter, at the blackbirds and the squirrels who dashed from tree-top to tree-top in mad bounds. They knew that all the little creatures on the grounds had nothing to fear. But they understood their flight when they smelt Him, for no forest creature could bear His presence.

Presently Friend Hare hopped up. He hesitated, sat still and then hopped on again.

"What is it?" Karus called after him impatiently.

But Friend Hare only looked around with bewildered eyes and could not even speak. He was completely terrified.

"What's the use of asking?" said Ronno gloomily.

Friend Hare gasped for breath. "We are surrounded," he said in a lifeless voice. "We can't escape on any side. He is everywhere."

At the same instant they heard His voice. Twenty or thirty strong, He cried, "Ho! ho! Ha! ha!" It roared like the sound of winds and storms. He beat on the tree trunks as though they were drums. It was wracking and terrifying. A distant twisting and rending of parted bushes rang out. There was a snapping and cracking of broken boughs.

He was coming.

He was coming into the heart of the thicket.

Then short whistling flute-like trills sounded

together with the loud flap of soaring wings. A
pheasant rose from under His very feet. The deer
heard the wing-beats of the pheasant grow fainter
as he mounted into the air. There was a loud
crash like thunder. Then silence. Then a dull
thud on the ground.

"He is dead," said Bambi's mother, trembling.

"The first," Ronno added.

The young doe, Marena, said, "In this very
hour many of us are going to die. Perhaps I shall
be one of them." No one listened to her, for a
mad terror had seized them all.

Bambi tried to think. But His savage noises
grew louder and louder and paralyzed Bambi's
senses. He heard nothing but those noises. They
numbed him while amidst the howling, shouting
and crashing he could hear his own heart pounding. He felt nothing but curiosity and did not
even realize that he was trembling in every limb.
From time to time his mother whispered in his
ear, "Stay close to me." She was shouting, but in
the uproar it sounded to Bambi as if she were
whispering. Her "Stay close to me," encouraged
him. It was like a chain holding him. Without
it he would have rushed off senselessly, and he

heard it at the very moment when his wits were wandering and he wanted to dash away.

He looked around. All sorts of creatures were swarming past, scampering blindly over one another. A pair of weasels ran by like thin snake-like streaks. The eye could scarcely follow them. A ferret listened as though bewitched to every shriek that desperate Friend Hare let out.

A fox was standing in a whole flurry of fluttering pheasants. They paid no attention to him. They ran right under his nose and he paid no attention to them. Motionless, with his head thrust forward, he listened to the onrushing tumult, lifting his pointed ears and snuffed the air with his nose. Only his tail moved, slowly wagging with his intense concentration.

A pheasant dashed up. He had come from where the danger was worst, and was beside himself with fear.

"Don't try to fly," he shouted to the others. "Don't fly, just run! Don't lose your head! Don't try to fly! Just run, run, run!"

He kept repeating the same thing over and over again as though to encourage himself. But he no longer knew what he was saying.

[137]

"Ho! ho! ha! ha!" came the death cry from quite near apparently.

"Don't lose your head," screamed the pheasant. And at the same time his voice broke in a whistling gasp and, spreading his wings, he flew up with a loud whir. Bambi watched how he flew straight up, directly between the tree, beating his wings. The dark metallic blue and greenish-brown markings on his body gleamed like gold. His long tail feathers swept proudly behind him. A short crash like thunder sounded sharply. The pheasant suddenly crumpled up in mid-flight. He turned head over tail as though he wanted to catch his claws with his beak, and then dropped violently to earth. He fell among the others and did not move again.

Then everyone lost his senses. They all rushed toward one another. Five or six pheasants rose at one time with a loud whirr. "Don't fly," cried the rest and ran. The thunder cracked five or six times and more of the flying birds dropped lifeless to the ground.

"Come," said Bambi's mother. Bambi looked around. Ronno and Karus had already fled. Old Nettla was disappearing. Only Marena was still beside them. Bambi went with his mother, Marena following them timidly. All around them was a roaring and shouting, and the thunder was crashing. Bambi's mother was calm. She trembled quietly but she kept her wits together.

"Bambi, my child," she said, "keep behind me all the time. We'll have to get out of here and across the open place. But now we'll go slowly."

The din was maddening. The thunder crashed ten, twelve times as He hurled it from His hands.

"Watch out," said Bambi's mother. "Don't run. But when we have to cross the open place, run as fast as you can. And don't forget, Bambi, my child, don't pay any attention to me when we get out there. Even if I fall, don't pay any attention to me, just keep on running. Do you understand, Bambi?"

His mother walked carefully step by step amidst the uproar. The pheasants were running up and down, burying themselves in the snow. Suddenly they would spring out and begin to run again. The whole Hare family was hopping to and fro, squatting down and then hopping again. No one said a word. They were all spent with terror and numbed by the din and thunderclaps.

It grew lighter in front of Bambi and his mother. The clearing showed through the bushes. Behind them the terrifying drumming on the tree trunks came crashing nearer and nearer. The breaking branches snapped. There was a roaring of "Ha, ha! Ho, ho!"

Then Friend Hare and two of his cousins rushed past them across the clearing. Bing! Ping! Bang! roared the thunder. Bambi saw how Friend Hare struck an elder in the middle of his flight and lay with his white belly turned upward. He quivered a little and then was still. Bambi stood petrified. But from behind him came the cry, "Here they are! Run! Run!"

There was a loud clapping of wings suddenly opened. There were gasps, sobs, showers of feathers, flutterings. The pheasants took wing and the whole flock rose almost at one instant. The air was throbbing with repeated thunderclaps and the dull thuds of the fallen and the high, piercing shrieks of those who had escaped.

Bambi heard steps and looked behind him. He was there. He came bursting through the bushes on all sides. He sprang up everywhere, struck about Him, beat the bushes, drummed on

[140]

the tree trunks and shouted with a fiendish voice.

"Now," said Bambi's mother. "Get away from here. And don't stay too close to me." She was off with a bound that barely skimmed the snow. Bambi rushed out after her. The thunder crashed around them on all sides. It seemed as if the earth would split in half. Bambi saw nothing. He kept running. A growing desire to get away from the tumult and out of reach of that scent which seemed to strangle him, the growing impulse to flee, the longing to save himself were loosed in him at last. He ran. It seemed to him as if he saw his mother hit but he did not know if it was really she or not. He felt a film come over his eyes from fear of the thunder crashing behind him. It had gripped him completely at last. He could think of nothing or see nothing around him. He kept running.

The open space was crossed. Another thicket took him in. The hue and cry still rang behind him. The sharp reports still thundered. And in the branches above him there was a light pattering like the first fall of hail. Then it grew quieter. Bambi kept running.

[141]

A dying pheasant, with its neck twisted, lay on the snow, beating feebly with its wings. When he heard Bambi coming he ceased his convulsive movements and whispered: "It's all over with me." Bambi paid no attention to him and ran on.

A tangle of bushes he blundered into forced him to slacken his pace and look for a path. He pawed the ground impatiently with his hoofs. "This way!" called someone with a gasping voice. Bambi obeyed involuntarily and found an opening at once. Someone moved feebly in front of him. It was Friend Hare's wife who had called.

"Can you help me a little?" she said. Bambi looked at her and shuddered. Her hind leg dangled lifelessly in the snow, dyeing it red and melting it with warm, oozing blood. "Can you help me a little?" she repeated. She spoke as if she were well and whole, almost as if she were happy. "I don't know what can have happened to me," she went on. "There's really no sense to it, but I just can't seem to walk. . . ."

In the middle of her words she rolled over on her side and died. Bambi was seized with horror again and ran.

"Bambi!"

He stopped with a jolt. A deer was calling him. Again he heard the cry. "Is that you, Bambi?"

Bambi saw Gobo floundering helplessly in the snow. All his strength was gone; he could no longer stand on his feet. He lay there half buried and lifted his head feebly. Bambi went up to him excitedly.

"Where's your mother, Gobo?" he asked, gasping for breath. "Where's Faline?" Bambi spoke quickly and impatiently. Terror still gripped his heart.

"Mother and Faline had to go on," Gobo answered resignedly. He spoke softly, but as seriously and as well as a grown deer. "They had to leave me here. I fell down. You must go on, too, Bambi."

"Get up," cried Bambi. "Get up, Gobo! You've rested long enough. There's not a minute to lose now. Get up and come with me!"

"No, leave me," Gobo answered quietly. "I can't stand up. It's impossible. I'd like to, but I'm too weak."

"What will happen to you?" Bambi persisted.

"I don't know. Probably I'll die," said Gobo simply.

[143]

The uproar began again and re-echoed. New crashes of thunder followed. Bambi shrank together. Suddenly a branch snapped. Young Karus pounded swiftly through the snow, galloping ahead of the din.

"Run," he called when he saw Bambi. "Don't stand there if you can run!" He was gone in a flash and his headlong flight carried Bambi along with it. Bambi was hardly aware that he had begun to run again and only after an interval did he say, "Good-by, Gobo." But he was already too far away. Gobo could no longer hear him.

He ran till nightfall through the woods that was filled with shouting and thunder. As darkness closed in, it grew quiet. Soon a light wind carried away the horrible scent that spread everywhere. But the excitement remained.

The first friend whom Bambi saw again was Ronno. He was limping more than ever.

"Over in the oak grove the fox has a burning fever from his wound," Ronno said. "I just passed him. He's suffering terribly. He keeps biting the snow and the ground."

"Have you seen my mother?" asked Bambi.

Bambi was hardly aware that he had begun to run again.

"No." answered Ronno evasively, and walked quickly away.

Later during the night Bambi met old Nettla with Faline. All three were delighted to meet.

"Have you seen my mother?" asked Bambi.

"No," Faline answered. "I don't even know where my own mother is."

"Well," said old Nettla cheerfully. "Here's a nice mess. I was so glad that I didn't have to bother with children any more and now I have to look after two at once. I'm heartily grateful."

Bambi and Faline laughed.

They talked about Gobo. Bambi told how he had found him, and they grew so sad they began to cry. But old Nettla would not have them crying. "Before everything else you have got to get something to eat. I never heard of such a thing. You haven't had a bite to eat this livelong day!"

She led them to places where there were still a few leaves that had not completely withered. Old Nettla was wonderfully gentle. She ate nothing herself, but made Bambi and Faline eat heartily. She pawed away the snow from the grassy spots and ordered them to eat with, "The grass is good here." Or else she would say, "No, wait. We'll find something better farther on." But between whiles she would grumble. "It's perfectly ridiculous the trouble children give you."

Suddenly they saw Aunt Ena coming and rushed towards her. "Aunt Ena," cried Bambi. He had seen her first. Faline was beside herself with joy and bounded around her. "Mother," she cried. But Ena was weeping and nearly dead from exhaustion.

"Gobo is gone," she cried. "I've looked for him. I went to the little place where he lay when he broke down in the snow . . . there was nothing there . . . he is gone . . . my poor little Gobo. . . ."

Old Nettla grumbled, "If you had looked for his tracks it would have been more sensible than crying," she said.

"There weren't any tracks," said Aunt Ena. "But . . . His . . . tracks were there. He found Gobo."

She was silent. Then Bambi asked despondently, "Aunt Ena, have you seen my mother?"

"No," answered Aunt Ena gently.

Bambi never saw his mother again.

CHAPTER XI

AT LAST THE WILLOWS shed their catkins. Everything was turning green, but the young leaves on the trees and bushes were still tiny. Glowing with the soft, early morning light they looked fresh and smiling like children who have just awakened from sleep.

Bambi was standing in front of a hazel bush, beating his new antlers against the wood. It was very pleasant to do that. And an absolute necessity besides, since skin and hide still covered his splendid antlers. The skin had to come off, of course, and no sensible creature would ever wait until it split of its own accord. Bambi pounded his antlers till the skin split and long strips of it dangled about his ears. As he pounded on the hazel stems again and again, he felt how much stronger his antlers were than the wood. This feeling shot through him in a rush of power and

[149]

pride. He beat more fiercely on the hazel bush and tore its bark into long pieces. The white body of the tree showed naked and quickly turned a rusty red in the open air. But Bambi paid no attention to that. He saw the bright wood of the tree flash under his strokes and it heartened him. A whole row of hazel bushes bore traces of his work.

"Well, you are nearly grown now," said a cheerful voice close by.

Bambi tossed his head and looked around him. There sat the squirrel observing him in a friendly way. From overhead came a short, shrill laugh, "Ha! Ha!"

Bambi and the squirrel were both half frightened. But the woodpecker who was clinging to an oak trunk called down, "Excuse me, but I always have to laugh when I see you deer acting like that."

"What is there to laugh at?" asked Bambi politely.

"O!" said the woodpecker, "you go at things in such a wrong-headed way. In the first place, you ought to try big trees, for you can't get anything out of those little wisps of hazel stalks."

"Excuse me," said the woodpecker, "but I always have to laugh
when I see you deer acting like that."

"What should I get out of them?" Bambi asked.

"Bugs," said the woodpecker with a laugh. "Bugs and grubs. Look, do like this." He drummed on the oak trunk, tack! tack! tack! tack!

The squirrel rushed up and scolded him. "What are you talking about?" he said. "The Prince isn't looking for bugs and grubs."

"Why not?" said the woodpecker in high glee. "They taste fine." He bit a bug in half, swallowed it and began drumming again.

"You don't understand," the squirrel went on scolding. "A noble lord like that has far other, far higher aims. You're only casting reflection on yourself by such talk."

"It's all the same to me," answered the woodpecker. "A fig for higher aims," he cried cheerfully and fluttered away. The squirrel bustled down again.

"Don't you remember me?" he said putting on a pleased expression.

"Very well," answered Bambi in a friendly way. "Do you live up there?" he asked pointing to the oak.

The squirrel looked at him good-humoredly. "You're mixing me up with my grandmother,"

[153]

he said. "I knew you were mixing me up with her. My grandmother used to live up there when you were just a baby, Prince Bambi. She often told me about you. The ferret killed her long ago, last winter, you may remember it."

"Yes," Bambi nodded. "I've heard about it."

"Well, afterwards my father settled here," the squirrel went on. He sat erect and held both forepaws politely over his white chest. "But maybe you've got me mixed up with my father, too. Did you know my father?"

"I'm sorry," Bambi replied. "But I never had that pleasure."

"I thought so," the squirrel exclaimed satisfied. "Father was so surly and so shy. He had nothing to do with anybody."

"Where is he now?" Bambi inquired.

"O," said the squirrel, "the owl caught him a month ago. Yes. . . . And now I'm living up there myself. I'm quite content, since I was born up there."

Bambi turned to go.

"Wait," cried the squirrel quickly, "I didn't mean to talk about all that. I wanted to say something quite different."

[154]

Bambi stopped. "What is it?" he asked patiently.

"Yes," said the squirrel, "what is it?" He thought a little while and then gave a quick skip and sat erect, balancing with his splendid tail. He looked at Bambi. "Right you are," he chattered on. "Now I know what it was. I wanted to say that your antlers are almost grown now, and that you are going to be a remarkably handsome person."

"Do you really think so?" said Bambi joyfully.

"Remarkably handsome," cried the squirrel, and pressed his forepaws rapturously against his white chest. "So tall, so stately and with such long bright prongs to your antlers. You don't often see the like."

"Really?" Bambi asked. He was so delighted that he immediately began to beat the hazel stems again. He tore off long ribbons of bark.

All the while the squirrel kept on talking. "I must say that very few have antlers like those at your age. It doesn't seem possible. I saw you several times from a distance last summer, and I can hardly believe that you're the same creature, you were such a thin little shaver then."

[155]

Bambi suddenly grew silent. "Good-by," he said hastily. "I have to go now." And he ran off.

He didn't like to be reminded of last summer. He had had a difficult time of it since then. At first, after his mother's disappearance, he had felt quite lost. The long winter was interminable. Spring came hesitatingly and it was late before things began to turn green. Without old Nettla Bambi might not even have pulled through at all, but she looked after him and helped him where she could. In spite of that he was alone a good deal.

He missed Gobo at every turn; poor Gobo, who was dead too, like the rest of them. Bambi thought of him often during that winter, and for the first time he really began to appreciate how good and lovable Gobo had been.

He seldom saw Faline. She stayed with her mother most of the time, and seemed to have grown unusually shy. Later when it had finally grown warm Bambi began to feel his old self once more. He flourished his first antler on high and was very proud of it. But bitter disappointment soon followed.

The other bucks chased him whenever they saw

him. They drove him away angrily. They would not let him come near them until finally he was afraid to take a step for fear of being caught. He was afraid to show himself anywhere and slunk along hidden trails in a very downcast frame of mind.

As the summer days grew warmer a remarkable restlessness seized him. His heart felt more and more oppressed with a sense of longing that was both pleasant and painful. Whenever he chanced to see Faline or one of her friends, though only at a distance, a rush of incomprehensible excitement crept over him. Often it happened that he recognized her track, or the air he snuffed told him she was near. Then he would feel himself irresistibly drawn towards her. But when he gave way to his desire he always came to grief. Either he met no one and, after wandering around for a long while, had to admit that they were avoiding him, or he ran across one of the bucks who immediately sprang at him, beat and kicked him and chased him disgracefully away. Ronno and Karus had treated him worst of all. No, that hadn't been a happy time.

And now the squirrel had stupidly reminded

him of it. Suddenly he became quite wild and started to run. The tit-mice and hedge sparrows flitted, frightened, through the bushes as he passed, and asked each other in a fluster, "What was that?" Bambi did not hear them. A couple of magpies chattered nervously, "What happened?" The jay cried angrily, "What is the matter with you?" Bambi paid no attention to him. Overhead the yellow-bird sang from tree to tree, "Good morning, I'm ha-appy." Bambi did not answer. The thicket was very bright and shot through with sunbeams. Bambi did not stop to think about such things.

Suddenly there was a loud whirr of wings. A whole rainbow of gorgeous colors flashed from under Bambi's very feet and shone so close to his eyes that he stopped, dazzled. It was Jonello, the pheasant. He had flown up in terror, for Bambi had nearly stepped on him. He fled away scolding.

"I never heard of such a thing," he cried in his split, cackling voice. Bambi stood still in astonishment and stared after him.

"It turned out all right this time, but it really was inconsiderate," said a soft, twittering voice close to the ground. It was Jonellina, the pheas-

[158]

ant's wife. She was sitting on the ground, hovering over her eggs. "My husband was terribly frightened," she went on in an irritable tone. "And so was I. But I don't dare stir from this spot. I wouldn't stir from this spot no matter what happened. You could step on me and I wouldn't move."

Bambi was a little embarrassed. "I beg your pardon," he stammered, "I didn't mean to do it."

"O, not at all," the pheasant's wife replied. "It was nothing so dreadful after all. But my husband and I are so nervous at present. You can understand why. . . ."

Bambi didn't understand why at all and went on. He was quieter now. The forest sang around him. The light grew more radiant and warmer. The leaves on the bushes, the grass underfoot and the moist, steaming earth began to smell more sweetly. Bambi's young strength swelled within him and streamed through all his limbs so that he walked around stiffly with awkward restrained movements like a mechanical thing.

He went up to a low alder shrub and, lifting his feet high, beat on the earth with such savage blows that the dirt flew. His two sharp-pointed hoofs cut the turf that grew there. They scraped away the wood-vetch and leeks, the violets and snowbells, till the bare earth was furrowed in front of him. Every blow sounded dully.

Two moles, who were grubbing among the tangled roots of an old sycamore tree, grew anxious and, looking out, saw Bambi.

"That's a ridiculous way to do things," said one mole. "Who ever heard of anybody digging that way?"

The other mole drew down one corner of his mouth in a scornful sneer. "He doesn't know anything, you can see that right off," he said. "But that's the way it is when people meddle with things they know nothing about."

Suddenly Bambi listened, tossed up his head, listened again, and peered through the leaves. A flash of red showed through the branches. The prongs of an antler gleamed indistinctly. Bambi snorted. Whoever it might be who was circling around him, whether it was Karus or somebody else, didn't matter. "Forward!" thought Bambi as he charged. "I'll show them that I'm not afraid of them," he thought as though suddenly exultant. "I'll show them that they'd better look out for me."

The branches rustled with the fury of his charge, the bushes cracked and broke. Then Bambi saw the other deer right in front of him. He did not recognize him, for everything was swimming before his eyes. He thought of nothing but "Forward!" His antlers lowered, he rushed on. All his strength was concentrated in his shoulders. He was ready for the blow. Then he smelt his opponent's hide. But he saw nothing ahead of him but the red wall of his flank. Then the other stag made a very slight turn and Bambi, not meeting the resistance he expected, charged past him into the empty air. He nearly went head over heels. He staggered, pulled himself together and made ready for a fresh onslaught.

Then he recognized the old stag.

Bambi was so astonished that he lost his self-possession. He was ashamed to run away as he would have liked to do. But he was also ashamed to stay there. He didn't move.

"Well?" asked the old stag, quietly and gently. His voice was so frank and yet so commanding it pierced Bambi to the heart. He was silent.

"Well?" the old stag repeated.

"I thought, . . ." Bambi stammered, "I

thought . . . it was Ronno . . . or. . . ." He stopped and risked a shy glance at the old stag. And this glance confused him still more. The old stag stood motionless and powerful. His head had turned completely white by now, and his proud dark eyes glowed in their depths.

"Why don't you charge me . . . ?" the old stag asked.

Bambi looked at him, filled with a wonderful ecstasy, and shaken by a mysterious tremor. He wanted to cry out, "It's because I love you," but he merely answered, "I don't know. . . ."

The old stag looked at him. "It's a long time since I've seen you," he said. "You've grown big and strong."

Bambi did not answer. He trembled with joy. The old stag went on examining him critically. Then he came unexpectedly up to Bambi who was terribly frightened.

"Act bravely," said the old stag.

He turned around and in the next moment had disappeared. Bambi remained in that place for a long while.

CHAPTER XII

IT WAS SUMMER and sizzling hot. The same longing he had felt before began to stir again in Bambi. But much more strongly now than then. It seethed in his blood and made him restless. He strayed far afield.

One day he met Faline. He met her quite unexpectedly, for his thoughts were so confused, his senses so clouded by the restless desire that raged within him, that he did not even recognize Faline. She was standing in front of him. Bambi stared at her speechless for a while. Then he said as though fascinated, "How beautiful you have grown, Faline!"

"So you recognize me again?" Faline replied.

"How could I help recognizing you?" cried Bambi. "Didn't we grow up together?"

Faline sighed. "It's a long time since we've seen each other," she said. Then she added,

"People grow to be strangers," but she was already using her gay bantering tone again. They remained together.

"I used to walk on this path with my mother when I was a child," Bambi said after a while.

"It leads to the meadow," said Faline.

"I saw you for the first time on the meadow," said Bambi a little solemnly. "Do you remember?"

"Yes," Faline replied. "Gobo and me." She sighed softly and said, "Poor Gobo. . . ."

Bambi repeated, "Poor Gobo."

Then they began to talk about old times and asked each other every minute, "Do you remember?" Each saw that the other still remembered everything. And they were both pleased at that.

"Do you remember how we used to play tag on the meadow?" Bambi reminisced.

"Yes, it was like this," said Faline and she was off like an arrow. At first Bambi hung back, somewhat surprised, and then he rushed after her. "Wait! wait!" he cried joyously.

"I can't wait," teased Faline, "I'm in too much

At last Bambi caught up with her and barred the way.

of a hurry." And bounding lightly away, she ran in a circle through the grass and bushes. At last Bambi caught up with her and barred the way. Then they stood quietly side by side. They laughed contentedly. Suddenly Faline leaped into the air as though some one had hit her, and bounded off anew. Bambi rushed after her. Faline raced around and around, always managing to elude him.

"Stop!" Bambi panted. "I want to ask you something."

Faline stopped.

"What do you want to ask me?" she inquired curiously.

Bambi was silent.

"O, so you're only fooling me," said Faline, and started to turn away.

"No," said Bambi quickly. "Stop! stop! I wanted. . . . I wanted to ask you . . . do you love me, Faline? . . ."

She looked at him more curiously than before, and a little guardedly. "I don't know," she said.

"But you must know," Bambi insisted. "I know very well that I love you. I love you terribly, Faline. Tell me, don't you love me?"

"Maybe I do," she answered coyly.

"And will you stay with me?" Bambi demanded passionately.

"If you ask me nicely," Faline said happily.

"Please do, Faline, dear, beautiful, beloved Faline," cried Bambi beside himself with love. "Do you hear me? I want you with all my heart."

"Then I'll certainly stay with you," said Faline gently, and ran away.

In ecstasy, Bambi darted after her again. Faline fled straight across the meadow, swerved about and vanished into the thicket. But as Bambi swerved to follow her there was a fierce rustling in the bushes and Karus sprang out.

"Halt!" he cried.

Bambi did not hear him. He was too busy with Faline. "Let me pass," he said hurriedly, "I haven't time for you."

"Get out," Karus commanded angrily. "Get away from here this minute or I'll shake you until there's no breath left in your body. I forbid you to follow Faline."

The memory of last summer when he had been so often and so miserably hunted awakened in

Bambi. Suddenly he became enraged. He did not say a word, but without waiting any longer rushed at Karus with his antlers lowered.

His charge was irresistible and, before he knew what had happened, Karus was lying in the grass. He was up again quicker than a flash, but was no sooner on his feet than a new attack made him stagger.

"Bambi," he cried. "Bam. . . ." he tried to cry again, but a third blow, that glanced off his shoulder, nearly choked him with pain.

Karus sprang to one side in order to elude Bambi who came rushing on again. Suddenly he felt strangely weak. At the same time he realized with a qualm that this was a life and death struggle. Cold terror seized him. He turned to flee from the silent Bambi who came rushing after him. Karus knew that Bambi was furious and would kill him without mercy, and that thought numbed his wits completely. He fled from the path and, with a final effort, burst through the bushes. His one hope was of escape.

All at once Bambi ceased chasing him. Karus did not even notice this in his terror, and kept

[169]

straight on through the bushes as fast as he could go. Bambi had stopped because he had heard Faline's shrill call. He listened as she called again in distress and fear. Suddenly he faced about and rushed back.

When he reached the meadow he saw Ronno pursuing Faline who had fled into the thicket.

"Ronno," cried Bambi. He did not even realize that he had called.

Ronno, who could not run very fast because of his lameness, stood still.

"O, there's our little Bambi," he said scornfully, "do you want something from me?"

"I do," said Bambi quietly but in a voice which control and overpowering anger had completely altered. "I want you to let Faline alone and to leave here immediately."

"Is that all?" sneered Ronno. "What an insolent gamin you've got to be. I wouldn't have thought it possible."

"Ronno," said Bambi still more softly, "it's for your own sake. If you don't go now you'll be glad to run later, but then you'll never be able to run again."

"Is that so?" cried Ronno in a rage. "Do you

dare to talk to me like that? It's because I limp,
I suppose. Most people don't even notice it. Or
maybe you think I'm afraid of you, too, because
Karus was such a pitiful coward. I give you fair
warning. . . ."

"No, Ronno," Bambi broke in, "I'll do all the
warning. Go!" His voice trembled. "I always
liked you, Ronno. I always thought you were very
clever and respected you because you were older
than I am. I tell you once and for all, go. I
haven't any patience left."

"It's a pity you have so little patience," Ronno
said with a sneer, "a great pity for you, my boy.
But be easy, I'll soon finish you off. You won't
have long to wait. Maybe you've forgotten how
often I used to chase you."

At the thought of that Bambi had nothing
more to say. Nothing could hold him back. Like
a wild beast he tore at Ronno who met him with
his head lowered. They charged together with a
crash. Ronno stood firm but wondered why
Bambi did not blench back. The sudden charge
had dazed him, for he had not expected that
Bambi would attack him first. Uneasily he felt

[171]

Bambi's giant strength and saw that he must keep himself well in hand.

He tried to turn a trick as they stood forehead pressed against forehead. He suddenly shifted his weight so that Bambi lost his balance and staggered forward.

Bambi braced with his hind legs and hurled himself on Ronno with redoubled fury before he had time to regain his footing. A prong broke from Ronno's antlers with a loud snap. Ronno thought his forehead was shattered. The sparks danced before his eyes and there was a roaring in his ears. The next moment a terrific blow tore open his shoulder. His breath failed him and he fell to the ground with Bambi standing over him furiously.

"Let me go," Ronno groaned.

Bambi charged blindly at him. His eyes flashed. He seemed to have no thought of mercy.

"Please stop," whined Ronno pitifully. "Don't you know that I'm lame? I was only joking. Spare me. Can't you take a joke?"

Bambi let him alone without a word. Ronno rose wearily. He was bleeding and his legs tottered. He slunk off in silence.

[172]

Bambi started for the thicket to look for Fa-line, but she came out of her own accord. She had been standing at the edge of the woods and had seen it all.

"That was wonderful," she said laughingly. Then she added softly and seriously, "I love you."

They walked on very happily together.

CHAPTER XIII

ONE DAY THEY WENT to look for the little clearing in the depth of the woods where Bambi had last met the old stag. Bambi told Faline all about the old stag and grew enthusiastic.

"Maybe we'll meet him again," he said. "I'd like you to see him."

"It would be nice," said Faline boldly. "I'd really like to chat with him once myself." But she wasn't telling the truth for, though she was very inquisitive, she was afraid of the old stag.

The twilight was already dusky gray. Sunset was near.

They walked softly side by side where the leaves hung quivering on the shrubs and bushes and permitted a clear view in all directions. Presently there was a rustling sound near by. They stopped and looked towards it. Then the old stag marched slowly and powerfully through the

[174]

bushes, into the clearing. In the drab twilight he seemed like a gigantic gray shadow.

Faline uttered an involuntary cry. Bambi controlled himself. He was terrified, too, and a cry stuck in his throat. But Faline's voice sounded so helpless that pity seized him and made him want to comfort her.

"What's the matter?" he whispered solicitously, while his voice quavered, "what's the matter with you? He isn't going to hurt us."

Faline simply shrieked again.

"Don't be so terribly upset, beloved," Bambi pleaded. "It's ridiculous to be so frightened by him. After all he's one of our own family."

But Faline wouldn't be comforted. She stood stock-still, staring at the stag who went along unconcerned. Then she shrieked and shrieked.

"Pull yourself together," Bambi begged. "What will he think of us?"

But Faline was not to be quieted. "He can think what he likes," she cried bleating again. "Ah-oh! Baoh! . . . It's terrible to be so big!"

She bleated again, "Baoh! Leave me," she went on, "I can't help it, I have to bleat. Baoh, baoh, baoh!"

[175]

The stag was standing in the little clearing, looking for tidbits in the grass.

Fresh courage came to Bambi who had one eye on the hysterical Faline, the other on the placid stag. With the encouragement he had given Faline he had conquered his own fears. He began to reproach himself for the pitiful state he was in whenever he saw the old stag, a state of mingled terror and excitement, admiration and submissiveness.

"It's perfectly absurd," he said with painful decision. "I'm going straight over to tell him who I am."

"Don't," cried Faline. "Don't! Baoh! Something terrible will happen. Baoh!"

"I'm going anyway," answered Bambi.

The stag who was feasting so calmly, not paying the slightest attention to the weeping Faline, seemed altogether too haughty to him. He felt offended and humiliated. "I'm going," he said. "Be quiet. You'll see, nothing will happen. Wait for me here."

He went, but Faline did not wait. She hadn't the least desire or courage to do so. She faced about and ran away crying, for she thought it was

The stag immediately lifted his head and looked at him.

the best thing she could do. Bambi could hear her going farther and farther away, bleating, "Ba-oh! Baoh!"

Bambi would gladly have followed her. But that was no longer possible. He pulled himself together and went forward.

Through the branches he saw the stag standing in the clearing, his head close to the ground. Bambi felt his heart pounding as he stepped out.

The stag immediately lifted his head and looked at him. Then he gazed absently straight ahead again. The way in which the stag gazed into space, as though no one else were there, seemed as haughty to Bambi as the way he had stared at him.

Bambi did not know what to do. He had come with the firm intention of speaking to the stag. He wanted to say, "Good day, I am Bambi. May I ask to know your honorable name also?"

Yes, it had all seemed very easy, but now it appeared that the affair was not so simple. What good were the best of intentions now? Bambi did not want to seem ill-bred as he would be if he went off without saying a word. But he did not want to seem forward either, and he would be if he began the conversation.

The stag was wonderfully majestic. It delighted Bambi and made him feel humble. He tried in vain to arouse his courage and kept asking himself, "Why do I let him frighten me? Am I not just as good as he is?" But it was no use. Bambi continued to be frightened and felt in his heart of hearts that he really was not as good as the old stag. Far from it. He felt wretched and had to use all his strength to keep himself steady.

The old stag looked at him and thought, "He's handsome, he's really charming, so delicate, so poised, so elegant in his whole bearing. I must not stare at him, though. It really isn't the thing to do. Besides, it might embarrass him." So he stared over Bambi's head into the empty air again.

"What a haughty look," thought Bambi. "It's unbearable, the opinion such people have of themselves."

The stag was thinking, "I'd like to talk to him, he looks so sympathetic. How stupid never to speak to people we don't know." He looked thoughtfully ahead of him.

"I might as well be air," said Bambi to him-

[180]

self. "This fellow acts as though he were the only thing on the face of the earth."

"What should I say to him?" the old stag was wondering. "I'm not used to talking. I'd say something stupid and make myself ridiculous . . . for he's undoubtedly very clever."

Bambi pulled himself together and looked fixedly at the stag. "How splendid he is," he thought despairingly.

"Well, some other time, perhaps," the stag decided and walked off, dissatisfied but majestic.

Bambi remained filled with bitterness.

CHAPTER XIV

THE FOREST SWELTERED under a scorching sun. Since it rose it had driven even the tiniest cloudlet from the sky, and shone all alone in the wide blue depths that were pallid now with heat. Over the meadows and the tree-tops the air quivered in glassy, transparent ripples as it does over a flame. Not a leaf was moving, not a blade of grass. The birds were silent and sat hidden among the shady leaves, never stirring from their places. All the paths and trails in the thicket were empty. Not a creature was abroad. The forest lay as though hurt by the blinding light. The earth and the trees, the bushes, the beasts, breathed in the intense heat with a kind of sluggish satisfaction.

Bambi was asleep.

He had made merry with Faline all night. He had pranced around with her until broad day-

light, and in his bliss had even forgotten to eat.
But he had grown so tired that he did not feel
hungry any more. His eyes fell shut. He lay
down where he happened to be standing in the
middle of the bushes, and fell asleep at once.

The bitter acrid odor that streamed from the
sun-warmed juniper, and the penetrating scent of
spurge laurel, mounted to his head while he slept
and gave him new strength. Suddenly he awoke
in a daze. Had Faline called him? Bambi
looked around. He remembered seeing Faline as
he lay down, standing close beside him near the
white-thorn, nibbling the leaves. He had supposed
she would remain near him, but she was gone.
Apparently she had grown tired of being alone
by now and was calling for him to come and look
for her.

As Bambi listened he wondered how long he
could have slept and how often Faline had called.
He wasn't sure. Veils of sleep still clouded his
thought.

Then she called again. With a sidewise spring
Bambi turned in the direction the sound came
from. Then he heard it again. And suddenly he
felt perfectly happy. He was wonderfully re-

freshed, quieted and strengthened, but racked by a terrific appetite.

The call came again clearly, thin as a bird's twittering, tender and full of longing: "Come, come!" it said.

Yes, that was her voice. That was **Faline**. Bambi rushed away so fast that the dry branches barely crackled as he burst through the bushes and the hot green leaves scarcely rustled.

But he had to stop short in the midst of his course, and swerve to one side, for the old stag was standing there, barring his path.

Bambi had no time for anything but love. The old stag was indifferent to him now. He would meet him again somewhere later on. He had no time for old stags now, however noble they might be. He had thoughts for Faline alone. He greeted the stag hastily and tried to hurry by.

"Where are you going?" asked the old stag earnestly.

Bambi was somewhat embarrassed and tried to think of an evasion, but he changed his mind and answered truthfully, "To her."

"Don't go," said the old stag.

For a second a single angry spark flared up in

Bambi's mind. Not go to Faline? How could the mean old stag ask that? "I'll simply run off," Bambi thought. And he looked quickly at the old stag. But the deep look that met him in the old stag's eyes held him fast. He quivered with impatience but he did not run away.

"She's calling me," he said in explanation. He said it in a tone which clearly bleated, "Don't keep me talking here."

"No," said the old stag, "she isn't calling."

The call came once again, thin as a bird's twittering, "Come!"

"Listen," Bambi cried excitedly, "there it is again."

"I hear it," said the old stag, nodding.

"Well, good-by," Bambi flung back hurriedly.

"Stop!" the old stag commanded.

"What do you want?" cried Bambi, beside himself with impatience. "Let me go. I have no time. Please, Faline is calling. . . . You ought to see that. . . ."

"I tell you," the old stag said, "that it isn't she."

Bambi was desperate. "But," he said, "I know her voice."

[185]

"Listen to me," the old stag went on.

Again the call came. Bambi felt the ground burning under his feet. "Later," he pleaded, "I'll come right back."

"No," said the old stag sadly, "you'll never come back, never again."

The call came again. "I must go! I must go!" cried Bambi who was nearly out of his wits.

"Then," the old stag declared in a commanding voice, "we'll go together."

"Quickly," cried Bambi and bounded off.

"No, slowly," commanded the old stag in a voice that forced Bambi to obey. "Stay in back of me. Move one step at a time."

The old stag began to move forward. Bambi followed, sighing with impatience.

"Listen," said the old stag without stopping, "no matter how often that call comes, don't stir from my side. If it's Faline, you'll get to hear her soon enough. But it isn't Faline. Don't let yourself be tempted. Everything depends now on whether you trust me or not."

Bambi did not dare to resist, and surrendered in silence.

The old stag advanced slowly and Bambi fol-

The old stag advanced slowly and Bambi followed him.

lowed him. O how cleverly the old stag moved! Not a sound came from under his hoofs. Not a leaf was disturbed. Not a twig snapped. And yet they were gliding through thick bushes, slinking through the ancient tangled thicket. Bambi was amazed and had to admire him in spite of his impatience. He had never dreamed that anybody could move like that.

The call came again and again. The old stag stood still, listening and nodding his head. Bambi stood beside him, shaken with desire, and suffering from restraint. He could not understand it at all.

Several times the old stag stopped, although no call had come, and lifted his head, listening and nodding. Bambi heard nothing. The old stag turned away from the direction of the call and made a detour. Bambi raged inwardly because of it.

The call came again and again. At last they drew nearer to it, then still nearer. At last they were quite near.

The old stag whispered, "No matter what you see, don't move, do you hear? Watch everything I do and act just as I do, cautiously. And don't lose your head."

[189]

They went a few steps farther and suddenly that sharp, arresting scent that Bambi knew so well struck them full in the face. He swallowed so much of it that he nearly cried out. He stood as though rooted to the ground. For a moment his heart seemed pounding in his throat. The old stag stood calmly beside him and motioned with his eyes.

He was standing there.

He was standing quite close to them leaning against the trunk of an oak, hidden by hazel bushes. He was calling softly, "Come, come!"

Bambi was completely bewildered. He was so terrified that he began to understand only by degrees that it was He who was imitating Faline's voice. It was He who was calling, "Come, come!"

Cold terror shot through Bambi's body. The idea of flight gripped him and tugged at his heart.

"Be still," whispered the old stag quickly and commandingly as if he meant to forestall any outbreak of fear. Bambi controlled himself with an effort.

The old stag looked at him a little scornfully at first, it seemed to Bambi. He noticed it in spite of the state he was in. But the stag changed at once to a serious and kindly look.

Bambi peered out with blinking eyes to where He was standing, and felt as if he could not bear His horrible presence much longer.

As if he had read this thought, the old stag whispered to him, "Let's go back," and turned about.

They glided away cautiously. The old stag moved with a marvelous zigzag course whose purpose Bambi did not understand. Again he followed with painfully controlled impatience. The longing for Faline had harassed him on the way over; now the impulse to flee was beating through his veins.

But the old stag walked on slowly, stopping and listening. He would begin a new zigzag, then stop again, going very slowly ahead.

By this time they were far from the danger spot. "If he stops again," thought Bambi, "it ought to be all right to speak to him by now, and I'll thank him."

But at that moment the old stag vanished under his very eyes into a thick tangle of dogwood shrubs. Not a leaf stirred, not a twig snapped as the stag slipped away.

[191]

Bambi followed and tried to get through as noiselessly, and to avoid every sound with as much skill. But he was not so lucky. The leaves swished gently, the boughs bent against his flanks and sprang up again with a loud twang; dry branches broke against his chest with sharp piercing snaps.

"He saved my life," Bambi kept thinking. "What can I say to him?"

But the old stag was nowhere to be seen. Bambi came out of the bushes. Around him was a sea of yellow, flowering goldenrod. He raised his head and looked around. Not a leaf was moving as far as he could see. He was all alone.

Freed from all control, the impulse to flee suddenly carried him away. The goldenrods parted with a loud swish beneath his bounding hoofs as though under the stroke of a scythe.

After wandering about for a long time he found Faline. He was breathless, tired and happy and deeply stirred.

"Please, beloved," he said, "please don't ever call me again. We'll search until we find each other, but please don't ever call me . . . for I can't resist your voice."

CHAPTER XV

A FEW DAYS LATER they were walking carefree together through an oak thicket on the far side of the meadow. They had to cross the meadow in order to reach their old trail where the tall oak stood.

As the bushes grew thinner around them they stopped and peered out. Something red was moving near the oak. Both of them looked at it.

"Who can it be?" whispered Bambi.

"Probably Ronno or Karus," said Faline.

Bambi doubted it. "They don't dare come near me any more," Bambi said, peering sharply ahead. "No," he decided, "that's not Karus or Ronno. It's a stranger."

Faline agreed, surprised, and very curious. "Yes," she said, "it's a stranger. I see it, too, now. How curious!"

They watched him.

[193]

"How carelessly he acts," exclaimed **Faline.**

"Stupid," said Bambi, "really stupid. He acts like a little child, as if there were no danger."

"Let's go over," Faline proposed. Her curiosity was getting the better of her.

"All right," Bambi answered. "Let's go, I want to have a better look at the fellow."

They took a few steps and then Faline stopped, "Suppose he wants to fight you," she said. "He's strong."

"Bah," said Bambi holding his head cocked and putting on a disdainful air, "look at the little antlers he has. Should I be afraid of that? The fellow is fat and sleek enough, but is he strong? I don't think so. Come along."

They went on.

The stranger was busy nibbling meadow grass and did not notice them until they were a good way across the meadow. Then he ran forward to meet them. He gave joyful playful skips that made a curiously childish impression. Bambi and Faline stopped, surprised, and waited for him. When he was a few steps off he stood still likewise.

After a while he asked, "Don't you know me?"

[194]

BAMBI

Bambi had lowered his head prepared for battle. "Do you know us?" he retorted.

The stranger interrupted him. "Bambi," he cried reproachfully, yet confidently.

Bambi was startled to hear his name spoken. The sound of that voice stirred an old memory in his heart. But Faline had rushed towards the stranger.

"Gobo," she cried and became speechless. She stood there silent without moving. She couldn't breathe.

"Faline," said Gobo softly, "Faline, sister, you knew me anyway." He went to her and kissed her mouth. The tears were running down his cheeks. Faline was crying too, and couldn't speak.

"Well, Gobo," Bambi began. His voice trembled and he felt very bewildered. He was deeply moved and very much surprised. "Well, so you're not dead," he said.

Gobo burst out laughing. "You see that I'm not dead," he said; "at least I think you can see that I'm not."

"But what happened that time in the snow?" Bambi persisted.

"O then?" Gobo said thoughtfully. "He rescued me then."

[195]

"And where have you been all this time?" asked Faline in astonishment.

"With Him," Gobo replied, "I've been with Him all the time."

He grew silent and looked at Faline and at Bambi. Their helpless astonishment delighted him. Then he added, "Yes, my dears, I've seen a lot more than all of you put together in your old forest." He sounded somewhat boastful, but they paid no attention to it. They were still too much absorbed in their great surprise.

"Tell us about it," cried Faline beside herself with joy.

"O," said Gobo with satisfaction, "I could talk all day about it and never reach the end."

"Well then, go ahead and talk," Bambi urged.

Gobo turned to Faline and grew serious. "Is mother still alive?" he asked timidly and softly.

"Yes," cried Faline gladly. "She's alive but I haven't seen her for a long while."

"I'm going to see her right away," said Gobo with decision. "Are you coming too?"

They all went.

They did not speak another word the whole way. Bambi and Faline felt Gobo's impatient

"Faline, sister, you knew me anyway." Gobo went to her and kissed her mouth.

longing to see his mother, so both of them kept silent. Gobo walked ahead hurriedly and did not speak. They let him do as he liked.

Only sometimes when he hurried blindly over a cross-trail or when, in a sudden burst of speed, he took the wrong turning, they called gently to him, "This way," Bambi would whisper, or Faline would say, "No, no, we go this way now."

A number of times they had to cross wide clearings. They noticed that Gobo never stopped at the edge of the thicket, never peered around for a moment when he walked into the open, but simply ran out without any precaution. Bambi and Faline exchanged astonished glances whenever this happened, but they never said a word and followed Gobo with some hesitation. They had to wander around sometime and search high and low.

Gobo recollected his childhood paths at once. He was delighted with himself, never realizing that Bambi and Faline were leading him. He looked around at them and called, "How do you like the way I can still find my way around?" They did not say anything, but they exchanged glances again.

[199]

Soon afterwards they came to a small leafy hollow. "Look," cried Faline and glided in. Gobo followed her and stopped. It was the glade in which they were both born and had lived with their mother as little children. Gobo and Faline looked into each other's eyes. They did not say a word. But Faline kissed her brother gently on the mouth. Then they hurried on.

They walked to and fro for a good hour. The sun shone brighter and brighter through the branches and the forest grew stiller and stiller. It was the time for lying down and resting. But Gobo didn't feel tired. He walked swiftly ahead, breathing deeply with impatience and excitement, and gazed aimlessly about him. He shrank together whenever a weasel slunk through the bushes at his feet. He nearly stepped on the pheasants, and when they scolded him, flying up with a loud flapping of wings, he was terribly frightened. Bambi marveled at the strange, blind way Gobo moved around.

Presently Gobo stopped and turned to them both. "She isn't anywhere here," he cried in despair.

Faline soothed him. "We'll soon find her," she

[200]

said, deeply moved, "soon, Gobo." She looked at him. He still had that dejected look she knew so well.

"Shall we call her?" she asked smiling. "Shall we call her the way we used to when we were children?"

Bambi went away a few steps. Then he saw Aunt Ena. She had already settled herself to rest and was lying quietly in a nearby hazel bush.

"At last," he said to himself. At the same moment Gobo and Faline came up. All three of them stood together and looked at Ena. She had raised her head quietly and looked sleepily back at them.

Gobo took a few hesitating steps and cried softly, "Mother."

She was on her feet in a flash and stood as though transfixed. Gobo sprang to her quickly. "Mother," he began again. He tried to speak but couldn't utter a word.

His mother looked deep into his eyes. Her rigid body began to move. Wave after wave of trembling broke over her shoulders and down her back.

She did not ask any questions. She did not want

[201]

any explanation or history. She kissed Gobo slowly on the mouth. She kissed his cheeks and his neck. She bathed him tirelessly in her kisses, as she had when he was born.

Bambi and Faline had gone away.

CHAPTER XVI

THEY WERE ALL STANDING around in the middle of the thicket in a little clearing. Gobo was talking to them.

Even Friend Hare was there. Full of astonishment, he would lift one spoonlike ear, listen attentively, and let it fall back, only to lift it again at once.

The magpie was perched on the lowest branch of a young beech and listened in amazement. The jay was sitting restlessly on an ash opposite and screamed every once in a while in wonder.

A few friendly pheasants had brought their wives and children and were stretching their necks in surprise as they listened. At times they would jerk them in again, turning their heads this way and that in speechless wonder.

The squirrel had scurried up and was gesturing, wild with excitement. At times he would

slide to the ground, at times he would run up
some tree or other. Or he would balance with
his tail erect and display his white chest. Every
now and again he tried to interrupt Gobo and say
something, but he was always told sternly to keep
quiet.

Gobo told how he had lain helpless in the snow
waiting to die.

"The dogs found me," he said. "Dogs are
terrible. They are certainly the most terrible creatures in the world. Their jaws drip blood and
their bark is pitiless and full of anger." He
looked all around the circle and continued, "Well,
since then I've played with them just as I would
with one of you." He was very proud. "I don't
need to be afraid of them any more, I'm good
friends with them now. Nevertheless, when they
begin to grow angry, I have a roaring in my ears
and my heart stops beating. But they don't really
mean any harm by it and, as I said, I'm a good
friend of theirs. But their bark is terribly
loud."

"Go on," Faline urged.

Gobo looked at her. "Well," he said, "they
would have torn me to pieces, but He came."

[204]

"The dogs found me."

Gobo paused. The others hardly breathed.

"Yes," said Gobo, "He came. He called off the dogs and they quieted down at once. He called them again and they crouched motionless at His feet. Then He picked me up. I screamed but He petted me. He held me in His arms. He didn't hurt me. And then He carried me away."

Faline interrupted him. "What does 'carry' mean?" she asked.

Gobo began to explain it in great detail.

"It's very simple," Bambi broke in, "look at what the squirrel does when he takes a nut and carries it off."

The squirrel tried to speak again. "A cousin of mine . . ." he began eagerly. But the others cried out at once, "Be still, be still, let Gobo go on."

The squirrel had to keep quiet. He was desperate and, pressing his forepaws against his white chest, he tried to begin a conversation with the magpie. "As I was saying, a cousin of mine. . . ." he began. But the magpie simply turned her back on him.

Gobo told of wonders. "Outside it will be cold

[207]

and the storm is howling. But inside there's not a breath of wind and it's as warm as in summer-time," he said.

"Akh!" screamed the jay.

"The rain may be pouring outside so that everything is flooded. But not a drop of it gets inside and you keep dry."

The pheasants craned their necks and twisted their heads.

"Everything outside may be snowed under, but inside I was warm," said Gobo; "I was even hot. They gave me hay to eat and chestnuts, potatoes and turnips, whatever I wanted."

"Hay?" they all cried at once, amazed, incredulous and excited.

"Sweet, new-mown hay," Gobo repeated calmly, and gazed triumphantly around.

The squirrel's voice cut in, "A cousin of mine. . . ."

"Keep quiet," cried the others.

"Where does He get hay and all the rest of the things in winter," asked Faline eagerly.

"He grows them," Gobo answered, "He grows what He wants and keeps what He wants."

Faline went on questioning him: "Weren't you

[208]

ever afraid, Gobo, when you were with Him?"
she asked.

Gobo smiled a very superior smile. "No, dear
Faline," he said, "not any more. I got to know
that He wouldn't hurt me. Why should I have
been afraid? You all think He's wicked. But He
isn't wicked. If He loves anybody or if anybody
serves Him, He's good to him. Wonderfully good!
Nobody in the world can be as kind as He can."

While Gobo was talking that way the old stag
suddenly stepped noiselessly from the bushes.

Gobo didn't notice him and went on talking.
But the others saw the old stag and held their
breath in awe.

The old stag stood motionless, watching Gobo
with deep and serious eyes.

Gobo said, "Not only He, but all His children
loved me. His wife and all of them used to pet
me and play with me." He broke off suddenly.
He had seen the old stag.

A silence followed.

Then the old stag asked in his quiet commanding voice, "What kind of a band is that you have
on your neck?"

Everybody looked at it and noticed for the first

time the dark strip of braided horsehair around Gobo's neck.

Gobo answered uneasily, "That? Why that's part of the halter I wore. It's His halter and it's the greatest honor to wear His halter, it's. . . ." He grew confused and stammered.

Everyone was silent. The old stag looked at Gobo for a long time, piercingly and sadly.

"You poor thing!" he said softly at last, and turned and was gone.

In the astonished silence that followed, the squirrel began to chatter again. "As I was saying, a cousin of mine stayed with Him, too. He caught him and shut him up, oh, for the longest while, till one day my father. . . ."

But nobody was listening to the squirrel. They were all walking away.

CHAPTER XVII

ONE DAY MARENA APPEARED AGAIN.
She was almost full grown the winter that
Gobo disappeared, but she had hardly ever been
seen since, for she lived alone, going her own
ways.

She had stayed slender and looked quite young.
But she was quiet and serious and gentler than
any of the others. She had heard from the squirrel and the jay, the magpie and the thrushes and
pheasants that Gobo had returned from his wonderful adventures. So she came back to see him.

Gobo's mother was very proud and happy over
her visit. Gobo's mother had grown rather proud
of her good fortune. She was delighted to hear
the whole forest talking about her son. She
basked in his glory and wanted everybody to
know that her Gobo was the cleverest, ablest and
best deer living.

"What do you think of him, Marena?" she exclaimed. "What do you think of our Gobo?" She didn't wait for an answer but went on, "Do you remember how old Nettla said he wasn't worth much because he shivered a little in the cold? Do you remember how she prophesied that he'd be nothing but a care to me?"

"Well," Marena answered, "you've had plenty of worry over Gobo."

"That's all over with now," his mother exclaimed. She wondered how people could still remember such things. "O, I'm sorry for poor old Nettla. What a pity that she couldn't live to see what my Gobo's become!"

"Yes, poor old Nettla," said Marena softly, "it's too bad about her."

Gobo liked to hear his mother praise him that way. It pleased him. He stood around and basked as happily in her praises as in the sunshine.

"Even the old Prince came to see Gobo," his mother told Marena. She whispered it as though it were something solemn and mysterious. "He never let anyone so much as get a glimpse of him before, but he came on account of Gobo."

[212]

*Marena was quiet and serious and gentler than any
of the others.*

"Why did he call me a poor thing?" Gobo broke in in a discontented tone. "I'd like to know what he meant by that."

"Don't think about it," his mother said to comfort him, "he's old and queer."

But at last Gobo meant to ease his mind. "All day long it keeps running through my head," he said. "Poor thing! I'm not a poor thing. I'm very lucky. I've seen more and been through more than all the rest of you put together. I've seen more of the world and I know more about life than anyone in the forest. What do you think, Marena?"

"Yes," she said, "no one can deny that."

From then on Marena and Gobo were always together.

CHAPTER XVIII

BAMBI WENT TO LOOK for the old stag. He roamed around all night long. He wandered till the sun rose and dawn found him on unbeaten trails without Faline.

He was still drawn to Faline at times. At times he loved her just as much as ever. Then he liked to roam about with her, to listen to her chatter, to browse with her on the meadow or at the edge of the thicket. But she no longer satisfied him completely.

Before, when he was with Faline, he hardly ever remembered his meetings with the old stag, and when he did it was only casually. Now he was looking for him and felt an inexplicable desire driving him to find him. He only thought of Faline between whiles. He could always be with her if he wanted to. He did not much care to stay with the others. Gobo or Aunt Ena he avoided when he could.

[216]

The words the old stag had let fall about Gobo kept ringing in Bambi's ears. They made a peculiarly deep impression on him. Gobo had affected him strangely from the very first day of his return. Bambi didn't know why, but there was something painful to him in Gobo's bearing. Bambi was ashamed of Gobo without knowing why. And he was afraid for him, again without knowing why. Whenever he was together with his harmless, vain, self-conscious and self-satisfied Gobo, the words kept running through his head, "Poor thing!" He couldn't get rid of them.

But one dark night when Bambi had again delighted the screech-owl by assuring him how badly he was frightened, it suddenly occurred to him to ask, "Do you happen to know where the old stag is now?"

The screech-owl answered in his cooing voice that he didn't have the least idea in the world. But Bambi perceived that he simply didn't want to tell.

"No," he said, "I don't believe you, you're too clever. You know everything that's happening in the forest. You certainly must know where the old stag is hiding."

⌈217⌉

The screech-owl, who was all fluffed up, smoothed his feathers against his body and made himself small. "Of course I know," he cooed still more softly, "but I oughtn't to tell you, I really oughtn't."

Bambi began to plead. "I won't give you away," he said. "How could I, when I respect you so much?"

The owl became a lovely, soft gray-brown ball again and rolled his big cunning eyes a little as he always did when he felt in a good humor. "So you really do respect me," he asked, "and why, pray?"

Bambi did not hesitate. "Because you're so wise," he said sincerely, "and so good-natured and friendly, besides. And because you're so clever at frightening people. It's so very clever to frighten people, so very, very clever. I wish I could do it, it would be a great help to me."

The screech-owl had sunk his bill into his downy breast and was happy.

"Well," he said, "I know that the old stag would be glad to see you."

"Do you really think so?" cried Bambi while his heart began to beat faster for joy.

[218]

"Yes, I'm sure of it," the owl answered. "He'd be glad to see you, and I think I can venture to tell you where he is now."

He laid his feathers close to his body and suddenly grew thin again.

"Do you know the deep ditch where the willows stand?"

Bambi nodded yes.

"Do you know the young oak thicket on the farther side?"

"No," Bambi confessed, "I've never been on the farther side."

"Well, listen carefully then," the owl whispered. "There's an oak thicket on the far side. Go through that. Then there are bushes, hazel and silver poplar, thorn and shadbush. In the midst of them is an old uprooted beech. You'll have to hunt for it. It's not so easy to see it from your height as it is from the air. You'll find him under the trunk. But don't tell him I told you."

"Under the trunk?" said Bambi.

"Yes," the screech-owl laughed, "there's a hollow in the ground there. The trunk lies right across it. And he sleeps under the trunk."

[219]

"Thank you," said Bambi sincerely. "I don't know if I can find it, but I'm very grateful anyhow." He ran quickly away.

The screech-owl flew noiselessly after him and began to hoot right beside him. "Oi, oi!" Bambi shrank together.

"Did I frighten you?" asked the owl.

"Yes," he stammered, and that time he told the truth.

The owl cooed with satisfaction and said, "I only wanted to remind you again. Don't tell him I told you."

"Of course not," Bambi assured him and ran on.

When Bambi reached the ditch the old stag rose before him out of the pitch black night so noiselessly and suddenly that Bambi drew back in terror.

"I'm no longer where you were going to look for me," said the stag.

Bambi was silent.

"What is it you want?" asked the stag.

"Nothing," Bambi stammered, "nothing, excuse me, nothing at all."

After a while the old stag spoke, and his voice

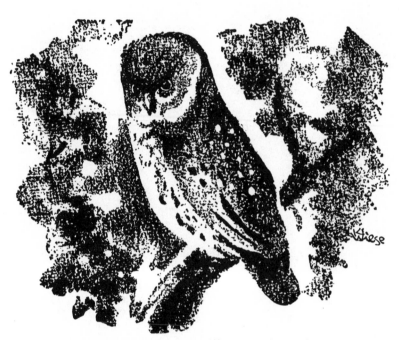

"Did I frighten you?" asked the owl.

sounded gentle. "This isn't the first time you've been looking for me," he said.

He waited. Bambi did not answer. The old stag went on, "Yesterday you passed close by me twice, and again this morning, very close."

"Why," said Bambi gathering courage, "why did you say that about Gobo?"

"Do you think that I was wrong?"

"No," cried Bambi sorrowfully, "no, I feel that you were right."

The old stag gave a barely perceptible nod and his eyes rested on Bambi more kindly than ever before.

"But why?" Bambi said, "I don't understand it."

"It's enough that you feel it. You will understand it later," the old stag said. "Good-by."

CHAPTER XIX

EVERYBODY SOON SAW that Gobo had habits which seemed strange and suspicious to the rest of them. He slept at night when the others were awake. But in the daytime, when the rest of them were looking for places to sleep in, he was wide awake and went walking. When he felt like it he would even go out of the thicket without any hesitation and stand with perfect peace of mind in the bright sunshine on the meadow.

Bambi found it impossible to keep silent any longer. "Don't you ever think of the danger?" he asked.

"No," Gobo said simply, "there isn't any for me."

"You forget, my dear Bambi," Gobo's mother broke in, "you forget that He's a friend of Gobo's. Gobo can take chances that the rest of you cannot take." She was very proud.

Bambi did not say anything more.

[224]

*Gobo would stand with perfect peace of mind in the bright
sunshine on the meadow.*

One day Gobo said to him, "You know, it seems strange to me to eat when and where I like."

Bambi did not understand. "Why is it strange, we all do it," he said.

"O, you do," said Gobo superiorly, "but I'm a little different. I'm accustomed to having my food brought to me or to being called when it's ready."

Bambi stared pityingly at Gobo. He looked at Faline and Marena and Aunt Ena. But they were all smiling and admiring Gobo.

"I think it will be hard for you to get accustomed to the winter, Gobo," Faline began, "we don't have hay or turnips or potatoes in the winter time."

"That's true," answered Gobo reflectively, "I hadn't thought about that yet. I can't even imagine how it would feel. It must be dreadful."

Bambi said quietly, "It isn't dreadful. It's only hard."

"Well," Gobo declared grandly, "if it gets too hard for me I'll simply go back to Him. Why should I go hungry? There's no need for that."

Bambi turned away without a word and walked off.

When Gobo was alone again with Marena he began to talk about Bambi. "He doesn't understand me," he said. "Poor old Bambi thinks I'm still the silly little Gobo that I once was. He can never get used to the fact that I've become something unusual. Danger! . . . What does he mean by danger? He means well enough by me, but danger is something for him and the likes of him, not for me."

Marena agreed with him. She loved him and Gobo loved her and they were both very happy.

"Well," he said to her, "nobody understands me the way you do. But anyhow I can't complain. I'm respected and honored by everybody. But you understand me best of all. When I tell the others how good He is, they listen and they don't think I'm lying, but they stick to their opinion that He's dreadful."

"I've always believed in Him," said Marena dreamily.

"Really?" Gobo replied airily.

"Do you remember the day when they left you lying in the snow?" Marena went on. "I said that day that sometime He'd come to the forest to play with us."

[228]

"No," Gobo replied yawning, "I don't remember that."

A few weeks passed, and one morning Bambi and Faline, Gobo and Marena were standing together again in the old familiar hazel thicket. Bambi and Faline were just returning from their wanderings, intending to look for their hiding place when they met Gobo and Marena. Gobo was about to go out on the meadow.

"Stay with us instead," said Bambi, "the sun will soon be rising and then nobody will go out in the open."

"Nonsense," said Gobo, scornfully, "if nobody else will go, I will."

He went on, Marena following him.

Bambi and Faline had stopped. "Come along," said Bambi angrily to Faline, "come along. Let him do what he pleases."

They were going on, but suddenly the jay screamed loudly from the far side of the meadow. With a bound Bambi had turned and was running after Gobo. Right by the oak he caught up with him and Marena.

"Did you hear that?" he cried to him.

"What?" asked Gobo puzzled.

Again the jay screamed on the far side of the meadow.

"Did you hear that?" Bambi repeated.

"No," said Gobo calmly.

"That means danger," Bambi persisted.

A magpie began to chatter loudly and, immediately after her, another and then a third. Then the jay screamed again and far overhead the crows gave warning.

Faline began to plead. "Don't go out there, Gobo! It's dangerous."

Even Marena begged, "Stay here. Stay here to-day, beloved one. It's dangerous."

Gobo stood there, smiling in his superior way. "Dangerous! dangerous! What has that to do with me?" he asked.

His pressing need gave Bambi an idea. "At least let Marena go first," he said, "so we can find out. . . ."

He hadn't finished before Marena had slipped out.

All three stood and looked at her, Bambi and Faline breathlessly, Gobo with obvious patience, as if to let the others enjoy their foolish whims.

They saw how Marena walked across the

meadow step by step, with hesitant feet, her head up. She peered and snuffed in all directions. Suddenly she turned like a flash with one high bound and, as though a cyclone had struck her, rushed back into the thicket.

"It's He, He," she whispered, her voice choking with terror. She was trembling in every limb. "I, I saw Him," she stammered, "it's He. He's standing over by the alders."

"Come," cried Bambi, "come quickly."

"Come," Faline pleaded. And Marena who could hardly speak whispered, "Please come now, Gobo, please."

But Gobo remained unmoved. "Run as much as you like," he said, "I won't stop you. If He's there I want to talk with Him."

Gobo could not be dissuaded.

They stood and watched how he went out. They stayed there, moved by his great confidence, while at the same time a terrible fear for him gripped them.

Gobo was standing boldly on the meadow looking around for the alders. Then he seemed to see them and to have discovered Him. Then the thunder crashed.

Gobo leaped into the air at the report. He suddenly turned around and fled back to the thicket, staggering as he came.

They still stood there, petrified with terror, while he came on. They heard him gasping for breath. And as he did not stop but bounded wildly forward, they turned and surrounded him and all took flight.

But poor Gobo dropped to the ground. Marena stopped close to him, Bambi and Faline a little farther off, ready to flee.

Gobo lay with his bloody entrails oozing from his torn flank. He lifted his head with a feeble twisting motion.

"Marena," he said with an effort, "Marena. . . ." He did not recognize her. His voice failed.

There was a loud careless rustling in the bushes by the meadow. Marena bent her head towards Gobo. "He's coming," she whispered frantically, "Gobo, He's coming! Can't you get up and come with me?"

Gobo lifted his head again feebly with a writhing motion, beat convulsively with his hoofs and then lay still.

With a crackling, snapping and rustling He parted the bushes and stepped out.

[232]

Marena saw Him from quite near. She slunk slowly back, disappearing through the nearest bushes, and hastened to Bambi and Faline.

She looked back once again and saw how He was bending over and seizing the wounded deer.

Then they heard Gobo's wailing death shriek.

CHAPTER XX

BAMBI WAS ALONE. He walked beside
the water that ran swiftly among the reeds and
swamp-willows.

He went there more and more often now that
he was staying by himself. There were few trails
there, and he hardly ever met any of his friends.
That was just what he wanted. For his thoughts
had grown serious and his heart heavy. He did
not know what was happening within him. He
did not even think about it. He merely recalled
things aimlessly, and his whole life seemed to
have become darker.

He used to stand for hours on the bank. The
current, that flowed round a gentle bend there,
occupied his entire thought. The cool air from
the ripples brought him strange, refreshing, acrid
smells that aroused forgetfulness and a sense of
trust in him.

[234]

The ducks talked endlessly to one another in a friendly, serious, capable way.

Bambi would stand and watch the ducks paddling companionably together. They talked endlessly to one another in a friendly, serious, capable way.

There were a couple of mother ducks, each with a flock of young ones around her. They were constantly teaching their young ones things. And the little ones were always learning them. Sometimes one of the other of the mothers would give a warning. Then the young ducks would dash off in all directions. They would scatter and glide away perfectly noiselessly. Bambi saw how the smallest ones, who could not fly yet, would paddle among the thick rushes without moving a stem that might betray them by swaying. He would see the small dark bodies creep here and there among the reeds. Then he could see nothing more.

Later one of the mothers would give a short call and in a flash they would all flock around her again. In an instant they would reassemble their flotilla and go on cruising quietly about as before. Bambi marveled anew at it each time. It was a constant source of wonder to him.

After one such alarm, Bambi asked one of the

[237]

mothers, "What was it? I was looking closely and I didn't see anything."

"It was nothing at all," answered the duck.

Another time one of the children gave the signal, turning like a flash and staring through the reeds. Presently he came out on the bank where Bambi was standing.

"There wasn't anything," the young one replied, shaking its tail feathers in a grown-up way and carefully putting the tips of its wings in place. Then it paddled through the water again.

Nevertheless Bambi had faith in the ducks. He came to the conclusion that they were more watchful than he, that they heard and saw things more quickly. When he stood watching them, that ceaseless tension that he felt within himself at other times relaxed a little.

He liked to talk with the ducks, too. They didn't talk the nonsense that he so often heard from the others. They talked about the broad skies and the wind and about distant fields where they feasted on choice tidbits.

From time to time Bambi saw something that looked like a fiery streak in the air beside the brook. "Srrrri!" the humming bird would cry

[238]

softly darting past like a tiny whirring speck. There was a gleam of green, a glow of red, as he flashed by and was gone. Bambi was thrilled and wanted to see the bright stranger near to. He called to him.

"Don't bother calling him," the sedge-hen said to Bambi from among the reed clumps, "don't bother calling. He'll never answer you."

"Where are you?" asked Bambi peering among the reeds.

But the sedge-hen only laughed loudly from an entirely different place, "Here I am. That cranky creature you just called to won't talk to anyone. It's useless to call him."

"He's so handsome," said Bambi.

"But bad," the sedge-hen retorted from still another place.

"What makes you think him bad?" Bambi inquired.

The sedge-hen answered from an altogether different place, "He doesn't care for anything or anybody. Let anything happen that wants to, he won't speak to anybody and never thanked anybody for speaking to him. He never gives anybody warning when there's danger.

[239]

He's never said a word to a living soul."

"The poor . . ." said Bambi.

The sedge-hen went on talking, and her cheery, piping voice sounded from the far side again. "He probably thinks that people are jealous of his silly markings and doesn't want them to get too good a look at him."

"Certain other people don't let you get a good look at them either," said Bambi.

In a twinkling the sedge-hen was standing in front of him. "There's nothing to look at in my case," she said simply. Small and gleaming with water, she stood there in her sleek feathers, her trim figure restless, animated and satisfied. In a flash she was gone again.

"I don't understand how people can stand so long in one spot," she called from the water. And added from the far side, "It's tiresome and dangerous to stay so long in one spot." Then from the other side she cried gayly once or twice. "You have to keep moving," she cried happily, "you've got to keep moving if you want to keep whole and hearty."

A soft rustling in the grass startled Bambi. He looked around. There was a reddish flash among the bushes. It disappeared in the reeds.

[240]

At the same time a sharp warm smell reached his nostrils. The fox had slunk by.

Bambi wanted to cry out and stamp on the ground as a warning. But the sedges rustled as the fox parted them in quick leaps. The water splashed and a duck screamed desperately. Bambi heard her wings flapping and saw her white body flash through the leaves. He saw how her wings beat the fox's face with sharp blows. Then it grew still.

At the same moment the fox came out of the bushes holding the duck in his jaws. Her neck hung down limply, her wings were still moving, but the fox paid no attention to that. He looked sidewise at Bambi with sneering eyes and crept slowly into the thicket.

Bambi stood motionless.

A few of the old ducks had flown up with a rush of wings and were flying around in helpless fright. The sedge-hen was crying warnings from all directions. The tit-mice chirped excitedly in the bushes. And the young orphaned ducks splashed about the sedge, crying with soft voices.

The hummingbird flew along the bank.

"Please tell us," the young ducks cried, "please, tell us, have you seen our mother?"

[241]

"Srrri," cried the hummingbird shrilly, and flew past sparkling, "what has she got to do with me?"

Bambi turned and went away. He wandered through a whole sea of goldenrod, passed through a grove of young beeches, crossed through old hazel thickets until he reached the edge of the deep ditch. He roamed around it, hoping to meet the old stag. He had not seen him for a long while, not since Gobo's death.

Then he caught a glimpse of him from afar and ran to meet him. For a while they walked together in silence, then the old stag asked: "Well, do they still talk about him the way they used to?"

Bambi understood that he referred to Gobo and replied, "I don't know. I'm nearly alone now." He hesitated, "But I think of him very often."

"Really," said the old stag, "are you alone now?"

"Yes," said Bambi expectantly, but the old stag remained silent.

They went on. Suddenly the old stag stopped. "Don't you hear anything?" he asked.

Bambi listened. He didn't hear anything.

[242]

"Come," cried the old stag and hurried forward. Bambi followed him. The stag stopped again. "Don't you hear anything yet?" he asked.

Then Bambi heard a rustling that he did not understand. It sounded like branches being bent down and repeatedly springing up again. Something was beating the earth dully and irregularly.

Bambi wanted to flee but the old stag cried, "Come with me," and ran in the direction of the noise. Bambi at his side ventured to ask, "Isn't it dangerous?"

"It's terribly dangerous," the old stag answered mysteriously.

Soon they saw branches being pulled and tugged at from below and shaken violently. They went nearer and saw that a little trail ran through the middle of the bushes.

Friend Hare was lying on the ground. He flung himself from side to side and writhed. Then he lay still and writhed again. Each of his motions pulled at the branches over him.

Bambi noticed a dark threadlike leash. It ran right from the branch to Friend Hare and was twisted around his neck.

Friend Hare must have heard someone coming,

[243]

for he flung himself wildly into the air and fell to the ground. He tried to escape and rolled, jerking and writhing in the grass.

"Lie still," the old stag commanded. Then sympathetically, with a gentle voice that went to Bambi's heart, he repeated in his ear, "Be easy, Friend Hare, it's I. Don't move now. Lie perfectly still."

The Hare lay motionless, flat on the ground. His throttled breath rattled softly in his throat.

The old stag took the branch between his teeth, and twisted it. He bent down. Then he walked around putting his weight cunningly against it. He held it to the earth with his hoof and snapped it with a single blow of his antlers.

Then he nodded encouragingly to the Hare. "Lie still," he said, "even if I hurt you."

Holding his head on one side, he laid one prong of his antlers close to the Hare's neck and pressed into the fur behind his ear. He made an effort and nodded. The Hare began to writhe.

The old stag immediately drew back. "Lie still," he commanded, "it's a question of life and death for you." He began over again. The Hare lay still gasping. Bambi stood close by, speechless with amazement.

One of the old stag's antlers, pressing against the Hare's fur, had slipped under the noose. The old stag was almost kneeling and twisted his head as though he were charging. He drove his antlers deeper and deeper under the noose, which gave at last and began to loosen.

The Hare could breathe again and his terror and pain burst from him instantly. "E-e-eh!" he cried bitterly.

The old stag stopped. "Keep quiet!" he cried, reproaching him gently, "keep quiet." His mouth was close to the Hare's shoulder, his antlers lay with a prong between the spoonlike ears. It looked as if he had spitted the Hare.

"How can you be so stupid as to cry at this time?" he grumbled gently. "Do you want the fox to come? Do you? I thought not. Keep quiet then."

He continued to work away, slowly exerting all his strength. Suddenly the noose broke with a loud snap. The Hare slipped out and was free, without realizing it for a moment. He took a step and sat down again dazed. Then he hopped away, slowly and timidly at first, then faster and faster. Presently he was running with wild leaps.

Bambi looked after him. "Without so much as a thank you," he exclaimed in surprise.

"He's still terrified," said the old stag.

The noose lay on the ground. Bambi touched it gently. It creaked, terrifying Bambi. That was a sound such as he had never heard in the woods.

"He?" asked Bambi softly.

The old stag nodded.

They walked on together in silence. "Take care when you're going along a trail," said the old stag, "test all the branches. Prod them on all sides of you with your antlers. And turn back at once if you hear that creak. And when you've shed your antlers be doubly cautious. I never use trails any more."

Bambi sank into troubled thought.

"He isn't here," he whispered to himself in profound astonishment.

"No, He's not in the forest now," the old stag answered.

"And yet He is here," said Bambi shaking his head.

The old stag went on and his voice was full of bitterness. "How did your Gobo put it . . . ? Didn't Gobo tell you He is all-powerful and all-good."

"He was good to Gobo," Bambi whispered.

The old stag stopped. "Do you believe that, Bambi?" he asked sadly. For the first time he had called Bambi by his name.

"I don't know," cried Bambi hurt, "I don't understand it."

The old stag said slowly, "We must learn to live and be cautious."

CHAPTER XXI

ONE MORNING BAMBI came to grief.
The pale gray dawn was just creeping through
the forest. A milky-white mist was rising from the
meadow and the stillness that precedes the coming of light was everywhere. The crows were not
awake yet, nor the magpies. The jays were asleep.

Bambi had met Faline the night before. She
looked sadly at him and was very shy.

"I'm so much alone now," she said gently.

"I'm alone too," Bambi answered with some
hesitation.

"Why don't you stay with me any more?"
Faline asked sorrowfully, and it hurt him to see
the gay and lively Faline so serious and downcast.

"I want to be alone," he replied. And gently
as he tried to say it, it sounded hard. He felt it
himself.

Faline looked at him and asked softly, "Do you love me still?"

"I don't know," Bambi answered in the same tone.

She walked silently away from him, leaving him alone.

He stood under the great oak at the meadow's edge and peered out cautiously, drinking in the pure and odorless morning air. It was moist and fresh from the earth, the dew, the grass and the wet woods. Bambi breathed in great gulps of it. All at once his spirit felt freer than for a long time. He walked happily onto the mist-covered meadow.

Then a sound like thunder crashed.

Bambi felt a fearful blow that made him stagger.

Mad with terror, he sprang back into the thicket and kept running. He did not understand what had happened. He could not grasp a single idea. He could only keep running on and on. Fear gripped his heart so that his breath failed as he rushed blindly on. Then a killing pain shot through him, so that he felt that he could not bear it. He felt something hot running over his left shoulder. It was like a thin, burning thread coming from where the pain shot through him. Bambi had to stop running. He was forced to walk slower. Then he saw that he was limping. He sank down.

It was comfortable just to lie there and rest.

"Up, Bambi! Get up!" the old stag was standing beside him and nudging his shoulder gently.

Bambi wanted to answer, "I can't," but the old stag repeated, "Up! Up!" And there was such compulsion in his voice and such tenderness that Bambi kept silent. Even the pain that shot through him stopped for a minute.

Then the old stag said hurriedly and anxiously, "Get up! You must get away, my son." My son! The words seemed to have escaped him. In a flash Bambi was on his feet.

"Good," said the old stag, breathing deeply and speaking emphatically, "come with me now and keep close beside me."

He walked swiftly ahead. Bambi followed him but he felt a burning desire to let himself drop to the ground, to lie still and rest.

The old stag seemed to guess it and talked to him without stopping. "Now you'll have to bear every pain. You can't think of lying down now. You mustn't think of it even for a moment. That's enough to tire you in itself. You must save yourself, do you understand me, Bambi? Save yourself. Or else you are lost. Just remember that He is behind you, do you understand, Bambi? And He will kill you without mercy. Come on. Keep close to me. You'll soon be all right. You must be all right."

Bambi had no strength left to think with. The pain shot through him at every step he took. It took away his breath and his consciousness. The hot trickle, burning his shoulder, seared him like some deep heartfelt trouble.

The old stag made a wide circle. It took a long time. Through his veil of pain and weakness, Bambi was amazed to see that they were passing the great oak again.

The old stag stopped and snuffed the ground. "He's still here," he whispered. "It's He. And that's His dog. Come along. Faster!" They ran.

Suddenly the old stag stopped again. "Look," he said, "that's where you lay on the ground."

Bambi saw the crushed grasses where a wide

[251]

pool of his own blood was soaking into the earth.

The old stag snuffed warily around the spot. "They were here, He and His dog," he said. "Come along!" He went ahead slowly, snuffing again and again.

Bambi saw the red drops gleaming on the leaves of the bushes and the grass stems. "We passed here before," he thought. But he couldn't speak.

"Aha!" said the old stag and seemed almost joyful, "we're behind them now."

He continued for a while on the same path. Then he doubled unexpectedly and began a new circle. Bambi staggered after him. They came to the oak again but on the opposite side. For the second time they passed the place where Bambi had fallen down. Then the old stag went in still another direction.

"Eat that," he commanded suddenly, stopping and pushing aside the grasses. He pointed to a pair of short dark-green leaves growing close together near the ground.

Bambi obeyed. They tasted terribly bitter and smelt sickeningly.

"How do you feel now?" the stag asked after a while.

[252]

"Better," Bambi answered quickly. He **was** suddenly able to speak again. His senses had cleared and his fatigue grew less.

"Let's move on again," the old stag commanded after another pause. After Bambi had been following him for a long time he said, "At last!" They stopped.

"The bleeding has stopped," said the old stag, "the blood's stopped flowing from your wound. It isn't emptying your veins now. And it can't betray you any more either. It can't show Him and His dog where to find you and kill you."

The old stag looked worried and tired but his voice sounded joyful. "Come along," he went on, "now you can rest."

They reached a wide ditch which Bambi had never crossed. The old stag climbed down and Bambi tried to follow him. But it cost him a great effort to climb the steep slope on the farther side. The pain began to shoot violently through him again. He stumbled, regained his feet, and stumbled again, breathing hard.

"I can't help you," said the old stag, "you'll have to get up yourself." Bambi reached the top. He felt the hot trickle on his shoulder again. He

[253]

felt his strength ebbing for the second time.

"You're bleeding again," said the old stag, "I thought you would. But it's only a little," he added in a whisper, "and it doesn't make any difference now."

They walked very slowly through a grove of lofty beeches. The ground was soft and level. They walked easily on it. Bambi felt a longing to lie down there, to stretch out and never move his limbs again. He couldn't go any further. His head ached. There was a humming in his ears. His nerves were quivering, and fever began to rack him. There was a darkness before his eyes. He felt nothing but a desire for rest and a detached amazement at finding his life so changed and shattered. He remembered how he had walked whole and uninjured through the woods that morning. It was barely an hour ago, and it seemed to him like some memory out of a distant, long-vanished past.

They passed through a scrub-oak and dogwood thicket. A huge, hollow beech trunk, thickly entangled with the bushes, lay right in front of them, barring the way.

"Here we are," Bambi heard the old stag say-

Bambi lay on the warm earth with the mouldering bark of the fallen tree above him.

ing. He walked along the beech trunk and Bambi walked beside him. He nearly fell into a hollow that lay in front of him.

"Here it is," said the old stag at the moment, "you can lie down here."

Bambi sank down and did not move again.

The hollow was still deeper under the beech trunk and formed a little chamber. The bushes closed thickly across the top so that whoever was within lay hidden.

"You'll be safe here," said the old stag.

Days passed.

Bambi lay on the warm earth with the mouldering bark of the fallen tree above him. He felt his pain intensify and then grow less and less until it died away more and more gently.

Sometimes he would creep out and stand swaying weakly on his unsteady legs. He would take a few steps to look for food. He ate plants now that he had never noticed before. Now they appealed to his taste and attracted him by their strange, enticing acrid smell. Everything that he had disdained before and would spit out if it got accidentally into his mouth, seemed appetizing to him. He still disliked many of the little leaves

[257]

and short, coarse shoots, but he ate them anyway, as though he were compelled to, and his wound healed faster. He felt his strength returning.

He was cured, but he didn't leave the hollow yet. He walked around a little at night, but lay quietly on his bed by day. Not until the fever had entirely left his body did Bambi begin to think over all that had happened to him. Then a great terror awoke in him, and a profound tremor passed through his heart. He could not shake himself free of it. He could not get up and run about as before. He lay still and troubled. He felt terrified, ashamed, amazed and troubled by turns. Sometimes he was full of despair, at others of joy.

The old stag was always with him. At first he stayed day and night at Bambi's side. Then he left him alone at times, especially when he saw Bambi deep in thought. But he always kept close at hand.

One night there was thunder and lightning and a downpour of rain, although the sky was clear and the setting sun was streaming down. The blackbirds sang loudly in all the neighboring tree-tops, the finches warbled, the tit-mice chirped in the bushes. Among the grasses or from under the bushes, the metallic, throaty cackling of the pheasants sounded at intervals. The woodpecker laughed exultantly and the doves cooed their fervid love.

Bambi crept out of the hollow. Life was beautiful. The old stag was standing there as though he expected Bambi. They sauntered on together. But Bambi did not return to the hollow or the old stag again.

CHAPTER XXII

O N E N I G H T when the air was whispering
with the autumnal fall of leaves the screech-owl
shrieked piercingly among the branches. Then
he waited.

But Bambi had spied him already through the
thinning leaves, and stopped.

The screech-owl flew nearer and shrieked
louder. Then he waited again. But Bambi did
not say anything.

Then the owl could restrain himself no longer.
"Aren't you frightened?" he asked, displeased.

"Well," Bambi replied, "a little."

"Is that so?" the screech-owl cooed in an
offended tone. "Only a little. You used to get
terribly frightened. It was really a pleasure to
see how frightened you'd get. But for some reason or other you're only a little frightened now."
He grew angrier and repeated, "Only a little!"

[260]

The screech-owl was getting old, and that was why he was so much vainer and so much more sensitive than before.

Bambi wanted to answer, "I wasn't ever frightened before either," but he decided to keep that to himself. He was sorry to see the good old screech-owl sitting there so angry. He tried to soothe him. "Maybe it's because I thought of you right away," he said.

"What?" said the screech-owl becoming happy again, "you really did think of me?"

"Yes," Bambi answered with some hesitation, "as soon as I heard you screech. Otherwise, of course, I'd have been as scared as ever."

"Really?" cooed the owl.

Bambi hadn't the heart to deny it. What difference did it make anyhow? Let the little old child enjoy himself.

"I really did," he assured him, and went on, "I'm so happy, for a thrill goes through me when I hear you so suddenly."

The screech-owl fluffed up his feathers into a soft, brownish-gray, downy ball. He was happy. It's nice of you to think of me," he cooed tenderly, "very nice. We haven't seen each other for a long time."

"A very long time," said Bambi.

"You don't use the old trails any more, do you?" the screech-owl inquired.

"No," said Bambi slowly, "I don't use the old trails any more."

"I'm also seeing more of the world than I used to," the screech-owl observed boastfully. He didn't mention that he had been driven from his old hereditary haunts by a pitiless younger rival. "You can't stay forever in the same spot," he added. Then he waited for an answer.

But Bambi had gone away. By now he understood almost as well as the old stag how to disappear suddenly and noiselessly.

The screech-owl was provoked. "It's a shame. . . ." he cooed to himself. He shook his feathers, sank his bill deep into his breast and silently philosophized, "You should never imagine you can be friends with great folks. They can be as nice as pie but when the time comes they haven't a thought for you, and you're left sitting stupidly by yourself as I'm sitting here now. . . ."

Suddenly he dropped to the earth like a stone. He had spied a mouse. It squeaked once in his talons. He tore it to pieces, for he was furious.

He crammed the little morsel faster than usual. Then he flew off. "What do all your great folks mean to me?" he asked. "Not a thing." He began to screech so piercingly and ceaselessly that a pair of wood-doves whom he passed awoke and fled from their roost with loud wingbeats.

* *

*

The storm swept the woods for several days and tore the last leaves from the branches. Then the trees stood stripped.

Bambi was wandering homewards in the gray dawn in order to sleep in the hollow with the old stag.

A shrill voice called him once or twice in quick succession. He stopped. Then the squirrel scampered down from the branches in a twinkling and sat on the ground in front of him.

"Is it really you?" he shrilled, surprised and delighted. "I recognized you the minute you passed me but I couldn't believe. . . ."

"Where did you come from?" asked Bambi.

The merry little face in front of him grew quite troubled. "The oak is gone," he began plaintively, "my beautiful old oak, do you remember it? It was awful. He chopped it down!"

Bambi hung his head sadly. His very soul felt sorry for the wonderful old tree.

"As soon as it happened," the squirrel related, "everybody who lived in the tree fled and watched how He bit through the trunk with a gigantic flashing tooth. The tree groaned aloud when it was wounded. It kept on groaning and the tooth kept gnawing, it was dreadful to hear it. Then the poor beautiful tree fell out on the meadow. Everybody cried."

Bambi was silent.

"Yes," sighed the squirrel, "He can do anything. He's all-powerful." He gazed at Bambi out of his big eyes, and pointed his ears. But Bambi kept silent.

"Then we were all homeless," the squirrel went on, "I don't even know where the others scattered to. I came here. But I won't find another tree like that in a hurry."

"The old oak," said Bambi to himself, "I knew it from the time I was a child."

"O well," said the squirrel. "But to think it's really you," he went on delightedly. "Everybody

[264]

*"My beautiful old oak, do you remember it?   It was awful.
He chopped it down!"*

said you must be dead long ago. Of course there were some people now and then who said you were still alive. Once in a while someone said he had seen you. But nobody could find out any-thing definite. And so I thought it was only gossip," the squirrel gazed at him inquisitively, "since you didn't come back any more."

Bambi could see how curious he was and how he was fishing for an answer.

Bambi kept silent. But a gentle anxious curi-osity was stirring in him, too. He wanted to ask about Faline, about Aunt Ena, and Ronno and Karus, about all his childhood companions. But he kept silent.

The squirrel still sat in front of him, studying him. "What antlers!" he cried admiringly. "What antlers! Nobody in the whole forest, ex-cept the old Prince, has antlers like that."

Once Bambi would have felt elated and flat-tered by such praise. But he only said, "Maybe."

The squirrel nodded quickly with his head. "Really," he said, surprised, "you're beginning to get gray."

Bambi wandered on.

The squirrel perceived that the conversation

was over and sprang through the bushes. "Good day," he shouted down. "Good-by. I'm very glad I met you. If I see any of your acquaintances I'll tell them you're still alive. They'll all be glad."

Bambi heard him and again felt that gentle stirring in his heart. But he said nothing. When he was still a child the old stag had taught him that you must live alone. Then and afterwards the old stag had revealed much wisdom and many secrets to him. But of all his teachings this had been the most important; you must live alone, if you wanted to preserve yourself, if you understood existence, if you wanted to attain wisdom, you had to live alone.

"But," Bambi had once objected, "we two are always together now."

"Not for very much longer," the old stag had answered quickly. That was a few weeks ago. Now it occurred to Bambi again, and he suddenly remembered how even the old stag's very first words to him had been about singleness. That day when Bambi was still a child calling for his mother, the old stag had come to him and asked him, "Can't you stay by yourself?"

Bambi wandered on.

CHAPTER XXIII

THE FOREST WAS AGAIN under snow, lying silent beneath its deep white mantle. Only the crows' calls could be heard. Now and then came a magpie's noisy chattering. The soft twittering of the tit-mice sounded timidly. Then the frost hardened and everything grew still. The air began to hum with the cold.

One morning a dog's baying broke the silence.

It was a continuous hurrying bay that pressed on quickly through the woods, eager and clear and harrying with loud yelps.

Bambi raised his head in the hollow under the fallen tree, and looked at the old stag who was lying beside him.

"That's nothing," said the old stag in answer to Bambi's glance, "nothing that need bother us."

Still they both listened.

They lay in their hollow with the old beech

[269]

trunk like a sheltering roof above them. The deep snow kept the icy draught from them, and the tangled bushes hid them from curious eyes.

The baying grew nearer. It was angry and panting and relentless. It sounded like the bark of a small hound. It came constantly closer.

Then they heard panting of another kind. They heard a low labored snarling under the angry barking. Bambi grew uneasy, but the old stag quieted him again. "We don't need to worry about it," he said. They lay silent in their warm hollow and peered out.

The footsteps drew nearer and nearer through the branches. The snow dropped from the shaken boughs and clouds of it rose from the earth.

Through the snow and over the roots and branches, the fox came springing, crouching and slinking. They were right; a little, short-legged hound was after him.

One of the fox's forelegs was crushed and the fur torn around it. He held his shattered paw in front of him, and blood poured from his wound. He was gasping for breath. His eyes were staring with terror and exertion. He was beside himself with rage and fear. He was desperate and exhausted.

[270]

The fox came springing, crouching and slinking. A little, short-legged hound was after him.

Once in a while he would face around and snarl so that the dog was startled and would fall back a few steps.

Presently the fox sat down on his haunches. He could go no farther. Raising his mangled forepaw pitifully, with his jaws open and his lips drawn back, he snarled at the dog.

But the dog was never silent for a minute. His high, rasping bark only grew fuller and deeper. "Here," he yapped, "here he is! Here! Here! Here!" He was not abusing the fox. He was not even speaking to him, but was urging on someone who was still far behind.

Bambi knew as well as the old stag did that it was He the dog was calling.

The fox knew it too. The blood was streaming down from him and fell from his breast into the snow, making a fiery red spot on the icy white surface, and steaming slowly.

A weakness overcame the fox. His crushed foot sank down helpless, but a burning pain shot through it when it touched the cold snow. He lifted it again with an effort and held it quivering in front of him.

"Let me go," said the fox beginning to speak,

[273]

"let me go." He spoke softly and beseechingly. He was quite weak and despondent.

"No! No! No!" the dog howled.

The fox pleaded still more insistently. "We're relations," he pleaded, "we're brothers almost. Let me go home. Let me die with my family at least. We're brothers almost, you and I."

"No! No! No!" the dog raged.

Then the fox rose so that he was sitting perfectly erect. He dropped his handsome pointed muzzle on his bleeding breast, raised his eyes and looked the dog straight in the face. In a completely altered voice, restrained and embittered, he growled, "Aren't you ashamed, you traitor!"

"No! No! No!" yelped the dog.

But the fox went on, "You turncoat, you renegade." His maimed body was taut with contempt and hatred. "You spy," he hissed, "you blackguard, you track us where He could never find us. You betray us, your own relations, me who am almost your brother. And you stand there and aren't ashamed!"

Instantly many other voices sounded loudly round about.

[274]

"Traitor!" cried the magpie from the tree.

"Spy!" shrieked the jay.

"Blackguard!" the weasel hissed.

"Renegade!" snarled the ferret.

From every tree and bush came chirpings, peepings, shrill cries, while overhead the crows cawed, "Spy! Spy!" Everyone had rushed up, and from the trees or from safe hiding places on the ground, they watched the contest. The fury that had burst from the fox released an embittered anger in them all. And the blood spilt on the snow, that steamed before their eyes, maddened them and made them forget all caution.

The dog stared around him. "Who are you?" he yelped. "What do you want? What do you know about it? What are you talking about? Everything belongs to Him, just as I do. But I, I love Him. I worship Him, I serve Him. Do you think you can oppose Him, poor creatures like you? He's all-powerful. He's above all of you. Everything we have comes from Him. Everything that lives or grows comes from Him." The dog was quivering with exaltation.

"Traitor!" cried the squirrel shrilly.

"Yes, traitor!" hissed the fox. "Nobody is a traitor but you, only you."

The dog was dancing about in a frenzy of devotion. "Only me?" he cried, "you lie. Aren't there many many others on His side? The horse, the cow, the sheep, the chickens, many, many of you and your kind are on His side and worship Him and serve Him."

"They're rabble!" snarled the fox, full of a boundless contempt.

Then the dog could contain himself no longer and sprang at the fox's throat. Growling, spitting, and yelping, they rolled in the snow, a writhing, savagely snapping mass from which fur flew. The snow rose in clouds and was spattered with fine drops of blood. At last the fox could not fight any more. In a few seconds he was lying on his back, his white belly uppermost. He twitched and stiffened and died.

The dog shook him a few times, then let him fall on the trampled snow. He stood beside him, his legs planted, calling in a deep, loud voice, "Here! Here! He's here!"

The others were horrorstruck and fled in all directions.

[276]

"Dreadful," said Bambi softly to the old stag in the hollow.

"The most dreadful part of all," the old stag answered, "is that the dogs believe what the hound just said. They believe it, they pass their lives in fear, they hate Him and themselves and yet they'd die for His sake."

CHAPTER XXIV

THE COLD BROKE, and there was a warm spell in the middle of the winter. The earth drank great draughts of the melting snows so that wide stretches of soil were everywhere visible. The blackbirds were not singing yet, but when they flew from the ground where they were hunting worms, or when they fluttered from tree to tree, they uttered a long-drawn joyous whistle that was almost a song. The woodpecker began to chatter now and then. Magpies and crows grew more talkative. The tit-mice chirped more cheerily. And the pheasants, swooping down from their roosts would stand in one spot preening their feathers and uttering their metallic throaty cacklings.

One such morning Bambi was roaming around as usual. In the gray dawn he came to the edge of the hollow. On the farther side where he had

The pheasants, swooping down from their roosts, would stand in one spot.

lived before something was stirring. Bambi stayed hidden in the thicket and peered across. A deer was wandering slowly to and fro, looking for places where the snow had melted, and cropping whatever grasses had sprung up so early.

Bambi wanted to turn at once and go away, for he recognized Faline. His first impulse was to spring forward and call her. But he stood as though rooted to the spot. He had not seen Faline for a long time. His heart began to beat faster. Faline moved slowly as though she were tired and sad. She resembled her mother now. She looked as old as Aunt Ena, as Bambi noticed with a strangely pained surprise.

Faline lifted her head and gazed across as though she sensed his presence. Again Bambi started forward, but he stopped again, hesitating and unable to stir.

He saw that Faline had grown old and gray.

"Gay, pert little Faline, how lovely she used to be," he thought, "and how lively!" His whole youth suddenly flashed before his eyes. The meadow, the trails where he walked with his mother, the happy games with Gobo and Faline, the nice grasshoppers and butterflies, the fight

[281]

with Karus and Ronno when he had won Faline
for his own. He felt happy again, and yet he
trembled.

Faline wandered on, her head drooped to the
ground, walking slowly, sadly and wearily away.
At that moment Bambi loved her with an overpowering, tender melancholy. He wanted to rush
through the hollow that separated him from the
others. He wanted to overtake her, to talk with
her, to talk to her about their youth and about
everything that had happened.

He gazed after her as she went off, passing
under the bare branches till finally she was lost
to sight.

He stood there a long time staring after her.

Then there was a crash like thunder. Bambi
shrank together. It came from where he was
standing. Not even from a little way off but right
beside him.

Then there was a second thunderclap, and right
after that another.

Bambi leaped a little farther into the thicket,
then stopped and listened. Everything was still.
He glided stealthily homewards.

The old stag was there before him. He had

not lain down yet, but was standing beside the fallen beech trunk expectantly.

"Where have you been so long?" he asked so seriously that Bambi grew silent.

"Did you hear it?" the old stag went on after a pause.

"Yes," Bambi answered, "three times. He must be in the woods."

"Of course," the old stag nodded, and repeated with a peculiar intonation, "He is in the woods and we must go."

"Where?" the word escaped Bambi.

"Where He is now," said the old stag, and his voice was solemn.

Bambi was terrified.

"Don't be frightened," the old stag went on, "come with me and don't be frightened. I'm glad that I can take you and show you the way. . . ." He hesitated and added softly, "before I go."

Bambi looked wonderingly at the old stag. And suddenly he noticed how aged he looked. His head was completely gray now. His face was perfectly gaunt. The deep light was extinguished in his eyes, and they had a feeble, greenish luster and seemed to be blind.

[283]

Bambi and the old stag had not gone far before they caught the first whiff of that acrid smell that sent such dread and terror to their hearts.

Bambi stopped. But the old stag went on directly towards the scent. Bambi followed hesitantly.

The terrifying scent grew stronger and stronger. But the old stag kept on without stopping. The idea of flight sprang up in Bambi's mind and tugged at his heart. It seethed through his mind and body, and nearly swept him away. But he kept a firm grip on himself and stayed close behind the old stag.

Then the horrible scent grew so strong that it drowned out everything else, and it was hardly possible to breathe.

"Here He is," said the old stag moving to one side.

Through the bare branches, Bambi saw him lying on the trampled snow a few steps away.

An irresistible burst of terror swept over Bambi and with a sudden bound he started to give in to his impulse to flee.

"Halt!" he heard the old stag calling. Bambi looked around and saw the stag standing calmly where He was lying on the ground. Bambi was amazed and, moved by a sense of obedience, a boundless curiosity and quivering expectancy, he went closer.

"Come near," said the old stag, "don't be afraid."

He way lying with His pale, naked face turned upwards, His hat a little to one side on the snow. Bambi who did not know anything about hats, thought His horrible head was split in two. The poacher's shirt, open at the neck, was pierced where a wound gaped like a small red mouth. Blood was oozing out slowly. Blood was drying on His hair and around His nose. A big pool of it lay on the snow which was melting from the warmth.

"We can stand right beside Him," the old stag began softly, "and it isn't dangerous."

Bambi looked down at the prostrate form whose limbs and skin seemed so mysterious and terrible to him. He gazed at the dead eyes that stared up sightlessly at him. Bambi couldn't understand it all.

"Bambi," the old stag went on, "do you remember what Gobo said and what the dog said, what they all think, do you remember?"

Bambi could not answer.

"Do you see, Bambi," the old stag went on, "do you see how He's lying there dead, like one of us? Listen, Bambi. He isn't all-powerful as they say. Everything that lives and grows doesn't come from Him. He isn't above us. He's just the same as we are. He has the same fears, the same needs, and suffers in the same way. He can be killed like us, and then He lies helpless on the ground like all the rest of us, as you see Him now."

There was a silence.

"Do you understand me, Bambi?" asked the old stag.

"I think so," Bambi said in a whisper.

"Then speak," the old stag commanded.

Bambi was inspired, and said trembling, "There is Another who is over us all, over us and over Him."

"Now I can go," said the old stag.

He turned away, and they wandered side by side for a stretch.

Presently the old stag stopped in front of a

tall oak. "Don't follow me any further, Bambi,"
he began with a calm voice, "my time is up. Now
I have to look for a resting place."

Bambi tried to speak.

"Don't," said the old stag cutting him short,
"don't. In the hour which I am approaching we
are all alone. Good-by, my son. I loved you
dearly."

CHAPTER XXV

DAWN OF THE SUMMER'S DAY came hot, without a breath of wind or the usual morning chill. The sun seemed to come up faster than usual. It rose swiftly and flashed like a torch with dazzling rays.

The dew on the meadows and bushes was drawn up in an instant. The earth was perfectly dry so that the clods crumbled. The forest had been still from an early hour. Only a woodpecker hammered now and then, or the doves cooed their tireless, fervid tenderness.

Bambi was standing in a little clearing, forming a narrow glade in the heart of the thicket.

A swarm of midges danced and hummed around his head in the warm sunshine.

There was a low buzzing among the leaves of the hazel bushes near Bambi, and a big maybeetle crawled out and flew slowly by. He flew

[288]

among the midges, up and up, till he reached the tree-top where he intended to sleep till evening. His wing-covers folded down hard and neatly and his wings vibrated with strength.

The midges divided to let the may-beetle pass through, and closed behind him again. His dark brown body, over which shone the vibrant glassy shimmer of his whirring wings, flashed for a moment in the sunshine as he disappeared.

"Did you see him?" the midges asked each other.

"That's the old may-beetle," some of them hummed.

Others said, "All of his offspring are dead. Only one is still alive. Only one."

"How long will he live?" a number of midges asked.

The others answered, "We don't know. Some of his offspring live a long time. They live forever almost. . . . They see the sun thirty or forty times, we don't know exactly how many. Our lives are long enough, but we see the daylight only once or twice."

"How long has the old beetle been living?" some very small midges asked.

"He has outlived his whole family. He's as old as the hills, as old as the hills. He's seen more and been through more in this world than we can even imagine."

Bambi walked on. "Midge buzzings," he thought, "midge buzzings."

A delicate frightened call came to his ears.

He listened and went closer, perfectly softly, keeping among the thickest bushes, and moving noiselessly as he had long known to do.

The call came again, more urgent, more plaintively. Fawns' voices were wailing, "Mother! Mother!"

Bambi glided through the bushes and followed the calls.

Two fawns were standing side by side, in their little red coats, a brother and sister, forsaken and despondent.

"Mother! Mother!" they called.

Before they knew what had happened Bambi was standing in front of them. They stared at him speechlessly.

"Your mother has no time for you now," said Bambi severely.

He looked into the little brother's eyes.

[290]

Two fawns were standing side by side, in their little red coats.

"Can't you stay by yourself?" he asked.

The little brother and sister were silent.

Bambi turned and, gliding into the bushes, disappeared before they had come to their senses. He walked along.

"The little fellow pleases me," he thought, "perhaps I'll meet him again when he's larger. . . ."

He walked along. "The little girl is nice too," he thought, "Faline looked like that when she was a fawn."

He went on, and vanished in the forest.

THE YEARLING

Marjorie Kinnan Rawlings

THE
YEARLING

Decorations by
Edward Shenton

CHARLES SCRIBNER'S SONS
NEW YORK : 1938

THE YEARLING

· 1 ·

A COLUMN of smoke rose thin and straight from the cabin chimney. The smoke was blue where it left the red of the clay. It trailed into the blue of the April sky and was no longer blue but gray. The boy Jody watched it, speculating. The fire on the kitchen hearth was dying down. His mother was hanging up pots and pans after the noon dinner. The day was Friday. She would sweep the floor with a broom of ti-ti and after that, if he were lucky, she would scrub it with the corn shucks scrub. If she scrubbed the floor she would not miss him until he had reached the Glen. He stood a minute, balancing the hoe on his shoulder.

The clearing itself was pleasant if the unweeded rows of young shafts of corn were not before him. The wild bees had found the chinaberry tree by the front gate. They burrowed into the fragile clusters of lavender bloom as greedily as though there were no other flowers in the scrub; as though they had forgotten the yellow jessamine of March; the sweet bay and the magnolias ahead of them in May. It occurred to him that he might follow the swift line of flight of the black and gold bodies, and so find a bee-tree, full of amber honey. The winter's cane syrup was gone and most of the jellies. Finding a bee-tree was nobler work than hoeing, and the corn could wait another day. The afternoon was alive with a soft stirring. It bored into him as the bees bored into the chinaberry blossoms, so that he must be gone across the clearing, through the pines and down the road to the running branch. The bee-tree might be near the water.

He stood his hoe against the split-rail fence. He walked down the cornfield until he was out of sight of the cabin. He swung himself over the fence on his two hands. Old Julia the hound had followed his father in the wagon to Grahamsville, but Rip the bull-dog and Perk the new feice saw the form clear the fence and ran toward him. Rip barked deeply but the voice of the small mongrel was high and shrill. They wagged deprecatory short tails when they recognized him. He sent them back to the yard. They watched after him indifferently. They were a sorry pair, he thought, good for nothing but the chase, the catch and the kill. They had no interest in him except when he brought them their plates of table scraps night and morning. Old Julia was a gentle thing with humans, but her worn-toothed devotion was only for his father, Penny Baxter. Jody had tried to make up to Julia, but she would have none of him.

"You was pups together," his father told him, "ten year gone, when you was two year old and her a baby. You hurted the leetle thing, not meanin' no harm. She cain't bring herself to trust you. Hounds is often that-a-way."

He made a circle around the sheds and corn-crib and cut south through the black-jack. He wished he had a dog like

Grandma Hutto's. It was white and curly-haired and did tricks. When Grandma Hutto laughed and shook and could not stop, the dog jumped into her lap and licked her face, wagging its plumed tail as though it laughed with her. He would like anything that was his own; that licked his face and followed him as old Julia followed his father. He cut into the sand road and began to run east. It was two miles to the Glen, but it seemed to Jody that he could run forever. There was no ache in his legs, as when he hoed the corn. He slowed down to make the road last longer. He had passed the big pines and left them behind. Where he walked now, the scrub had closed in, walling in the road with dense sand pines, each one so thin it seemed to the boy it might make kindling by itself. The road went up an incline. At the top he stopped. The April sky was framed by the tawny sand and the pines. It was as blue as his homespun shirt, dyed with Grandma Hutto's indigo. Small clouds were stationary, like bolls of cotton. As he watched, the sunlight left the sky a moment and the clouds were gray.

"There'll come a little old drizzly rain before night-fall," he thought.

The down grade tempted him to a lope. He reached the thick-bedded sand of the Silver Glen road. The tar-flower was in bloom, and fetter-bush and sparkleberry. He slowed to a walk, so that he might pass the changing vegetation tree by tree, bush by bush, each one unique and familiar. He reached the magnolia tree where he had carved the wild-cat's face. The growth was a sign that there was water nearby. It seemed a strange thing to him, when earth was earth and rain was rain, that scrawny pines should grow in the scrub, while by every branch and lake and river there grew magnolias. Dogs were the same everywhere, and oxen and mules and horses. But trees were different in different places.

"Reckon it's because they can't move none," he decided. They took what food was in the soil under them.

3

The east bank of the road shelved suddenly. It dropped below him twenty feet to a spring. The bank was dense with magnolia and loblolly bay, sweet gum and gray-barked ash. He went down to the spring in the cool darkness of their shadows. A sharp pleasure came over him. This was a secret and a lovely place.

A spring as clear as well water bubbled up from nowhere in the sand. It was as though the banks cupped green leafy hands to hold it. There was a whirlpool where the water rose from the earth. Grains of sand boiled in it. Beyond the bank, the parent spring bubbled up at a higher level, cut itself a channel through white limestone and began to run rapidly down-hill to make a creek. The creek joined Lake George, Lake George was a part of the St. John's River, the great river flowed northward and into the sea. It excited Jody to watch the beginning of the ocean. There were other beginnings, true, but this one was his own. He liked to think that no one came here but himself and the wild animals and the thirsty birds.

He was warm from his jaunt. The dusky glen laid cool hands on him. He rolled up the hems of his blue denim breeches and stepped with bare dirty feet into the shallow spring. His toes sunk into the sand. It oozed softly between them and over his bony ankles. The water was so cold that for a moment it burned his skin. Then it made a rippling sound, flowing past his pipe-stem legs, and was entirely delicious. He walked up and down, digging his big toe experimentally under smooth rocks he encountered. A school of minnows flashed ahead of him down the growing branch. He chased them through the shallows. They were suddenly out of sight as though they had never existed. He crouched under a bared and overhanging live-oak root where a pool was deep, thinking they might reappear, but only a spring frog wriggled from under the mud, stared at him, and dove under the tree root in a spasmodic terror. He laughed.

4

"I ain't no 'coon. I'd not ketch you," he called after it.

A breeze parted the canopied limbs over him. The sun dropped through and lay on his head and shoulders. It was good to be warm at his head while his hard calloused feet were cold. The breeze died away, the sun no longer reached him. He waded across to the opposite bank where the growth was more open. A low palmetto brushed him. It reminded him that his knife was snug in his pocket; that he had planned as long ago as Christmas, to make himself a flutter-mill.

He had never built one alone. Grandma Hutto's son Oliver had always made one for him whenever he was home from sea. He went to work intently, frowning as he tried to recall the exact angle necessary to make the mill-wheel turn smoothly. He cut two forked twigs and trimmed them into two Y's of the same size. Oliver had been very particular to have the cross-bar round and smooth, he remembered. A wild cherry grew half-way up the bank. He climbed it and cut a twig as even as a polished pencil. He selected a palm frond and cut two strips of the tough fiber, an inch wide and four inches long. He cut a slit lengthwise in the center of each of them, wide enough to insert the cherry twig. The strips of palm frond must be at angles, like the arms of a windmill. He adjusted them carefully. He separated the Y-shaped twigs by nearly the length of the cherry cross-bar and pushed them deep into the sand of the branch bed a few yards below the spring.

The water was only a few inches deep but it ran strongly, with a firm current. The palm-frond mill-wheel must just brush the water's surface. He experimented with depth until he was satisfied, then laid the cherry bar between the twigs. It hung motionless. He twisted it a moment, anxiously, helping it to fit itself into its forked grooves. The bar began to rotate. The current caught the flexible tip of one bit of palm frond. By the time it lifted clear, the rotation of the bar brought the angled tip of the second into contact with the stream. The small leafy

5

paddles swung over and over, up and down. The little wheel was turning. The flutter-mill was at work. It turned with the easy rhythm of the great water-mill at Lynne that ground corn into meal.

Jody drew a deep breath. He threw himself on the weedy sand close to the water and abandoned himself to the magic of motion. Up, over, down, up, over, down—the flutter-mill was enchanting. The bubbling spring would rise forever from the earth, the thin current was endless. The spring was the beginning of waters sliding to the sea. Unless leaves fell, or squirrels cut sweet bay twigs to drop and block the fragile wheel, the flutter-mill might turn forever. When he was an old man, as old as his father, there seemed no reason why this rippling movement might not continue as he had begun it.

He moved a stone that was matching its corners against his sharp ribs and burrowed a little, hollowing himself a nest for his hips and shoulders. He stretched out one arm and laid his head on it. A shaft of sunlight, warm and thin like a light patchwork quilt, lay across his body. He watched the flutter-mill indolently, sunk in the sand and the sunlight. The movement was hypnotic. His eyelids fluttered with the palm-leaf paddles. Drops of silver slipping from the wheel blurred together like the tail of a shooting star. The water made a sound like kittens lapping. A rain frog sang a moment and then was still. There was an instant when the boy hung at the edge of a high bank made of the soft fluff of broom-sage, and the rain frog and the starry dripping of the flutter-mill hung with him. Instead of falling over the edge, he sank into the softness. The blue, white-tufted sky closed over him. He slept.

When he awakened, he thought he was in a place other than the branch bed. He was in another world, so that for an instant he thought he might still be dreaming. The sun was gone, and all the light and shadow. There were no black boles of live oaks, no glossy green of magnolia leaves, no pattern of gold lace

6

where the sun had sifted through the branches of the wild cherry. The world was all a gentle gray, and he lay in a mist as fine as spray from a waterfall. The mist tickled his skin. It was scarcely wet. It was at once warm and cool. He rolled over on his back and it was as though he looked up into the soft gray breast of a mourning dove.

He lay, absorbing the fine-dropped rain like a young plant. When his face was damp at last and his shirt was moist to the touch, he left his nest. He stopped short. A deer had come to the spring while he was sleeping. The fresh tracks came down the east bank and stopped at the water's edge. They were sharp and pointed, the tracks of a doe. They sank deeply into the sand, so that he knew the doe was an old one and a large. Perhaps she was heavy with fawn. She had come down and drunk deeply from the spring, not seeing him where he slept. Then she had scented him. There was a scuffled confusion in the sand where she had wheeled in fright. The tracks up the opposite bank had long harried streaks behind them. Perhaps she had not drunk, after all, before she scented him, and turned and ran with that swift, sand-throwing flight. He hoped she was not now thirsty, wide-eyed in the scrub.

He looked about for other tracks. The squirrels had raced up and down the banks, but they were bold, always. A raccoon had been that way, with his feet like sharp-nailed hands, but he could not be sure how recently. Only his father could tell for certain the hour when any wild things had passed by. Only the doe had surely come and had been frightened. He turned back again to the flutter-mill. It was turning as steadily as though it had always been there. The palm-leaf paddles were frail but they made a brave show of strength, rippling against the shallow water. They were glistening from the slow rain.

Jody looked at the sky. He could not tell the time of day in the grayness, nor how long he may have slept. He bounded up the west bank, where open gallberry flats spread without obstructions. As he stood, hesitant whether to go or stay, the rain ended as gently as it had begun. A light breeze stirred from the southwest. The sun came out. The clouds rolled together into great white billowing feather bolsters, and across the east a rainbow arched, so lovely and so various that Jody thought he would burst with looking at it. The earth was pale green, the air itself was all but visible, golden with the rain-washed sunlight, and all the trees and grass and bushes glittered, varnished with the rain-drops.

A spring of delight boiled up within him as irresistibly as the spring of the branch. He lifted his arms and held them straight from his shoulders like a water-turkey's wings. He began to whirl around in his tracks. He whirled faster and faster until his ecstasy was a whirlpool, and when he thought he would explode with it, he became dizzy and closed his eyes and dropped to the ground and lay flat in the broom-sage. The earth whirled under him and with him. He opened his eyes and the blue April sky and the cotton clouds whirled over him. Boy and earth and trees and sky spun together. The whirling stopped, his head cleared and he got to his feet. He was light-headed and giddy, but something in him was relieved, and the April day could be borne again, like any ordinary day.

He turned and galloped toward home. He drew deep breaths of the pines, aromatic with wetness. The loose sand that had pulled at his feet was firmed by the rain. The return was comfortable going. The sun was not far from its setting when the long-leaf pines around the Baxter clearing came into sight. They stood tall and dark against the red-gold west. He heard the chickens clucking and quarreling and knew they had just been fed. He turned into the clearing. The weathered gray of the split-rail fence was luminous in the rich spring light. Smoke curled thickly from the stick-and-clay chimney. Supper would be ready on the hearth and hot bread baking in the Dutch oven. He hoped his father had not returned from

Grahamsville. It came to him for the first time that perhaps he should not have left the place while his father was away. If his mother had needed wood, she would be angry. Even his father would shake his head a little and say, "Son——" He heard old Cæsar snort and knew his father was ahead of him.

The clearing was in a pleasant clatter. The horse whinnied at the gate, the calf bleated in its stall and the milch cow answered, the chickens scratched and cackled and the dogs barked with the coming of food and evening. It was good to be hungry and to be fed and the stock was eager with an expectant certainty. The end of winter had been meager; corn short, and hay, and dried cow-peas. But now in April the pastures were green and succulent and even the chickens savored the sprouts of young grass. The dogs had found a nest of young rabbits that evening, and after such tid-bits the scraps from the Baxter supper table were a matter of some indifference. Jody saw old Julia lying under the wagon, worn out from her miles of trotting. He swung open the front paling gate and went to find his father.

Penny Baxter was at the wood-pile. He still wore the coat of the broadcloth suit that he had been married in, that he now wore as badge of his gentility when he went to church, or off trading. The sleeves were too short, not because Penny had grown, but because the years of hanging through the summer dampness, and being pressed with the smoothing iron and pressed again, had somehow shrunk the fabric. Jody saw his father's hands, big for the rest of him, close around a bundle of wood. He was doing Jody's work, and in his good coat. Jody ran to him.

"I'll git it, Pa."

He hoped his willingness, now, would cover his delinquency. His father straightened his back.

"I near about give you out, son," he said.

"I went to the Glen."

9

"Hit were a mighty purty day to go," Penny said. "Or to go anywhere. How come you to take out such a fur piece?"

It was as hard to remember why he had gone as though it had been a year ago. He had to think back to the moment when he had laid down his hoe.

"Oh." He had it now. "I aimed to foller the honey-bees and find a bee-tree."

"You find it?"

Jody stared blankly.

"Dogged if I ain't forgot 'til now to look for it."

He felt as foolish as a bird-dog caught chasing field mice. He looked at his father sheepishly. His father's pale blue eyes were twinkling.

"Tell the truth, Jody," he said, "and shame the devil. Wa'n't the bee-tree a fine excuse to go a-ramblin'?"

Jody grinned.

"The notion takened me," he admitted, "afore I studied on the bee-tree."

"That's what I figgered. How come me to know, was when I was drivin' along to Grahamsville, I said to myself, 'There's Jody now, and the hoein' ain't goin' to take him too long. What would I do this fine spring day, was I a boy?' And then I thought, 'I'd go a-ramblin'.' Most anywhere, long as it kivered the ground."

A warmth filled the boy that was not the low golden sun. He nodded.

"That's the way I figgered," he said.

"But your Ma, now," Penny jerked his head toward the house, "don't hold with ramblin'. Most women-folks cain't see for their lives, how a man loves so to ramble. I never let on you wasn't here. She said, 'Where's Jody?' and I said, 'Oh, I reckon he's around some'eres.'"

He winked one eye and Jody winked back.

"Men-folks has got to stick together in the name o' peace. You carry your Ma a good bait o' wood now."

Jody filled his arms and hurried to the house. His mother was kneeling at the hearth. The spiced smells that came to his nose made him weak with hunger.

"That ain't sweet 'tater pone, is it, Ma?"

"Hit's sweet 'tater pone, and don't you fellers be too long a time now, piddlin' around and visitin'. Supper's done and ready."

He dumped the wood in the box and scurried to the lot. His father was milking Trixie.

"Ma says to git done and come on," he reported. "Must I feed old Cæsar?"

"I done fed him, son, sich as I had to give the pore feller." He stood up from the three-legged milking stool. "Carry in the milk and don't trip and waste it outen the gourd like you done yestiddy. Easy, Trixie——"

He moved aside from the cow and went to the stall in the shed, where her calf was tethered.

"Here, Trixie. Soo, gal——"

The cow lowed and came to her calf.

"Easy, there. You greedy as Jody."

He stroked the pair and followed the boy to the house. They washed in turn at the water-shelf and dried their hands and faces on the roller towel hanging outside the kitchen door. Ma Baxter sat at the table waiting for them, helping their plates. Her bulky frame filled the end of the long narrow table. Jody and his father sat down on either side of her. It seemed natural to both of them that she should preside.

"You-all hongry tonight?" she asked.

"I kin hold a barrel o' meat and a bushel o' biscuit," Jody said.

"That's what you say. Your eyes is bigger'n your belly."

"I'd about say the same," Penny said, "if I hadn't learned better. Goin' to Grahamsville allus do make me hongry."

"You git a snort o' 'shine there, is the reason," she said.

"A mighty small one today. Jim Turnbuckle treated."

"Then you shore didn't git enough to hurt you."

Jody heard nothing; saw nothing but his plate. He had never been so hungry in his life, and after a lean winter and slow spring, with food not much more plentiful for the Baxters than for their stock, his mother had cooked a supper good enough for the preacher. There were poke-greens with bits of white bacon buried in them; sand-buggers made of potato and onion and the cooter he had found crawling yesterday; sour orange biscuits and at his mother's elbow the sweet potato pone. He was torn between his desire for more biscuits and another sand-bugger and the knowledge, born of painful experience, that if he ate them, he would suddenly have no room for pone. The choice was plain.

"Ma," he said, "kin I have my pone right now?"

She was at a pause in the feeding of her own large frame. She cut him, dexterously, a generous portion. He plunged into its spiced and savory goodness.

"The time it takened me," she complained, "to make that pone—and you destroyin' it before I git my breath——"

"I'm eatin' it quick," he admitted, "but I'll remember it a long time."

Supper was done with. Jody was replete. Even his father, who usually ate like a sparrow, had taken a second helping.

"I'm full, thank the Lord," he said.

Ma Baxter sighed.

"If a feller'd light me a candle," she said, "I'd git shut o' the dishwashin' and mebbe have time to set and enjoy myself."

Jody left his seat and lit a tallow candle. As the yellow flame wavered, he looked out of the east window. The full moon was rising.

"A pity to waste light, ain't it," his father said, "and the full moon shinin'."

He came to the window and they watched it together.

"Son, what do it put in your head? Do you mind what we said we'd do, full moon in April?"

"I dis-remember."

Somehow, the seasons always took him unawares. It must be necessary to be as old as his father to keep them in the mind and memory, to remember moon-time from one year's end to another.

"You ain't forgot what I told you? I'll swear, Jody. Why, boy, the bears comes outen their winter beds on the full moon in April."

"Old Slewfoot! You said we'd lay for him when he come out!"

"That's it."

"You said we'd go where we seed his tracks comin' and goin' and criss-crossin', and likely find his bed, and him, too, comin' out in April."

"And fat. Fat and lazy. The meat so sweet, from him layin' up."

"And him mebbe easier to ketch, not woke up good."

"That's it."

"When kin we go, Pa?"

"Soon as we git the hoein' done. And see bear-sign."

"Which-a-way will we begin huntin' him?"

"We'd best to go by the Glen springs and see has he come out and watered there."

"A big ol' doe watered there today," Jody said. "Whilst I was asleep. I built me a flutter-mill, Pa. It run fine."

Ma Baxter stopped the clatter of her pots and pans.

"You sly scaper," she said. "That's the first I knowed you been off. You gittin' slick as a clay road in the rain."

He shouted with laughter.

"I fooled you, Ma. Say it, Ma, I got to fool you oncet."

"You fooled me. And me standin' over the fire makin' potato pone——"

She was not truly angry.

"Now, Ma," he cajoled her, "suppose I was a varmint and didn't eat nothin' but roots and grass."

"I'd not have nothin' then to rile me," she said.

At the same time he saw her mouth twist. She tried to straighten it and could not.

"Ma's a-laughin'! Ma's a-laughin'! You ain't riled when you laugh!"

He darted behind her and untied her apron strings. The apron slipped to the floor. She turned her bulk quickly and boxed his ears, but the blows were feather-light and playful. The same delirium came over him again that he had felt in the afternoon. He began to whirl around and around as he had done in the broom-sage.

"You knock them plates offen the table," she said, "and you'll see who's riled."

"I cain't he'p it. I'm dizzy."

"You're addled," she said. "Jest plain addled."

It was true. He was addled with April. He was dizzy with Spring. He was as drunk as Lem Forrester on a Saturday night. His head was swimming with the strong brew made up of the sun and the air and the thin gray rain. The flutter-mill had made him drunk, and the doe's coming, and his father's hiding his absence, and his mother's making him a pone and laughing at him. He was stabbed with the candle-light inside the safe comfort of the cabin; with the moonlight around it. He pictured old Slewfoot, the great black outlaw bear with one toe missing, rearing up in his winter bed and tasting the soft air and smelling the moonlight, as he, Jody, smelled and tasted them. He went to bed in a fever and could not sleep. A mark was on him from the day's delight, so that all his life, when

April was a thin green and the flavor of rain was on his tongue, an old wound would throb and a nostalgia would fill him for something he could not quite remember. A whip-poor-will called across the bright night, and suddenly he was asleep.

· 2 ·

Penny Baxter lay awake beside the vast sleeping bulk of his wife. He was always wakeful on the full moon. He had often wondered whether, with the light so bright, men were not meant to go into their fields and labor. He would like to slip from his bed and perhaps cut down an oak for wood, or finish the hoeing that Jody had left undone.

"I reckon I'd ought to of crawled him about it," he thought.

In his day, he would have been thoroughly thrashed for slipping away and idling. His father would have sent him back to the spring, without his supper, to tear out the flutter-mill.

"But that's it," he thought. "A boy ain't a boy too long."

As he looked back over the years, he himself had had no boyhood. His own father had been a preacher, stern as the Old Testament God. The living had come, however, not from the Word, but from the small farm near Volusia on which he had raised a large family. He had taught them to read and write and to know the Scriptures, but all of them, from the time they could toddle behind him down the corn rows, carrying the sack of seed, had toiled until their small bones ached and their growing fingers cramped. Rations had been short and hookworm abundant. Penny had grown to maturity no bigger than a boy. His feet were small, his shoulders narrow, his ribs and hips jointed together in a continuous fragile framework. He had stood among the Forresters one day, like an ash sapling among giant oaks.

Lem Forrester looked down at him and said, "Why, you leetle ol' penny-piece, you. You're good money, a'right, but hit jest don't come no smaller. Leetle ol' Penny Baxter——"

The name had been his only one ever since. When he voted, he signed himself "Ezra Ezekial Baxter," but when he paid his taxes, he was put down as "Penny Baxter" and made no protest. But he was a sound amalgam; sound as copper itself; and with something, too, of the copper's softness. He leaned backward in his honesty, so that he was often a temptation to store-keepers and mill-owners and horse-traders. Store-keeper Boyles at Volusia, as honest as he, had once given him a dollar too much in change. His horse being lame, Penny had walked the long miles back again to return it.

"The next time you came to trade would have done," Boyles said.

"I know," Penny answered him, "but 'twa'n't mine and I wouldn't of wanted to die with it on me. Dead or alive, I only want what's mine."

The remark might have explained, to those who puzzled at him, his migration to the adjacent scrub. Folk who lived along the deep and placid river, alive with craft, with dugouts and scows, lumber rafts and freight and passenger vessels, side-wheel steamers that almost filled the stream, in places, from bank to bank, had said that Penny Baxter was either a brave man or a crazy one to leave the common way of life and take his bride into the very heart of the wild Florida scrub, populous with bears and wolves and panthers. It had been understandable for the Forresters to go there, for the growing family of great burly quarrelsome males needed all the room in the county, and freedom from any hindrance. But who would hinder Penny Baxter?

It was not hindrance— But in the towns and villages, in farming sections where neighbors were not too far apart, men's minds and actions and property overlapped. There were intrusions on the individual spirit. There were friendliness and mutual help in time of trouble, true, but there were bickerings and watchfulness, one man suspicious of another. He had grown from under the sternness of his father into a world less direct, less honest, in its harshness, and therefore more disturbing.

He had perhaps been bruised too often. The peace of the vast aloof scrub had drawn him with the beneficence of its silence. Something in him was raw and tender. The touch of men was hurtful upon it, but the touch of the pines was healing. Making a living came harder there, distances were troublesome in the buying of supplies and the marketing of crops. But the clearing was peculiarly his own. The wild animals seemed less predatory to him than people he had known. The forays of bear and wolf and wild-cat and panther on stock were understandable, which was more than he could say of human cruelties.

In his thirties he had married a buxom girl, already twice his size, loaded her in an ox-cart along with the rudiments of housekeeping, and jogged with her to the clearing, where with his own hands he had reared a cabin. He had chosen his land as well as a man might choose in the brooding expanse of scrawny sand pines. He had bought of the Forresters, who lived a safe four miles away, high good land in the center of a pine island. The island was called by such a name, in an arid forest, because it was literally an island of long-leaf pines, lifted high, a land-mark, in the rolling sea that was the scrub. There were other such islands scattered to the north and west, where some acci-dent of soil or moisture produced patches of luxuriant growth; even of hammock, the richest growth of all. Live oaks were here and there; the red bay and the magnolia; wild cherry and sweet gum; hickory and holly.

A scarcity of water was the only draw-back to the location. The water level lay so deep that wells were priceless. Water for inhabitants of Baxter's Island must come, until bricks and mor-tar were cheaper, from the great sink-hole on the western boundary of the hundred-acre tract. The sink-hole was a phe-nomenon common to the Florida limestone regions. Under-ground rivers ran through such sections. The bubbling springs that turned at once into creeks and runs were outbreaks of these. Sometimes a thin shell of surface soil caved in and a great cavern was revealed, with or without a flow of water. The sink-hole included with Penny Baxter's land contained, unfor-tunately, no flowing spring. But a pure filtered water seeped day and night through the high banks and formed a pool at the bottom. The Forresters had tried to sell Penny poor land in the scrub itself, but with cash to back him, he had insisted on the island.

He had said to them, "The scrub's a fitten place for the game to raise, and all the wild things. Foxes and deer and panther-cats and rattlesnakes. I cain't raise young uns in a pure thicket."

The Forresters had slapped their thighs and roared with laughter from their beards.

Lem had bellowed, "How many ha' pennies is in a penny? You'll do good, be you daddy to a fox-cub."

Penny could hear him now, after all the years. He turned over in his bed, cautiously, not to awaken his wife. He had indeed planned boldly for sons and daughters, moving in pro-lific plenty among the long-leaf pines. The family had come.

Ora Baxter was plainly built for child-bearing. But it had seemed as though his seed were as puny as himself.

"Or Lem put a mouth on me," he thought.

The babies were frail, and almost as fast as they came, they sickened and died. Penny had buried them one by one in a cleared place among the black-jack oaks, where the poor loose soil made the digging easier. The plot grew in size until he was compelled to fence it in against the vandalism of hogs and pole-cats. He had carved little wooden tombstones for all. He could picture them now, standing white and straight in the moonlight. Some of them had names: Ezra Jr.; Little Ora; William T. The others bore only such legends as Baby Baxter, aged 3 mos. 6 days. On one, Penny had scratched laboriously with his pocket-knife, "She never saw the light of day." His mind moved back down the years, touching them, as a man touches fence-posts in his passing.

There had been a hiatus in the births. Then, when the loneliness of the place had begun to frighten him a little, and his wife was almost past the age of bearing, Jody Baxter was born and thrived. When the baby was a toddling two-year-old, Penny had gone to the war. He had taken his wife and child to the river, to live with his crony, Grandma Hutto, for the few months he expected to be away. He had come back at the end of four years with the mark of age on him. He had gathered up his wife and boy and taken them back to the scrub with gratitude for its peace and isolation.

Jody's mother had accepted her youngest with something of detachment, as though she had given all she had of love and care and interest to those others. But Penny's bowels yearned over his son. He gave him something more than his paternity. He found that the child stood wide-eyed and breathless before the miracle of bird and creature, of flower and tree, of wind and rain and sun and moon, as he had always stood. And if, on a soft day in April, the boy had prowled away on his boy's business, he could understand the thing that had drawn him. He understood, too, its briefness.

His wife's bulk stirred and she made a sound in her sleep. He would act on any such occasion, he knew, as a bulwark for the boy against the mother's sharpness. The whip-poor-will flew farther into the forest and took up his lament again, sweet with distance. The moonlight moved beyond the focus of the bed-room window.

"Leave him kick up his heels," he thought, "and run away. Leave him build his flutter-mills. The day'll come, he'll not even care to."

· 3 ·

Jody opened his eyes unwillingly. Sometime, he thought, he would slip away into the woods and sleep from Friday until Monday. Daylight was showing through the east window of his small bedroom. He could not be certain whether it was the pale light that had awakened him, or the stirring of the chickens in the peach trees. He heard them fluttering one by one from their roost in the branches. The daylight lay in orange streaks. The pines beyond the clearing were still black against it. Now in April the sun was rising earlier. It could not be very late. It was good to awaken by himself before his mother called him. He turned over luxuriously. The dry corn shucks of his mattress rustled under him. The Dominick rooster crowed boisterously under the window.

"You crow now," the boy said. "See kin you rout me out."

The bright streaks in the east thickened and blended. A golden flush spread as high as the pines, and as he watched, the sun itself lifted, like a vast copper skillet being drawn to hang among the branches. A light wind stirred, as though the growing light had pushed it out of the restless east. The sacking curtains eddied out into the room. The breeze reached the bed and brushed him with the cool softness of clean fur. He lay for a moment in torment between the luxury of his bed and the coming day. Then he was out of his nest and standing on the deerskin rug, and his breeches were hanging handily, and his shirt right side out by good fortune, and he was in them, and dressed, and there was not any need of sleep, or anything but the day, and the smell of hot cakes in the kitchen.

"Hey, ol' Ma," he said at the door. "I like you, Ma."

"You and them hounds and all the rest o' the stock," she said. "Mighty lovin' on a empty belly and me with a dish in my hand."

"That's the way you're purtiest," he said, and grinned.

He went whistling to the water-shelf and dipped into the wooden bucket to fill the wash-basin. He soused his hands and face in the water, deciding against the strong lye soap. He wet his hair and parted and smoothed it with his fingers. He took down the small mirror from the wall and studied himself a moment.

"I'm turrible ugly, Ma," he called.

"Well, there ain't been a purty Baxter since the name begun."

He wrinkled his nose at the mirror. The gesture made the freckles across the bridge blend together.

"I wisht I was dark like the Forresters."

"You be proud you ain't. Them fellers is black as their hearts. You a Baxter and all the Baxters is fair."

"You talk like I wasn't no kin to you."

"My folks runs to fairness, too. They ain't none of 'em puny, though. Iffen you'll learn yourself to work, you'll be your Pa all over."

The mirror showed a small face with high cheek bones. The face was freckled and pale, but healthy, like a fine sand. The hair grieved him on the occasions when he went to church or any doings at Volusia. It was straw-colored and shaggy, and no matter how carefully his father cut it, once a month on the Sunday morning nearest the full moon, it grew in tufts at the back. "Drakes' tails," his mother called them. His eyes were wide and blue. When he frowned, in close study over his reader, or watching something curious, they narrowed. It was then that his mother claimed him kin.

"He do favor the Alverses a mite," she said.

Jody turned the mirror to inspect his ears; not for cleanliness, but remembering the pain of the day when Lem Forrester had held his chin with one vast hand and pulled his ears with the other.

"Boy, your ears is set up on your head like a 'possum's," Lem said.

Jody made a leering grimace at himself and returned the mirror to the wall.

"Do we got to wait for Pa to eat breakfast?" he asked.

"We do. Set it all in front of you and there'd likely not be enough left for him."

He hesitated at the back door.

"And don't you slip off, neither. He ain't but to the corn-crib."

From the south, beyond the black-jacks, he heard the bell-like voice of old Julia, giving tongue in great excitement. He thought he heard, too, his father, giving her a command. He bolted away before his mother's sharp voice could stop him. She, too, had heard the dog. She followed to the door and called after him.

"Don't you and your Pa be gone too long now, follerin' that

THE YEARLING

fool hound. I'm o' no mind to set around waitin' breakfast and you two piddlin' around in the woods."

He could no longer hear either old Julia or his father. He was in a frenzy for fear the excitement was over; the intruder gone and perhaps dog and father with it. He crashed through the black-jacks in the direction from which the sounds had come. His father's voice spoke, close at hand.

"Easy, son. What's done 'll wait for you."

He stopped short. Old Julia stood trembling, not in fear but in eagerness. His father stood looking down at the crushed and mangled carcass of black Betsy, the brood sow.

"He must of heered me darin' him," Penny said. "Look careful, boy. See do you see what I see."

The sight of the mutilated sow sickened him. His father was looking beyond the dead animal. Old Julia had her sharp nose turned in the same direction. Jody walked a few paces and examined the sand. The unmistakable tracks made his blood jump. They were the tracks of a giant bear. And from the print of the right front paw, as big as the crown of a hat, one toe was missing.

"Old Slewfoot!"

Penny nodded.

"I'm proud you remembered his track."

They bent together and studied the signs and the direction in which they had both come and gone.

"That's what I call," Penny said, "carryin' the war into the enemy's camp."

"None o' the dogs bayed him, Pa. Lessen I didn't hear, for sleepin'."

"None of 'em bayed him. He had the wind in his favor. Don't you think he didn't know what he was doin'. He slipped in like a shadow and done his meanness and slipped out afore day."

A chill ran along Jody's backbone. He could picture the

shadow, big and black as a shed in motion, moving among the black-jacks and gathering in the tame and sleeping sow with one sweep of the great clawed paw. Then the white tusks followed into the backbone, crushing it, and into the warm and palpitating flesh. Betsy had had no chance even to squeal for help.

"He'd a'ready fed," Penny pointed out. "He ate no more'n a mouthful. A bear's stomach is shrunk when he first comes outen his winter bed. That's why I hate a bear. A creetur that kills and eats what he needs, why, he's jest like the rest of us, makin' out the best he kin. But an animal, or a person either, that'll do harm jest to be a-doin'—— You look in a bear's face and you'll see he's got no remorse."

"You aim to carry in old Betsy?"

"The meat's bad tore up, but I reckon there's sausage left. And lard."

Jody knew that he should feel badly about old Betsy, but all that he could feel was excitement. The unwarranted kill, inside the sanctuary of the Baxter acres, had made a personal enemy of the big bear that had evaded all the stock owners for five years. He was wild to begin the hunt. He acknowledged to himself, as well, a trace of fear. Old Slewfoot had struck close to home.

He took one hind leg of the sow and Penny the other. They dragged it to the house with Julia reluctant at their heels. The old bear-dog could not understand why they did not set out at once on the chase.

"I'll swear," Penny said, "I'm daresome to break the news to your Ma."

"She'll rare for certain," Jody agreed.

"Betsy was sich a fine brood sow. My, she was fine."

Ma Baxter was waiting for them by the gate.

"I been a-callin' and I been a-callin'," she hailed them. "What you got there, piddlin' around so long? Oh dear goodness, oh dear goodness—my sow, my sow."

She threw her arms toward the sky. Penny and Jody passed through the gate and back of the house. She followed, wailing.

"We'll hang the meat to the cross-piece, son," Penny said. "The dogs'll not reach it there."

"You might tell me," Ma Baxter said. "The least you kin do is tell me, how come her dead and tore to ribbons right under my nose."

"Old Slewfoot done it, Ma," Jody said. "His tracks was certain."

"And them dogs asleep right here in the clearin'?"

The three had already appeared, nosing about the fresh smell of the blood. She threw a stick in their direction.

"You no-account creeturs! Hornin' in on our rations and leavin' sich as this to happen."

"Ain't a dog borned as smart as that bear," Penny said.

"They could of barked."

She threw another stick and the dogs slunk away.

The family went to the house. In the confusion, Jody went first into the kitchen, where the smell of breakfast tortured him. His mother could not be too disturbed to notice what he was doing.

"You git right back here," she called, "and wash your dirty hands."

He joined his father at the water-shelf. Breakfast was on the table. Ma Baxter sat, swaying her body in distress, and did not eat. Jody heaped his plate. There were grits and gravy, hot cakes, and buttermilk.

"Anyway," he said, "we got meat to eat for a whiles now."

She turned on him.

"Meat now, and none this winter."

"I'll ask the Forresters out of a sow," Penny said.

"Yes, and be beholden to them rascals." She began to wail again. "That blasted bear— I'd like to git my hands on him."

"I'll tell him when I see him," Penny said mildly between mouthfuls.

Jody burst out laughing.

"That's right," she said. "Make a fun-box outen me."

Jody patted her big arm.

"Hit jest come to me, Ma, how you'd look—you and ol' Slewfoot mixin' it."

"I'd bet on your Ma," Penny said.

"Nobody but me don't take life serious," she lamented.

· 4 ·

Penny pushed back his plate and stood up from the table.
"Well, son, we got our day's work laid out for us."

Jody's heart fell. Hoeing——

"We stand a right good chancet o' comin' up with that bear today."

The sun was bright again.

"Fetch me my shot-bag and my powder horn. And the tinder horn."

Jody jumped to bring them.

"Look at him move," his mother said. "To see him hoe, you'd think he was a snail. Say 'huntin'' and he's quick as a otter."

She went to the kitchen safe and took out one of the few remaining glasses of jelly. She spread the jelly on the left-over stack of hot cakes and tied them in a piece of cloth and dropped them in Penny's knapsack. She took the remains of the sweet potato pone and set aside a piece for herself, then added the pone, wrapped in a fragment of paper, to the knapsack. She looked again at the pone she had saved, and with a quick motion dropped it in the sack with the other.

"This ain't much dinner," she said. "Mebbe you'll be soon back."

"Don't look for us 'til you see us," Penny said. "Anyways, no man never starved to death in a day."

"To hear Jody tell it," she said, "he kin starve to death about a hour after breakfast."

Penny swung the knapsack and tinder horn over his shoulder.

"Jody, take the big knife and go cut a good strip offen that 'gator tail."

The meat, dry-cured for the feeding of the dogs, hung in the smoke-house. Jody ran to it and swung open the heavy timbered door. The smoke-house was dark and cool, odorous with the smell of hams and bacons, dusty with the ash of hickory. The rafters, studded with square-headed nails for the hanging of meats, were now almost bare. Three shoulders of ham hung, lean and withered, and two bacon sides. A haunch of jerked venison swung beside the smoked alligator meat. Old Slewfoot had indeed done damage. Betsy the broodsow would have filled the room with her plump progeny by the coming fall. Jody hacked away a piece of alligator. The meat was dry but tender. He touched his tongue to it. Its saltiness was not unpleasing. He joined his father in the yard.

At sight of the old muzzle-loading shotgun, Julia lifted her voice in a wail of delight. Rip shot from under the house to join her. Perk, the new feice, wagged his tail stupidly and without understanding. Penny patted the dogs in turn.

"You'll likely not be so merry, time the day be done," he

told them. "Jody-boy, you best put on your shoes. Hit'll be rough goin', places."

It seemed to Jody that he would burst if there was further delay. He dashed in to his room and routed out his heavy cowhide brogans from under the bed. He slipped his feet into them and raced after his father as though the hunt would be done and over before he reached him. Old Julia was loping ahead, her long nose against the trail of the bear.

"The trail'll not be too cold, Pa? Reckon he won't be gone too fur yonder to ketch up with him?"

"He'll be fur yonder, but we got a heap better chancet o' ketchin' up with him, do we let him take it easy and give him time to lay up. A bear that knows he's follered moves a sight faster'n one that figgers the world's his own, to prowl and feed in."

The trail led south through the black-jacks. After the rain of the afternoon before, the great nubbed tracks made a plain pattern across the sand.

"He's got a foot like a Georgia nigger," Penny said.

The black-jacks ended as though they had been sown by hand and there had been no more seed in the sack. The land was lower and the growth was of large pines.

"Pa, how big you reckon he be?"

"He's big. He ain't full weight right now, account of his stomach bein' shrunk up from layin' up, and empty. But look at that track. Hit's sizable enough to prove him. And look at the way it's deeper at the back. A deer track'll prove the same. A deer or bear that's fat and heavy'll sink in that-a-way. A leetle ol' light doe or yearlin' 'll walk tippy-toed, and you'll not see more than the front of their hooves. Oh, he's big."

"You'll not be scairt when we come up with him, Pa?"

"Not lessen things goes mighty wrong. I'm fearful, always, for the pore dogs. They're the scapers gits the worst of it."

Penny's eyes twinkled.

"I don't reckon you'll be scairt, son?"

"Not me." He thought a moment. "But if I was to be scairt, must I climb a tree?"

Penny chuckled.

"Yes, son. Even if you ain't scairt, hit's a good place to watch the ruckus."

They walked in silence. Old Julia moved certainly. Rip the bulldog was content to follow at her heels, snuffing where she snuffed, stopping when she hesitated. She blew through her soft nose when the grasses tickled it. The feice made dashes to one side or another and once tore wildly after a rabbit that bolted from under his nose. Jody whistled after him.

"Leave him go, son," Penny told him. "He'll join up agin when it comes to him he's lonesome."

Old Julia gave a thin high wail and looked over her shoulder.

"The wise old scaper's changin' his direction," Penny said. "Likely he's headin' for the saw-grass ponds. Iffen that's his notion, we kin mebbe slip around and surprise him."

Some understanding came to Jody of the secret of his father's hunting. The Forresters, he thought, would have plunged after old Slewfoot the moment they had found his kill. They would have shouted and bellowed, their pack of dogs would have bayed until the scrub echoed with it, for they encouraged them in it, and the wary old bear would have had full warning of their coming. His father got game, ten to their one. The little man was famous for it.

Jody said, "You shore kin figger what a creetur'll do."

"You belong to figger. A wild creetur's quicker'n a man and a heap stronger. What's man got that a bear ain't got? A mite more sense. He cain't out-run a bear, but he's a sorry hunter if he cain't out-study him."

The pines were becoming scattering. There was suddenly a strip of hammock land, and a place of live oaks and scrub

THE YEARLING

palmettos. The undergrowth was thick, laced with cat-briers. Then hammock, too, ended, and to the south and west lay a broad open expanse that looked at first sight to be a meadow. This was the saw-grass. It grew knee-deep in water, its harsh saw-edged blades rising so thickly that it seemed a compact vegetation. Old Julia splashed into it. The rippling of the water showed the pond. A gust of air passed across the open area, the saw-grass waved and parted, and the shallow water of a dozen ponds showed clearly. Penny watched the hound intently. The treeless expanse seemed to Jody more stirring than the shadowy forest. At any moment the great black form might rear itself high.

He whispered, "Will we cut around?"

Penny shook his head. He answered in a low voice.

"Wind's wrong. Don't seem to me like he's headin' acrost it, nohow."

The hound splashed in a zigzag trail where solid ground edged the saw-grass. Here and there the scent was lost in the water. Once she dipped her head to lap, not in thirst, but for the very taste of the trail. She moved confidently down the middle of the pond. Rip and Perk found their short legs too deep in muck for comfort. They retreated to higher ground and shook themselves, watching Julia anxiously. Perk barked shortly, and Penny slapped him, for quiet. Jody stepped cautiously behind his father. A blue heron flew low over him without warning, and he started. The pond water was cold an instant against his legs, his breeches were clammy, the muck sucked at his shoes. Then the water was comfortable, and it was good to walk in the wet coolness, leaving sandy whirlpools behind.

"He's feedin' on the fire-plant," Penny murmured.

He pointed to the flat arrow-shaped leaves. Edges showed jagged tooth-marks. Others were bitten clear of the stalk.

"Hit's his spring tonic. A bear'll make for it first thing, time

33

he comes out in the spring." He leaned close and touched a leaf whose ragged edge was turning brown. "Dogged if he wa'n't here a night ago, too. That's how come him to have appetite for a nip o' pore old Betsy."

The hound too paused. The scent lay now, not underfoot, but on the reeds and grasses where the strong-smelling fur had brushed. She laid her long nose against a bulrush and stared into space, then, satisfied as to direction, splashed due south at a lively pace. Penny spoke now freely.

"He's done feedin'. Old Julia says he's clippin' it for home."

He moved to higher land, keeping the hound in sight. He walked briskly, chatting.

"Many's the time I've seed a bear feedin' on the fire-plant in the moonlight. He'll snort and shuffle, and splash and grunt. He'll rip them leaves offen the stems and cram 'em in his ugly ol' mouth like a person. Then he'll nose along and chaw, like a dog chawin' grass. And the night-birds cryin' over him, and the bull-frogs hollerin' like nigger-dogs, and the Mallards callin' 'Snake! Snake! Snake!' and the drops o' water on the leaves o' the fire-plant shinin' bright and red as a bull-bat's eyes——"

It was as good as seeing it, to hear Penny tell of it.

"I'd shore love to see a bear feedin' on the fire-plant, Pa."

"Well, you live long as me, and you'll see that and a heap more things, is strange and curious."

"Did you shoot 'em, Pa, while they was feedin'?"

"Son, I've helt back my shot and contented myself with watchin' many a time when creeturs was feedin' harmless and innocent. It goes agin me to crack down at sich a time. Or when creeturs is matin'. Now and agin, when it was git meat or the Baxters go hongry, I've done what I've no likin' to do. And don't you grow up like the Forresters, killin' meat you got no use for, for the fun of it. That's evil as the bears. You hear me?"

"Yes, sir."

Old Julia gave a sharp cry. The trail cut at right angles, to the east.

"I feared it," Penny said. "The bay——"

The red bay thicket seemed impenetrable. This land of sudden changes gave good cover for the game. Old Slewfoot in his careless feeding had never been far from shelter. The bay saplings stood as close together as the palings of a stockade. Jody wondered how the bear had managed to work his bulk among them. But here and there the saplings thinned, or were young and limber, and he could see, plainly marked, a common trail. Other creatures had used it. Tracks crossed and crisscrossed. Wild-cat had followed deer, lynx had followed wild-cat, and all about were the paw-prints of the small things, 'coons and rabbits and 'possums and skunks, feeding cautiously aside from their predatory kin.

Penny said, "I reckon I best load."

He clucked to Julia to wait for him. She lay down knowingly to rest and Rip and Perk dropped willingly beside her. Jody had been carrying the powder horn over his shoulder. Penny opened it and shook a measure of powder down the muzzle. From his shot-bag he pulled a wisp of dried black Spanish moss, inserted it for wadding, and packed it with the ramrod. He dropped in a measure of low-mould shot, more wadding, and at the last, a cap, and used the ramrod lightly again.

"All right, Julia. Git him."

The morning's trailing had been a leisurely business; a pleasant jaunting rather than a hunt. Now the dark bay thicket closed in over their heads, jorees flew from the denseness with an alarming whir of wings, the earth was soft and black, and there were scurryings and rustlings on either side in the bushes. On the trail, a bar of sunlight lay occasionally where the thicket parted. The scent, for all the comings and goings, was not confused, for the taint of bear hung heavy in the leafy tunnel. The short fur of the bulldog stood on end. Old Julia ran swiftly. Penny and Jody were forced to stoop to follow. Penny swung the muzzle-loader in his right hand, its barrel tipped at an angle, so that if he stumbled and the charge went off, he would not touch the running dogs before him. A branch crashed behind and Jody clutched at his father's shirt. A squirrel ran chattering away.

The thicket thinned. The ground dropped lower and became a swamp. The sunlight came through in patches as big as a basket. There were giant ferns here, taller than their heads. One lay crushed where the bear had moved across it. Its spiced sweetness lay heavy on the warm air. A young tendril sprang back into an upright position. Penny pointed to it. Slewfoot, Jody understood, had passed not many minutes before. Old Julia was feverish. The trail was food and drink. Her nose skimmed the damp ground. A scrub jay flew ahead, warning the game, and crying *"Plick-up-wha-a-a."*

The swamp dipped to a running branch no broader than a fence post. The print of the nubbed foot spanned it. A water moccasin lifted a curious head, then spun down-stream in smooth brown spirals. Across the branch, palmettos grew. The great track continued across the swamp. Jody noticed that the back of his father's shirt was wet. He touched his own sleeve. It was dripping. Suddenly Julia bayed and Penny began to run.

"The Creek!" he shouted. "He's tryin' to make the Creek!"

Sound filled the swamp. Saplings crashed. The bear was a black hurricane, mowing down obstructions. The dogs barked and bayed. The roaring in Jody's ears was his heart pounding. A bamboo vine tripped him and he sprawled and was on his feet again. Penny's short legs churned in front of him like paddles. Slewfoot would make Juniper Creek before the dogs could halt him at bay.

A clear space opened at the creek's bank. Jody saw a vast black shapeless form break through. Penny halted and lifted his gun. On the instant, a small brown missile hurled itself at the shaggy head. Old Julia had caught up with her enemy. She leaped and retreated, and in the moment of retreat, was at him again. Rip darted in beside her. Slewfoot wheeled and slashed at him. Julia flashed at his flank. Penny held his fire. He could not shoot, for the dogs.

Old Slewfoot was suddenly, deceptively, indifferent. He seemed to stand baffled, slow and uncertain, weaving back and forth. He whined, like a child whimpering. The dogs backed off an instant. The moment was perfect for a shot and Penny swung his gun to his shoulder, drew a bead on the left cheek, and pulled the trigger. A harmless pop sounded. He cocked the hammer again and pulled the trigger once more. The sweat stood out on his forehead. Again the hammer clicked futilely. Then a black storm broke. It roared in on the dogs with incredible swiftness. White tusks and curved claws were streaks of lightning across it. It snarled and whirled and gnashed its teeth and slashed in every direction. The dogs were as quick. Julia made swift sorties from the rear, and when Slewfoot wheeled to rake at her, Rip leaped for the hairy throat.

Jody was in a paralysis of horror. He saw that his father had cocked the hammer again and stood half-crouching, licking his lips, fingering the trigger. Old Julia bored in at the bear's right flank. He wheeled, not on her, but on the bulldog at his left. He caught him sideways and sent him sprawling into the bushes. Again Penny pulled the trigger. The explosion that followed had a sizzling sound, and Penny fell backward. The gun had back-fired.

Rip returned to his attempts for the bear's throat and Julia took up her worrying from the rear. The bear stood again at bay, weaving. Jody ran to his father. Penny was already on his feet. The right side of his face was black with powder. Slewfoot shook free of Rip, whirled to Julia and caught her to his chest with his cupped claws. She yelped sharply. Rip hurled himself at the back and buried his teeth in the hide.

Jody screamed, "He's killin' Julia!"

Penny ran desperately into the heart of the fracas. He jammed the gun-barrel in the bear's ribs. Even in her pain, Julia had taken a grip on the black throat above her. Slewfoot snarled and turned suddenly and plunged down the bank of the creek and into the deep water. Both dogs kept their hold. Slewfoot swam madly. Only Julia's head showed above water, below the bear's snout. Rip rode the broad back with bravado. Slewfoot made the far bank and scrambled up its side. Julia loosed her hold and dropped limply on the earth. The bear plunged toward the dense thicket. For a moment more Rip stayed with him. Then, confused, he too dropped away and turned back uncertainly to the creek. He snuffed at Julia and sat down on his haunches and howled across the water. There was a crashing in the distant undergrowth, then silence.

Penny called, "Here, Rip! Here, Julia!"

Rip wagged his stumpy tail and did not stir. Penny lifted his hunting horn to his lips and blew caressingly. Jody saw Julia lift her head, then fall back again.

Penny said, "I got to go fetch her."

He slipped off his shoes and slid down the bank into the water. He struck out strongly. A few yards from shore the current laid hold of him as though he were a log and shot him down-stream at a fierce clip. He struggled against it, fighting for distance. Jody saw him stagger to his feet far down the run, wipe the water from his eyes and push his way back up the shore to his dogs. He leaned to examine the hound, then gathered her under one arm. This time he went some distance up-stream before taking to the creek. When he dropped into the water, stroking with his free arm, the current picked him up and deposited him almost at Jody's feet. Rip paddled behind him, landed and shook himself. Penny laid the old hound down gently.

"She's bad hurt," he said.

He took off his shirt and trussed the dog in it. He tied the sleeves together to make a sling and hoisted it on his back.

"This settles it," he said. "I got to git me a new gun."

The powder burn on his cheek had already turned into a blister.

"What's wrong, Pa?"

"Near about ever'thing. The hammer's loose on the cylinder. I knowed that. I been havin' to cock it two-three times right along. But when it back-fired, that belongs to mean the mainspring's got weak. Well, le's git goin'. You tote the blasted ol' gun."

The procession started homeward through the swamp. Penny cut north and west.

"Now I'll not rest 'til I git that bear," he said. "Jest give me a new gun—and time."

Suddenly Jody could not endure the sight of the limp bundle in front of him. There were tricklings of blood down his father's thin bare back.

"I want to go ahead, Pa."

Penny turned and eyed him.

"Don't go gittin' faintified on me."

"I kin break a trail for you."

"All right. Go ahead. Jody—take the knapsack. Git you some bread. Eat a bite, boy. You'll feel better."

Jody fumbled blindly in the sack and pulled out the parcel of pancakes. The brierberry jelly was tart and cool on his tongue. He was ashamed to have it taste so good. He bolted several of the cakes. He handed some to his father.

"Rations is mighty comfortin'," Penny said.

A whine sounded in the bushes. A small cringing form was following them. It was Perk, the feice. Jody kicked at him in a fury.

39

"Don't bother him," Penny said. "I suspected him all along. There's dogs is bear-dogs and there's dogs jest isn't bear-dogs."

The feice dropped in at the end of the line. Jody tried to break trail, but fallen trees lay, thicker than his body, and would not be stirred. Bull-briers, tougher than his father's muscles, snared him, and he could only push his way around them or crawl beneath. Penny with his burden had to shift for himself. The swamp was close and humid. Rip was panting. The pancakes lay soothingly in Jody's belly. He reached in the knapsack for the sweet potato pone. His father refused his share and Jody divided it with Rip. The little feice, he thought, deserved nothing.

It was good to clear the swamp at last and come into the open pine woods. Even the scrub that followed after for a mile or two, seemed light and penetrable. Pushing through the low scrub oaks, the scrub palmettos, the gallberry bushes and the ti-ti, was less laborious than crossing the swamp. It was late afternoon when the high pines of Baxter's Island showed ahead. The procession filed down the sand road from the east and into the clearing. Rip and Perk ran ahead to the hollowed cypress watering trough kept for the chickens. Ma Baxter sat rocking on the narrow veranda, a mound of mending in her lap.

"A dead dog and no bear, eh?" she called.

"Not dead yit. Git me water and rags and the big needle and thread."

She rose quickly to help. Jody was always amazed at the capability of her great frame and hands when there was trouble. Penny laid old Julia down on the veranda floor. She whimpered. Jody bent to stroke her head and she bared her teeth at him. He trailed his mother disconsolately. She was tearing an old apron into strips.

"You kin fetch the water," she told him, and he scurried to the kettle.

40

Penny returned to the veranda with an armful of crocus sacks to make a bed for the hound. Ma Baxter brought the surgical equipment. Penny unwrapped his blood-soaked shirt from the dog and bathed the deep gashes. Old Julia made no protest. She had known claws before. He sewed the two deepest cuts and rubbed pine gum into all of them. She yelped once and then was silent as he worked. A rib, he said, was broken. He could do nothing for that, but if she lived, it would mend. She had lost much blood. Her breath came short. Penny gathered her up, bed and all.

Ma Baxter demanded, "Now where you carryin' her?"

"To the bedroom. I got to watch her tonight."

"Not to my bedroom, Ezra Baxter. I'll do for her what's got to be done, but I'll not have you poppin' in and outen the bed all night, wakin' me. I didn't half sleep, last night."

"Then I'll sleep with Jody and bed Julia there," he said. "I'll not leave her alone in no shed tonight. Fetch me cold water, Jody."

He carried her to Jody's room and laid her in the corner on the pile of sacking. She would not drink, or could not, and he opened her mouth and poured water down her dry throat.

"Leave her rest now. We'll go do our chores."

The clearing possessed this evening a strange coziness. Jody gathered the eggs from the hay-mow, milked the cow and turned the calf in to her, and cut wood for his mother. Penny, as always, went to the sink-hole with a wooden ox-yoke supporting two wooden buckets over his thin shoulders. Ma Baxter cooked supper of poke-greens and dried cow-peas. She fried a frugal slice of the fresh pork.

"A piece o' bear meat 'd go mighty good tonight," she lamented.

Jody was hungry but Penny had little appetite. He left the table twice to offer Julia food, which she rejected. Ma Baxter rose heavily to clear the table and wash the dishes. She asked for no details of the hunt. Jody longed to talk of it, to cast away the spell of the tracking, and the fight, and the fear that had struck him. Penny was silent. No one noticed the boy and he dipped deeply into the dish of cow-peas.

The sun set red and clear. Shadows lay long and black in the Baxter kitchen.

Penny said, "I'm wore out. I could do with bed."

Jody's feet were raw and blistered from the cowhide shoes. "Me, too," he said.

"I'll set up a whiles," Ma Baxter said. "I ain't done much today, excusin' fret and worry, and mess with the sausage."

Penny and Jody went to their room. They undressed on the side of the narrow bed.

"Now if you was big as your Ma," Penny said, "we couldn't lay in it without somebody fell on the floor."

There was room enough for the two thin bony bodies. The red faded from the west and the room was dusky. The hound slept and whimpered in her sleep. The moon rose, an hour past the full, and the small room lay in a silver brightness. Jody's feet burned. His knees twitched.

Penny said, "You wakeful, son?"

"I cain't stop walkin'."

"We went a fur piece. How you like bear-huntin', boy?"

"Well—" He rubbed his knees. "I like thinkin' about it."

"I know."

"I liked the trackin' and the trailin'. I liked seein' the sap-lin's broke down, and the ferns in the swamp."

"I know."

"I liked old Julia bayin' now and agin——"

"But the fightin's right fearsome, ain't it, son?"

"Hit's mighty fearsome."

"Hit's sickenin', the dogs gittin' bloodied and sich as that. And son, you ain't never seed a bear kilt. But mean as they be, hit's someway piteeful when they go down and the dogs tears their throats and they cry out jest like a person, and lay down and die before you."

Father and son lay in silence.

"If the wild creeturs'd only leave us be," Penny said.

"I wisht we could kill 'em all off," Jody said. "Them that steals offen us and does us harm."

" 'Tain't stealin', in a creetur. A creetur's got his livin' to make and he makes it the best way he kin. Same as us. Hit's panther nature and wolf nature and bear nature to kill their meat. County lines is nothin' to them, nor a man's fences. How's a creetur to know the land's mine and paid for? How's a bear to know I'm dependin' on my hogs for my own rations? All he knows is, he's hongry."

Jody lay staring into the brightness. Baxter's Island seemed to him a fortress ringed around with hunger. Now in the moonlight eyes were shining, red and green and yellow. The hungry would dart in to the clearing in swift forays, and kill and eat and slink away again. Pole-cats and 'possums would raid the hen-roost, wolf or panther might slay the calf before daylight, old Slewfoot might come again to murder and feed.

"A creetur's only doin' the same as me when I go huntin' us meat," Penny said. "Huntin' him where he lives and beds and raises his young uns. Hit's a hard law, but it's the law. 'Kill or go hongry.' "

Yet the clearing was safe. The creatures came, but they went away again. Jody began to shiver and could not tell why.

"You cold, son?"

"I reckon."

He saw old Slewfoot wheel, and slash and snarl. He saw old Julia leap, and be caught and crushed, and hold on, and then fall away, broken and bleeding. But the clearing was safe.

"Move close, son. I'll warm you."

He edged closer to his father's bones and sinews. Penny slipped an arm around him and he lay close against the lank thigh. His father was the core of safety. His father swam the swift creek to fetch back his wounded dog. The clearing was safe, and his father fought for it, and for his own. A sense of snugness came over him and he dropped asleep. He awakened once, disturbed. Penny was crouched in the corner in the moonlight, ministering to the hound.

· 5 ·

Penny said at breakfast, "Well, it's trade for a new gun, or court trouble."

Old Julia was better. Her wounds were clean, without swelling. She was exhausted from loss of blood and wanted only to sleep. She had lapped a little milk from the gourd Penny held for her.

"How you aim to buy a new gun," Ma Baxter asked, "and not money scarcely for taxes?"

"I said 'trade'," Penny corrected.

"Ary day you git the best of a trade, I'll eat my wash-pot."

"Now Ma, I wouldn't even crave to beat a man. But there's trades where all is satisfied."

"What you got to trade with?"

"The feice."

"Who'd have him?"

"He's a good ketch-dog."

"Good to ketch biscuits."

"You know as good as I do, the Forresters is fools for dogs."

"Ezra Baxter, do you go tradin' with the Forresters, you'll do good to come home wearin' your breeches."

"Well, that's where me and Jody is headin' for, today."

Penny spoke with a firmness against which the bulk of his wife was sheer air. She sighed.

"All right. Leave me without nobody to split my wood or fetch me water or care do I drop in my tracks. Go. Take him."

"I ain't never left you without wood nor water."

Jody listened anxiously. He would rather visit the Forresters than eat.

"Jody has got to mix with men and learn the ways o' men," Penny said.

"The Forresters' is a fine place to begin. Do he learn from them, he'll learn to have a heart as black as midnight."

"He might learn from them, not to. Anyways, that's where we're goin'."

He rose from the table.

"I'll fetch water and Jody, you go split a good bait o' wood."

"You want to tote lunch?" she called after him.

"I'd not insult my neighbors that-a-way. We'll noon with them."

Jody hurried to the wood-pile. Every blow of the axe on the fat pine brought him closer to the Forresters and his friend Fodder-wing. He split a plentiful amount and carried enough to the kitchen to fill his mother's wood-box. His father had not yet returned from the sink-hole with his load of water. Jody hurried to the lot and saddled the horse. If the horse were ready and waiting, they might get off before his mother discovered some fresh pretext for detaining him. He saw Penny coming down the sand road from the west, bowed under the ox-yoke with the two heavy wooden buckets brimming with water. He ran to help him ease the load to the ground, for a lack of balance would tumble the buckets headlong, and the tedious hauling would have to be done all over again.

"Cæsar's saddled," he said.

"And the woods is a-fire, I take it." Penny grinned. "All right. Leave me put on my tradin' coat and tie up Rip and git my gun and we're long gone."

The saddle had been bought of the Forresters, having proved a trifle small for any of their great butts. It held Penny and Jody together in comfort.

"Git in front, son. But do you keep out-growin' me, you'll be obliged to ride behind, for I cain't see the road before me. Here, Perk! Heel up."

The feice fell in behind. He stopped once and looked back over his shoulder.

"I hope it's your last look," Penny told him.

Cæsar, well rested, went into a steady trot. His old back was broad, the saddle was wide, and riding so, with his father braced behind him, was as comfortable, Jody thought, as a rocking chair. The sand road was a sunny ribbon, leaf-shadowed. West, by the sink-hole, the road forked, one branch continuing on to Forresters' Island, the other turning north. Ancient axe-marks on venerable long-leaf pines blazed the turn to the northerly trail.

"Did you or the Forresters make them blazes?" Jody asked.

"Them was cut before me and the Forresters was ever heered tell of. Why, son, some's so deep, and them pines grows so slow, I'd not be surprised was some of 'em Spanish blazes. That teacher never learned you no history last year? Why, boy, the Spaniards made this trail. This right here, that we're leavin' now, is the old Spanish trail clear acrost Floridy. It split back near Fort Butler. The south un goes to Tampa. Hit's the Dragoon trail. This un here's the Black Bear."

Jody turned big eyes to his father.

"You reckon the Spaniards fit the bears?"

"I reckon they had to, when they stopped to camp. They had Injuns to fight and bears and panther-cats. Same as us, only we ain't got the Injuns."

Jody stared about him. The pine-woods were suddenly populous.

"Is there any Spaniards hereabouts now?"

"There's nary a man livin', Jody, has even heered his grand-pappy say he'd ever seed a Spaniard. The Spaniards come from acrost the ocean, and went tradin' and fightin' and marchin' acrost Floridy, and no man knows where they're gone."

The business of the spring woods went forward leisurely in the golden morning. Red-birds were mating, and the crested males were everywhere, singing until Baxter's Island dripped with the sweetness of the sound.

"Hit's better'n fiddlin' and guitarin', ain't it?" Penny said.

Jody came back to the scrub with a start. He had been half-way across the ocean with the Spaniards.

The sweet gums were in full new leaf. The flowers of red-bud and jessamine and dogwood had come and gone, but huckleberries and ti-ti and dog-tongue were in full bloom. The road ran to the west through a mile of tender green, of white and rosy blossoming. Wild honey-bees hummed in the small lacelike flowers of the St. Augustine grapes. The road narrowed past an abandoned clearing. Cæsar slowed to a walk. The scrub closed in around them. Scrub oak and gall-berry and myrtle bushes brushed their legs. The growth was thick and low and there was only occasional shade. The April sun was high and strong. Cæsar was sweating and the stirrup leathers rubbed and squeaked.

Two miles of the way were hot and silent. Only jorees darted among the bushes. A fox crossed, dragging his brush, and a yellow shape that might have been a wild-cat shot almost invisibly into the myrtle. Then the road widened, the vegetation withdrew, and the landmark that was the tall trees of Forresters' Island lifted ahead. Penny dismounted and picked up the feice and mounted again, holding the dog in his arms.

Jody said, "Why you totin' him?"

"Jest never you mind."

They passed into hammock, cool and deep, arched with palms and live oaks. The road wound about and the weathered gray of the Forrester cabin showed under a giant oak. A pond shone beyond and below it.

Penny said, "Now don't you torment Fodder-wing."

"I don't never torment him. He's my friend."

"That's good. He's the second settin' and he ain't to blame for hatchin' out peculiar."

"He's my best friend. Except Oliver."

"You better stick to Oliver. His tales is tall as Fodder-wing's, but at least he knows when he's lyin'."

Suddenly the quiet of the forest exploded. A commotion broke loose inside the cabin. The sound came of chairs hurled across its width, a large object crashed, glass shattered, heavy feet stamped on the plank floor and the voices of male Forresters beat against the walls. A female voice shrilled above the tumult. The door flew wide and a pack of dogs streamed into the open. Ma Forrester flailed at them with a hearthbroom as they raced for safety. Her sons crowded behind her.

Penny called, "Hit safe for a feller to git down here?'"

The Forresters roared greetings to the Baxters and commands to the dogs. Ma Forrester lifted her gingham apron in both hands and waved it up and down like a flag. The shouts of welcome were so mingled with orders to the dogs that Jody was uncomfortable, faintly uncertain of the reception.

"Git down and come in! Git away, you blasted bacon-thieves! Hi-yuh! Howdy! Git to tarnation!"

Ma Forrester swooped after the dogs and they scattered into the forest.

"Penny Baxter! Jody! Git down and come in!"

Jody dropped to the ground and she thumped him on the back. She smelled of snuff and of wood-smoke. The odor did not offend him but he was obliged to think of the delicate sweet scent of Grandma Hutto. Penny dismounted. He held the feice tenderly. The Forresters milled about him. Buck led the horse away to the corral. Mill-wheel caught Jody up and swung him over one shoulder and to the ground again, as though he swung a puppy.

Beyond, down the cabin steps, Jody saw Fodder-wing hurrying toward him. The humped and twisted body moved in a series of contortions, like a wounded ape. Fodder-wing lifted his walking stick and waved it. Jody ran to meet him. Fodder-wing's face was luminous.

He cried, "Jody!"

They stood, embarrassed and delighted.

A sense of pleasure came over Jody that he felt with no one else. His friend's body was no more unnatural to him than the body of a chameleon or a 'possum. He took the word of grown folks that Fodder-wing was witless. He himself would have known better than to do the thing that had given Fodder-wing his name. The youngest Forrester had conceived the idea that if he could attach himself to something light and airy, he could float from the roof-tree of the barn as gently as any bird. He had attached great bundles of fodder, cow-pea hay, to his arms, and jumped. He had survived, miraculously, adding a few broken bones further to contort the hunch-backed frame with which he had been born. It was a crazy thing to do, of course. Yet privately, Jody felt, something of the sort might work. He had, himself, often thought of kites, very large kites. And some secret understanding was his of the crippled boy's longing for flight; for lightness; for a moment's freedom from his body, earth-bound and bent and stumbling.

He said, "Hey."

Fodder-wing said, "I got a baby 'coon."

He had, always, a new pet.

"Le's go see it."

Fodder-wing led him back of the cabin to a collection of boxes and cages that sheltered his changing assortment of birds and creatures.

"My eagle died," Fodder-wing said. "He was too wild to pen."

The pair of black swamp rabbits was not new.

"They won't raise no young uns," Fodder-wing complained. "I'm fixin' to turn 'em a-loose."

A fox-squirrel worked an endless treadle.

"I'll give him to you," Fodder-wing offered. "I kin git me another."

Jody's hopes lifted and fell.

"Ma won't let me keep nothin'."

His heart swelled, aching for the fox-squirrel.

"Here's the 'coon. Here, Racket!"

A black nose protruded between narrow slats. A tiny black paw, like a nigger baby's hand, reached out. Fodder-wing lifted a slat and brought out the 'coon. It clung to his arm and gave a strange chirring cry.

"You kin hold him. He'll not bite you."

Jody cuddled the 'coon against him. He thought he had never seen or touched a thing so delightful. The gray fur was as soft as his mother's outing flannel nightgown. The pointed face was masked across the eyes with a black bar. The bushy tail was beautifully ringed. The 'coon nibbled at his flesh and cried again.

"He wants his sugar-teat," Fodder-wing said maternally.

"Le's take him to the house whilst the dogs is out. He's mighty skeert o' the dogs, but he'll git used to 'em. He don't like no commotion."

"What was you-all fightin' about," Jody asked, "when we come up?"

"I wasn't into it," Fodder-wing said with disdain. "It was them."

"What was it?"

"One o' the dogs wet in the middle o' the floor. They couldn't agree whose dog 'twas, done it."

· 6 ·

THE 'coon sucked greedily at his sugar-teat. He lay on his back, cupped in Jody's arm, and clutched the sugar-filled cloth with his fore feet. He closed his eyes blissfully. His small paunch was already round with milk and shortly he pushed the sugar-teat away and scrambled to be free. Jody lifted him to his shoulder. The 'coon parted his hair and felt along his neck and ears with his small, restless hands.

"His hands is never still," Fodder-wing said.

Pa Forrester spoke from the shadows beyond the hearth. Jody had not noticed him, he sat so quiet.

"I had me a 'coon when I were a young un," he said. "Hit were gentle as a kitten for two yare. Then one day hit bit a chunk outen my shin." He spat into the fire. "This un'll grow up to bite. Hit's 'coon nature."

Ma Forrester came into the cabin and went to her pots and pans. Her sons trooped in behind her; Buck and Mill-wheel, Gabby and Pack, Arch and Lem. Jody looked puzzled at the dried and wizened pair that had bred these mountainous men. They were all much alike, except Lem and Gabby. Gabby was shorter than the rest and not unduly bright. Lem alone was clean-shaven. He was as tall as any of them, but thinner, and not so dark, and had the least to say. He often sat apart, brooding and sulky, while Buck and Mill-wheel, the most boisterous, caroused.

Penny Baxter came in, lost among them. Pa Forrester continued his discourse on the nature of 'coons. No one listened but Jody, but the old man relished his own words.

"That 'coon'll grow up to where he's big as a dog. He'll whop ary dog on the yard. A 'coon lives for one thing, to whop a dog. He'll lie on his back in the water and fight a hull pack o' dogs. He'll drown 'em, one by one. And bite? A 'coon'll bite one more time after he's dead."

Jody was torn between the desire to follow him, and his interest in the talk of the other Forresters. He was surprised to see that his father still carried the worthless feice tenderly in his arms. Penny crossed the room.

"Howdy, Mr. Forrester. Proud to see you. How's your health?"

"Howdy, sir. I'm right smart tol'able, seein' as how I be near about done for. Truth to tell, I'd ought to be dead this minute and gone to glory, but I keep puttin' it off. Seems like I'm better acquainted here."

Ma Forrester said, "Set down, Mr. Baxter."

Penny drew a rocker and sat down.

Lem Forrester called across the room, "Your dog lame?"

"Why, no. I've never knowed him to go lame. I jest figger on keepin' him outen the jaws o' them blood-hounds o' yourn."

"Valuable, eh?" Lem asked.

"Not him. He ain't wuth a good twist o' t'baccy. Don't you-all aim to detain him when I leave here, for he's not wuth stealin'."

"You takin' mighty good keer of him, iffen he's that sorry."

"So I be."

"You had him on bear?"

"I've had him on bear."

Lem came close and breathed down heavily.

"Do he track good? Do he holt a bear at bay?"

"He's mighty sorry. Sorriest bear-dog I ever owned or follered."

Lem said, "I never heered a man run down his own dog that-a-way."

Penny said, "Well, I'll admit he's likely-lookin', and most ary man'd want him, lookin' at him, and I jest wouldn't put no notion o' tradin' in your minds, for you'd git fooled and cheated."

"You figger on huntin' some on your way back?"

"Why, a man allus has huntin' in his mind."

"Hit's mighty quare you toted a dog along wouldn't be no good to you."

The Forresters looked about at one another. They fell silent. Their black eyes were riveted on the feice.

"The dog's no good and my old muzzle-loadin' shotgun is no good," Penny said. "I'm in a pure fix."

The black eyes darted to the walls of the cabin, where the Forrester arms hung. The array, Jody thought, would stock a gun-shop. The Forresters made good money trading horses, selling venison and making moonshine. They bought guns as other men would buy flour and coffee.

"I never heered tell o' you failin' to git meat," Lem said.

"I failed yestiddy. My gun wouldn't shoot and when it did, hit back-fired."

"What was you huntin'?"

"Old Slewfoot."

A roar broke.

"Where's he feedin'? Which-a-way did he come from? Where's he gone?"

Pa Forrester thumped the floor with his cane.

"You fellers shut up and leave Penny tell it. He cain't tell a thing, and you-all bellerin' like bulls."

Ma Forrester banged a pot-lid and lifted a pan of corn-bread as big, Jody thought, as a syrup kettle. The good smells from the hearth were overwhelming.

She said, "Don't git Mr. Baxter started 'til he's et. Where's your manners?"

"And where's your manners," Pa Forrester reproached his sons, "not givin' comp'ny the chancet to wet his whistle afore dinner?"

Mill-wheel went into a bedroom and returned with a demijohn. He pulled out the corn-cob stopper and handed the jug to Penny.

"You'll excuse me," Penny said, "if I don't drink deep. I ain't got as big a place to put it as you fellers."

They laughed uproariously. Mill-wheel passed the jug about the room.

"Jody?"

Penny said, "He ain't old enough."

Pa Forrester said, "Why, I were weaned on it."

Ma Forrester said, "Pour me a noggin. In my cup."

She ladled food into pans big enough to wash in. The long trenchered table was covered with steam. There were dried cow-peas boiled with white bacon, a haunch of roast venison, a platter of fried squirrel, swamp cabbage, big hominy, biscuits, cornbread, syrup and coffee. A raisin pudding waited at the side of the earth.

"If I'd of knowed you was comin'," she said, "I'd of cooked somethin' fitten. Well, draw up."

Jody looked at his father to see whether he too was excited by the savory plenty. Penny's face was somehow grave.

"All this here is fine enough for the governor," he said.

Ma Forrester said uncomfortably, "I reckon you folks gives thanks, to your table. Pa, hit won't hurt you none to ask a blessin', long as we got comp'ny."

The old man looked about unhappily and folded his hands.

"Oh Lord, once more Thou hast done see fit to bless our sinnin' souls and bellies with good rations. Amen."

The Forresters cleared their throats and fell to. Jody sat opposite his father, and between Ma Forrester and Fodder-wing. He found his plate piled high. Buck and Mill-wheel slipped choice morsels to Fodder-wing. He passed them on under the table to Jody. The Forresters ate with concentration, silent for once. The food melted away before them. An argument arose between Lem and Gabby. Their father pounded on the table with his withered fist. They protested a moment at the intervention, then subsided. Pa Forrester leaned close to Penny and murmured in a low voice.

"My boys is rough, I know. They don't do what they ought. They drink a heap and they fight and ary woman wants to git away from 'em has got to run like a doe. But I'll say this for 'em—they ain't nary one of 'em has ever cussed his mammy or his pappy at the table."

· 7 ·

Pa Forrester said, "Well, neighbor, let's have the news about that tormented bear."

Ma Forrester said, "Yes, and you scapers git the dishes washed afore you git too deep into it, too."

Her sons rose hurriedly, each with his own plate and some larger dish or pan. Jody stared at them. He would as soon have expected them to tie ribbons in their hair. She tweaked his ear on her way to her rocker.

"I got no girls," she said. "If these fellers wants me to cook for 'em, they kin jest clean up after me."

Jody looked at his father, pleading mutely that this piece of heresy be not taken home to Baxter's Island. The Forresters made short work of the dishes. Fodder-wing hobbled after them, gathering the scraps for all the animals. Only by feeding the pack of dogs himself, could he be sure of saving tid-bits for his pets as well. He smiled to himself, that there would be so much today to take to them. There was even enough cold food left for supper. Jody gaped at the abundance. The Forresters finished their work in a clatter, and hung the iron pots and kettles on nails near the hearth. They drew up their cowhide chairs and hand-hewn benches around Penny. Some lit corn-cob pipes and others shaved parings of tobacco from dark plugs. Ma Forrester lipped a little snuff. Buck picked up Penny's gun and a small file and began to work on the loose hammer.

"Well," Penny began, "he takened us plumb by surprise."

Jody shivered.

"He slipped in like a shadow and killed our brood-sow. Laid her open, end to end, and only ate a mouthful. Not hongry. Jest low-down and mean."

Penny paused to light his own pipe. The Forresters bent to him with blazing splinters of fat pine.

"He come as quiet as a black cloud, into the wind. Made a circle to git his wind right. So quiet, the dogs never heered nor scented him. Even this un—even this un—" he leaned to stroke the feice at his feet—"was fooled."

The Forresters exchanged glances.

"We set out after breakfast, Jody and me and all three o' the dogs. We tracked that bear acrost the south scrub. We tracked him along the edge o' the saw-grass ponds. We tracked him thu Juniper Bay. We tracked him thu the swamp, the trail gittin' hotter and hotter. We come up with him——"

The Forresters gripped their knees.

"We come up with him, men, right smack at the edge o' Juniper Creek, where the water flows swiftest and deepest."

The story, Jody thought, was even better than the hunt. He saw it all again, the shadows and the fern, the broken palmettos and the running branch water. He was bursting with the excitement of the story. He was bursting, too, with pride in his father. Penny Baxter, no bigger than a dirt-dauber, could out-hunt the best of them. And he could sit, as he sat now, weaving a spell of mystery and magic, that held these huge hairy men eager and breathless.

He made the fight an epic thing. When his gun back-fired, and old Slewfoot crushed Julia to his breast, Gabby swallowed his tobacco and rushed to the fire-place, spitting and choking. The Forresters clenched their fists, and sat precariously at the edges of their seats, and listened with their mouths open.

"Gawd," Buck breathed, "I'd o' loved to o' been there."

"And where's Slewfoot gone?" Gabby begged.

"No man knows," Penny told them.

There was silence.

Lem said at last, "You ain't never oncet mentioned that dog you got there."

"Don't press me," Penny said. "I done told you he's wuth-less."

"I notice he come outen it in mighty good shape. Not a mark on him, is there?"

"No, there's nary mark on him."

"Takes a mighty clever dog to fight a bear and not git ary scratch on him."

Penny puffed on his pipe.

Lem rose and walked to him, towering over him. He cracked his knuckles. He was sweating.

"I want two things," he said hoarsely. "I want to be in at the death o' ol' Slewfoot. And I want that dog there."

"Oh my, no," Penny said mildly. "I'd not cheat you, tradin' him."

"No use lyin' to me. Name your trade."

"I'll trade you old Rip, instead."

"Think you're foxy. I got better dogs than Rip right now."

Lem went to the wall and took down from its nails a gun. It was a London Fine Twist. The double barrels shone. The stock was walnut, warm and glowing. The twin hammers were jaunty. The fittings were chased and intricate. Lem swung it to his shoulder, sighted it. He handed it to Penny.

"Right from England. No more muzzle-loadin'. Fill your own shell-cases easy as spittin'. Stick your shells in—breech her —cock her—Bam! Bam! Two shots. Shoots as true as a eagle flies. Swap even."

"Oh my, no," Penny said. "This here gun is valuable."

"There's more where it come from. Don't argue with me, man. When I want a dog, I want a dog. Take the gun for him or by God I'll come and steal him."

"Well, all right, then," Penny said, "if that's the way it stands. But you got to promise before witnesses not to beat the very puddin' outen me after you've hunted him."

"Shake." A hairy paw closed over Penny's hand. "Here, boy!"

Lem whistled to the feice. He took him by the scruff of the neck and led him outside, as though fearful even now of losing him.

Penny teetered in his chair. He balanced the gun indifferently across his knees. Jody could not take his eyes from its perfection. He was filled with awe that his father had out-witted a Forrester. He wondered if Lem would keep his promise. He had heard of the intricacies of trading, but it had never occurred to him that one man could get the best of another by the simple expedient of telling him the truth.

Talk went on into the afternoon. Buck had tightened up Penny's old muzzle-loader so that he thought it could be counted on. The Forresters were unhurried; unoccupied. Tales were told of old Slewfoot's smartness; of other bears before him; but none so clever as he. Chases were described in every detail. Dogs twenty years dead were called by name and by performance. Fodder-wing grew tired of them and wanted to go to the pond and fish for minnows. But Jody could not bear to leave this telling of old tales. Pa and Ma Forrester chirped and shrilled occasionally, then dozed off in between, like sleepy crickets. At last their infirmities took them over, and they slept soundly, side by side in their rockers, their dried old frames stiff even in their slumber. Penny stretched and rose.

He said, "I hate to leave good comp'ny."

"Spend the night. We'll have a fox-chase."

"I thank you, but I don't like to leave my place without no man on it."

Fodder-wing tugged at his arm.

"Leave Jody stay with me. He ain't half seed my things."

Buck said, "Leave the young un stay, Penny. I got to go to Volusia tomorrow. I'll ride him by your place."

"His Ma'll rare," Penny said.

"That's what Ma's is good for. Eh, Jody?"

"Pa, I'd be mighty proud to stay. I ain't played none in a long while."

"Not since day before yestiddy. Well, stay, then, if these folks is shore you're welcome. Lem, don't kill the boy if you try out the feice afore Buck gits him home to me."

They shouted with laughter. Penny shouldered the new gun with his old one and went for his horse. Jody followed. He reached out one hand and stroked the smoothness of the gun.

"If 'twas anybody in the world but Lem," Penny murmured, "I'd be too shamed to go home with it. I've owed Lem a trimmin' since he named me."

"You told him the truth."

"My words was straight, but my intentions was crooked as the Ocklawaha River."

"What'll he do when he finds out?"

"He'll want to tear me down. And after that, I'm hopin' he'll laugh. Good-by, son, 'til tomorrer. Be good now."

The Forresters followed to see him off. Jody waved after his father with a new sense of aloneness. He was almost tempted to call him back; to run after him and climb up in the saddle and ride home with him to the snugness of the clearing.

Fodder-wing called, "The 'coon's fishin' in a puddle, Jody! Come see!"

He ran to watch the 'coon. It was paddling about in a small pool of water, feeling with its human hands for something only instinct told it could be there. He played with Fodder-wing and the 'coon the rest of the afternoon. He helped to clean the squirrel's box and build a cage for a crippled red-bird. The Forresters had game chickens, as wild as themselves. The hens laid their eggs all over the adjacent woods, in brierberry tangles, under piles of brush, and the snakes ate as many as the hens hatched. He went with Fodder-wing to collect the eggs. A hen was setting. Fodder-wing gave her the eggs they had gathered. There were fifteen in all.

"This un's a good mother," he said. It appeared that he took charge of all such matters.

Again Jody longed for something of his own. Fodder-wing would give him the fox squirrel, even, he believed, the baby 'coon. But past experience had taught him not to aggravate his mother with another mouth, no matter how small, to feed. Fodder-wing talked to the setting hen.

"You stay on the nest now, you hear me? You hatch all them eggs into biddies. I want yellow biddies this time. None o' them black uns."

They turned back toward the cabin. The 'coon came crying to meet them. It scrambled up Fodder-wing's crooked legs and back and snugged down, clasping his neck. It closed its small white teeth over his skin and shook its head with pretended ferocity. Fodder-wing let Jody carry it to the cabin. It looked up at him with inquiring bright eyes, aware of his strangeness; then accepted him. The Forresters had scattered over their land at chores which they took leisurely, in their stride. Buck and

Arch drove the penned cows and their calves to the pond to water. Mill-wheel fed the string of horses in the corral. Pack and Lem had disappeared into the dense woods north of the cabin; perhaps, Jody speculated, to their still. There was ease and abundance here, as well as violence. There were so many of them to do things. Penny Baxter carried the work of a clearing almost as large as theirs, alone. Jody remembered guiltily the unhoed rows of corn he had left behind him. But Penny would not mind finishing them.

Pa and Ma Forrester were still asleep in their chairs. The sun was red in the west. Darkness came quickly into the cabin, for the live oaks kept out light that would have been still bright at the Baxters' clearing. One by one the brothers trooped into the cabin. Fodder-wing started up the fire on the hearth to heat the left-over coffee. Jody saw Ma Forrester open one careful eye, then close it again. Her sons piled the cold food on the table with a clatter that would have awakened an owl in the daytime. She sat up and prodded Pa Forrester in the ribs and joined the rest at their supper. This time they cleaned every platter. There was not even food left for the dogs. Fodder-wing mixed a pan of cold cornbread with a bucket of clabber and took it outside for them. He swung crookedly from side to side, tilting the bucket, and Jody ran to help him.

After supper, the Forresters smoked and talked of horses. The cattle-men in the county, and farther to the west, were complaining of a scarcity. Wolves and bears and panthers had raised havoc with the spring's colts. The traders who came usually from Kentucky with strings of horses had not appeared. The Forresters agreed that it would be profitable to go north and west and trade for cattle ponies. Jody and Fodder-wing lost interest in the talk and went into a corner to play mumblede-peg. Ma Baxter would never have allowed pocket knives to be flipped into her clean smooth floors. Here, a few splinters more or less could make no difference. Jody sat up erect from the game.

"I know something I bet you don't know."

"What?"

"The Spaniards used to cross the scrub right in front of our gate."

"Why, I knowed that." Fodder-wing hunched close and began to whisper excitedly. "I've seed 'em."

Jody stared at him.

"What you seed?"

"I've seed the Spaniards. They're tall and dark and have shiny helmets and they ride black horses."

"You couldn't see 'em. There ain't none left. They've done left here, jest like the Injuns."

Fodder-wing closed one eye wisely.

"That's what folks tell you. You listen to me. Next time you go west o' your sink-hole—you know that big magnolia? With dogwood all around it? You look behind that magnolia. There's allus a Spaniard on a black horse ridin' past that magnolia."

The hair stiffened on Jody's neck. This was, of course, another of Fodder-wing's tales. This was why his father and mother said Fodder-wing was crazy. But he longed to believe it. It would do no harm at least to look behind the magnolia.

The Forresters stretched and knocked out their pipes or spat out their tobacco. They went into their bedrooms, dropping their suspenders and loosening their breeches. There was a bed for each, for no two of them could sleep together in any double bed. Fodder-wing led Jody to his own bed in a shed-like room under the kitchen eaves.

"You kin have the pillow," he told him.

Jody wondered if his mother would ask him if he had washed his feet. How freely the Forresters lived, he thought, tumbling into bed without it. Fodder-wing began a tall tale about the end of the world. It was empty and dark, he said, with only clouds to ride on. At first Jody was interested. Then the tale became dull and rambling. He dropped off to sleep and dreamed of Spaniards, riding clouds instead of horses.

He awakened with a start late in the night. Din filled the cabin. His first thought was that the Forresters were fighting again. But the shouts held a community of purpose, and Ma Forrester called encouragement. A door was banged open and several of the dogs were halloo-ed inside. A light shone in the doorway of Fodder-wing's room and the dogs and men poured in. The men were stark naked, and they looked thinner and less bulky, but they seemed as tall as the cabin. Ma Forrester held a lighted tallow candle. Her grasshopper frame was lost inside a long gray flannel nightgown. The dogs shot under the bed and out again. Jody and Fodder-wing scrambled to their feet. No one troubled to explain the commotion. The boys followed after the hunt. It led through every room and ended with a mad exit of the dogs through the torn mosquito netting that covered one window.

"They'll git him outside," Ma Forrester said, suddenly placid. "Pesky varmint."

"Ma's got the best ear for varmints," Fodder-wing said proudly.

"I guess anybody'd hear him did he come scratchin' around their bed-post," she said.

Pa Forrester hobbled into the room on his cane.

"The night's near about done," he said. "I'd ruther have a snort o' whiskey than sleep agin."

Buck said, "Pa, you got the most sense for sich a ol' buzzard."

He went to a cupboard and brought out the demi-john. The old man uncorked it and tipped it back and drank.

Lem said, "Don't take no sense to crave liquor. Give it here."

He took a deep draught and passed the jug on. He wiped his mouth and rubbed his bare stomach. He went to the wall and felt along it for his fiddle. He twanged the strings carelessly, then sat down and began to scrape a tune.

Arch said, "You ain't got that right," and brought his guitar and sat on the bench beside him.

Ma Forrester set the candle on the table.

She asked, "You naked jay-birds fixin' to set up 'til day?"

Arch and Lem were deep in their chords and no one answered her. Buck took his mouth-organ from a shelf and began a tune of his own. Arch and Lem stopped to listen, then fell in with his melody.

Pa Forrester said, "Dog take it, that's purty."

The demi-john went around again. Pack brought out his Jew's-harp and Mill-wheel his drum, Buck changed his plaintive song for a lively dance tune, and the idle music swung into full volume. Jody and Fodder-wing dropped on the floor between Lem and Arch.

Ma Forrester said, "Now you needn't think I aim to go to bed and miss nothin'."

She unbanked the fire on the hearth and threw on fat-wood and moved the coffee-pot close.

"You hootin' owls 'll eat breakfast soon this mornin' or I'll know why," she said. She winked at Jody. "Kill two birds with one stone. Have a frolic and git breakfast done with."

He winked back at her. He felt bold and gay and tremulous. He could not understand how his mother could disapprove of such frolicksome people.

The music was out of tune and thunderous. It sounded like all the wild-cats in the scrub rounded up together, but it had a rhythm and a gusto that satisfied the ear and soul. The wild chords went through Jody as though he too were a fiddle and Lem Forrester drew long fingers across him.

Lem said to him in a low voice, "Iffen I only had my sweetheart here, to sing and dance."

Jody asked brashly, "Who-all's your sweetheart?"

"My leetle ol' Twink Weatherby."

"Why, she's Oliver Hutto's gal."

Lem lifted his fiddle-bow. Jody thought for an instant he meant to strike him. Then he went on with his fiddling, but his eyes smoldered.

"You say that agin in your life, boy, and you'll not have a tongue left to say it with. Understand?"

"Yes, Lem. Could be I was wrong," he added eagerly.

"I'm jest tellin' you."

He felt depressed a while, and disloyal to Oliver. Then the music caught him up again as though a great gust of wind lifted him across the tree-tops. The Forresters went from dance-tunes to songs, and Pa and Ma Forrester joined the singing with shrill, wavering voices. Daylight came, and the mocking-birds in the live oaks sang so clear and loud the Forresters heard them, and laid down their pieces, and saw the dawn in the cabin.

Breakfast covered the table with some scantiness, for a For-rester breakfast, for Ma had been too much occupied to do much cooking. The men pulled on only their breeches, for the food was ready and smoking. After breakfast, they washed above their beards, and put on their boots and shirts, and went leisurely about their day's business. Buck saddled his big roan stallion and swung Jody up behind him on the rump, for there was not room for a feather with him in the saddle.

Fodder-wing followed limping to the edge of the clearing, with the raccoon on his shoulder, and waved his stick in fare-well until they were out of sight. Jody rode home with Buck to Baxter's Island and waved after him as he went on. He was still in a daze. It was only as he swung open the gate under the chinaberry that he remembered he had forgotten to look be-hind the magnolia tree for a Spaniard riding.

· 8 ·

Jody clicked the gate behind him. The unmistakable smell of roasting meat filled the air. He ran around the side of the cabin. Resentment was mixed with his eagerness. Resisting the open kitchen door, he hurried to his father. Penny stepped out of the smoke-house and hailed him.

The truth, a tangled pain and pleasure, was before him. A large deer hide was stretched on the smoke-house wall.

Jody wailed, "You been huntin' and didn't wait on me." He stamped his foot. "I ain't never goin' to leave you go off without me agin."

"Easy, son, 'til you hear. Be proud things come so bountiful."

His wrath cooled. Curiosity bubbled like a spring.

"Tell me quick, Pa, how come."

Penny sat down on his heels in the sand. Jody dropped flat beside him.

"A buck, Jody. I near about run him down."

Again he was furious.

"Why'n't it wait 'til I got home?"

"Didn't you pleasure yourself at the Forresters? You cain't git all your 'coons up one tree."

"Hit could of waited. They ain't never enough time. Hit go too fast."

Penny laughed.

"Well, son, you nor me nor no man, ain't never yit learnt to halt it."

"Were the buck runnin'?"

"Jody, I'll declare. I ain't never had meat stand and wait for me, the way that buck stood in the road. He didn't pay the horse no mind. Jest stood there. My first thought was, ' 'Tarnation, and me with no shells to my new gun.' Then I unbreeched the gun and looked in, and bless Heaven, I mought o' knowed a Forrester would have ary gun full-loaded. There was two shells in the gun, and there stood the buck, jest waitin'. I cracked down and he dropped. Right in the road, handy as a sack o' meal. I h'isted him over old Cæsar's rump and away we goed. Tell you what come to me. 'Me bringin' in venison,' I figgered, 'Ma won't crawl me for leavin' Jody with Fodderwing.' "

"What did she say when she seed the new gun and the meat?"

"She said, 'If 'twas anybody but a honest fool like you, I'd swear you'd been out thievin'.' "

They chuckled together. The odors from the kitchen were savory. The hours with the Forresters were forgotten. There was no reality but the day's dinner. Jody went into the kitchen.

"Hey, Ma. I'm home."

"Well, must I laugh or cry?"

Her ample figure was bent over the hearth. The day was warm and sweat ran down her heavy neck.

"We got us a shootin' Pa, ain't we, Ma?"

"Yes, and a good thing, too, with you off all the time."

"Ma——"

"What is it?"

"We eatin' venison today?"

She turned from the fire.

"Merciful Heaven, don't you never think o' nothin' but your empty belly?"

"You cook venison so good, Ma."

She was mollified.

"We eatin' it today. I was feared it'd not keep, and the weather warm."

"The liver'll not keep, neither."

"Well, for pity's sake, we cain't eat ever'thing to oncet. If you'll fill my wood-box this evenin', could be we'd eat liver tonight."

He prowled among the dishes.

"Git outen my kitchen, lessen you want to torment me to death. Then what'd you do for dinner?"

"I'd cook it."

"Yes, you and the dogs."

He ran out of the house to his father.

"How's old Julia?"

It seemed to him he had been away a week.

"Doin' fine. Give her a month, and she'll have ol' Slewfoot hollerin'."

"Is the Forresters aimin' to he'p us hunt him?"

"We never come to no agreement. I'd ruther they hunted their way and leave me hunt mine. I don't much care who gits him, long as we keep him offen our stock."

"Pa, I never told you. I was scairt when the dogs was fightin' him. I was too scairt even to run."

"Hit didn't pleasure me none, neither, when I found I didn't have me a gun."

"But you told it to the Forresters like as if we was mighty bold-hearted."

"Well, son, that's what makes a tale."

Jody examined the deer hide. It was large and handsome, red with spring. The game seemed for him to be two different animals. On the chase, it was the quarry. He wanted only to see it fall. When it lay dead and bleeding, he was sickened and sorry. His heart ached over the mangled death. Then when it was cut into portions, and dried and salted and smoked; or boiled or baked or fried in the savory kitchen or roasted over the camp-fire, it was only meat, like bacon, and his mouth watered at its goodness. He wondered by what alchemy it was changed, so that what sickened him one hour, maddened him with hunger, the next. It seemed as though there were either two different animals or two different boys.

The hides did not change. They kept their aliveness. Whenever he stepped with bare feet on the soft deer-skin beside his bed, he half expected to feel it start under him. Penny, small body though he was, had a scattering of black hair across his thin chest. As a boy, he had slept naked in winter in a bear-skin, with the fur next to him. Ma Baxter said he had grown hair on his chest from so sleeping. It was her joke, but Jody half believed it.

The clearing was filled as abundantly as the Forresters'. His mother had ground the slaughtered sow into sausage. Stuffed casings hung in the smoke-house. A slow hickory fire smoked under them. Penny left his work to drop a few chips of wood on the smoldering embers.

Jody said, "Must I chop wood or finish hoein' the corn?"

"Now, Jody, you know good and well I couldn't let the weeds take the corn. I finished the hoein'. Wood's the thing."

He was glad to go to the wood-pile, for if he did not do

something to occupy his mind, hunger would force him to gnaw the dogs' alligator meat or pick up the chickens' scraps of cornbread. The time went slowly at first, and he was tormented with the desire to follow his father's activities. Then Penny disappeared in the mule lot and Jody swung the axe without distraction. He carried an armful of wood to his mother as an excuse to see how dinner was progressing. He was relieved to see it on the table. She was pouring the coffee.

"Call your Pa," she said. "And wash them turrible hands. I'll guarantee you ain't touched water since you left home."

Penny came at last. The ham of venison filled the center of the table. He drew his carving knife with maddening deliberation across the meat.

Jody said, "I'm so hongry, my belly thinks my throat is cut."

Penny laid down the knife and looked at him.

Ma Baxter said, "Now if that ain't a purty somethin' to say. Where'd you learn to say that?"

"Well, that's what the Forresters say."

"I knowed it. That's the kind o' thing you learn o' them low-down rascals."

"They ain't low-down, Ma."

"Ever' one of 'em's lower'n a doodle-bug. And black-hearted to boot."

"They ain't black-hearted. They're purely friendly. Ma, they fiddle and play and sing better'n the fiddlers' convention. We was up long before day, singin' and frolickin'. It was fine."

"That's all right if they got nothin' better to do."

Meat was before them, piled high on the plates. The Baxters fell to.

· 9 ·

A soft rain fell in the night. The April morning that followed was clear and luminous. The young corn lifted pointed
leaves and was inches higher. The cow-peas in the field beyond
were breaking the ground. The sugar-cane was needle-points
of greenness against the tawny earth. It was strange, Jody
thought, whenever he had been away from the clearing, and
came home again, he noticed things that he had never noticed
before, but that had been there all the time. Young mulberries
were clustered along the boughs, and before he went to the
Forresters' he had not even seen them. The Scuppernong grape-
vine, a gift from his mother's kin in Carolina, was in bloom for
the first time, fine and lace-like. The wild golden bees had
found its fragrance, and were standing on their heads to guzzle
its thin honey.

For two days he had filled his stomach so richly that this morning he felt a little languid and was not truly hungry. His father was up and out ahead of him, as usual. Breakfast was ready in the kitchen and his mother was tending the sausages in the smoke-house. The woodbox was low and Jody idled outside to fill it. He was in a mood for work, but it must be something gentle and unhurried. He made two leisurely trips to fill the woodbox. Old Julia was dragging herself around in search of Penny. Jody stooped to stroke her head. She seemed to share the sense of well-being that filled the clearing; or perhaps she understood that she had been spared a time longer to run through swamp and scrub and hammock. She wagged her long tail and stood quiet under his petting. The deepest wound was still raw and angry, but the others were healing. Jody saw his father, moving across the road toward the house from the barns and lot. He dangled a strange object. He called to Jody.

"I got a mighty cur'ous somethin'."

Jody ran to him. The limp object was an animal, at once strange and familiar. It was a raccoon, but instead of being the usual iron-gray, it was all a creamy white. He could not believe his eyes.

"How come it white, Pa? Is it a ol' grand-daddy 'coon?"

"That's what's so cur'ous. A 'coon don't never git to where he's white-headed. No sir, hit's one o' them rare things the books calls a albino. Borned white. And look, them rings on its tail, them that's due to be dark, they ain't no more'n cream-colored."

They crouched in the sand and examined the 'coon.

"Were it in the trap, Pa?"

"In the trap. Bad hurted but not dead. I'll declare, I hated a-killin' of it."

Jody felt a sense of loss, that he had not known the albino 'coon alive.

"Leave me tote him, Pa."

He cradled the dead animal in his arms. The pale fur seemed softer than the ordinary. The belly fur was as soft as the fluff of new-hatched biddies. He stroked it.

"I'd of loved to of ketched him leetle, Pa, and raised him."

"He'd of been a purty pet, a'right, but likely jest as mean as ary other 'coon."

They turned in at the gate and around the side of the house to the kitchen.

"Fodder-wing said none of his 'coons wasn't never pertickler mean."

"Yes, but a Forrester wouldn't scarcely notice if he was to git bit."

"Likely he'd bite right back, eh, Pa?"

They laughed together, picturing their neighbors. Ma Baxter met them at the door. Her face brightened, seeing the animal.

"You got him. Good. That's what's been goin' with my hens."

"But Ma," Jody protested. "Look at him. He's white. He's a cur'ossity."

"He's a thievin' varmint right on," she said indifferently. "Is the hide wuth more'n usual?"

Jody looked at his father. Penny was deep in the wash-basin. He opened one bright eye among the soap-suds and winked at his son.

"Likely ain't wuth a nickel," he said carelessly. "Jody's been a-wantin' of a leetle knapsack. Jest as good to leave him use up the hide."

Next to having the albino 'coon alive, nothing could be finer than a knapsack of the soft curious fur. Jody's mind was full of it. He could not eat his breakfast. He wanted to show his gratitude.

"I kin clean the water troughs, Pa," he said.

Penny nodded.

"I keep hopin' each year, come spring, to hire us a deep well dug. Then them water troughs could fill with trash and welcome. But bricks is mighty high."

"I'd not know what 'twas, not to be sparin' o' my water," Ma Baxter said. "For twenty years, I been sparin'."

"Now be patient, Ma," Penny said.

His face furrowed. Jody knew that the lack of abundant water was a trial to his father, and a greater hardship than for mother or son. Jody was held accountable for wood, but it was Penny himself who slung the ox yoke across his narrow shoulders, hung the great hewn cypress buckets at either end, and trudged up and down the sandy road from the clearing to the sink-hole, where seepage alone built pools of water, amber-colored from leaf-mould, and filtered by the sand. It was as though the labor were Penny's apology to his family for having established them on land so arid, when creeks and rivers and good wells flowed not many miles away. For the first time, Jody wondered why his father had chosen to inhabit this place. Thinking of the pools on the steep side of the sink-hole that must be cleared, he was almost tempted to wish that they lived on the river, with Grandma Hutto. Yet the clearing, the island of tall pines, made up the world. Life in other places was only a tale that was told, as Oliver Hutto told of Africa and China and Connecticut.

His mother said, "You better put a biscuit-two and some meat in your pocket. You ain't et."

He filled his pockets.

"You know what I wisht I had, Ma? A pouch like a 'possum, to tote things."

"The Lord put your stomach inside you o' purpose. He meant you to put your rations inside you when your Ma sets 'em on the table."

He rose and ambled to the door.

Penny said, "You git on to the sink-hole, son, and I'll foller time I've skinned out your 'coon hide."

The day was bright and windy. Jody took a grubbing hoe from the shed behind the house and strolled toward the road. The mulberry trees by the fence were a sharp green. His mother's favorite hen clucked to her biddies from the slat coop. He scooped up a small ball of yellow down and held it against his cheek, its cheepings shrill in his ear. He released it and it scurried for shelter under the fat hen's wings. The yard would soon need hoeing.

The walk from the front steps to the gate needed hoeing, too. The walk was bordered with cypress slats, but the weeds crept under and over, and grew impudently among the Amaryllis that lined the pathway. The lavender petals of the chinaberry blooms were falling. Jody scuffed his bare toes through them and went through the gate. He hesitated. The barns were tempting. There might be a new hatching of biddies. The calf might have a different look from yesterday. And if he could think of a good reason to give himself for prowling about, the increasingly unwelcome job of cleaning the water troughs might be that much longer postponed. Then it occurred to him that if he finished the cleaning in short order, he might be through for the day. He swung the grubbing hoe over his shoulder and set off at a trot toward the sink-hole.

The end of the world, he thought, might be like the sink-hole. Fodder-wing had said that it was empty and dark, with only clouds to ride on. But no one knew. Certainly reaching it must feel as it felt to reach the edge of the sink-hole. Jody wished that he had been the first to discover it. He turned the corner of the fence row. He left the road and took the trail. It was narrow, hemmed in by briers. He pretended that he did not know there was a sink-hole. He passed a dogwood tree.

It was a landmark. He closed his eyes and whistled carelessly. He put his feet ahead of him slowly. In spite of his determination, in spite of squeezing his eyelids tight, he could not make himself go farther with his eyes shut. He opened them and walked with a sense of relief the last few steps to the edge of the great limestone sink.

A small world lay at his feet. It was deep and concave, like a great bowl. Fodder-wing said that a bear as big as God had scooped out a pawful of earth to get a lily-root. Jody knew the truth from his father. It was only that underground rivers ran through the earth and swirled and eddied beneath the surface, and changed their courses. This was especially so where there were streaks of limestone, as here. The limestone was soft and crumbling before the air touched and hardened it. Sometimes, without reason, without warning, after long rains, perhaps, a section of earth sank in, gently and almost without sound, and a deep cavity marked the place where once had run, darkly and unseen, a river. Sometimes the sink-hole was a few feet only in depth and width. Baxter's sink-hole was sixty feet deep. It was so wide that Penny's old muzzle-loader could not hit a squirrel from one side to the other. The sink-hole was as round as though it had been dug so on purpose. Staring into it, it seemed to Jody that the truth of its fashioning was more fantastic than the tales of Fodder-wing.

The hole was older than Penny Baxter. Penny said he could remember when the trees that lined its steep banks were no larger much than saplings. Now they were of great size. A magnolia that grew half-way up the east bank had a trunk as broad as the mill-stone with which the Baxters ground their meal. A hickory was as thick as a man's thigh. A live oak spread its branches across half the sink-hole. Smaller trees, sweet gum and dogwood, ironwood and holly, grew lushly up and down the banks. Palmettos thrust tall spears among them. Giant ferns grew from top to bottom. Jody looked down into a great cupped garden, feathered with green leaves, cool and moist and, always, mysterious. The sink-hole was set in the arid scrub, at the core of the pine island, like a lush green heart.

The trail to the bottom of the sink-hole led down the west bank. It was worn deep into the sand and limestone by the years of Penny Baxter's feet, leading his stock to water. In the dryest weather, there was a continual seepage which dripped down the banks and came to gather at the bottom in a shallow pool. This water was stagnant, and clouded by the comings and goings of the animals who watered there. Only Penny's hogs used it for drinking and wallowing. For the other stock, and for his own family's use, Penny had an ingenious arrangement. Up the east, or opposite, bank from the trail, he had cut out of the limestone strata a series of troughs to catch and hold the filtered seepage. The lowest trough was shoulder-high from the bottom of the sink-hole. Here he led the cow and calf to water, and his horse. Here in his young manhood he had led the yoke of cream-colored oxen with which he had cleared his land. A few yards higher up, he had cut a pair of deeper troughs. Here his wife brought her block and paddle and came to do her washing. A portion of the bank bore a milky whitewash from the years of her soap-suds. For her annual quilt-washing, she caught rain water.

At the last, high above the stock trough and the wash troughs, lay a deep, narrow trough that gathered water used only for cooking and drinking. The bank above was so steep that none of the larger animals disturbed the water. The deer that came, the bears, the panthers, all used the west trail and watered either at the pool itself, or at the stock trough. Squirrels drank from the upper trough, and occasionally a wild-cat, but for the most it was untouched by anything but Penny's gourd, dipping into it to fill his cypress buckets.

Jody jolted down the trail, bracing himself against the steepness with the grubbing hoe. It made a clumsy stock, catching in the wild grape vines. The descent always excited him. Step by step the banks lifted above him. Step by step he passed the tops of trees. A breath of wind eddied into the green bowl, stirring waves of coolness. The leaves fluttered their thin hands. The ferns bent a moment to the ground. A red-bird swung in an arc across the sink-hole. It turned and dropped down to the pool, like a bright leaf falling. Seeing the boy, it whirred up and away. Jody knelt by the pool.

The water was clear, for the hogs were feeding to the north in the marshy prairies, and had no need of the sink-hole. A small green frog eyed the boy from a partly submerged twig. The nearest water was a couple of miles away. It seemed amazing that frogs should travel so far, to settle in a small and distant pool. He wondered if the first frog migrants had known that there was water here, when they hopped to the rim of the sink-hole and hesitated on their green haunches. Penny said that once in rainy weather he had seen a line of frogs in single file, like marching soldiers, crossing the dry flat-woods. Did they move blindly or with knowledge? Penny did not know. Jody flipped a frond of fern into the pool and the frog dove and hid himself in the soft muck.

A sense of aloneness that was not lonely came to the boy. He decided that when he was grown he would build himself a little house beside the pool. The animals would become used to it, and he would look out of the windows on moonlit nights and see them drinking.

He crossed the flat floor of the sink-hole and climbed a few feet to reach the stock trough. It was awkward, bringing the grubbing hoe over his shoulder and into the trough. He discarded it and went at his work with his two hands. An accumulation of leaves and sand had left a thick layer. He dug and scraped vigorously. He worked against the creeping moisture, trying to hold the trough dry and empty for an instant.

The seepage had returned by the time he took his hands away. The limestone trough was white and clean. He left it with satisfaction and moved higher up the bank to the more laborious work of scouring out the larger wash troughs. Constant use kept these comparatively free from leaves, but the soapsuds in time made them slippery. He climbed a sweet gum and gathered an armful of Spanish moss. It made good scouring material. He scooped sand from a bare spot on the bank and used it with the moss.

He was tired when he reached the drinking trough at the top. The incline was so steep that by resting his belly flat against the bank, he needed only to lower his head, like a fawn, to drink. He ran his tongue up and down the length of the trough. He darted it in and out and leaned back to watch the ripples. He wondered whether a bear lapped water like a dog or sucked it in like a deer. He imagined himself a bear and drank both ways, deciding. Lapping was slower, but he choked when he sucked the water in. He could not decide. Penny would know how a bear drank. He had probably actually seen them.

Jody buried his face completely in the water. He turned it from side to side, so that first one cheek and then the other was laved and cooled. He stood on his head in the trough, resting his weight on the palms of his hands. He tried to see how long he could hold his breath. He made bubbles. He heard his father's voice at the bottom of the sink-hole.

"Son, how come that water to feel so good to you? Put the same thing in the wash-basin, you act like 'twas something nasty."

He turned, dripping.

"Pa, I never heered you comin'."

"You had your dirty leetle ol' face too deep in what your pore Pa was fixin' to take a drink of."

"I wa'n't dirty, Pa. The water ain't riled."

"I ain't that thirsty."

Penny climbed the bank and examined the lower troughs. He nodded. He leaned over the rim of the wash trough and chewed a twig.

"I declare," he said, "your Ma purely shocked me when she said 'twenty years'. I jest hadn't never set down and reckoned the time. The years has slipped by me, one by one, me not noticin' nor countin'. Ever' spring, I'd figger to git your Ma a well dug. Then I'd need a ox, or the cow'd bog down and perish, or one o' the young uns'd put in and die and I'd have no heart for well-diggin', and medicine to pay for. Bricks so turrible high— When I begun diggin' oncet, and got no water at thirty feet, I knowed I was in for it. But twenty years is too long to ask ary woman to do her washin' on a seepage hillside."

Jody listened gravely.

He said, "We'll git her a well one day."

"Twenty years—" Penny repeated. "But always somethin' interferin'. And the war— And then the land to be cleared all over agin."

He stood leaning against the trough, looking backward along the years.

"When I first come here," he said, "when I picked this place and come to it, I hoped——"

The morning's question came to Jody's mind again.

"How come you to pick it, Pa?"

"Well, I picked it because—" His face puckered, his mind seeking words. "I jest craved peace, was all." He smiled. "Out here I got it, excusin' the bears and panthers and wolves and wild-cats—and now and agin, your Ma."

They sat in silence. The squirrels began to stir in the tree-tops. Suddenly Penny poked Jody in the ribs with his elbow.

"Look at that scaper, peekin' at us."

He pointed to a sweet gum. A half-grown raccoon was peering around the side of the trunk, a dozen feet from the ground. It saw itself observed and pulled back out of sight. In an instant the masked face looked again.

Penny said, "I reckon we be as cur'ous to the creeturs as they be to us."

"How come some is skeert and some is bold?"

"That I don't know. It depend, likely, on how young a creetur is scairt. They don't seem to be no rule for it. I mind me, oncet, I'd been huntin' all mornin'—this were over on Wild-cat Prairie—and I set down under a live oak and made me a leetle fire to warm me and cook me a bit o' bacon. Well, whilst I was settin' there, a fox walked right up t'other side o' the fire and laid down. I looked at him and he looked at me. I figgered mebbe he were hongry. I takened a piece o' meat and I jobbed it on a long stick and I helt it out to him. I helt it right over his nose. Now a fox is mighty wild and I ain't never knowed one to git that hongry to where he wouldn't run. And you know that fox laid there right on, lookin' at me, and never et nor run."

"I'd love to of seed him. What you figger made him lay there, Pa, lookin' at you?"

"Hit's been a puzzlement to me all these years since it happened. All I kin figger is, the dogs had run him until he got heated and his brains was cooked. I figger, for some reason, that fox were cold-out crazy."

The 'coon had moved into full view.

Jody said, "Pa, I wisht I had me somethin' to pet and play with, like Fodder-wing. I wisht I had me a 'coon, or a bear cub, or sich as that."

Penny said, "You know how your Ma rares. I'd not mind it, for I love the creeturs. But times has been hard and rations scarce, and your Ma's the one to say."

"I'd love a baby fox, or a baby panther. Kin you tame 'em, do you git 'em young?"

"You kin tame a 'coon . You kin tame a bear. You kin tame a wild-cat and you kin tame a panther." He pondered. His mind went back to his father's sermons. "You kin tame ary-thing, son, excusin' the human tongue."

· 10 ·

Jody lay comfortably ill, recovering from the fever. His mother called it the fever, so he did not argue. He thought privately that too many half-ripe brierberries might have something to do with his ailment. Treatment for such things was always much more violent than treatment for the fever. His mother had observed his shaking, had laid her big hand on his forehead and said, "Git into the bed. You got chills and fever." He had said nothing.

She came into the room now with a cup of steaming liquid. He eyed it anxiously. For two days she had been giving him lemon-leaf tea. It was aromatic and pleasant. When he had grumbled about its tartness, she had added a teaspoon of jelly to it. He wondered if now, in the mysterious wisdom that sometimes descended on her, she had discovered the truth.

If she guessed that his trouble had been the colic, the medicine she held would be either snake-root tonic, or a blood purifier made from Queen's Delight, both of which he abominated.

"If your Pa'd only plant me a root o' fever grass," she said, "I could git both o' you well o' the fever in no time. 'Tain't decent, not havin' fever-grass in the yard."

"What you got in the cup, Ma?"

"None o' your business. Open your mouth."

"I got a right to know. Supposin' you kilt me and I never knowed what medicine you give me."

"Hit's mullein tea, if you got to know. Hit come to me, could be you was comin' down with the measles."

"'Tain't the measles, Ma."

"How do you know? You ain't never had 'em. Open your mouth. If 'tain't the measles, this here won't hurt you. If 'tis the measles, hit'll bring out the rash."

The thought of bringing out a rash was tempting. He opened his mouth. She grasped him by the hair and poured half the cupful down his throat. He sputtered and fought.

"I won't take no more. 'Tain't the measles."

"Well, you'll die if 'tis, and the rash don't break out."

He opened his mouth again and took the rest of the mullein tea. It was bitter, but not nearly as bad as some of her concoctions. The bitter brew she made from pomegranate peelings, or that from pitcher-plant root, was infinitely worse. He lay back on his moss-stuffed pillow.

"If 'tis the measles, Ma, how soon will the rash come?"

"Soon as you git to sweatin' from the tea. Kiver up."

She left the room and he resigned himself to waiting for the sweat. Being sick was something of a treat. He would not willingly go through the first night again, when cramps had tied him in knots. But the convalescence, the solicitude of his mother and his father, was definitely pleasant. He felt a faint

87

sense of guilt that he had not told about the brierberries. She would have given him a purge, and it would all have been over with by the next morning. Penny had done all the work of the clearing alone for two days. He had hitched old Cæsar to the plow and plowed over the sugar-cane and hilled it up, had worked the corn and the cow-peas and the small patch of tobacco. He had hauled water from the sink-hole, cut wood, fed and watered the stock.

But perhaps, Jody speculated, he did have the fever. Perhaps he was coming down with the measles. He felt his face and stomach. There was no rash yet, no sweat. He flounced back and forth in the bed to hurry the heating. He realized that he felt as well as ever; better, actually, than before the plenitude of meat had tempted him into over-eating. He recalled the quantities of fresh sausage and of venison that he had eaten without his mother's stopping him. Perhaps after all the brierberries had had nothing to do with it. He was sweating at last.

He called, "Hey, Ma, come see! The sweat's done come."

She came to him and examined him.

"You feel as good as I do," she said. "Git outen that bed."

He threw back the covers and stepped out onto the deer-skin rug. For a moment he was light-headed.

"You feel all right?" she asked.

"Yessum. Sort o' weakified."

"Well, you ain't et nothin'. Git into your shirt and breeches and come git you some dinner."

He dressed quickly and followed her to the kitchen. The food was still warm. She laid out biscuits for him, and a plate of hash, and poured him a cup of sweet milk. She watched him eat.

"I hoped you'd git up a leetle mite pacified," she said.

"Kin I have some more hash, Ma?"

"I should say not. You've et enough now, to fill a alligator."

"Where's Pa?"

"To the lot, I reckon."

He strolled in search of him. Penny was sitting idly, for once, on the gate.

"Well, son," he said, "you look right peert."

"I feel good."

"You ain't got the measles, or the child-bed fever, or the smallpox?" The blue eyes twinkled.

Jody shook his head.

"Pa——"

"Yes, son."

"I don't figger there was nothin' ailded me but green brier-berries."

"That's about what I figgered. I never said nothin' to your Ma, for she's death on a belly-full of green brierberries."

Jody sighed with relief.

Penny said, "I been settin' here studyin'. The moon'll be right in a hour-two. What say you and me git us a couple o' bobs and go fishin'?"

"In the creek?"

"I sort o' crave to fish some o' them saw-grass ponds over where ol' Slewfoot was feedin'."

"I'll bet we kin ketch us a cattywampus in one o' them ponds."

"We kin sure pleasure ourselves tryin'."

They went together to the shed back of the house to gather their paraphernalia. Penny discarded an old hook and rigged two new ones. He cut short hairs from the tail of the deer he had shot and made lures of the gray and white wisps. He tied them invisibly to the fish-hooks.

"If I was a fish, I'd strike at this myself," he said.

He went to the house and spoke briefly with his wife.

"Me and Jody is goin' bobbin' for bass."

"I thought you was give out and Jody was ailin'."

"That's why we're goin' fishin'," he said.

She followed to the door and watched after them.

"If you don't git no bass," she called, "ketch me a leetle bream I kin fry crisp and eat bones and all."

"We'll not come back without somethin'," he promised.

The afternoon was warm but the way seemed short. In a way, Jody thought, fishing was better than hunting. It was not so exciting, but neither was there terror. The heart beat at a reasonable cadence. There was time to look about, and see the increase of green leaves in the live oaks and magnolias. They stopped at a familiar pond. It was shallow from too long dryness. Penny found a grasshopper and threw it into the water. There was no strike; no hungry swirl of waters.

"I'm feered the fish has died outen here," he said. "These leetle ol' ponds in the middle o' no-where has allus been a puzzlement to me. I cain't see how the fish lives here, year on year."

He caught another grasshopper and hurled it without result.

"The pore fish," he said. "Helpless in a world o' their own. 'Stead o' fishin' for 'em, I'd ought to come out here and feed 'em."

He lifted his bamboo rod over his shoulder.

"Mebbe the Lord figgers the same about me," he chuckled. "Mebbe he looks down and says, 'There's Penny Baxter tryin' to make out on that clearin'.' " He added, "But hit's a good clearin'. Likely the fish is as content as me."

Jody said, "Look, Pa, there's people."

Human beings were a stranger sight in the lonely place of live oak islands and saw-grass ponds and prairies, than the creatures. Penny shaded his eyes. A file of half a dozen men and women was entering the scrub road they had just left behind.

"Hit's the Minorcans," he said. "Huntin' gophers."

Jody saw now the sacks over their shoulders. The small dusty land-turtles whose deep burrows were an indication of the poorest soil, were the last food most inhabitants of the scrub considered edible.

"I've allus wondered," Penny said, "didn't they make a medicine mebbe outen the gophers. Don't seem like they'd come here clear from the coast to hunt them things jest to eat."

"Let's slip back clost and look at 'em," Jody said.

"I'd not pry on the pore things," Penny said. "The Minorcans is a people was mighty bad put upon. My father knowed their hull history. A English feller carried 'em to New Smyrna, over by the ocean and the Indian River. He promised 'em a pure Heaven and put 'em to work. And when times got bad and the crops failed, he left 'em to nigh about starve to death. There wasn't many left."

"Is they like gypsies?"

"No, for gypsies is wild. The men is dark, like gypsies, but the women is fair when they're young. They mind their own business and live peaceable."

The procession disappeared into the scrub. Jody tingled, and the hair stirred on the back of his neck. It was like seeing Spaniards. It was as though phantoms, dark and shadowy, and not men and women, had passed before him, weighted with their strange burden of gophers and injustice.

Penny said, "Now the bass had ought to be thick as tadpoles in that pond right over there."

They were in territory a little west of the prairie's rim where old Slewfoot had fed on fire-plant. Dry weather sucked up much of the water and the marsh had broad areas that were now firm and dry. The ponds showed plainly. They had withdrawn from the saw-grass and only lily pads troubled the water's surface. A Blue Peter ran across them, bright with yellow legs and painted face. A slight breath of air rippled across the marsh and the water rippled under it. The lily pads tipped, an instant, their broad shining leaves to the glint of the sun.

"Jest enough of a riffle," Penny said, "and the moon jest right."

He fastened lengths of line to the two poles and attached the deer-hair bobs.

"Now you work your bob acrost the north end and I'll try the south. Don't make no fuss, walkin'."

Jody stood a moment to watch his father make an expert cast across the pond. He marveled at the skill of the knotted hands. The bob lay at the edge of a cluster of lily pads. Penny began to jerk it slowly across the water. It dipped and bobbed with the irregular rhythm of a live insect. There was no strike and Penny drew in his line and cast again in the same place. He called to invisible fish, lurking near the weedy bottom.

"Now Grandpappy, I kin see you settin' there on your stoop." He jerked the bob more slowly. "You better lay down your pipe and come git your dinner."

Jody tore himself from the fascination of his father's performance and moved to his end of the pond. He cast badly for a time, tangling his line and laying his bob in the most unlikely places; over-reaching the narrow pond and enmeshing the hook in the tough saw-grass. Then something of harmony came to him. He felt his arm swing in a satisfying arc. His wrist flexed at the proper moment. He laid the bob exactly where he had meant to, at the edge of a patch of switch-grass.

Penny called, "Mighty nice, son. Leave it lay jest a minute. Then git ready the first second you jerk it."

He had not known his father was watching. He was tense. He jerked his pole cautiously and the bob flipped across the water. There was a swirl, a silver form shot half clear of the water, an open mouth as big as a cook-pot enveloped the bob.

A weight like a millstone dropped at the end of his line, fought like a wild-cat, and pulled him off-balance. He braced himself against the frenzy to which he was irrevocably attached.

Penny called, "Take it easy. Don't let him git under them bonnets. Keep the tip o' your pole up. Don't give him no slack."

Penny left him to the struggle. His arms ached from the strain. He was afraid to tug too hard for fear of breaking the line. He dared not yield an inch for fear a sudden slackness would tell of the loss of the giant. He longed for magic words from his father, indicating some miracle by which he might land his fish and be done with the torment. The bass was sulking. It made a dash for the grasses, where it might tangle the line around their stems and so rip free. It came to Jody that if he walked around the edge of the pond, keeping a taut line, he might lead the bass into shallow water and flounder him at the edge. He worked cautiously. He was tempted to drop the pole and clutch the line itself and come to grips with his adversary. He began to walk away from the pond. He gave his pole a heave and landed the bass, flouncing, in the grass. He dropped the pole and ran, to move the catch to a final safety. The bass would weigh ten pounds. Penny came to him.

"Boy, I'm proud of you. Nobody couldn't of handled him better."

Jody stood panting. Penny thumped him on the back, as excited as he. He looked down, unbelieving, at the stout form and the great maw.

"I feel as good as if 'twas ol' Slewfoot," he said, and they grinned together and pummeled each other's backs.

"Now I got to go beat you," Penny said.

They took separate ponds. Penny called that he was licked and beaten. He began fishing for Ma Baxter's bream with a hand-line and bonnet worms. Jody cast and cast again, but there was never the mad swirl of waters, the great leap, the live and struggling weight. He caught a small bass and held it up to show his father.

"Throw him back," Penny called. "We don't need him for eatin'. Leave him to grow up big as t'other one. Then we'll come back agin and ketch him."

Jody put the small fish back reluctantly and watched it swim away. His father was stern about not taking more of any-thing, fish or game, than could be eaten or kept. Hope of another monster dwindled as the sun finished its spring arc of the daylight sky. He cast leisurely, taking his pleasure in his increasing dexterity of arm and wrist. The moon was now wrong. It was no longer feed-time. The fish were not striking. Suddenly he heard his father whistle like a quail. It was the signal they used together in squirrel hunting. Jody laid down his pole and looked back to make sure he could identify the tuft of grass where he had covered his bass from the rays of the sun. He walked cautiously to where his father beckoned.

Penny whispered, "Foller me. We'll ease up clost as we dare."

He pointed. "The whoopin' cranes is dancin'."

Jody saw the great white birds in the distance. His father's eye, he thought, was like an eagle's. They crouched on all fours and crept forward slowly. Now and then Penny dropped flat on his stomach and Jody dropped behind him. They reached a clump of high saw-grass and Penny motioned for concealment behind it. The birds were so close that it seemed to Jody he might touch them with his long fishing pole. Penny squatted on his haunches and Jody followed. His eyes were wide. He made a count of the whooping cranes. There were sixteen.

The cranes were dancing a cotillion as surely as it was danced at Volusia. Two stood apart, erect and white, making a strange music that was part cry and part singing. The rhythm was irregular, like the dance. The other birds were in a circle. In the heart of the circle, several moved counter-clock-wise. The musicians made their music. The dancers raised their wings and lifted their feet, first one and then the other. They sunk their heads deep in their snowy breasts, lifted them and sunk again. They moved soundlessly, part awkwardness, part grace. The dance was solemn. Wings fluttered, rising and falling like out-stretched arms. The outer circle shuffled around and around. The group in the center attained a slow frenzy.

Suddenly all motion ceased. Jody thought the dance was over, or that the intruders had been discovered. Then the two musicians joined the circle. Two others took their places. There was a pause. The dance was resumed. The birds were reflected in the clear marsh water. Sixteen white shadows reflected the motions. The evening breeze moved across the sawgrass. It bowed and fluttered. The water rippled. The setting sun lay rosy on the white bodies. Magic birds were dancing in a mystic marsh. The grass swayed with them, and the shallow waters, and the earth fluttered under them. The earth was dancing with the cranes, and the low sun, and the wind and sky.

Jody found his own arms lifting and falling with his breath, as the cranes' wings lifted. The sun was sinking into the sawgrass. The marsh was golden. The whooping cranes were washed with gold. The far hammocks were black. Darkness came to the lily pads, and the water blackened. The cranes were whiter than any clouds, or any white bloom of oleander or of lily. Without warning, they took flight. Whether the hour-long dance was, simply, done, or whether the long nose of an alligator had lifted above the water to alarm them, Jody could not tell, but they were gone. They made a great circle against the sunset, whooping their strange rusty cry that sounded only in their flight. Then they flew in a long line into the west, and vanished.

Penny and Jody straightened and stood up. They were cramped from the long crouching. Dusk lay over the saw-grass, so that the ponds were scarcely visible. The world was shadow, melting into shadow. They turned to the north. Jody found his bass. They cut to the east, to leave the marsh behind them, then north again. The trail was dim in the growing darkness. It joined the scrub road and they turned once more east, continuing now in a certainty, for the dense growth of the scrub bordered the road like walls. The scrub was black and the road was a dark gray strip of carpet, sandy and sound-less. Small creatures darted across in front of them and scurried in the bushes. In the distance, a panther screamed. Bull-bats shot low over their heads. They walked in silence.

At the house, bread was baked and waiting, and hot fat was in the iron skillet. Penny lighted a fat-wood torch and went to the lot to do his chores. Jody scaled and dressed the fish at the back stoop, where a ray of light glimmered from the fire on the hearth. Ma Baxter dipped the pieces in meal and fried them crisp and golden. The family ate without speaking.

She said, "What ails you fellers?"

They did not answer. They had no thought for what they ate nor for the woman. They were no more than conscious that she spoke to them. They had seen a thing that was unearthly. They were in a trance from the strong spell of its beauty.

· 11 ·

THE fawns were being born. Jody saw through the scrub the delicate tracery of their small pointed hooves. Wherever he went, to the sink-hole, for wood into the black-jacks south of the lot, to the traps, Penny was obliged to keep about for varmints, he walked with eyes on the ground, watching for signs of their comings and their goings. The larger hoof-marks of the does usually preceded them. But the does were wary. Often the doe-sign was in one place, where the mother had fed alone, and the wavering fawn-sign was some distance away, where the infant had been left in the greater safety of heavy cover. Often there were twin fawns. When Jody found the double set of tracks he could scarcely contain himself.

He thought always then, "I could leave one for the mammy and take one for myself."

He broached the matter to his mother one evening.

"Ma, we got milk a-plenty. Cain't I git me a leetle ol' fawn for a pet for me? A spotted fawn, Ma. Cain't I?"

"I should jest say not. What you mean, milk a-plenty? They ain't a extry drop left from sun to sun."

"It could have my milk."

"Yes, and fatten the blasted fawn and you grow up puny. Much as we all got to do, what on earth do you want with one o' them things, blayting around here day and night?"

"I want one. I want a 'coon, but I know a 'coon gits mischievous. I'd love a bear cub, but I know they're liable to be mean. I jest want something—" he puckered his face so that his freckles ran together—"I jest want something all my own. Something to foller me and be mine." He struggled for words. "I want something with dependence to it."

His mother snorted.

"Well, you'll not find that no-where. Not in the animal world nor in the world o' man. Now Jody, I'll not have you pesterin' me. You say another word, 'fawn' or ''coon' or 'bear cub,' and I'll take a bresh to you."

Penny listened quietly from his corner.

In the morning he said, "We'll go hunt us a buck today, Jody. Likely we'll find a fawn beddin'. Hit's near about as much pleasure seein' 'em wild, as havin' 'em tame."

"Will we take both dogs?"

"Nobody but old Julia. She ain't had a work-out since she was hurt. A slow hunt'll do her good."

Ma Baxter said, "That last venison didn't last no time. But we did jerk right smart of it, come to think of it. Git a few hams in the smoke-house and hit'll look natural agin."

Her good nature rose and fell with the food supply.

Penny said, "Jody, looks like you've fell heir to the old muzzle-loader. But don't git too put out now, do it fail you like it failed me."

He could not imagine being impatient about it. It was enough to have the use of it for himself. His mother had sewed the cream-colored 'coonskin into a knapsack for him. He filled it with shot and caps and wadding and filled the powder horn.

Penny said, "Ma, I been studyin'. I jest about got to go to Volusia to git me shell cases. Lem only th'owed in a few shells with the gun. And I'd love some rale coffee. I've had a bait o' them wild coffee beans."

"Me, too," she agreed. "And I need me some thread and a paper o' needles."

"Now the bucks," he said, "seems to be feedin' toward the river. I been seein' a perfect shower o' tracks headin' that-a-way. I believe me and Jody kin hunt on in that direction, and do we git us a buck or two, we kin trade the saddles and haunches to Volusia for what we need. Then we kin say 'Howdy' to Grandma Hutto."

She frowned.

"You'll git to visitin' with that sassy old woman and like as not you'll be gone a couple o' days. I think you'd ought to leave Jody with me."

Jody squirmed and looked at his father.

Penny said, "We'll be back tomorrer. How's Jody to learn to hunt and be a man if his daddy don't carry him along and learn him?"

"Hit's a good excuse," she said. "Hit's jest men-folks likin' to prowl off together."

"Then you come make the hunt with me, sweetheart, and leave Jody here."

Jody laughed out. The picture of his mother's great frame pushing through the bay-heads made him shout in spite of himself.

"Oh go on," she said, and laughed. "Git it over and done with."

"You know you enjoy gittin' shut of us now and agin," Penny told her.

99

"Hit's my only rest," she admitted. "Leave me Grandpa's gun loaded."

The ancient Long Tom, Jody thought, was more of a menace to her than to any intruders. She was an inaccurate and incompetent shot, and the gun was as fallible as Penny's muzzle-loader, but he could understand the comfort to her of its presence. He brought it from the shed for his father to load, grateful that she had not demanded his own newly acquired piece.

Penny whistled to old Julia and the man and boy and hound set out eastward in mid-morning. The May day was warm and close. The sun beat down through the scrub. The small hard leaves of the scrub oaks were flat pans to hold the heat. The sand burned Jody's feet through his cowhide shoes. In spite of the heat, Penny walked at a fast gait. It was all Jody could do to follow him. Julia loped ahead. There was as yet no scent. Penny stopped once and stared about the horizon.

Jody asked, "What you see, Pa?"

"Nothin', son, and very leetle o' that."

A mile east of the clearing, he changed his direction. There were suddenly deer tracks in a great plenty. Penny studied them, for size and sex and freshness.

"Here's two big ol' bucks travelin' together," he said at last. "They come this way before day."

"How kin you tell about tracks so?"

"Jest by bein' used to 'em."

Jody could see little difference between them and some of the other hoof-marks. Penny stooped and traced them with his finger.

"Now you know to tell a doe from a buck. A doe's track is pointed and fine. And ary one kin tell how fresh a track be, for a old track has sand blowed into it. And now if you'll notice, a deer's toes is spraddled when he's runnin'. They're close together when he walks." He indicated the fresh tracks to the hound. "Here, Julia, git him!"

Julia bent her long nose to the trail. It led out of the scrub, toward the south-east, into an open area of gallberry flats. Here was bear sign as well.

Jody asked, "Must I shoot a bear, do I git the chancet?"

"Bear or buck, hit's all right. Jest be sure you got a good chancet. Don't go wastin' your shot."

The flats were not hard going, but the sun was blazing. The gallberry bushes ended and there was a welcome stretch of pines. The shadows were cooling. Penny pointed out a bear gnaw. It was a clawed area on a tall pine tree, shoulder high to a man. The resin dripped from it.

"I've watched a bear at it," Penny said, "many a time. He'll stretch up and he'll claw. He'll turn his head sideways and he'll nag and gnaw. Then he'll back up and rub his shoulders agin the resin. Some folks says it's to keep the bees from stingin' when he robs a bee-tree, but I've allus figgered 'twas jest a way o' boastin'. A buck'll boast jest about the same way. He'll rub his head and horns agin a saplin' jest to prove hisself."

Julia lifted her nose and Penny and Jody stopped short. There was a commotion ahead. Penny motioned Julia to heel and they crept close. An opening showed and they halted. Twin bear cubs were high in a slim pine sapling, using it for a swing. The sapling was tall and limber and the yearling cubs were rocking it back and forth. Jody had swung in the same fashion. For an instant the cubs were not bears, but boys like himself. He would have liked to climb the sapling and rock with them. It bent half-way to the ground as they swung their weight, swayed upright again, then low on the other side. The cubs made now and then an amiable talking.

Julia could not resist barking. The cubs stopped their play, astonished, and stared down at the humans. They were not alarmed. It was their first sight of mankind and they seemed to feel, as Jody felt, only curiosity. They cocked their black furry heads from one side to the other. One scrambled to a higher limb, not for safety, but for a better view. He curled one arm around the sapling and gaped down below him. His black beady eyes were bright.

"Oh Pa," Jody begged, "let's ketch us one."

Penny himself was tempted.

"They're a mite big for tamin'." He brought himself to his senses. "Now what ails us? Jest how long would it take your Ma to run him off, and me and you with him?"

"Pa, look at him cut his eyes."

"That's likely the mean un. Of twin bear cubs, one'll be gentle and t'other'll be mean."

"Let's ketch the gentle un. Please, Pa."

The cubs craned their necks. Penny shook his head.

"Come along, boy. Le's git on with our hunt and leave 'em to their play."

He lingered behind while his father took up the bucks' trail again. He thought once that the cubs were about to come down the sapling to him, but they only scrambled about from one limb to another and turned their heads to watch him. He ached to touch them. He imagined them sitting on their haunches and begging, as Oliver Hutto described trained bears as doing; nesting in his lap, warm and furry and intimate; sleeping on the foot of his bed; even under the covers with him, if the nights were cold. His father was almost out of sight under the pines. He ran after him. He looked back over his shoulder and waved his hand to the bear cubs. They lifted their black noses, as though the air might tell them, what their eyes had not, the nature of their observers. In their first sign of alarm, he saw them clamber down the sapling and slip away to the west beyond the gallberries. He caught up to his father.

"Do you ever ask your Ma into leavin' you have sich as that," Penny told him, "you belong to git one young enough to train easy."

The thought was encouraging. The yearling cubs would indeed be large to handle.

"Now I never had nothin' much to pet nor play with, neither," Penny said. "There was sich a mess of us. Neither farmin' nor the Bible pays a man too good, and Pa was like your Ma, he jest wouldn't feed no creeturs. He done well to fill our bellies. Then he put in and died, and since I was the oldest rat in the barn, I had to look after the rest of 'em 'til they was old enough to shuffle around for theirselves."

"Well, a bear cub could near about make his own livin', couldn't he?"

"Yes—offen your Ma's chickens."

Jody sighed and applied himself with his father to the buck tracks. The pair of deer was keeping close together. It was odd, he thought, that the bucks could be so friendly through the spring and summer. Then when their horns were grown, and they began to run with the does in the autumn, they would drive the fawns away from the does, and battle fiercely. One buck was larger than the other.

"That un there's a buck big enough to ride," Penny said.

A patch of hammock joined the pines. Dogbane grew thickly here, lifting its yellow bells. Penny studied the multitude of tracks.

"Now boy," he said, "you been wantin' to see fawns. Me and Julia'll go on and make a circle. You climb up this here live oak and scrooch down in the branches and I believe you'll see somethin'. Hide your gun here in the bushes. You'll not want it."

Jody settled himself halfway up the live oak. Penny and Julia disappeared. The shade of the oak was cool. A light breeze moved through its leaves. Jody's shaggy hair was wet. He pushed it out of his eyes and wiped his face on his blue sleeve, then settled himself to quiet. Silence took over the scrub. Far away a hawk cried shrilly and was gone. No bird stirred in any branches. No creature moved or fed. No bees droned, or any insect. It was high noon. Everything living was resting in the heat of the sun's meridian. Everything except Penny and old Julia, who moved now somewhere among the scrub oaks and the myrtle. Bushes crackled below him. He thought his father was returning. He almost betrayed himself with a quick movement. A bleat sounded. A fawn was moving from under the protection of a low clump of palmettos. It must have been there all the time. Penny had known. Jody held his breath.

A doe bounded over the palmettos. The fawn ran to her, wobbling on unsteady legs. She bent her head to it and made a low sound in greeting. She licked its small anxious face. It was all eyes and ears. It was spotted. Jody had never seen one so young. The doe threw up her head and tasted the air with her wide nostrils. A taint lay on it of the human enemy. She kicked up her heels and made a sortie about the live oak. She discovered the trail of hound and man. She followed it backward and forward, throwing up her head at every few steps. She stopped and listened, her ears pricked tall above her great luminous eyes.

The fawn bleated. The doe quieted. She seemed satisfied that the danger had come and gone. The fawn nuzzled her full udders and began to nurse. It butted her bag with its knobby head and switched its short tail in a gluttonous ecstasy. The doe was not content. She broke away from it and moved directly underneath the live oak. The boughs below Jody obscured his view, but he could see that she had traced his scent to the tree and was lifting her head to locate him. Her nose followed the odor of his hands, the leather of his shoes, the sweat of his clothing, as surely as a man's eyes followed a blazed trail. The fawn followed, greedy for the warm milk. Suddenly the doe wheeled and kicked the fawn sprawling into the bushes. She cleared them in a great bound and galloped away.

Jody scrambled down from his perch and ran to the place where he had seen the fawn tumble. It was not there. He hunted the ground carefully. The tiny hoof-marks crossed and criss-crossed and he could not tell one track from another. He sat down disconsolately to wait for his father. Penny returned, red of face and wet with sweat.

"Well, son," he called, "what did you see?"

"A doe and a fawn. The fawn were right here all the while. He nursed his mammy and she smelled me and run off. And I cain't find the fawn no-where. You reckon Julia kin track him?"

Penny dropped down on the ground.

"Julia kin track ary thing that makes a trail. But don't let's torment the leetle thing. Hit's right clost this minute, and likely scairt to death."

"His mammy shouldn't of left him."

"That's where she was smart. Most ary thing would take out after her. And she's learned the fawn to lay up so still hit'll not git noticed."

"Hit were mighty cute spotted, Pa."

"Was the spots all in a line, or helter-skelter?"

"They was in a line."

"Then hit's a leetle ol' buck-fawn. Wasn't you proud to see it so clost?"

"I was proud, but I'd shore love to ketch him and keep him."

Penny laughed and opened his knapsack and took out the lunch. Jody protested. He was for once more anxious to hunt than to eat.

Penny said, "We got to noon somewhere, and a deer is mighty like to run over us right here. When you noon, you jest as good to noon where the game walks."

Jody brought his gun from its hiding place and sat down to eat. He was abstracted and only the flavor of fresh brierberry jam brought him back to a consciousness of his food. The jam was thin and not sweet enough, sugar being scarce. Old Julia was still a little weak. She lay stretched out on her side. Her battle scars showed white against her dark hide. Penny lay on his back.

He said lazily, "Them two bucks is like to circle back through here to bed up right soon, if the wind don't change. If you was of a notion to go climb one o' them high pine trees about a quarter to the east, hit'd make a mighty good stand."

Jody picked up his gun and started away. He would give anything to bring down a buck alone.

Penny called after him, "Don't try for too long a shot. Take your time. And don't let the gun kick you outen the tree."

Tall scattered pines lifted ahead from a desolate flat of gall-berry bushes. Jody chose one that commanded a view of a wide area. Nothing could cross in any direction without his seeing it. It was hard work to climb the straight trunk with the gun in one hand. His knees and shins were raw when he reached the lowest branches. He rested a moment then climbed as high as he dared in the tree-top. The pine swayed in an imperceptible breeze. It seemed alive, stirring with a breath of its own.

He recalled the bear cubs, rocking the sapling. He began to swing his tree-top, but it was over-balanced with his weight and that of his gun. It cracked ominously and he held quiet. He looked about him. He knew now how a hawk felt, surveying the world from high places. An eagle stared down as he was staring, high and wise and predatory and keen. He swung his head in a slow circle. For the first time he could believe that the world was round. By turning his head quickly, he could almost see the whole horizon at once.

He thought that his vision covered the entire area. He was startled to see movement. He had seen nothing approaching. But a large buck was feeding toward him. Early huckleberries were offering food. The buck was still out of range. He debated climbing down from the pine tree and stalking it, but knew that the animal, more alert than he, would be gone before he could lift his gun. He could only wait, and pray that it would feed within a reasonable distance. It moved with a maddening slowness.

For a time he thought it meant to feed away from him, to the south. Then it began to move directly toward him. He brought his gun up behind the shelter of the branches. His heart pounded. He could not tell for the life of him whether the deer was near or far. It loomed large, yet he was conscious that such details as eyes and ears were still not plain to him. He waited for what seemed an interminable period. The buck lifted his head. Jody drew a bead on the stout neck.

He pulled the trigger. At the instant that he did so, he realized that he had not made sufficient allowance for his height above the game. He had over-shot. Yet it seemed to him that he must have touched the animal, for it leaped into the air with something more than alarm. It cleared the gallberry bushes with a high bounding, making long cradled arcs. It passed directly under the pine-tree. If he had had his father's new double-barreled gun, he would have had another shot. In a few seconds he heard Penny's gun. He was quivering. He climbed down from the pine and pushed his way back to the patch of hammock. The buck lay in the shade of the live oak. Penny had already begun the dressing.

Jody called, "Did I hit him?"

"You hit him. You done a mighty good job. Like as not, he'd of fell a piece on, but I takened a shot at him as he come by, jest to make sure. You was a might high."

"I know it. The minute I shot, I knowed I was high."

"Well, that's the way you learn. Next time, you'll know. Now here's your shot, here, and there's mine."

Jody knelt down to examine the fine frame. Again, a sickness came over him at the sight of the glazed eyes and the bleeding throat.

He said, "I wisht we could git our meat without killin' it."

"Hit's a pity, a'right. But we got to eat."

Penny was working deftly. His hunting knife, a flat saw-file ground down to an edge, with only a corn-cob for handle, was not overly sharp, but he had already drawn the venison and cut off the heavy head. He skinned it below the knees, crossed the legs and tied them, slipped his arms through the junctures, and stood up with the carcass neatly balanced on his back for carrying.

"Now Boyles may want the hide when we skin it out at Volusia," he said, "but if you'd like to carry the hide to Grandma Hutto for a present, we'll jest refuse him."

"I reckon she'd be proud to have it for a rug, a'right. I wisht I'd shot it by myself, to give her."

"That's jest all right. The hide's yours. I'll carry her a fore-quarter, for my portion. She's got nobody but us to hunt for her, with Oliver gone to sea. That mindless Yankee hangs around her is no good for sich as that." Penny said innocently, "Now mebbe you'd ruther carry the hide to your sweetheart."

Jody scowled blackly.

"Pa, you know I got no sweetheart."

"You ain't goin' back on Eulalie after I seed you holdin' hands at the doin's?"

"I was not holdin' hands. It was a game they was playin'. If you say that agin, Pa, I'll jest die."

Penny seldom teased his son, but now and then an occasion was irresistible.

"Grandma's my sweetheart," Jody said.

"All right. I jest wanted to git it straight."

The sand road was long and hot. Penny was wet with sweat, but he walked easily under his burden.

Jody said, "Kin I tote it a ways?" but Penny shook his head.

"These fellers only fits a man's back," he said.

They crossed Juniper Creek, then, after two miles of narrow

road, picked up the main road to the river and to Volusia. Penny stopped to rest. In late afternoon they passed Captain McDonald's house and Jody knew they were nearing Fort Butler. Around a bend in the road, the dry growth of pines and scrub oak disappeared. There was a new lushness. Sweet gums and bay were here, and, like sign-posts indicating the river, cypress. Wild azaleas were blooming late in the low places, and the passion flower opened its lavender corollas along the road.

They reached the St. John's River. It was dark and aloof. It seemed to slide toward the ocean indifferent to its own banks and to the men who crossed or used it. Jody stared at it. It was a pathway to the world. Penny shouted across it to summon the ferry from the Volusia side. A man crossed over for them with a rough raft of hewn logs. They crossed back, watching the slow sweep of the river current. Penny paid his ferryage and they walked up the curving shell road and into the Volusia store.

Penny hailed the proprietor, "Howdy, Mr. Boyles. How do this feller look to you?"

"Too good for the steam-boat. But Cap'll want it."

"What's venison worth?"

"The same. A dollar and a half a saddle. I'll swear, those city folks travelling up and down the river— Hollering for venison, and 'tain't half as good as pork, and you and me, we know it."

Penny hauled the deer to the big meat block and began the skinning.

"Yes," he agreed, "but if a feller's pot-bellied and cain't git out and shoot it for hisself, I reckon venison has a mighty fancy taste to him."

They laughed together. Penny was a welcome trader at the store, as much for his wit and his stories, as his business. Boyles himself was judge and arbiter and encyclopedia for the small community. He stood now in the close odorous dusk of his store like a captain in the hold of his ship. His wares included the necessities and scanty luxuries of the whole country-side, from plows, wagons, buggies and implements, through food staples to whiskey and hardware, dry goods and notions and medicines.

"Now one fore-quarter I'll call back by for tomorrer to carry home to my wife. T'other one goes to Grandma Hutto," Penny said.

"Bless her old soul," Boyles said. "Why I say 'old soul' I don't know. If a man's wife was as young-hearted as Grandma Hutto, why, living'd be a feast."

Jody walked along the length of the glass case under the counter. There were sweet crackers and an assortment of candies. There were Barlow knives and the new Rogers. There were shoe-strings, buttons, thread and needles. The coarser wares were on shelves that lined the walls. Buckets and pitchers, lard-oil lamps and basins, the new kerosene lamps, coffee pots and cast-iron skillets and Dutch ovens, nestled together like strange birds, fledglings in one nest. Beyond the utensils were the dress goods; calico and Osnaburg, denim and shoddy, domestic and homespun. A few bolts of alpaca and linsey and broadcloth were thick with dust. There was little sale for such luxuries, especially in the summer. At the back of the store were the groceries, hams and cheeses and bacons. There were barrels of sugar and flour and meal and grits and green coffee beans; sacks of potatoes; kegs of syrup; barrels of whiskey. Nothing here was tempting and Jody wandered back to the glass case. A rusty mouth organ lay on top of a pile of licorice strings. He was tempted for a moment to trade in his deer hide and buy the mouth organ, so that he could play to Grandma Hutto or accompany the Forresters. But Grandma would probably prefer the deer hide. Boyles called to him.

"Young man, your daddy doesn't come to trade too often. I'll treat you to a dime's worth of anything you take a notion to."

He looked over the assortment hungrily.

"I reckon the mouth organ's wuth more'n a dime."

"Well, yes, but it's been there a good while now. Take it and welcome."

Jody cast a last look at the candies. But Grandma Hutto would have sweets for him.

He said, "Thank you, sir."

Boyles said, "Your boy's mannerly, Mr. Baxter."

"He's right smart of a comfort," Penny said. "We lost so many young uns, I think sometimes I set too much store by him."

Jody glowed with a sense of virtue. He longed to be good and noble. He turned back of the counter to garner the reward of his character. He glanced up at a motion by the door. Boyles' niece, Eulalie, stood gaping at him. He was flooded instantly with hate. He hated her because his father had teased him. He hated her hair, hanging in tight pig-tails. He hated her freckles, more lavish than his own. He hated her squirrel-teeth, her hands, her feet, and every bone in her lank body. He leaned over swiftly and picked a small potato from a sack and lifted it. She eyed him venomously. Slowly, she flickered her tongue at him like a garter snake. She clasped two fingers over her nose in a gesture of malodorous disgust. He hurled the potato. It struck her on the shoulder and she retreated with shrieks of anguish.

Penny said, "Why, Jody."

Boyles advanced, frowning.

Penny said sternly, "Git right outen here. Mr. Boyles, he cain't have the mouth organ."

He went outside into the hot sunlight. He was humiliated. Yet if he had it to do over again, he would throw another potato at her, a larger one. When his business was done, Penny joined him.

He said, "I'm sorry you seed fit to shame me. Mebbe your

Ma's right. Mebbe you hadn't ought to have no truck with the Forresters."

Jody scuffled his feet in the sand.

"I don't keer. I hate her."

"I don't know what to say. How on earth come you to do it?"

"I jest hate her. She made a face at me. She's ugly."

"Well, son, you cain't go thru life chunkin' things at all the ugly women you meet."

Jody spat unrepentant in the sand.

"Well," Penny said, "I don't know what Grandma Hutto'll say."

"Oh Pa, don't tell her. Please don't tell her."

Penny was ominously silent.

"I'll be mannerly, Pa."

"I don't know whether she'll take this hide from you now or not."

"Leave me have it, Pa. I'll not chunk nothin' at nobody agin, if you'll not tell Grandma."

"All right. This time. But don't let me ketch you at sich as that agin. Take your deer-hide."

His spirits lifted. The menacing cloud moved away. They turned north up a path that paralleled the river. Magnolias were in bloom along it. Beyond, there was a lane of oleanders. These too were blossoming. Red-birds flew ahead down the lane. The oleanders led to a gate in a white picket fence. Grandma Hutto's flower garden was a bright patchwork quilt thrown down inside the pickets. Her small white cottage was bound to the substantial earth with vines of honeysuckle and jessamine. Everything here was dear and familiar. Jody ran down the path through the garden; through the patch of indigo, in feathery, rose-lavender bloom.

He called, "Hey! Grandma!"

Light steps sounded inside the cottage and she was on the door-step.

"Jody! You scamp."

He ran to her.

Penny called, "Don't knock her down, boy."

She braced her small frame. He squeezed her until she squeaked.

"You tormented bear cub," she said.

She began to laugh, and he tipped back his head to laugh with her and watch her face. It was pink and wrinkled. Her eyes were as black as gallberries. They opened and shut when she laughed, and the wrinkles rippled out from the sides. She shook up and down, and her small plump breast quivered like a quail dusting. Jody sniffed at her like a puppy.

He said, "Ummm, Grandma, you smell good."

Penny said, "That's more'n you kin say for us, Grandma. We're a dirty pair o' somebodies."

" 'Tain't nothin' but huntin' smell," Jody said. "Deer-hide and leaves and sich. And sweatin'."

"It's a dandy smell," she said. "I'm jest lonesome for boy-smell and man-smell."

Penny said, "Anyway, here's our excuse-us. Fresh venison."

"And the hide," Jody said. "For a rug for you. Hit's mine. I wounded it."

She lifted her hands in the air. Their gifts became at once of great value. It seemed to Jody that he could bring in a panther single-handed, in return for her approval. She touched meat and hide.

Penny said, "Now don't dirty them leetle hands."

She drew gallantry from men as the sun drew water. Her pertness enchanted them. Young men went away from her with a feeling of bravado. Old men were enslaved by her silver curls. Something about her was forever female and made all men virile. Her gift infuriated all women. Ma Baxter had returned to the clearing from her four years in her house with an acute dislike. The older woman returned it with good measure.

Penny said, "Leave me tote the meat to the kitchen. And I'd best tack the hide to your shed wall, to cure for you."

Jody called, "Here, Fluff!"

The white dog came racing. He bounded at Jody like a ball and leaped at his face to lick it.

Grandma said, "He's as proud to see you as if 'twas some of his kin-folks."

Fluff caught sight of old Julia, sitting sedately on her haunches. He stiffened and advanced to her. Julia sat without stirring, her long ears drooping.

Grandma said, "I like that dog. She looks jest like my Aunt Lucy."

Penny went to the rear of the cottage with the venison and the hide. They were all welcome here, father and son and battle-scarred hound. Jody felt more at home than when he returned to his own mother.

He said, "I reckon you wouldn't be so proud to see me, did you have to put up with me all the time."

Grandma chuckled.

"You've heard your Ma say that. Did she quarrel about you comin'?"

"Not so turrible as sometimes."

"Your father," she said tartly, "married a woman all Hell couldn't amuse."

She lifted a finger in the air.

"I'll bet you want to go swimmin'."

"In the river?"

"Smack in the river. When you come out, I'll give you clean clothes. Some of Oliver's."

She did not caution him against alligators or moccasins or

against the river current. It was good to have it taken for granted that he had a little sense of his own. He ran down the path to the landing. The river flowed deep and dark. It made a rippling sound against the banks, but the great liquid heart of it moved silently. Only the swift progress of fallen leaves showed the current. Jody hesitated a moment on the wooden landing, then dove in. He came up gasping with the coldness and struck upstream. He kept close to the bank, where the current ran less swiftly.

He made almost no progress. The dark vegetation towered on either side of the river. He was pinned between banks of live oaks and cypresses. He pretended that an alligator was behind him and swam desperately. He passed one spot and then, laboriously, another, dog-paddling. He wondered if he could swim as far as the upper landing, where the ferry crossed and the river steamers halted. He fought his way toward it. A cypress knee offered anchorage and he clung to it and caught his wind. He set out again. The landing looked far away. His shirt and breeches interfered with his freedom. He wished he had gone in naked. Grandma would not have minded. He wondered what his mother would have said if he had told her the Forresters had played and sung naked.

He looked over his shoulder. Hutto's landing had disappeared around the bend. He was suddenly not happy in the fluid darkness. He turned around. The current caught him and he shot downstream. He struggled to approach the bank. Watery tentacles held him. He thought in a panic that he might be swept on to Volusia Bar, to great Lake George itself, even, perhaps, the sea. He fought blindly, reaching for whatever might be solid under him. He found himself grounding a little above the landing. In relief, he drifted cautiously down to it and climbed up on the wooden platform. He drew a deep breath. The panic left him and he was exhilarated by the cold water and the danger. Penny was on the landing.

His father said, "That were right smart of a tussle. Reckon I'll jest ease around the edge to git me my wash."

He dropped cautiously from the landing.

He said, "Now I don't aim to take my feet offen the ground. My day for capers is over."

He came out of the water shortly. They returned to the rear of the cottage. Grandma Hutto had clean clothes waiting for them. For Penny, there were garments of the long-dead Mr. Hutto, musty with age. For Jody, there were shirt and breeches that Oliver had worn and outgrown many years ago.

Grandma said, "They say you git to use things again, if you save them, ever' seven years. How many is two times seven, Jody?"

"Fourteen."

Penny said, "Don't ask him no further. That school teacher me and the Forresters boarded last winter didn't scarcely know, hisself."

"Well, lots of things is more important than book-learnin'."

"I know that, but a feller needs to know to read and write and figger. But Jody's gittin' along right good with what I kin make out to learn him."

They dressed in the shed. They smoothed back their hair with their hands and felt clean and strange in the borrowed clothing. Jody's freckled face shone. His tawny hair lay wet and smooth. They put on their own shoes and wiped away the dust with their discarded shirts. Grandma Hutto called to them and they went into the cottage.

Jody smelled its familiar odor. He had never been able to disentangle its elements. The sweet lavender she used on her clothing was plain. There were dried grasses in a jar before the fire-place. There was the unmistakable smell of honey, which she kept in a cupboard. There was pastry; tarts and cookies and fruit cakes. There was the smell of the soap she used on Fluff's fur. There was the pervasive scent of flowers from the garden outside the windows. And above it all, it came to him at last, lay the smell of the river. The river itself was fluid through the cottage and around it, leaving a whirlpool of odorous dampness and decaying fern. He looked through the open door. A path led through marigolds to the water. The river shone in the late sunlight, Guinea-gold, like the bright flowers. Its flow drew Jody's mind with it to the ocean, where Oliver rode the storms in ships, and knew the world.

Grandma brought Scuppernong wine and spice cakes. Jody was allowed a glass of wine. It was as clear as Juniper Springs. Penny smacked his lips over it, but Jody wished it was something sweeter, blackberry shrub, perhaps. He ate spice cakes absently, and stopped in shame to see that he had emptied the plate. This, at home, would be catastrophe. Grandma went to the cupboard and filled the plate again.

She said, "Don't you spoil your dinner."

"I never know, 'til it's too late."

She went to the kitchen and he followed her. She began to slice venison to broil. He frowned anxiously. The meat was no great treat to the Baxters. She opened the oven door and he became aware that other things were being cooked. She had an iron cook stove. Food from it was more mysterious than from the open hearth at home. The closed door concealed all manner of things behind its black bosom. The cake had dulled his appetite a little, but the good odors brought it back again.

He wandered back and forth from Grandma to his father. Penny sat sunk in quiet in a padded chair in the front room. Shadows lay over him and absorbed him. There was not here the excitement of a visit to the Forresters. There was instead a snugness that covered him like a warm quilt in winter. It was meat and drink to Penny, harassed at home by all his duties. Jody offered to help in the kitchen, but Grandma sent him away. He rambled into the yard and played with Fluff. Old Julia watched them wonderingly. Romping was as alien to her as to her master. Her black and tan face wore the solemnity of the work-dog.

Dinner was ready. Grandma Hutto was the only person Jody knew who had a separate room to eat in. Every one else ate in the kitchen, from a scrubbed and bare pine table. Even as she brought in the food, he could not take his eyes from the white cloth and the blue plates.

Penny said, "Now we're a mighty sorry pair o' tramps to set down to all these pretties."

But he joked and gossiped with Grandma with an ease he did not have at his own table.

He said to her, "I'm surprised your sweetheart ain't showed up yit."

Her black eyes snapped.

"Anybody but you said that, Penny Baxter, he'd get pitched in the river."

"The way you done pore Easy hisself, eh?"

"Pity he didn't drown. A man that don't know when he's insulted."

"You'll be obliged to take him yit, to give you the legal right to throw him out."

Jody laughed boisterously. He could not listen to them and eat at the same time. He found himself getting behind and settled down to steady eating. There was a bass, fresh from Easy's fish-trap in the river, baked whole with a savory stuffing. The Irish potatoes were a treat, after the Baxter sweet potatoes three times a day. There was early mutton corn. The Baxters seldom ate new corn, for all that was raised seemed more desperately needed for the stock. Jody sighed with his inability to hold everything. He concentrated on light bread and mayhaw jelly.

Penny said, "He'll be so spoiled, his Ma'll have to break him in like a new bird-dog."

After dinner they walked together through the garden to

the river bank. Boats passed. The travellers waved to Grandma and she waved back. Toward sunset Easy Ozell turned into the path to the cottage to do the evening chores. Grandma eyed her approaching admirer.

"Now don't he look like the back end o' bad luck?"

Jody thought that Easy looked like a sick gray crane, with feathers draggled by the rain. His hair hung in gray wisps in his neck. He had a long thin gray mustache that drooped to his jaws. His arms hung like limp wings at his sides.

"Look at him," she said. "Tormented Yankee. His feet drag like a 'gator's tail."

"He shore ain't purty," Penny admitted, "but he's humble as a dog."

"I hate a pitiful man," she said. "And I hate anything is bow-legged. He's so bow-legged his breeches near about make a mark on the ground."

Easy shuffled back of the house. Jody heard him with the cow, and later at the wood-pile. When the evening's work was done, he came timidly to the front steps. Penny shook hands with him and Grandma nodded to him. He cleared his throat. Then as though his Adam's apple, working up and down, blocked his words, he gave up trying to speak and sat down on the bottom step. The talk flowed about him, and his gray face was bright with content. At twilight, Grandma disappeared inside the house. Easy rose stiffly to go.

He said to Penny, "My, if I could talk like you. Maybe she'd take to me better. You s'pose it's that, or won't she never forgive me, bein' a Yankee? If 'twas that, I'll declare, Penny, I'd spit on the flag."

"Well, you know a woman'll hold a idee like a 'gator'll hold a shoat. She cain't fergit the time the Yankees takened her needles and thread and she walked clean to St. Augustine with three hen's eggs to trade for a paper o' needles. Now if the Yankees had got beat, she'd mebbe forgive you."

"But I was beat, Penny. I myself was beat something awful. It was at Bull Run. You rebels whipped us something terrible. My, I hated it." His memories overcame him. He wiped his eyes. "You whipped us, and we was two to your one!"

He shuffled away.

"Now think o' that beat-down human aspirin' to Grandma," Penny said. "He's shore got a low eye for a high fence."

Inside the cottage, Penny tormented Grandma about Easy, as he had tormented Jody about Eulalie. But she gave back as good as she took, and the bout was good-natured. The subject reminded Jody of the matter that had been on his conscience.

He said, "Grandma, Lem Forrester said Twink Weatherby was his gal. I said she was Oliver's, and Lem didn't like it no leetle bit."

"Oliver'll likely take care o' Lem when he comes home," she said. "If a Forrester knows to fight fair."

She put them to bed in a room as white as the snow that Oliver told of. Jody stretched out beside his father between immaculate sheets.

He said, "Don't Grandma live nice?"

Penny said, "Hit's a way some women has." He added loyally, "But don't think hard o' your Ma for not doin' like Grandma. Your Ma ain't never had nothin' much to do with, and I'm to blame for that, not her. She cain't he'p it, livin' rough."

Jody said, "I wisht Grandma was really my Grandma. I wisht Oliver was shore enough kin."

"Well, folks that seems like kin-folks, is kin-folks. You ruther live here with Grandma?"

Jody pictured the cabin in the clearing. Hoot-owls would be crying, and perhaps the wolves would howl, or a panther scream. The deer would be drinking at the sink-hole, the bucks alone, the does with their fawns. The bear cubs would be curled up in their beds together. There was something at Baxter's Island that was better than white tablecloths and counterpanes.

"No, I'd not. I'd jest like to take Grandma home to live with us. But we'd have to make Ma mind her."

Penny chuckled.

"Pore boy," he said, "has got to grow up and learn women——"

· 12 ·

Jody heard the freight and passenger steamer pass the Hutto landing about daylight. He sat up in bed and looked out of the window. The lights of the steamer were pale under the early morning sky. The paddle wheels churned thickly through the water. The steamer blew its thin high whistle at Volusia. He thought he heard it stop and then go on up the river. Somehow, its passing concerned him. He could not go to sleep again. Outside in the yard old Julia growled. Penny stirred from his sleep. Watchfulness lived sentinel in his brain. Sounds no heavier than the wind aroused him.

He said, "The steamer stopped. Somebody's comin'."

Old Julia barked deeply, then whined and was still.

"Hit's somebody she knows."

Jody cried, "Hit's Oliver!" and jumped from the bed.

He ran naked through the cottage. Fluff awakened and dashed from his bed by Grandma's door, barking shrilly.

A voice shouted, "Turn out, you lazy landlubbers!"

Grandma ran from her bedroom. She had on a long white nightgown and a white nightcap. She fastened a shawl around her shoulders as she ran. Oliver took the steps in one bound like a buck and Jody and his mother were on him in a whirlwind. He lifted his mother by the waist and swung her. She thumped him with her small fists. Jody and Fluff yelped for attention. Oliver swung them in turn. Penny joined them sedately, fully dressed. They pumped hands in greeting. In the dim light of dawn, Oliver's teeth flashed white. Grandma's eye caught another flashing.

"Now you jest give me them ear-bobs, you pirate."

She stood on tip-toe to reach up to his ears. Gold hoops swung from the lobes. She unscrewed them and put them in her own ears. He laughed and shook her and Fluff barked in a frenzy. In the tumult, Penny spoke.

"Lord save us, Jody, you're plumb naked."

Jody froze in his tracks. He turned to run. Oliver caught him. Grandma pulled the shawl from her shoulders and tied it around his waist.

She said, "I'd of run naked, too, if I'd had to. Oliver don't come home but twice a year, do he, boy?"

He said, "Hit was dark when I set out, anyways."

The commotion quieted. Oliver picked up his duffel-bag and carried it inside. Jody trailed him.

"Where you been to this time, Oliver? Did you see whales?"

Penny said, "Leave the man ketch his breath, Jody. He cain't turn out tales for young uns like a spring turns water."

But Oliver was bursting with his tales.

"That's what a sailor comes home for," he said. "To see his Ma and his gal and to tell lies."

His ship had been in the tropics. Jody tore himself away

long enough to slip into his borrowed shirt and breeches. He called questions and Grandma called questions. The home-comer answered back and forth. Grandma dressed in a flow-ered dimity and arranged her silver curls with special care. She went to the kitchen to start breakfast. Oliver opened the mouth of his duffel-bag and dumped the contents in the middle of the floor.

Grandma said, "I can't look and cook at the same time."

Oliver said, "Then for the Lord's sake, Ma, cook."

"You're thin."

"I'm skin and bones, waitin' to get home to eat."

"Jody, come get that fire to roarin'. Slice that ham. Slice that bacon. Slice that venison."

She took bowls from cupboards, beat eggs and batter. Jody helped her, then ran back to Oliver. The sun rose and flooded the cottage. Oliver and Penny and Jody squatted on their haunches over the contents of the duffel-bag.

Oliver said, "I've got somethin' for everybody but Jody. Funny, I forgot him."

"You didn't. You ain't never yit forgot me."

"See can you pick out your present."

Jody passed over a roll of silk. That was of course for Grandma. He pushed aside Oliver's clothes, spiced and musty with strange foreign odors. A small packet was wrapped in flannel. Oliver took it out of his hands.

"That's for my gal."

A loose sack was filled with agates and translucent stones. Jody passed on. He lifted a parcel to his nose.

"T'baccy!"

"For your Pa. From Turkey."

"Why, Oliver." Penny opened it, marvelling. The rich aroma drifted across the room. "Why, Oliver. I cain't remember when I've had me a present."

Jody pinched a long narrow bundle. It was heavy and metallic.

"This is it!"

"You can't tell without seein' it."

Jody unwrapped the bundle madly. A hunting knife fell to the floor. The blade was keen and shining. Jody stared.

"Not a knife, Oliver——"

"Now if you'd rather have one of them ground-down files like your Pa has——"

Jody pounced. He swung the long blade to catch the light.

"There ain't nobody in the scrub," he said, "has got sich as that. Not even the Forresters has got sich a knife."

"That's what I figured. We can't let them black-beards get ahead of us."

Jody looked at the small flannel-swathed parcel Oliver held in one hand. He was torn between Oliver and the Forresters.

He burst out, "Oliver— Lem Forrester says Twink Weatherby is his gal."

Oliver laughed and tossed the parcel from one hand to the other.

He said, "No Forrester ever told the truth. Nobody takes my gal away from me."

Jody felt a wave of relief. He had told both Grandma and Oliver and washed his conscience clear, and Oliver was not disturbed. Then a memory came to him of Lem's dark face, brooding and sullen, as he scraped the strings of his fiddle. He put the picture from him. He sunk himself in the treasures his friend had brought home from far places across the sea.

Grandma, he noticed, did not touch her plate at breakfast. She kept Oliver's filled. Her bright eyes hovered over her son like hungry swallows. Oliver sat tall and straight at the table. His skin was bronzed where his shirt was open over his lean throat. His hair was sun-burned, with a red light in it. His eyes were the color which Jody imagined was the color of the sea, gray-blue, with a flashing of green. Jody ran his hand over his own snub nose and freckled skin. He felt surreptitiously across the back of his head, where the straw-colored drake's-tails stuck out stiffly. He was immensely dissatisfied with himself.

He asked, "Grandma, was Oliver borned good-lookin'?"

Penny said, "I kin answer that. I kin remember when he was uglier'n you and me both."

Oliver said complacently, "You'll grow up handsome as I am, Jody, if that's what's botherin' you."

"Jest half as handsome'd do," he said.

Oliver said, "I'll call you in to tell that to my gal today."

Grandma wrinkled her nose.

"Sailors belong to do their courtin' before they come home," she said.

"From what I hear," Penny offered, "sailors don't never quit courtin'."

"How about you, Jody?" Oliver asked. "You got a sweetheart yet?"

Penny said, "Why, ain't you heered, Oliver? Jody's sweet on Eulalie Boyles."

Jody felt a murderous fury creep over him. He wanted to roar like the Forresters and frighten every one with his rage. He stuttered.

"I—I hate girls. I hate Eulalie most of all."

Oliver said innocently, "Why, what's the matter with her?"

"I hate her ol' twitchy nose. She looks like a rabbit."

Oliver and Penny shouted and slapped each other.

Grandma said, "Now quit tormentin' the boy, both of you. Can't you remember that fur back, yourselves?"

His venom melted under his gratitude to her. Grandma was the only one who ever stood up for him. No, he thought, that was not true. Penny himself usually helped him fight his battles. When his mother was unreasonable, Penny always said, "Leave him be, Ory. I remember when I were a boy—" It came to him that his father only teased him here, in the hands of friends. When he needed help, Penny never failed him. He grinned.

He said to his father, "I jest dare you tell Ma I got a gal. She'd rare worse'n if I had me a varmint."

Grandma said, "Your Ma rares at you, do she?"

"At me and Pa both. Worse at Pa."

"She don't appreciate him," she said. "She jest don't know any better." She sighed. "A woman has got to love a bad man once or twice in her life, to be thankful for a good one."

Penny stared modestly at the floor. Jody was consumed with curiosity as to whether Mr. Hutto had been good or bad. He dared not ask. At any rate, Mr. Hutto had been so long dead that he supposed it no longer mattered. Oliver rose and stretched his long legs.

Grandma said, "You leavin' me, the very minute you get home?"

"Just for a little while. I got to go around and get acquainted in the neighborhood again."

"That little yellow-headed Twink, eh?"

"Sure." He leaned over her and tousled her curls. "Penny, you-all ain't goin' home today?"

"We got to do our tradin' and head for the scrub, Oliver. I hate it, I hate to miss the Sat'day frolic. We come on a Friday so's to git our venison to Boyles in time for the north boat today. And 'tain't right to leave Ory alone too long."

"No," Grandma said. "A panther might get her."

Penny looked at her quickly, but she was arranging the folds of her apron with great care.

Oliver said, "Well, see you over the river."

He was gone, slapping his sailor's cap on the back of his head. His whistle sounded after him. Jody was desolate. Something would happen to keep him from hearing Oliver's tales. He could feel it. He would have liked to sit on the river bank all morning while Oliver yarned. He had never had enough.

Oliver told a tale or two, and some one came, or Oliver stopped to do something else, and never finished.

"I ain't never yit had me a bait o' stories," he said.

Grandma said, "I've never had him long enough, neither." Penny loitered over his leaving.

"I hate to leave," he said, "pertickler, now Oliver's here."

"I miss Oliver worse," she said, "when he's here, and away from me, than when he's at sea."

Jody said, "Hit's Twink. Hit's gals does it. I don't never aim to have no gal."

He was resentful of Oliver's leaving them. The four of them made a close community, and Oliver had torn it to tatters. Penny basked in the peace of the cottage. He filled his pipe again and again with the foreign tobacco.

He said, "I do hate it, but we got to go. We got our tradin' to do, and hit's a fur piece home, a-foot."

Jody walked along the river bank and threw sticks for Fluff. He saw Easy Ozell running toward the cottage.

Easy called, "Git your Pa quick. Don't let Mis' Hutto hear."

Jody ran through the garden and called his father. Penny came outside.

Easy panted, "Oliver's fightin' the Forresters. He took a crack at Lem outside the store and all them fightin' Forresters come down on him. They're killin' him."

Penny ran for the store. Jody could not keep up with him. Easy trailed behind both of them.

Penny called over his shoulder, "I hope we kin settle it afore Grandma gits into it with a gun."

Jody called, "Pa, we fightin' for Oliver?"

"We're fightin' for whoever's takin' a lickin' and that's Oliver."

Jody's brain whirled like a wind-mill.

He said, "Pa, you said no man couldn't live on Baxter's Island without the Forresters was his friends."

"I said so. But I ain't goin' to see Oliver hurt."

Jody was numb. It seemed to him that Oliver deserved his punishment. He had gone away and left them, to see a girl. He was almost glad the Forresters were after him. Perhaps Oliver would come home from the fight and be done with his nonsense. Twink Weatherby— Jody spat into the sand. He thought of Fodder-wing. He could not bear never to be friends with him again.

He called to his father's back, "I ain't goin' to fight for Oliver."

Penny did not answer. His short legs churned. The fight was in the sandy road in front of the Boyles store. A cloud of dust rose ahead, like a whirlwind in the heat of summer. Jody heard the shouting of the watchers before he could make out the figures of the fighters. All of Volusia was there.

Penny panted, "That white 'possumed crowd don't keer who's kilt, long as they git to see a fight."

Jody saw Twink Weatherby on the outer circle. Men and women all called her pretty, but he wanted to tear out her soft yellow curls, one by one. Her small pointed face was white. Her wide blue eyes were fixed on the fighters. She twisted a handkerchief around and around in her fingers. Penny pushed his way through the crowd. Jody followed behind him. He clutched at his father's shirt.

It was true. The Forresters were killing Oliver. Oliver was fighting three of them at once, Lem and Mill-wheel and Buck. He looked like a buck deer Jody had once seen, wounded and bleeding, with the dogs tearing flesh from its throat and shoulders. Blood and sand covered his face. He was boxing warily, trying to take on one Forrester at a time. Lem and Buck rushed in on him together. Jody heard a heavy fist crack against bone. Oliver dropped in the sand. The crowd roared.

Jody's mind whirled in confusion. Oliver deserved it, for leaving the cottage and going to a girl. But three against one was never fair. Even when the dogs bayed a bear or panther, it seemed to him an uneven matter. The Forresters, his mother said, were black-hearted. He had never believed her. They sang and drank and frolicked and guffawed. They fed him lavishly and slapped him on the back and gave him Fodder-wing to play with. Was this black-hearted, for three to fight together against one? Yet Mill-wheel and Buck were fighting for Lem, keeping his girl for him. Was not that good? Was that not loyal? Oliver came to his knees, then wavered to his feet. He smiled through the dirt and blood. Jody's stomach turned over. Oliver was being killed.

Jody jumped on Lem's back. He clawed at his neck and thumped his head. Lem shook him off and turned and sent him sprawling. His face stung from the impact of the big hand. His hip ached from the fall.

Lem snapped, "You keep outen this, you leetle panther."

Penny called loudly, "Who's judgin' this fight?"

Lem said, "We're judgin' it."

Penny pushed in front of him. His voice was high against the shouting.

"If it take three men to whop one, I say that one is the better man."

Lem advanced on him.

He said, "I'm o' no mind to kill you, Penny Baxter. But I'll smack you flat as a skeeter if you don't git outen my way."

Penny said, "Fair is fair. If you aim to kill Oliver, shoot him honest and hang for murder. But be men."

Buck shuffled his feet in the sand.

He said, "We'd of fit him one at a time, but he lit right in."

Penny pressed his advantage.

"Whose fight is it? Who done what to who?"

Lem said, "He come back stealin', that's what he done."

Oliver wiped his sleeve across his face.

He said, "It's Lem that tried to steal."

"Steal what?" Penny pounded one fist inside the other. "Hounds, hogs, guns, or hosses?"

On the outer rim, Twink Weatherby began to cry.

Oliver said in a low voice, "This is no place to tell it, Penny."

"Then be this the place to fight it out? Like a pack o' dogs fightin' in the road? You two fellers fight it out alone another day."

Oliver said, "I'll fight a man anywhere, that says what Lem said."

Lem said, "And I'll say it again."

They started together. Penny pushed between them. He seemed to Jody like a small stout pine tree, bending against a hurricane. The crowd roared. Lem drew back his fist and struck Oliver over Penny's head. The blow sounded like the crack of a rifle. Oliver crumpled like a rag doll to the sand and lay still. Penny brought his knuckles under Lem's jaw. Buck and Mill-wheel came at him from the sides. Lem sunk his fist in Penny's ribs. Jody moved with a fury that caught him up from the outside, like a strong wind. He sunk his teeth in Lem's wrist. He kicked the big shins. Lem turned, like a bear annoyed by a puppy. He knocked Jody clear of his feet. It seemed to him that Lem struck him again in mid-air. He saw Oliver sway to his feet. He saw Penny's arms swinging like flails. He heard a roaring. It was close at first, then it faded. He dropped into blackness.

·13·

Jody thought, "I dreamed the fighting."

He stared at the ceiling in Grandma Hutto's spare bed-room. A freight steamer was thrashing up-stream. He heard the side-wheel paddles drinking the swift current of the river. They gulped great wet mouthfuls and let it spill out again. The steamer blew for the Volusia landing. He must certainly have only now awakened in the morning. The steamer's chugging filled the river bed and beat against the western wall that was the scrub. He had had a nightmare about Oliver Hutto, com-ing home to fight the Forresters. He turned his head to look out of the window and watch the passing vessel. A sharp pain shot through his neck and shoulder. He could only turn his head part-way. Memory went through him, thrusting like the pain.

He thought, "The fighting was true."

It was afternoon. The sun shone in the west across the river. A bright band lay across the counterpane. The pain stopped, but he felt faint and dizzy. There was movement in the room. A rocker creaked.

Grandma Hutto said, "His eyes are open."

He tried to turn his head toward her voice but could not, without pain. She leaned over him.

He said, "Hey, Grandma."

She spoke, not to him, but to his father.

"He's tough as you. He's all right."

Penny appeared on the other side of the bed. One wrist was bandaged and one eye was black. He grinned at Jody.

He said, "We was a big help, you and me."

A cold wet cloth slipped from Jody's forehead. Grandma took it away and laid her hand in its place. She reached her fingers back of his head and felt carefully for the source of pain. It was in his left jaw, where Lem had struck him, and in the back of his head, where he had hit the sand. It eased under her slow manipulation.

She said, "Say somethin', so I'll know your brains ain't jellied."

"I cain't think o' nothin' to say." He added, "Ain't it past dinner-time?"

Penny said, "The only serious hurt could come to him, is likely his belly."

He said, "I ain't hongry. I jest seed the sun and I was wonderin'."

She said, "That's all right, Punkin."

He asked, "Where's Oliver?"

"In the bed."

"Is he bad hurted?"

"Not bad enough to learn him sense."

"I don't know now," Penny said. "One more clip, and he'd not of had much left to learn with."

"Anyway, he's spoiled his pretty looks so no yellow-headed thing'll look at him for a while."

"You women is right smart hard on one another," Penny said. "Seems to me 'twas Oliver and Lem done most o' the lookin'."

Grandma rolled up the cold cloth and left the bedroom.

Penny said, " 'Twa'n't noways fair, gittin' a young un knocked dead. But I'm proud you was man enough to mix in it, when you seed a friend in trouble."

Jody stared at the sunlight.

He thought, "The Forresters are my friends, too."

As though he read his thoughts, Penny said, "This'll likely end neighborin' with the Forresters."

A twinge of pain shot from Jody's head into the pit of his stomach. He could not give up Fodder-wing. He decided that he would slip away some time and call to Fodder-wing from the bushes. He pictured the secret meeting. Perhaps they would be discovered and Lem would whip them both to death. Then Oliver would be sorry he had fought because of Twink Weatherby. Jody was more resentful at Oliver than at the Forresters. Something of Oliver that had belonged to him, and to Grandma, had been taken away and given to the yellow-headed girl who wrung her hands over the fighting.

Yet if he had it to do over again, he would still have to help Oliver. He recalled a wild-cat that the dogs had torn to pieces. Wild-cats deserved what they got. Yet at one moment, when the snarling mouth had gaped wide in agony, and the evil eyes had filmed in dying, he had been stabbed with pity. He had cried out, longing to help the creature in its torture. Too much pain was unjust. Too many against one were unjust. That was why it had been necessary to fight for Oliver, even if it lost him Fodder-wing. He closed his eyes, satisfied. Everything was all right when he understood it.

Grandma came into the bedroom with a tray.

"Now, Punkin, see can you sit up."

Penny slipped his hands under the pillow and Jody eased up slowly. He was stiff and sore, but he felt no worse than the time he had fallen out of the chinaberry tree.

Penny said, "I wisht pore Oliver had got off this light."

Grandma said, "He's lucky he didn't get his fine nose broke."

He ate his way painfully toward a plate of gingerbread. Because of the soreness, he was forced to leave a square. He looked at it.

Grandma said, "I'll save that for you."

Penny said, "Ain't it a treat, to have a woman reads your mind and then agrees with it."

"I mean."

Jody lay against his pillow. Violence broke into peace, and tore the world to tatters, and then, suddenly, all was peaceful again.

Penny said, "I got to be pushin' on. Ory'll be rarin'."

He stood in the doorway. He was a little stooped. He looked lonely.

Jody said, "I want to go with you."

Penny's face grew bright.

He said, "Now, boy." He was eager. "You shore you're fitten? Tell you what I'll do. Borry Boyles' ol' mare, the one goes home alone. We'll ride her back and turn her a-loose."

Grandma said, "Ora'll feel better about him, if he goes with you. I know what happens to Oliver where I can see him, ain't near as bad as what happens out of my sight."

Jody eased his body from the bed. He was dizzy. His head felt large and full. He was tempted to sink back on the smooth sheets.

Penny said, "Jody's a man, if I do say it."

He straightened and went to the door.

"Must I say good-by to Oliver?"

"Why, shore, but don't let on how bad he looks. He's proud."

He went to Oliver's room. Oliver's eyes were swollen shut, as though he had fallen in a nest of wasps. One cheek was purple. A white bandage was tied around his head. His lips were puffed. The fine sailor was laid low, and all because of Twink Weatherby.

Jody said, "Good-by, Oliver."

Oliver did not answer. Jody softened.

"I'm sorry Pa and me didn't git there quicker."

Oliver said, "Come here."

Jody went close to the bed.

"You do somethin' for me? Go tell Twink I'll meet her at the old grove Tuesday about dusk-dark."

Jody was frozen.

He burst out, "I won't do it. I hate her. Ol' yellow-headed somethin'."

"All right. I'll send Easy."

Jody scuffled the rug with one foot.

Oliver said, "I thought you were my friend."

Being friends, he thought, was a nuisance. Then he remembered the hunting knife and was filled with gratitude and shame.

"Well, all right. I don't want to, but I'll tell her."

Oliver laughed from the bed. He would laugh, Jody thought, if he lay dying.

"Good-by, Oliver."

"Good-by, Jody."

He left the room. Grandma was waiting.

He said, "It come out kind o' disappointin', didn't it, Grandma? Oliver fightin', and all."

Penny said, "Boy, be civil."

Grandma said, "The truth's civil enough. When bears with sore heads go courtin', there's always trouble. As long as this is the end and not the beginning——"

Penny said, "You know where to send for me."

They went down the path through the garden. Jody looked back over his shoulder. Grandma stood waving after them.

Penny stopped at Boyles' store for his supplies and for his forequarter of venison. Boyles was willing to lend the mare, if Penny would strap a length of good buckskin for boot laces on the saddle when he sent her home, in payment. The supplies, flour and coffee and powder and lead and shell cases for the new gun, were dropped in a sack. Boyles went to his lot and brought out the mare, saddled with a blanket.

"Don't turn her loose 'til morning," he said. "She can outrun a wolf, but I wouldn't want a panther dropping on her."

Penny turned away to lift his sacks. Jody sidled close to the storekeeper. He was reluctant to have his father know Oliver's secret.

He whispered, "I got to see Twink Weatherby. Where do she live?"

"What you want of her?"

"I got somethin' to say to her."

Boyles said, "A heap of us have something to say to her. Well, you'll have to bide your time. The young lady's put a kerchief on her yellow curls and slipped off on the freight boat to Sanford."

Jody felt a satisfaction as great as though he had driven her away himself. He borrowed a piece of paper and a thick pencil and printed a note to Oliver. It was laborious work, for his father's teachings had been supplemented only by one brief winter of instruction from the itinerant school teacher. He wrote:

Dear ollever; yor ol twinkk has dun gode up the rivver. im gladd. yor frend jody.

He read it over. He decided in favor of a greater kindness. He crossed out "im gladd" and wrote in its place "im sorry."

He felt virtuous. Something of the old glow for Oliver came back to him. Perhaps he could still hear his tales.

Crossing to the scrub side on the ferry, he stared down into the swift river. His thoughts were as turbulent as the current. Oliver had never failed him before. The Forresters were after all as rough as his mother insisted. He felt deserted. But he was sure Fodder-wing would not change. The gentle mind in the twisted body would be as aloof from the quarrel as his own. His father, of course, stood as unchangeable as the earth.

·14·

THE quail were nesting. The fluted covey call had been silent for some time. The coveys were dividing into pairs. The
cocks were sounding the mating call, clear and sweet and insistent.

One day in mid-June Jody saw a cock and a hen run from
the grape arbor with the scuttling hurry of paternity. He was
wise enough not to follow them, but prowled about under the
arbor until he found the nest. It held twenty cream-colored
eggs. He was careful not to touch them, for fear the quail
might desert them, as guineas did. A week later he went to the
arbor to look at the progress of the Scuppernongs. They were
like the smallest pellets of shot, but they were green and
sturdy. He lifted a length of vine, imagining the dusty golden
grapes in the late summer.

There was a stirring at his feet, as though the grass had exploded. The setting was hatched. The young quail, each no bigger than the end of his thumb, scattered like small wind-blown leaves. The mother quail cried out, and made alternate sorties after the brood, in defense, and at Jody, in attack. He stood quiet, as his father had taught him to do. The hen gathered her young together and took them away through the tall broom-sage grasses. Jody ran to find his father. Penny was working the field peas.

"Pa, the quail has hatched under the Scuppernong. And the grapes is makin'."

Penny rested on the plow handles. He was wet with sweat. He looked across the field. A hawk flew low, quartering.

He said, "If the hawks don't git the quail, and the 'coons don't git the Scuppernongs, we'll have a mighty good meal, about first frost."

Jody said, "I hate the hawks eatin' the quail, but I don't someway mind the 'coons eatin' the grapes."

"That's because you love quail-meat more'n you love grapes."

"No, 'tain't. Hit's because I hate hawks and I love 'coons."

"Fodder-wing learned you that," Penny said, "with all them pet 'coons."

"I reckon so."

"The hogs come up yit, boy?"

"Not yit."

Penny frowned.

"I purely hate to think the Forresters has trapped 'em. But they ain't never stayed off so long. If 'twas bears, they wouldn't all be gone to oncet."

"I been as far as the old clearin', Pa, and the tracks goes on west from there."

"Time I git done workin' these peas, we're jest obliged to take Rip and Julia and go track 'em."

"What'll we do, do the Forresters have 'em trapped?"

"Whatever we got to do, when the time comes."

"Ain't you skeert to face the Forresters agin?"

"No, for I'm right."

"Would you be skeert if you was wrong?"

"If I was wrong, I wouldn't face 'em."

"What'll we do, do we git beat up agin?"

"Take it for our share and go on."

"I'd ruther let the Forresters keep the hogs."

"And go without meat? A black eye'll quiet down a heap quicker'n a empty belly. You want to beg off goin'?"

He hesitated.

"I reckon not."

Penny turned back to his cultivating.

"Then go tell your Ma please Ma'am to fix us early supper."

Jody went to the house. His mother was rocking and sewing on the shady porch. A small blue-bellied lizard scuttled from under her chair. Jody grinned, thinking how quickly she would heave her frame from the rocker if she had known.

"Please, Ma'am, Pa says to fix us supper right now. We got to go huntin' the hogs."

"About time."

She finished her seam leisurely. He dropped on the step below her.

"We likely got to face the Forresters, Ma, if they got 'em trapped."

"Well, face 'em. Black-hearted thieves."

He stared at her. She had been furious at both him and his father because they had fought the Forresters at Volusia.

He said, "We're like to git beat up and bloodied agin, Ma."

She folded her sewing impatiently.

"Well, pity on us, we got to have our meat. Who'll git it if you don't?"

She went into the house. He heard her thumping the lid on the Dutch oven. He was confused. His mother talked much of "duty." He had always hated the very word. Why was it his duty to let the Forresters maul him again, to recover the hogs, if it had not been his duty to let them maul him in order to help his friend Oliver? It seemed more honorable to him to bleed for a friend than for a side of bacon. He sat idly, listening to the fluttered whirring of mocking-birds in the chinaberry. The jays were chasing the red-birds out of the mulberry trees. There was a squabble for food even in the safety of the clearing. But it seemed to him there was always enough here for every one. There was food and shelter for father and mother and son; for old Cæsar; for Trixie and her spotted calf; for Rip and Julia; for the chickens, clucking and crowing and scratching; for the hogs, grunting in at evening for a cob of corn; for the song-birds in the trees, and the quail nesting under the arbor; for all of these, there was enough at the clearing.

Out in the scrub, the war waged ceaselessly. The bears and wolves and panthers and wild-cats all preyed on the deer. Bears even ate the cubs of other bears, all meat being to their maws the same. Squirrels and wood-rats, 'possums and 'coons, must all scurry for their lives. Birds and small furred creatures cowered in the shadow of hawk and owl. But the clearing was safe. Penny kept it so, with his good fences, with Rip and old Julia, with a wariness that seemed to Jody to be unsleeping. Sometimes he heard a rustling in the night, and the door opened and closed, and it was Penny, slipping back to his bed from a silent hunt for some marauder.

There was intrusion back and forth, as well. The Baxters went into the scrub for flesh of deer and hide of wild-cat. And the predatory animals and the hungry varmints came into the clearing when they could. The clearing was ringed around with hunger. It was a fortress in the scrub. Baxter's Island was an island of plenty in a hungry sea.

He heard the trace chains clanking. Penny was returning to

the lot along the fence row. Jody ran ahead to open the lot gates for him. He helped with the unharnessing. He climbed the ladder into the loft and pitched down a forkful of cowpea hay into Cæsar's manger. There was no more corn and would not be until the summer's crop was made. He found a pile of hay with the dried peas still clinging to it and threw it down for Trixie. There would be more milk in the morning for both the Baxters and the spotted calf. The calf was inclined to leanness, for Penny was weaning it from the cow. The loft was heavy with heat, trapped under the thick hand-hewn slabs of the shingled roof. The hay crackled with a dry sweetness. It tickled his nostrils. He lay down in it a moment, abandoning himself to the resiliency. He was no more than comfortable when he heard his mother call. He scrambled down from the loft. Penny had finished milking. They went to the house together. Supper was on the table. There were only clabber and corn-bread, but there was enough.

Ma Baxter said, "You fellers try to git a shot at some meat while you're off."

Penny nodded.

"I'm totin' my gun o' purpose."

They set off to the west. The sun was still above the tree-tops. There had been no rain for several days, but now cumulus clouds were piled low in the north and west. From the east and south, a steel grayness crept toward the glaring brilliance of the west.

Penny said, "A good rain today'd near about leave us lay by the corn."

There was no breeze. The air lay over the road like a thick down comforter. It seemed to Jody that it was something that could be pushed away, if he could struggle up through it. The sand burned his bare calloused soles. Rip and Julia walked list-lessly, heads down, tails sagging, their tongues dripping from open jaws. It was not easy to follow the tracks of the hogs where the loose soil had been so long dry. Penny's eye was keener here than Julia's nose. The hogs had fed through the black-jack, crossed the abandoned clearing, and then headed for the prairie, where lily roots could be dug, and pools of cool water could be muddied and wallowed in. They did not range so far when food could be had close at home. Now was a barren and parlous season. There was no mast yet, of pine or oak or hickory, except what could be rooted deep under the leaves from last year's falling. Palmetto berries were still too green, even for the undiscerning taste of a hog. Three miles from Baxter's Island Penny crouched to examine the trail. He picked up a grain of corn and turned it over in his hand. He pointed to the hoof-marks of a horse.

"They baited them hogs," he said.

He straightened his back. His face was grave. Jody watched him anxiously.

"Well, son, we're obliged to follow."

"Clare to the Forresters?"

"Clare to wheresomever the hogs be. Mought be, we'll find 'em in a pen some'eres."

The trail zigzagged where the hogs had weaved back and forth for the scattered corn.

Penny said, "I kin understand the Forresters fightin' Oliver and I kin understand them rompin' on you and me. But I be dogged if I kin understand cold-out meanness."

A quarter of a mile beyond stood a rough hog-trap. It had been sprung but the pen was now empty. It was made of untrimmed saplings and a limber sapling had been baited to spring the gate behind the crowding hogs.

"Them rascals was nearby, waitin'," Penny said. "That pen wouldn't hold a hog no time."

A cart had turned around in the sand to the right of the pen. The wheel tracks led down a dim scrub road toward Forresters' Island.

Penny said, "All right, boy. Here's our way."

The sun was near the horizon. The cumulus clouds were white puff-balls, stained with the red and yellow wash of the sunset. The south was filled with darkness, like the smoke of gunpowder. A chill air moved across the scrub and was gone, as though a vast being had blown a cold breath and then passed by. Jody shivered and was grateful for the hot air that fell in behind it. A wild grape-vine trailed across the thin-rutted road. Penny leaned to pull it aside.

He said, "When there's trouble waitin' for you, you jest as good go to meet it."

The rattler struck him from under the grape-vine without warning. Jody saw the flash, blurred as a shadow, swifter than a martin, surer than the slashing claws of a bear. He saw his father stagger backward under the force of the blow. He heard him give a cry. He wanted to step back, too. He wanted to cry out with all his voice. He stood rooted to the sand and could not make a sound. It was lightning that had struck, and not a rattler. It was a branch that broke, it was a bird that flew, it was a rabbit running——

Penny shouted, "Git back! Hold the dogs!"

The voice released him. He dropped back and clutched the dogs by the scruff of their necks. He saw the mottled shadow lift its flat head, knee-high. The head swung from side to side, following his father's slow motions. He heard the rattles hum. The dogs heard. They winded. The fur stood stiff on their bodies. Old Julia whined and twisted out of his hand. She turned and slunk down the trail. Her long tail clung to her hindquarters. Rip reared on his hind feet, barking.

As slowly as a man in a dream, Penny backed away. The rattles sung. They were not rattles— Surely it was a locust humming. Surely it was a tree-frog singing— Penny lifted his gun to his shoulder and fired. Jody quivered. The rattler coiled and writhed in its spasms. The head was buried in the sand. The contortions moved down the length of the thick body, the rattles whirred feebly and were still. The coiling flattened into slow convolutions, like a low tide ebbing. Penny turned and stared at his son.

He said, "He got me."

He lifted his right arm and gaped at it. His lips lifted dry over his teeth. His throat worked. He looked dully at two punctures in the flesh. A drop of blood oozed from each.

He said, "He was a big un."

Jody let go his hold on Rip. The dog ran to the dead snake and barked fiercely. He made sorties and at last poked the coils with one paw. He quieted and snuffed about in the sand. Penny lifted his head from his staring. His face was like hickory ashes.

He said, "Ol' Death goin' to git me yit."

He licked his lips. He turned abruptly and began to push through the scrub in the direction of the clearing. The road would be shorter going, for it was open, but he headed blindly for home in a direct line. He plowed through the low scrub oaks, the gallberries, the scrub palmettos. Jody panted behind him. His heart pounded so hard that he could not see where he was going. He followed the sound of his father's crashing across the undergrowth. Suddenly the denseness ended. A patch of higher oaks made a shaded clearing. It was strange to walk in silence.

Penny stopped short. There was a stirring ahead. A doe-deer leaped to her feet. Penny drew a deep breath, as though breathing were for some reason easier. He lifted his shotgun and leveled it at the head. It flashed over Jody's mind that his father had gone mad. This was no moment to stop for game. Penny fired. The doe turned a somersault and dropped to the sand and kicked a little and lay still. Penny ran to the body and drew his knife from its scabbard. Now Jody knew his father was insane. Penny did not cut the throat, but slashed into the belly. He laid the carcass wide open. The pulse still throbbed in the heart. Penny slashed out the liver. Kneeling, he changed his knife to his left hand. He turned his right arm and stared again at the twin punctures. They were now closed. The forearm was thick-swollen and blackening. The sweat stood out on his forehead. He cut quickly across the wound. A dark blood gushed and he pressed the warm liver against the incision.

He said in a hushed voice, "I kin feel it draw——"

He pressed harder. He took the meat away and looked at it. It was a venomous green. He turned it and applied the fresh side.

He said, "Cut me out a piece o' the heart."

Jody jumped from his paralysis. He fumbled with the knife. He hacked away a portion.

Penny said, "Another."

He changed the application again and again.

He said, "Hand me the knife."

He cut a higher gash in his arm where the dark swelling rose the thickest. Jody cried out.

"Pa! You'll bleed to death!"

"I'd ruther bleed to death than swell. I seed a man die——"

The sweat poured down his cheeks.

"Do it hurt bad, Pa?"

"Like a hot knife was buried to the shoulder."

The meat no longer showed green when he withdrew it. The warm vitality of the doe's flesh was solidifying in death. He stood up.

He said quietly, "I cain't do it no more good. I'm goin' on home. You go to the Forresters and git 'em to ride to the Branch for Doc Wilson."

"Reckon they'll go?"

"We got to chance it. Call out to 'em quick, sayin', afore they chunk somethin' at you or mebbe shoot."

He turned back to pick up the beaten trail. Jody followed. Over his shoulder he heard a light rustling. He looked back. A spotted fawn stood peering from the edge of the clearing, wavering on uncertain legs. Its dark eyes were wide and wondering.

He called out, "Pa! The doe's got a fawn."

"Sorry, boy. I cain't he'p it. Come on."

An agony for the fawn came over him. He hesitated. It tossed its small head, bewildered. It wobbled to the carcass of the doe and leaned to smell it. It bleated.

Penny called, "Git a move on, young un."

Jody ran to catch up with him. Penny stopped an instant at the dim road.

"Tell somebody to take this road in to our place and pick me up in case I cain't make it in. Hurry."

The horror of his father's body, swollen in the road, washed over him. He began to run. His father was plodding with a slow desperation in the direction of Baxter's Island.

Jody ran down the wagon trail to the myrtle thicket where it branched off into the main road to Forresters' Island. The road, much used, had no growth of weeds or grass to make a footing. The dry shifting sand caught at the soles of his feet and seemed to wrap clinging tentacles around the muscles of his legs. He dropped into a short dog-trot that seemed to pull more steadily against the sand. His legs moved, but his mind and body seemed suspended above them, like an empty box on a pair of cart-wheels. The road under him was a treadmill. His legs pumped up and down, but he seemed to be passing the same trees and bushes again and again. His pace seemed so slow, so futile, that he came to a bend with a dull surprise. The curve was familiar. He was not far from the road that led directly into the Forrester clearing.

He came to the tall trees of the island. They startled him, because they meant that he was now so close. He came alive and he was afraid. He was afraid of the Forresters. And if they refused him help, and he got safely away again, where should he go? He halted a moment under the shadowy live oaks, planning. It was twilight. He was sure it was not time for darkness. The rain clouds were not clouds, but an infusion of the sky, and had now filled it entirely. The only light was a strand of green across the west, the color of the doe's flesh with the venom on it. It came to him that he would call to his friend Fodder-wing. His friend would hear him and come, and he might be allowed to approach close enough to tell his errand. It eased his heart to think of it, to think of his friend's eyes gentle with sorrow for him. He drew a long breath and ran wildly down the path under the oak trees.

He shouted, "Fodder-wing! Fodder-wing! Hit's Jody!"

In an instant now his friend would come to him from the house, crawling down the rickety steps on all fours, as he must do when in a hurry. Or he would appear from the bushes with his raccoon at his heels.

"Fodder-wing! Hit's me!"

There was no answer. He broke into the swept sandy yard.

"Fodder-wing!"

There was an early light lit in the house. A twist of smoke curled from the chimney. The doors and shutters were closed against the mosquitoes and against the night-time. The door swung open. In the light beyond, he saw the Forrester men rise to their feet, one after the other, as though the great trees in the forest lifted themselves by their roots and stirred toward him. He stopped short. Lem Forrester advanced to the stoop. He lowered his head and turned it a little sideways until he recognized the intruder.

"You leetle bastard. What you after here?"

Jody faltered, "Fodder-wing——"

"He's ailin'. You cain't see him no-ways."

It was too much. He burst out crying.

He sobbed, "Pa— He's snake-bit."

The Forresters came down the steps and surrounded him.

He sobbed loudly, with pity for himself and for his father, and because he was here at last and something was finished that he had set out to do. There was a stirring among the men, as though the leavening quickened in a bowl of bread-dough.

"Where's he at? What kind o' snake?"

"A rattlesnake. A big un. He's makin' it for home but he don't know kin he make it."

"Is he swellin'? Where'd it git him?"

"In the arm. Hit's bad swelled a'ready. Please ride for Doc Wilson. Please ride for him quick, and I won't he'p Oliver agin you no more. Please."

Lem Forrester laughed.

"A skeeter promises he won't bite," he said.

Buck said, "Hit's like not to do no good. A man dies right now, bit in the arm. He'll likely be dead afore Doc kin git to him."

"He shot a doe-deer and used the liver to draw out the pizen. Please ride for Doc."

Mill-wheel said, "I'll ride for him."

Relief flooded him like the sun.

"I shore thank you."

"I'd he'p a dog, was snake-bit. Spare your thanks."

Buck said, "I'll ride on and pick up Penny. Walkin's bad for a man is snake-bit. My God, fellers, we ain't got a drop o' whiskey for him."

Gabby said, "Ol' Doc'll have some. If he's purty tol'able sober, he'll have some left. If he's drunk all he's got, he kin blow his breath, and that'll make a powerful portion."

Buck and Mill-wheel turned away with torturing deliberation to the lot to saddle their horses. Their leisureliness frightened Jody as speed would not have done. If there was hope for his father, they would be hurrying. They were as slow and unconcerned as though they were burying Penny, not riding for assistance. He stood, desolate. He would like to see Fodder-

wing just a moment before he went away. The remaining Forresters turned back up the steps, ignoring him.

Lem called from the door, "Git goin', Skeeter."

Arch said, "Leave the young un be. Don't torment him,
and his daddy likely dyin'."

Lem said, "Die and good riddance. Biggety bantam."

They went into the house and closed the door. A panic came
over Jody, that they did not mean, any of them, to help at all;
that Buck and Mill-wheel had gone away to the corral for a
joke, and were laughing at him there. He was forsaken, and
his father was forsaken. Then the two men rode out and Buck
lifted his hand to him, not unkindly.

"No use to fret, boy. We'll do what we kin. We don't hold
nothin' agin folks in trouble."

They touched their heels to the horses' flanks and shot away.
Lightness filled him where he had been heavy as lead. It was
only Lem, then, who was an enemy. He settled his hate on him
with satisfaction. He listened until the hoof-beats faded from
his hearing, then set out down the road for home.

Now he was free to accept the facts. A rattlesnake had struck
his father, who might die of it. But help was on the way, and
he had done what he was supposed to do. His fear had a name,
and was no longer quite so terrible. He decided not to try to
run, but to walk steadily. He should have liked to ask the loan
of a horse for himself, but dared not.

A pattering of rain passed over him. A hush followed. The
storm might go around the scrub entirely, as often happened.
There was a faint luminosity in the air around him. He had
scarcely been conscious that he was carrying his father's gun.
He swung it over one shoulder and walked rapidly where the
road was firm. He wondered how long it would take Mill-
wheel to reach the Branch. He wondered, not whether old Doc
would be drunk, for that was known, but just how drunk he
would be. If Doc could sit up in bed, he was considered fit to go.

He had been at Doc's place once when he was very young. He remembered still the sprawling house with wide verandas, decaying, as old Doc was decaying, in the heart of a dense vegetation. He remembered the cockroaches and the lizards, as much at home inside the house as in the thick vines outside it. He remembered old Doc, deep in his cups, lying under a mosquito canopy, staring at the ceiling. When he was called, he sprawled to his feet and went about his business on uncertain legs, but with gentle heart and hands. He was known far and wide as a good doctor, drunk or no. If he could be reached in time, Jody thought, his father's life was certain.

He turned from the Forresters' lane into the road that ran east to his father's clearing. He had four miles ahead of him. On hard ground, he could make it in little over an hour. The sand was soft, and the very darkness seemed to hold him back and make his steps uneven. He would do well to reach home in an hour and a half, and it might take two. He broke now and then into a trot. The brightness in the air dropped into the darkness of the scrub like a water turkey dropping into the river. The growth on either side of the road pressed closer, so that the way was narrow.

He heard thunder in the east, and a flash of lightning filled the sky. He thought he heard foot-steps in the scrub oaks, but it was drops of rain, striking like shot on the leaves. He had never minded night or darkness, but Penny had always been in front of him. Now he was alone. He wondered, sickened, whether his father lay now in the road ahead of him, swollen with poison, or perhaps across Buck's saddle, if Buck had reached and found him. The lightning flashed again. He had sat with his father through many storms, under the live oaks. The rain had then been friendly, shutting them in together.

A snarl sounded in the bushes. Something incredibly swift flashed across the road in front of him and was gone, soundlessly. A musky taint lay on the air. He was not afraid of lynx or wild-cat, but a panther had been known to attack a horse. His heart thumped. He fingered the stock of his father's gun. It was useless, for Penny had shot both barrels, one at the rattler, one at the doe. He had his father's knife in his belt, and wished he had brought the long knife Oliver had given him. He had no scabbard for it, and it was dangerously sharp, Penny had said, to carry. When he was safe at home, lying under the grape arbor, or at the bottom of the sink-hole, he had pictured himself thrusting it with one sure plunge into the heart of bear or wolf or panther. There was no flush of pride now in the picture. A panther's claws were quicker than he.

Whatever the animal, it had gone its way. He walked more rapidly, stumbling in his haste. He thought he heard a wolf howl, but it was so far away that it might only have been the wind. The wind was rising. He heard it far off in the distance. It was as though it were blowing in another world, across a dark abyss. Suddenly it swelled. He heard it coming closer, like a moving wall. The trees ahead thrashed their limbs. The bushes rattled and flattened to the ground. There was a great roaring and the storm hit him like a blow.

He lowered his head and fought against it. He was drenched to the skin in an instant. The rain poured down the back of his neck and washed through his breeches. His clothes hung heavily and held him back. He stopped and turned his back to the wind and propped the gun at the side of the road. He took off his shirt and breeches and rolled them into a bundle. He took up the gun and went on naked through the storm. The rain on his bare skin made him feel clean and free. The lightning flashed and he was startled by his own whiteness. He felt suddenly defenceless. He was alone and naked in an unfriendly world; lost and forgotten in the storm and darkness. Something ran behind him and ahead of him. It stalked the scrub like a panther. It was vast and formless and it was his enemy. Ol' Death was loose in the scrub.

It came to him that his father was already dead, or dying. The burden of the thought was intolerable. He ran faster, to shake it off. Penny could not die. Dogs could die, and bears and deer and other people. That was acceptable, because it was remote. His father could not die. The earth might cave in under him in one vast sink-hole and he could accept it. But without Penny, there was no earth. Without him there was nothing. He was frightened as he had never been before. He began to sob. His tears ran salt into his mouth.

He begged of the night, as he had begged of the Forresters, "Please——"

His throat ached and his groins were shot with hot lead. The lightning showed an opening ahead of him. He had reached the abandoned clearing. He darted into it and crouched against the old rail fence for a moment's shelter. The wind washed over him more coldly than the rain. He shivered and rose and went on again. The stop had chilled him. He wanted to run, to warm himself, but he had strength only to plod slowly. The rain had packed the sand so that the walking was firm and easier. The wind lessened. The down-pour settled into a steady falling. He walked on in a dull misery. It seemed to him that he must walk forever, but suddenly he was passing the sink-hole and was at the clearing.

The Baxter cabin was bright with candles. Horses whinnied and pawed the sand. There were three tethered to the slat fence. He passed through the gate and into the cabin. Whatever was, was done. There was no bustle to greet him. Buck and Mill-wheel sat by the empty hearth, tilted back in their chairs. They were talking casually. They glanced at him, said "Hey, boy," and went on with their talk.

"You wasn't here, Buck, when ol' man Twistle died o' snake-bite. Penny must o' been right about whiskey not doin' no good. Twistle were drunk as a coot when he stepped on the rattler."

"Well, do I ever git snake-bit, fill me full jest for luck. I'd ruther die drunk than sober, ary day."

Mill-wheel spat into the fireplace.

"Don't fret," he said. "You will."

Jody was faint. He dared not ask them the question. He walked past them and into his father's bedroom. His mother sat on one side of the bed and Doc Wilson sat on the other. Old Doc did not turn his head. His mother looked at him and rose without speaking. She went to a dresser and took out a fresh shirt and breeches and held them out to him. He dropped his wet bundle and stood the gun against the wall. He walked slowly to the bed.

He thought, "If he's not dead now, he'll not die."

In the bed, Penny stirred. Jody's heart leaped like a rabbit jumping. Penny groaned and retched. Doc leaned quickly and held a basin for him and propped his head. Penny's face was dark and swollen. He vomited with the agony of one who has nothing to emit, but must vomit still. He fell back panting. Doc reached inside the covers and drew out a brick wrapped in flannel. He handed it to Ma Baxter. She laid Jody's garments at the foot of the bed and went to the kitchen to heat the brick again.

Jody whispered, "Is he bad?"

"He's bad, a'right. Looks as if he'd make it. Then again, looks as if he won't."

Penny opened his puffed eyes. The pupils were dilated until his eyes seemed black. He moved his arm. It was swollen as thick as a bullock's thigh.

He murmured thickly, "You'll ketch cold."

Jody fumbled for his clothes and pulled them on. Doc nodded.

"That's a good sign, knowin' you. That's the first he's spoken."

A tenderness filled Jody that was half pain, half sweetness.

In his agony, his father was concerned for him. Penny could not die. Not Penny.

He said, "He's obliged to make it, Doc, sir." He added, as he had heard his father say, "Us Baxters is all runty and tough."

Doc nodded.

He called to the kitchen, "Let's try some warm milk now."

With hope, Ma Baxter began to sniffle. Jody joined her at the hearth.

She whimpered, "I don't see as we'd deserve it, do it happen."

He said, "Hit'll not happen, Ma." But his marrow was cold again.

He went outside for wood to hurry the fire. The storm was moving on to the west. The clouds were rolling like battalions of marching Spaniards. In the east, bright spaces showed, filled with stars. The wind blew fresh and cool. He came in with an armful of fatwood.

He said, "Hit'll be a purty day tomorrow, Ma."

"Hit'll be a purty day iffen he's yit alive when day comes." She burst into tears. They dropped on the hearth and hissed. She lifted her apron and wiped her eyes. "You take the milk in," she said. "I'll make Doc and me a cup o' tea. I hadn't et nothin', waitin' for you-all, when Buck carried him in."

He remembered that he had eaten lightly. He could think of nothing that would taste good. The thought of food on his tongue was a dry thought, without nourishment or relish. He carried the cup of hot milk carefully, balancing it in his hands. Doc took it from him and sat close to Penny on the bed.

"Now boy, you hold his head up while I spoon-feed him."

Penny's head was heavy on the pillow. Jody's arms ached with the strain of lifting it. His father's breathing was heavy, like the Forresters when they were drunk. His face had changed color. It was green and pallid, like a frog's belly. At first his teeth resisted the intruding spoon.

Doc said, "Open your mouth before I call the Forresters to open it."

The swollen lips parted. Penny swallowed. A portion of the cupful went down. He turned his head away.

Doc said, "All right. But if you lose it, I'm comin' back with more."

Penny broke into a sweat.

Doc said, "That's fine. Sweatin's fine, for poison. Lord of the jay-birds, if we weren't all out of whiskey, I'd make you sweat."

Ma Baxter came to the bedroom with two plates with cups of tea and biscuits on them. Doc took his plate and balanced it on his knee. He drank with a mixture of gusto and distaste.

He said, "It's all right, but 'tain't whiskey."

He was the soberest Jody had ever heard of his being.

"A good man snake-bit," he said mournfully, "and the whole county out of whiskey."

Ma Baxter said dully, "Jody, you want somethin'?"

"I ain't hongry."

His stomach was as queasy as his father's. It seemed to him that he could feel the poison working in his own veins, attacking his heart, churning in his gizzard.

Doc said, "Blest if he ain't goin' to keep that milk down."

Penny was in a deep sleep.

Ma Baxter rocked and sipped and nibbled.

She said, "The Lord watches the sparrer's fall. Mought be He'll take a hand for the Baxters."

Jody went into the front room. Buck and Mill-wheel had lain down on the deer-skin rugs on the floor.

Jody said, "Ma and Doc's eatin'. You-all hongry?"

Buck said, "We'd jest done et when you come. Don't pay us no mind. We'll sleep here and wait-see how it comes out."

Jody crouched on his heels. He would have liked to talk with them. It would be good to talk of dogs and guns and hunting, of all the things that living men could do. Buck snored. Jody tiptoed back to the bedroom. Doc was nodding in his chair. His mother moved the candle from the bed-side and returned to her rocker. The runners swished a while and then were still. She too nodded.

It seemed to Jody that he was alone with his father. The vigil was in his hands. If he kept awake, and labored for breath with the tortured sleeper, breathing with him and for him, he could keep him alive. He drew a breath as deep as the ones his father was drawing. It made him dizzy. He was light-headed and his stomach was empty. He knew he would feel better if he should eat, but he could not swallow. He sat down on the floor and leaned his head against the side of the bed. He began to think back over the day, as though he walked a road backward. He could not help but feel a greater security here beside his father, than in the stormy night. Many things, he realized, would be terrible alone that were not terrible when he was with Penny. Only the rattlesnake had kept all its horror.

He recalled the triangular head, the lightning flash of its striking, the subsidence into alert coils. His flesh crawled. It seemed to him he should never be easy in the woods again. He recalled the coolness of his father's shot, and the fear of the dogs. He recalled the doe and the horror of her warm meat against his father's wound. He remembered the fawn. He sat upright. The fawn was alone in the night, as he had been alone. The catastrophe that might take his father, had made it motherless. It had lain hungry and bewildered through the thunder and rain and lightning, close to the devastated body of its dam, waiting for the stiff form to arise and give it warmth and food and comfort. He pressed his face into the hanging covers of the bed and cried bitterly. He was torn with hate for all death and pity for all aloneness.

· 15 ·

Jody moved through a tortuous dream. With his father beside him, he fought a nest of rattlesnakes. They crawled across his feet, trailing their rattles, clacking lightly. The nest resolved itself into one snake, gigantic, moving toward him on a level with his face. It struck and he tried to scream but could not. He looked for his father. He lay under the rattler, with his eyes open to a dark sky. His body was swollen to the size of a bear. He was dead. Jody began to move backward away from the rattler, one agonized step at a time. His feet were glued to the ground. The snake suddenly vanished and he stood alone in a vast windy place, holding the fawn in his arms. Penny was gone. A sense of sorrow filled him so that he thought his heart would break. He awakened, sobbing.

He sat up on the hard floor. Day was breaking over the clearing. A pale light lay in streaks beyond the pine trees. The room was filled with grayness. For an instant he was still conscious of the fawn against him. Then he remembered. He scrambled to his feet and looked at his father.

Penny was breathing with a greater ease. He was still swollen and fevered, but he looked no worse than when the wild honey bees had stung him. Ma Baxter was asleep in her rocker with her head thrown far back. Old Doc lay across the foot of the bed.

Jody whispered, "Doc!"

Doc grunted and lifted his head.

"What is it—what is it—what is it?"

"Doc! Look at Pa!"

Doc shifted his body and eased himself on one elbow. He blinked and rubbed his eyes. He sat up. He leaned over Penny.

"Lord o' the jay-birds, he's made it."

Ma Baxter said, "Eh?"

She sat upright.

"He dead?"

"Not by a long sight."

She burst out crying.

Doc said, "You sound like you're sorry."

She said, "You jest don't know what 'twould mean, him leavin' us here."

Jody had never heard her speak so gently.

Doc said, "Why, you got you another man here. Look at Jody, now. Big enough to plow and reap and do the huntin'."

She said, "Jody's a'right, but he ain't a thing but boy. Got his mind on nothin' but prowlin' and playin'."

He hung his head. It was true.

She said, "His Pa encourages him."

Doc said, "Well, boy, be glad you got encouragement. Most of us live our lives without it. Now, Ma'am, let's get some more milk down this feller, time he wakes."

Jody said eagerly, "I'll go milk, Ma."

She said with satisfaction, "About time."

He passed through the front room. Buck was sitting up on the floor, rubbing his head sleepily. Mill-wheel was still asleep.

Jody said, "Doc says Pa's done made it."

"I be dogged. I woked up, fixin' to go he'p bury him."

Jody went around the side of the house and took down the milk-gourd from the wall. He felt as light as the gourd. It seemed to him in his liberation that he might spread his arms and float over the gate like a feather. The dawn was still nebulous. A mocking-bird made a thin metallic sound in the chinaberry. The Dominick rooster crowed uncertainly. This was the hour at which Penny arose, allowing Jody to sleep a little later. The morning was still, with a faint fluttering of breeze through the tops of the tall pine trees. The sunrise reached long fingers into the clearing. As he clicked the lot-gate, doves flew from the pines with a whistling of wings.

He called exultantly after them. "Hey, doves!"

Trixie lowed, hearing him. He climbed into the loft for fodder for her. She was very patient, he thought, giving her milk in return for so poor a feeding. She munched hungrily. She lifted a hind leg once in threat when he was clumsy with the milking. He stripped two teats carefully, then turned the calf in with her to nurse on the other two. There was not as much milk as his father would have gotten from her. He decided that he would drink none himself so that his father might have all of it until he was well again.

The calf butted the sagging udders and sucked noisily. It was too big still to be nursing. The thought of the fawn returned to him. A leaden feeling came over him again. It would be desperate with hunger this morning. He wondered if it would try to nurse the cold teats of the doe. The open flesh of the dead deer would attract the wolves. Perhaps they had found the fawn and had torn its soft body to ribbons. His joy in the morning, in his father's living, was darkened and tainted. His mind followed the fawn and would not be comforted.

His mother took the milk-gourd without comment on the quantity. She strained the milk and poured a cupful and took it to the sick room. He followed her. Penny was awake. He smiled weakly.

He whispered thickly, "Ol' Death got to wait a while on me."

Doc said, "You belong to be kin to the rattlesnakes, man. How you done it without whiskey, I don't know."

Penny whispered, "Why, Doc, I'm a king snake. You know a rattler cain't kill a king snake."

Buck and Mill-wheel came into the room. They grinned.

Buck said, "You ain't purty, Penny, but by God, you're alive."

Doc held the milk to Penny's lips. He swallowed thirstily.

Doc said, "I can't take much credit for savin' you. Your time just hadn't come to make a die of it."

Penny closed his eyes.

He said, "I could sleep a week."

Doc said, "That's what I want you to do. I can't do no more for you."

He stood up and stretched his legs.

Ma Baxter said, "Who'll do the farmin' and him asleep?"

Buck said, "What's he got, belongs to be done?"

"Mostly the corn, needs another workin' to be laid by. The 'taters needs hoein', but Jody's right good at hoein', do he choose to stick to it."

"I'll stick, Ma."

Buck said, "I'll stay and work the corn and sich."

She was flustered.

She said stiffly, "I hates to be beholden to you."

"Hell, Ma'am, they ain't too many of us shiftin' for a livin' out here. I'd be a pore man, didn't I not stay."

She said meekly, "I'm shore obliged. If the corn don't make, we jest as good all three to die o' snake-bite."

Doc said, "This is the soberest I've waked up since my wife died. I'd be proud to eat breakfast before I go."

She bustled to the kitchen. Jody went to build up the fire.

She said, "I never figgered I'd be beholden to a Forrester."

"Buck ain't exactly a Forrester, Ma. Buck's a friend."

"Hit do look that-a-way."

She filled the coffee-pot with water and added fresh coffee to the grounds.

She said, "Go to the smoke-house and git that last side o' bacon. I'll not be out-done."

He brought it proudly. She allowed him to slice the meat.

He said, "Ma, Pa shot a doe and used the liver to draw out the pizen. He bled hisself and then laid on the liver."

"You should of carried back a haunch o' the meat."

"There wasn't no time to figger on sich as that."

"That's right, too."

"Ma, the doe had a fawn."

"Well, most does has fawns."

"This un was right young. Nigh about new-borned."

"Well, what about it? Go set the table. Lay out the brier-berry jelly. The butter's right strong but it's yit butter. Lay it out, too."

She was stirring up a cornpone. The fat was sizzling in the skillet. She poured in the batter. The bacon crackled in the pan. She turned and flattened the slices, so that they would brown evenly. He wondered if they would ever be able to fill up Buck and Mill-wheel, accustomed to the copiousness of Forrester victuals.

He said, "Make a heap o' gravy, Ma."

"Iffen you'll do without your milk, I'll make milk-gravy."

The sacrifice was nothing.

He said, "We could of kilt a chicken."

"I studied on it, but they're all too young or too old."

She turned the cornpone. The coffee began to boil.

He said, "I could of shot some doves or some squirrels this mornin'."

"A fine time to think of it. Go tell the men-folks to wash theirselves and come to table."

He called them. The three men went outside to the water-shelf and slapped water over their faces, dabbled their hands. He brought them a clean towel.

Doc said, "Blest if I don't get hungry when I'm sober."

Mill-wheel said, "Whiskey's a food. I could live on whiskey."

Doc said, "I've near about done it. Twenty years. Since my wife died."

Jody was proud of the table. There were not as many different dishes as the Forresters served, but there was enough of everything. The men ate greedily. At last they pushed away their plates and lit their pipes.

Mill-wheel said, "Seems like Sunday, don't it?"

Ma Baxter said, "Sickness allus do seem like Sunday, someway. Folks settin' around, and the men not goin' to the field."

Jody had never seen her so amiable. She had waited to eat until the men were done, for fear of their not having plenty. She sat now eating with relish. The men chatted idly. Jody allowed his thoughts to drift back to the fawn. He could not keep it out of his mind. It stood in the back of it as close as he had held it, in his dreaming, in his arms. He slipped from the table and went to his father's bedside. Penny lay at rest. His eyes were open and clear, but the pupils were still dark and dilated.

Jody said, "How you comin', Pa?"

"Jest fine, son. Ol' Death gone thievin' elsewhere. But wa'n't it a close squeak!"

"I mean."

Penny said, "I'm proud of you, boy, the way you kept your head and done what was needed."

"Pa——"

164

"Yes, son."

"Pa, you recollect the doe and the fawn?"

"I cain't never forget 'em. The pore doe saved me, and that's certain."

"Pa, the fawn may be out there yit. Hit's hongry, and likely mighty skeert."

"I reckon so."

"Pa, I'm about growed and don't need no milk. How about me goin' out and seein' kin I find the fawn?"

"And tote it here?"

"And raise it."

Penny lay quiet, staring at the ceiling.

"Boy, you got me hemmed in."

"Hit won't take much to raise it, Pa. Hit'll soon git to where it kin make out on leaves and acorns."

"Dogged if you don't figger the farrest of ary young un I've ever knowed."

"We takened its mammy, and it wa'n't no-ways to blame."

"Shore don't seem grateful to leave it starve, do it? Son, I ain't got it in my heart to say 'No' to you. I never figgered I'd see daylight, come dawn today."

"Kin I ride back with Mill-wheel and see kin I find it?"

"Tell your Ma I said you're to go."

He sidled back to the table and sat down. His mother was pouring coffee for every one.

He said, "Ma, Pa says I kin go bring back the fawn."

She held the coffee-pot in mid-air.

"What fawn?"

"The fawn belonged to the doe we kilt, to use the liver to draw out the pizen and save Pa."

She gasped.

"Well, for pity sake——"

"Pa says hit'd not be grateful, to leave it starve."

Doc Wilson said, "That's right, Ma'am. Nothing in the

world don't ever come quite free. The boy's right and his daddy's right."

Mill-wheel said, "He kin ride back with me. I'll he'p him find it."

She set down the pot helplessly.

"Well, if you'll give it your milk— We got nothin' else to feed it."

"That's what I aim to do. Hit'll be no time, and it not needin' nothin'."

The men rose from the table.

Doc said, "I don't look for nothing but progress, Ma'am, but if he takes a turn for the worse, you know where to find me."

She said, "Well. What do we owe you, Doc? We cain't pay right now, but time the crops is made——"

"Pay for what? I've done nothing. He was safe before I got here. I've had a night's lodging and a good breakfast. Send me some syrup when your cane's ground."

"You're mighty good, Doc. We been scramblin' so, I didn't know folks could be so good."

"Hush, woman. You got a good man there. Why wouldn't folks be good to him?"

Buck said, "You reckon that ol' horse o' Penny's kin keep ahead o' me at the plow? I'm like to run him down."

Doc said, "Get as much milk down Penny as he'll take. Then give him greens and fresh meat, if you can get it."

Buck said, "Me and Jody'll tend to that."

Mill-wheel said, "Come on, boy. We got to git ridin'."

Ma Baxter asked anxiously, "You'll not be gone long?"

Jody said, "I'll be back shore, before dinner."

"Reckon you'd not git home a-tall," she said, "if 'twasn't for dinner-time."

Doc said, "That's man-nature, Ma'am. Three things bring a man home again—his bed, his woman, and his dinner."

Buck and Mill-wheel guffawed. Doc's eye caught the cream-colored 'coonskin knapsack.

"Now ain't that a pretty something? Wouldn't I like such as that to tote my medicines?"

Jody had never before possessed a thing that was worth giving away. He took it from its nail, and put it in Doc's hands.

"Hit's mine," he said. "Take it."

"Why, I'd not rob you, boy."

"I got no use for it," he said loftily. "I kin git me another."

"Now I thank you. Every trip I make, I'll think, 'Thank you, Jody Baxter.'"

He was proud with old Doc's pleasure. They went outside to water the horses and feed them from the scanty stock of hay in the Baxter barn.

Buck said to Jody, "You Baxters is makin' out and that's about all, ain't it?"

Doc said, "Baxter's had to carry the work alone. Time the boy here gets some size to him, they'll prosper."

Buck said, "Size don't seem to mean much to a Baxter."

Mill-wheel mounted his horse and pulled Jody up behind him. Doc mounted and turned away in the opposite direction. Jody waved after him. His heart was light.

He said to Mill-wheel, "You reckon the fawn's yit there? Will you he'p me find him?"

"We'll find him, do he be alive. How you know it's a he?"

"The spots was all in a line. On a doe-fawn, Pa says the spots is ever' which-a-way."

"That's the female of it."

"What you mean?"

"Why, females is on-accountable."

Mill-wheel slapped the horse's flank and they broke into a trot.

"This female business. How come you and your Pa to pitch into us, when we was fightin' Oliver Hutto?"

"Oliver was gittin' the wust of it. Hit didn't seem right, a hull passel o' you-all whoppin' Oliver."

"You right. Hit were Lem's gal and Oliver's gal. They should of fit it out alone."

"But a gal cain't belong to two fellers at oncet."

"You jest don't know gals."

"I hate Twink Weatherby."

"I'd not look at her, neither. I got a widder-woman at Fort Gates, knows how to be faithful."

The matter was too complicated. Jody gave himself over to thoughts of the fawn. They passed the abandoned clearing.

He said, "Cut to the north, Mill-wheel. Hit were up here Pa got snake-bit and kilt the doe and I seed the fawn."

"What was you and your daddy doin' up this road?"

Jody hesitated.

"We was huntin' our hogs."

"Oh— Huntin' your hogs, eh? Well, don't fret about them hogs. I jest got a idee they'll be home by sundown."

"Ma and Pa'll shore be proud to see 'em come in."

"I had no idee, you-all was runnin' so tight."

"We ain't runnin' tight. We're all right."

"You Baxters has got guts, I'll say that."

"You reckon Pa'll not die?"

"Not him. His chitlin's is made o' iron."

Jody said, "Tell me about Fodder-wing. Is he shore enough ailin'? Or didn't Lem want I should see him?"

"He's purely ailin'. He ain't like the rest of us. He ain't like nobody. Seems like he drinks air 'stead o' water, and feeds on what the wild creeturs feeds on, 'stead o' bacon."

"He sees things ain't so, don't he? Spaniards and sich."

"He do, but dogged if they ain't times he'll make you think he do see 'em."

"You reckon Lem'll leave me come see him?"

"I'd not risk it yit. I'll git word to you one day when mebbe Lem's gone off, see?"

"I shore crave to see Fodder-wing."

"You'll see him. Now whereabouts you want to go, huntin' that fawn? Hit's gittin' right thick up this trail."

Suddenly Jody was unwilling to have Mill-wheel with him. If the fawn was dead, or could not be found, he could not have his disappointment seen. And if the fawn was there, the meeting would be so lovely and so secret that he could not endure to share it.

He said, "Hit's not fur now, but hit's powerful thick for a horse. I kin make it a-foot."

"But I'm daresome to leave you, boy. Suppose you was to git lost, or snake-bit, too?"

"I'll take keer. Hit'll take me likely a long time to find the fawn, if he's wandered. Leave me off right here."

"All right, but you go mighty easy now, pokin' in them palmeeters. This is rattlesnake Heaven in these parts. You know north here, and east?"

"There, and there. That fur tall pine makes a bearin'."

"That's right. Now do things go wrong again, you or Buck, one, ride back for me. So long."

"So long, Mill-wheel. I'm shore obliged."

He waved after him. He waited for the sound of the hooves to end, then cut to the right. The scrub was still. Only his own crackling of twigs sounded across the silence. He was eager almost past caution, but he broke a bough and pushed it ahead of him where the growth was thick and the ground invisible. Rattlers got out of the way when they had a chance. Penny had gone farther into the oak thicket than he remembered. He wondered for an instant if he had mistaken his direction. Then a buzzard rose in front of him and flapped into the air. He came into the clearing under the oaks. Buzzards sat in a circle around the carcass of the doe. They turned their heads on their long scrawny necks and hissed at him. He threw his bough at them and they flew into an adjacent tree. Their wings creaked and whistled like rusty pump-handles. The sand showed large cat-prints, he could not tell whether of wild-cat or of panther. But the big cats killed fresh, and they had left the doe to the carrion birds. He asked himself whether the sweeter meat of the fawn had scented the air for the curled nostrils.

He skirted the carcass and parted the grass at the place where he had seen the fawn. It did not seem possible that it was only yesterday. The fawn was not there. He circled the clearing. There was no sound, no sign. The buzzards clacked their wings, impatient to return to their business. He returned to the spot where the fawn had emerged and dropped to all fours, studying the sand for the small hoof-prints. The night's rain had washed away all tracks except those of cat and buzzards. But the cat-sign had not been made in this direction. Under a scrub palmetto he was able to make out a track, pointed and dainty as the mark of a ground-dove. He crawled past the palmetto.

Movement directly in front of him startled him so that he tumbled backward. The fawn lifted its face to his. It turned its head with a wide, wondering motion and shook him through with the stare of its liquid eyes. It was quivering. It made no effort to rise or run. Jody could not trust himself to move.

He whispered, "It's me."

The fawn lifted its nose, scenting him. He reached out one hand and laid it on the soft neck. The touch made him delirious. He moved forward on all fours until he was close beside it. He put his arms around its body. A light convulsion passed over it but it did not stir. He stroked its sides as gently as though the fawn were a china deer and he might break it. Its skin was softer than the white 'coonskin knapsack. It was sleek and clean and had a sweet scent of grass. He rose slowly and lifted the fawn from the ground. It was no heavier than old Julia. Its legs hung limply. They were surprisingly long and he had to hoist the fawn as high as possible under his arm.

He was afraid that it might kick and bleat at sight and smell of its mother. He skirted the clearing and pushed his way into the thicket. It was difficult to fight through with his burden. The fawn's legs caught in the bushes and he could not lift his own with freedom. He tried to shield its face from prickling vines. Its head bobbed with his stride. His heart thumped with the marvel of its acceptance of him. He reached the trail and walked as fast as he could until he came to the intersection with the road home. He stopped to rest and set the fawn down on its dangling legs. It wavered on them. It looked at him and bleated.

He said, enchanted, "I'll tote you time I git my breath."

He remembered his father's saying that a fawn would follow that had been first carried. He started away slowly. The fawn stared after him. He came back to it and stroked it and walked away again. It took a few wobbling steps toward him and cried piteously. It was willing to follow him. It belonged to him. It was his own. He was light-headed with his joy. He wanted to fondle it, to run and romp with it, to call to it to come to him. He dared not alarm it. He picked it up and carried it in front of him over his two arms. It seemed to him that he walked without effort. He had the strength of a Forrester.

His arms began to ache and he was forced to stop again. When he walked on, the fawn followed him at once. He allowed it to walk a little distance, then picked it up again. The distance home was nothing. He could have walked all day and into the night, carrying it and watching it follow. He was wet with sweat but a light breeze blew through the June morning, cooling him. The sky was as clear as spring water in a blue china cup. He came to the clearing. It was fresh and green after the night's rain. He could see Buck Forrester following old Cæsar at the plow in the cornfield. He thought he heard him curse the horse's slowness. He fumbled with the gate latch and was finally obliged to set down the fawn to manage it. It came to him that he would walk into the house, into Penny's bedroom, with the fawn walking behind him. But at the steps, the fawn balked and refused to climb them. He picked it up and went to his father. Penny lay with closed eyes.

Jody called, "Pa! Lookit!"

Penny turned his head. Jody stood beside him, the fawn clutched hard against him. It seemed to Penny that the boy's eyes were as bright as the fawn's. His face lightened, seeing them together.

He said, "I'm proud you found him."

"Pa, he wa'n't skeert o' me. He were layin' up right where his mammy had made his bed."

"The does learns 'em that, time they're borned. You kin step on a fawn, times, they lay so still."

"Pa, I toted him, and when I set him down, right off he follered me. Like a dog, Pa."

"Ain't that fine? Let's see him better."

Jody lifted the fawn high. Penny reached out a hand and touched its nose. It bleated and reached hopefully for his fingers.

He said, "Well, leetle feller. I'm sorry I had to take away your mammy."

"You reckon he misses her?"

"No. He misses his rations and he knows that. He misses somethin' else but he don't know jest what."

Ma Baxter came into the room.

"Look, Ma, I found him."

"I see."

"Ain't he purty, Ma? Lookit them spots all in rows. Lookit them big eyes. Ain't he purty?"

"He's powerful young. Hit'll take milk for him a long whiles. I don't know as I'd of give my consent, if I'd knowed he was so young."

Penny said, "Ory, I got one thing to say, and I'm sayin' it now, and then I'll have no more talk of it. The leetle fawn's as welcome in this house as Jody. It's hissen. We'll raise it without grudgment o' milk or meal. You got me to answer to, do I ever hear you quarrelin' about it. This is Jody's fawn jest like Julia's my dog."

Jody had never heard his father speak to her so sternly. The tone must hold familiarity for his mother, however, for she opened and shut her mouth and blinked her eyes.

She said, "I only said it was young."

"All right. So it is."

He closed his eyes.

He said, "If ever'body's satisfied now, I'd thank you to leave me rest. Hit puts my heart to jerkin', to talk."

Jody said, "I'll fix its milk, Ma. No need you should bother."

She was silent. He went to the kitchen. The fawn wobbled after him. A pan of morning's milk stood in the kitchen safe. The cream had risen on it. He skimmed the cream into a jug and used his shirt sleeve to wipe up the few drops he could not keep from spilling. If he could keep the fawn fom being any trouble to his mother, she would mind it less. He poured milk into a small gourd. He held it out to the fawn. It butted it suddenly, smelling the milk. He saved it precariously from spilling over the floor. He led the fawn outside to the yard and began again. It could make nothing of the milk in the gourd.

He dipped his fingers in the milk and thrust them into the fawn's soft wet mouth. It sucked greedily. When he withdrew them, it bleated frantically and butted him. He dipped his fingers again and as the fawn sucked, he lowered them slowly into the milk. The fawn blew and sucked and snorted. It stamped its small hooves impatiently. As long as he held his fingers below the level of the mik, the fawn was content. It closed its eyes dreamily. It was ecstasy to feel its tongue against his hand. Its small tail flicked back and forth. The last of the milk vanished in a swirl of foam and gurgling. The fawn bleated and butted but its frenzy was appeased. Jody was tempted to go for more milk, but even with his father's backing he was afraid to press his advantage too far. A doe's bag was as small as a yearling heifer's. Surely the fawn had had as much as its mother could have given it. It lay down suddenly, exhausted and replete.

He gave his attention to a bed for it. It would be too much to ask, to bring it into the house. He went to the shed behind the house and cleaned out a corner down to the sand. He went to the live oaks at the north end of the yard and pulled down armfuls of Spanish moss. He made a thick bed in the shed. A hen was on a nest close by. Her bright beady eyes watched him dubiously. She finished her laying and flew through the door, cackling. The nest was a new one, with six eggs in it. Jody gathered them carefully and took them to his mother in the kitchen.

He said, "You'll be proud to git these, Ma. Extry eggs."

"Hit's a good thing they's somethin' extry around to eat."

He ignored the comment.

He said, "The new nest is right next to where I fixed the fawn's bed. In the shed, where it'll not bother nobody."

She did not answer and he went outside where the fawn lay under a mulberry tree. He gathered it up and carried it to its bed in the dark shed.

"Now you belong to do whatever I tell you," he said. "Like

174

as if I was your mammy. I tell you to lay here 'til I come git you agin."

The fawn blinked its eyelids. It groaned comfortably and dropped its head. He tiptoed from the shed. No dog, he thought, could be more biddable. He went to the wood-pile and shaved fine splinters of fatwood for kindling. He arranged the pile neatly. He gathered an armful of black-jack oak and took it to his mother's wood-box in the kitchen.

He said, "Was it all right, Ma, the way I skimmed the cream?"

"Hit was all right."

He said, "Fodder-wing's ailin'."

"Is?"

"Lem wouldn't leave me see him. Lem's the only one is mad at us, Ma. On account of Oliver's gal."

"Uh-huh."

"Mill-wheel said he'd leave me know and I could slip in some time and see Fodder-wing when Lem ain't around."

She laughed.

"You're talkified as a old woman today."

She passed him on her way to the hearth and touched his head lightly.

She said, "I feel right good, myself. I never figgered your Pa'd see daylight today."

The kitchen was filled with peace. There was a clanking of harness. Buck passed through the gate from the field and crossed the road to the lot to put up old Cæsar for the noon hour.

Jody said, "I best go he'p him."

But it was the fawn that drew him from the contentment of the house. He slipped into the shed to marvel at its existence and his possession. When he returned with Buck from the lot, chattering of the fawn, he beckoned him to follow.

He said, "Don't skeer him. There he lies——"

Buck was not as satisfying as Penny in his response. He had seen so many of Fodder-wing's pets come and go.

"He'll likely go wild and run off," he said, and went to the water-shelf to wash his hands before dinner.

A chill came over Jody. Buck was worse than his mother to take away pleasure. He lingered a moment with the fawn, stroking it. It moved its sleepy head and nuzzled his fingers. Buck could not know of the closeness. It was all the better for being secret. He left the fawn and went to the basin and washed, too. The touch of the fawn had left his hands scented with a faint grassy pungency. He hated to wash it away, but decided that his mother might not find it as pleasant.

His mother had wet and combed her hair for dinner, not with coquetry, but with pride. She wore a clean sacking apron over her brown calico.

She said to Buck, "With only Penny to do, we ain't got the rations plentiful like you folks. But we do eat clean and decent."

Jody looked quickly to see if Buck would take offense. Buck ladled grits into his plate and scooped a hole in the center for the fried eggs and gravy.

"Now Miss Ory, don't fret about me. Jody and me'll slip off this evenin' and git you a mess o' squirrels and mebbe a turkey. I seed turkey sign the fur edge o' the pea field."

Ma Baxter filled a plate for Penny, and added a cup of milk.

"You take it to him, Jody."

He went to his father. Penny shook his head at the plate.

"Hit look jest plain nasty to me, son. Set up there and feed me a spoon o' the grits, and the milk. Hit wearies me to lift my arm."

The swelling had left his face, but his arm was still three times its normal size, and his breath came heavily. He swal-

lowed a few mouthfuls of the soft hominy and drank the milk.
He motioned the plate away.

"You gittin' along all right with your baby?"

Jody reported on the moss bed.

"You picked a good place. What you fixin' to name him?"

"I jest don't know. I want a name is real special."

Buck and Ma Baxter came into the bedroom and sat down
to visit. The day was hot and the sun high and there was no
hurry for anything.

Penny said, "Jody's in a tight for a name for the new Baxter."

Buck said, "Tell you, Jody, when you see Fodder-wing, he'll
pick a name. He's got a ear for sich things, jest like some folks
has got a ear for fiddle music. He'll pick you a name is purty."

Ma Baxter said, "Go eat your dinner, Jody. That spotted
fawn has takened your mind off your rations."

The opportunity was choice. He went to the kitchen and
heaped a plate with food and went to the shed. The fawn was
still drowsy. He sat beside it and ate his dinner. He dipped his
fingers in the grease-covered grits and held them out to it, but
it only snuffed and turned its head away.

He said, "You better learn somethin' besides milk."

The dirt daubers buzzed in the rafters. He scraped his plate
clean and set it aside. He lay down beside the fawn. He put
one arm across its neck. It did not seem to him that he could
ever be lonely again.

· 16 ·

THE fawn took up much of Jody's time. It tagged him wherever he went. At the wood-pile, it interfered with the swing of his axe. The milking had been assigned to him. He was forced to bar the fawn from the lot and it stood by the gate, peering between the bars, and bleated until he had finished. He stripped Trixie's teats until she kicked in protest. Each cupful of milk meant more nourishment for the fawn. It seemed to him that he could see it growing. It stood firm on its small legs and leaped and tossed its head and tail. He romped with it until they dropped together in a heap to rest and cool themselves.

The days were hot and humid. Penny sweat in his bed. Buck came dripping from the fields. He discarded his shirt and worked naked to the waist. His chest was thick with black hair. The perspiration glistened on it like rain drops on black dried moss. When she was sure he would not call for it, Ma Baxter washed and boiled the shirt and hung it in the scalding sunshine.

She said with satisfaction, "There's that much of him, now, won't stink."

Buck filled the Baxter cabin until it bulged.

Ma Baxter said to Penny, "First sight I catch o' that beard and chest in the mornin's, I take a start, for I think a bear's got in the house."

She was appalled at the amount of food he bolted three times a day. She could scarcely complain, since he more than made it up with the work he was doing and the game with which he supplied her. In the week he had been at the clearing, he had worked out the corn, the cow-peas and the sweet potatoes. He had cleared two acres of new ground to the west, between the pea-field and the sink-hole. He had cut down a dozen oaks and pines and sweet gums and innumerable saplings, burned the stumps and trimmed the fallen trees, so that Jody and Penny on the cross-cut saw might cut the limbs and trunks for fire-wood.

He said, "You plant Sea Island cotton on that new ground, come spring, and you'll make you a crop."

Ma Baxter said suspiciously, "You-all has got no cotton."

He said easily, "Us Forresters ain't farmers. We'll do the clarin', we'll plow a field now and agin, but it's our nature to make a livin' what I reckon you'd call rough and easy."

She said primly, "Rough ways lands folks in trouble."

He said, "You ever know my granddaddy? They called him Trouble Forrester."

She could not dislike him. He was as good-natured as a dog. She could only say to Penny in the privacy of night, "He works like a ox, but he's so tormented black. Ezra, he's black as a buzzard."

"Hit's his beard," Penny said. "Did I have a black beard like that un, I mought not look like no buzzard, but I'd shore look like a crow."

Penny's strength was slow in returning. The swelling from the poisoning had gone down. The skin was sloughing away where the rattler had struck him and he had cut the wounds to make the envenomed blood flow more freely. But at the least exertion, he was nauseated, and his heart pumped like the paddle-wheels on the river steamers, and he gasped for breath and must lie flat to recover himself. He was all wiry nerves, strung like harp-strings on a frail wooden body.

To Jody, the presence of Buck was a stimulation so great that he was feverish with it. The fawn alone would have had him delirious. The two together kept him in a daze, wandering from Penny's room to wherever Buck was working, to wherever the fawn might be, and around again.

His mother said, "You'd ought to be noticin' all what Buck is doin', so you kin do it when he's gone."

There was a tacit understanding among the three of them that Penny was to be spared.

The morning of the eighth day that Buck had been at the clearing, he called Jody to the cornfield. Vandals had visited it during the night. Half a row of corn had been stripped of its ears. Mid-way of the row lay a pile of corn-husks.

Buck said, "You know what done that?"

" 'Coons?"

"Hell, no. Foxes. Foxes love corn gooder'n I do. Two-three o' them bushy-tailed scapers come in last night and had them a pure picnic."

Jody laughed out.

"A fox picnic! I'd love to of seed it."

Buck said sternly, "You'd ought to be out at night with your gun, keepin' 'em out. Now we'll git 'em tonight. You got to learn to be serious. And this evenin' we'll rob that bee-tree by the sink-hole, and that'll learn you how to do that."

Jody went through the day impatiently. A hunt with Buck had a different quality from a hunt with his father. There was an excitement in anything the Forresters did that made him nervous and high-keyed. There was noise and confusion. A hunt with Penny held a satisfaction that was of more than the chase. There was always time to see a bird fly over, or to listen to a 'gator, bellowing in the swamp. He wished that Penny were able to be about, to rob the bee-tree with them; to go on the trail of the robber foxes. In mid-afternoon, Buck came from the new ground. Penny was sleeping.

Buck said to Ma Baxter, "I'll want a lard-pail and a axe and a heap o' rags to burn for smudges."

There were not many rags in the Baxter household. Clothes were worn and patched and mended until they dropped in ribbons. Flour sacks went into aprons and dish-towels and chair-backs that she embroidered on winter evenings; into backs for her patch-work quilts. Buck looked disgustedly at the small handful she gave him.

He said, "Well, reckon we kin use moss."

She said, "Don't you-all git stung, now. My grand-pappy got hisself stung oncet to where he was in the bed a fortnight."

"If we git stung, hit shore won't be o' purpose."

He started across the yard with Jody beside him. The fawn was close behind.

"You want your blasted baby to git stung to death? Then shut him up."

Jody led the fawn reluctantly to the shed and closed the door. He hated to be separated from it, even for honey-hunting. It seemed unjust that Penny should not be along. He had had his eye on the bee-tree all spring. He had waited for the proper time, when the bees should have gathered their nectar from the yellow jessamine, from the mulberry and the holly, the palmetto bloom and the chinaberry, the wild grapes and the peaches, and from the hawthorn and the wild plum. There would still be bloom from which they might make their own winter store. The red bay and the loblolly were in full blossom. There would soon be sumac and goldenrod and asters.

Buck said, "You know who'd purely love to be gittin' honey with us? Fodder-wing. He'll work amongst the bees so quiet, you'd figger they was makin' him a present o' the honey-comb."

They reached the sink-hole.

Buck said, "I don't see how you-all have made out, totin' your water so fur. If I wasn't about to be leavin', I'd shore he'p you dig a well nigh to the house."

"You fixin' to leave?"

"Well, yes. I'm fretted about Fodder-wing. And I ain't never lived this long without whiskey."

The bee-tree was a dead pine. Mid-way up its height, the wild honey-bees flew in and out of a deep cavity. It stood at the north edge of the sink-hole. Buck stopped by the live oaks to pull down armfuls of green Spanish moss. At the base of the pine he pointed to a pile of dried grass and feathers.

"The wood-ducks tried to nest there," he said. "They'll see a hole in a tree, and don't matter do it belong to a Lord God woodpecker, or one o' them big woodpeckers with a ivory bill, or a swarm o' bees, they'll take a notion to it and they'll try to nest in the hole. The bees has done drove these uns out."

He began to chop at the base of the dead pine. High in the air a humming sounded like a den of rattlers, far distant and turbulent. The blows of the axe echoed back and forth across the sink-hole. Squirrels, quiescent in the oaks and palm trees, began to chatter at the disturbance. Scrub jays cried shrilly. The pine shook. The humming grew into a roar. The bees sung across their heads like small shot.

Buck called, "Light me a smudge, boy. Be peert."

Jody made a loose ball of moss and rags and opened Buck's tinder horn. He struggled with flint and steel. Penny was so expert at starting a fire that it occurred to Jody in a panic that he had never done it himself. The sparks flashed to the scorched rags that constituted the tinder, but he blew them so violently that they flickered out almost as soon as they touched the cloth. Buck dropped the axe and ran to him and took the materials from him. He rubbed flint and steel together as vigorously as Jody had done, but he blew on the spark-touched rags with a judiciousness amazing in a Forrester. The rags blazed and he touched the fire to the moss. It began to smoke without blazing.

Buck ran back to the pine and put his muscles behind the axe. Its bright blade ate into the decayed center of the tree. Its long fibers split and ripped and shivered. The pine roared in the air as though a voice had come to it to cry out with in its falling. It crashed to earth and the bees were a cloud across its dead gaping heart. Buck snatched up the smudge and darted in as quick, for all his size, as a weasel. He stuffed the smoking ball into the cavity with one thrust and ran madly. He looked more than ever like a lumbering bear. He let out a howl and slapped at his chest and shoulders. Jody had to laugh at him. Then a needle-point of fire stabbed his own neck.

Buck shouted, 'Git down the sink-hole! Git to the water!"

They scrambled down the steep bank. The seepage pool at the bottom was shallow for lack of rains. The water did not quite cover them when they lay in it. Buck scooped up handfuls of mud and plastered Jody's hair and neck with it. His own thatch was a thick enough protection. A few bees followed and swung back and forth persistently. After a time Buck raised himself cautiously.

He said, "They're due to be quiet now. But ain't we a pair o' hogs."

Their breeches, their faces, their shirts, were caked with mud. It was not yet wash-day and Jody led the way up the south wall of the sink-hole to the wash-troughs. They soused their clothes in one and washed themselves from the other.

Buck said, "What you grinnin' about?"

Jody shook his head. He could imagine his mother saying, "If it takes bees to git a Forrester clean, I'll hive 'em a swarm."

Buck had half a dozen stings but Jody had escaped with two. They approached the bee tree cautiously. The smudge had been properly placed. The bees were drugged with the heavy smoke. They swarmed slowly around the cavity, searching for their queen.

Buck split a wider opening and used his sheath knife to hack away the edges. He cleaned away trash and splinters and reached in with the knife. He turned, amazed.

"Great day! They's a wash-tub o' honey here. The tree's full."

He brought out a slab, golden and dripping. The comb was rough and dark, but the honey was paler than fine syrup. They filled the lard-pail and carried it between them to the house. Ma Baxter gave them a cypress tub to take back with them.

Buck said, "Now a wash tub o' biscuits is all more is needed."

The return load was heavy. It was the largest yield, Buck said, he had ever seen from a bee-tree since he was a boy.

He said, "When I go home tomorrer and tell my folks, they'll not believe me."

She said slowly, "I reckon you'll want to carry some back with you."

"No more'n I kin carry in my belly. I got my eye on two-three trees in the swamp. Do they fail me, I'm like to come beggin'."

Ma Baxter said, "You've been mighty neighborly. Mebbe some day we'll have a plenty and kin do for you."

Jody said, "I wish you'd not go, Buck."

The big man shoved him playfully.

"With me gone, you'll not have no time to nuss that fawn."

Buck was plainly restless. He shuffled his feet at supper and paced up and down afterward. He looked at the sky.

He said, "A good clare night for ridin'."

Jody said, "How come you anxious all to oncet?"

Buck paused in his pacing.

"I git that-a-way. I like to come and I like to go. Wherever I be, I'm content a while, and then I jest someway ain't content no more. When me and Lem and Mill-wheel goes off hoss-tradin' to Kentucky, I'll swear, I figger I'll bust 'til I git home agin." He paused and stared into the sunset. He added in a low voice, "And I'm right smart fretted about Fodder-wing. I got a feelin' here—" he thumped his hairy chest—"he ain't doin' good."

"Wouldn't somebody of come?"

"That's it. If they didn't know your Pa was bad off, they'd of ridden over jest to say Howdy. They figgered your Pa needed he'p and they'd not like to toll me away, was the news bad or worrisome."

He waited nervously for dark. He wanted to be done with his job, and gone. Penny was as good a night-hunter as any Forrester. Jody was tempted to brag of the varmints his father had disposed of, but that might cut him out of a night-prowl with Buck. He held his tongue. He helped Buck prepare the fatwood splinters for the fire-pan.

Buck said, "My Uncle Cotton had red hair. They was a heap of it, stood up like a haystack, and red as a fightin' cock's comb. He was fire-huntin' one night, and the handle was a mite short, and a spark from the pan set his hair a-fire. And you know when he hollered to Pa for he'p, Pa didn't pay him no mind. He jest thought the moon had done rose and was shinin' through Uncle Cotton's hair."

Jody gaped.

"Is that true, Buck?"

Buck whittled busily.

"Now if you was to tell me a tale," he said, "I'd not ask you no sich of a question."

Penny called from his bedroom.

"I cain't stand it. I'm o' good notion not to leave you go without me."

They came to his room.

"If 'twas a panther hunt you was goin' on," he said, "I'll swear I'd feel good enough to go with you."

Buck said, "Now I'd jest carry you on a panther hunt, did I have my dogs."

"Why, my pair'll out-hunt your whole pack." He asked innocently, "How did you-all come out with that sorry dog I traded you?"

Buck drawled, "Why, that dog's proved out the fastest and the finest and the hardest-huntin' and the fearlessest of ary dog we've ever had on the place. All he needed was men to train him."

Penny chuckled.

He said, "I'm proud you was smart enough to make somethin' outen him. Where's he now?"

"Well, he was so blasted good, he put t'other dogs so to shame, Lem couldn't abide it, and he hauled off and shot him and buried him in the Baxter cemetery one night."

Penny said gravely, "I noticed the new grave and I figgered you-all had give outen buryin'-ground. I'll whittle a head-stone, time I git my strength. I'll carve on it, 'Here lies a Forrester, mourned by all his kin.'"

He grinned broadly and slapped the covers of his bed.

"Give in, Buck," he said, "give in."

Buck wiped his beard.

"All right," he said, "I'll take it for funnin'. But don't look to Lem to take it for ary thing but a cold-out insult."

Penny said, "No hard feelin's. I got none, and I hope you-all'll hold none, Lem nor nobody."

"Lem's different. He takes things personal."

186

"That grieves me. I pitched into the fight betwixt him and Oliver because they was too many of you on one side."

Buck said, "Well, blood's thicker'n water. We fight amongst ourselves now and agin, but when it's us and t'other feller, we allus fight on the same side o' the creek. But me and you has got no call to fall out."

Words began fights and words ended them.

Jody asked, "If fellers didn't say quarrelin' things, would they put in to fight?"

Penny said, "I'm feered so. I oncet seed a pair o' deef dummies havin' it. But they do say they got a sign language, and likely one passed the insult in a sign."

Buck said, "Hit's male nature, boy. Wait 'til you git to courtin' and you'll git your breeches dusted many a time."

"But nobody but Lem and Oliver was courtin', and here all us Baxters and all you Forresters was in to it."

Penny said, "They's no end to what a man'll fight for. I even knowed a preacher takened off his coat and fit ary man wouldn't agree to infant damnation. All a feller kin do, is fight for what he figgers is right, and the devil take the hindmost."

Buck said, "Listen. I think I heered a fox bark then in the hammock."

At first the night seemed silent. Then sounds drifted like clouds into their hearing. An owl hooted. A tree-frog scraped his fiddle and predicted rain.

Buck said, "There he be."

A thin bark sounded in the distance, shrill and mournful.

Buck said, "Now wouldn't that be music to my pore dogs? Wouldn't they sing to that sopranner?"

Penny said, "If you and Jody don't clean out the litter tonight, bring your dogs on the next moon and we'll have us a chase."

Buck said, "Let's us git goin', Jody. That yipper'll about make the cornfield time we do." He picked up Penny's shotgun from the corner. "I'll borry this tonight. Seems to me I've seed it before."

"Jest don't bury it beside the dog," Penny said. "Hit's ralely a good gun."

Jody packed his muzzle-loader over his shoulder. He went out with Buck. The fawn heard him and bleated from the shed. They walked under the mulberries and crossed the split-rail fence into the cornfield. Buck walked north down the first row. At the far end of the field he began walking across the ends of the rows. He stopped at each row and focussed the light from the fire-pan down the length of the field. Mid-way he stopped. He turned and nudged Jody. Where the light came to rest, two fiery green agates caught the light.

He murmured, "Slip half-way up the row. I'll keep the light on him. Don't git in the path o' the light. When his eyes looks as big as a shillin', give it to him, right between 'em."

Jody crept forward, hugging the corn at his left. The green lights were extinguished a moment, then stared again. He lifted his gun and allowed the light from the blazing splinters in the fire-pan to slip down the barrel. He pulled the trigger. The gun, as always, knocked him off balance. He started to run forward to ascertain his hit, but Buck hissed at him.

"Psst. You got him. Leave him lay. Come back."

He crept along the row. Buck handed him the shotgun.

"They's likely another here clost."

They crept from row to row. This time he saw the glowing eyes before Buck saw them. He advanced down the row as before. The shotgun was a delight to handle. It was lighter than the old muzzle-loader, not so long, and easier to sight. He shot with a feeling of confidence. Again Buck called him back and he retreated. But though they combed the rows carefully, and worked around the west end of the field and flashed the light down the corn rows from the south, there were no more bright green eyes.

Buck said aloud, "That's the crop for tonight. Let's see what we got."

Both shots had killed. One was a dog-fox and one a vixen, fat with Baxter corn.

Buck said, "Now they got a litter off in a den some'eres, but they'll be part-growed and kin make out by theirselves. Come fall, we'll have us a fox-chase."

The foxes were gray and in good condition, with full brushes. Jody carried them in complacently.

Approaching the cabin, they heard a commotion. Ma Baxter shrieked.

Buck said, "Your Ma wouldn't romp on your Pa while he was ailin', would she?"

"She don't never romp on him with nothin' but talkin'."

"I'd a heap ruther a woman tore me down with a lighter'd knot, than speakin' sharp."

Close to the cabin, they heard Penny shout.

Buck said, "Why, boy, the woman's killin' him."

Jody said, "Somethin's after the fawn!"

The yard itself was not often disturbed by anything more dangerous than the small varmints. Buck hurdled the fence and Jody vaulted it after him. A light shone from the doorway. Penny stood there dressed only in his breeches. Ma Baxter was beside him, flapping her apron. Jody thought he saw a dark form move off into the night, toward the grape arbor, followed by the dogs, baying.

Penny called, "Hit's a bear! Git him! Git him 'fore he makes the fence!"

Sparks showered from the fire-pan as Buck ran. The light reached out to a lumbering body galloping to the east under the peach trees.

Jody shouted, "Give me the fire-pan, Buck, and you do the shootin'."

He felt frightened and incompetent. They exchanged on the run. At the fence the bear turned at bay. He slashed at the dogs. His eyes and teeth shone in the spasmodic light. Then he turned to clamber over the fence. Buck shot. The bear tumbled. The dogs broke into a tumult. Penny came running. The light showed a kill. The dogs made a pretense of having done the job, and bayed and attacked proudly. Buck was smug.

He said, "This feller'd not of come around if he'd knowed they was a Forrester on the place."

Penny said, "He smelt things set him so wild, he'd not of noticed the hull tribe of you."

"What was that?"

"Jody's fawn and the new honey."

"Did he git to the fawn, Pa? Oh Pa, the fawn ain't hurt?"

"He never got to him. The door by luck was closed. Then he must of winded the honey and come traipsin' around by the stoop. I figgered it was you-all comin' back and I didn't pay no mind until he knocked the cover offen the honey. I could of shot him down right at the door, but here I was and no gun. All me and Ory could do was holler, but I reckon it was the fiercest hollerin' he'd ever run into, and he lit out."

Jody was weak at thought of what might have happened to the fawn. He ran to the shed to comfort it, and found it drowsy and unconcerned. He stroked it gratefully, then returned to the men and the bear. It was a two-year-old male, in good condition. Penny insisted on helping with the dressing. They dragged the carcass to the back yard and skinned it out by the light of the fire-pan; quartered it and hung the meat in the smokehouse.

Buck said, "Now I will beg a pail o' the fat for Ma, to make her some bear grease and cracklin's. There's things she jest won't fry without bear grease, and the old soul says bear cracklin's and sweet pertaters rests so easy on her gums. Why, them four teeth o' hers could chomp on 'em all day."

Ma Baxter developed generosity with the plenitude.

She said, "And a big piece o' the liver goes to pore leetle Fodder-wing. Hit'll give him strength."

Penny said, "I'm only sad this ain't old Slewfoot. My, wouldn't I love to draw the knife down his thievin' backbone."

The foxes could wait to be skinned until morning, for the meat would be used only to cook for the chickens, with pepper, for a tonic.

Buck said, "Did old man Easy Ozell ever ask you to come eat one o' his fox pilaus?"

Penny said, "He done so. And I said, 'No, thank you, Easy, I'll jest wait until you cook one o' your dogs.'"

Penny was thriving on the excitement. He sat on his heels beside Buck and exchanged tales of foxes and of dogs, of strange foods and the stranger people who ate them. The yarns for once failed to hold Jody's interest. He was anxious for every one to go to bed. At last Penny's new-found energy failed him, and he washed his hands and cleaned his skinning knife and joined his wife in the bed. Buck was wound up to talk half the night. Jody knew the signs and pretended to go to sleep on his pallet on the floor of his small room. Buck had been occupying his bed, his long hairy legs hanging unsupported a quarter of its length. Buck sat on the edge of the bed and talked until the lack of audience discouraged him. Jody heard him yawn and pull off his trousers and lie down on the corn shucks mattress on the creaking slats.

He waited until a deep rumbling snore sounded. Then he slipped from the house and groped his way to the shed. The fawn stood up at the sound. He felt his way to it and threw his arms around its neck. It nuzzled his cheek. He picked it up and carried it to the door. It had grown so fast in the brief time he had had it, that it was all he could do to carry it. He tiptoed into the yard with it and set it down. It followed him willingly. He crept into the house, keeping one hand on its smooth hard head to guide it. Its sharp heels clicked on the wooden floor. He lifted it again and stepped cautiously past his mother's bedroom and into his own.

He lay down on his pallet and drew the fawn down beside him. He often lay so with it in the shed, or under the live oaks in the heat of the day. He lay with his head against its side. Its ribs lifted and fell with its breathing. It rested its chin on his hand. It had a few short hairs there that prickled him. He had been cudgeling his wits for an excuse to bring the fawn inside at night to sleep with him, and now he had one that could not be disputed. He would smuggle it in and out as long as possible, in the name of peace. On the inevitable day when he should be discovered, what better reason was there than the menace—the constant danger, he would point out—of bears?

· 17 ·

THERE was not a field of sweet potatoes, but an endless sea.
Jody looked behind him at the rows he had finished hoeing.
They were beginning to make a respectable showing, but the
rows unfinished seemed to stretch to the horizon. The July heat
simmered on the earth. The sand was scalding to his bare feet.
The leaves of the sweet potato vines curled upward, as though
the dry soil, and not the sun, were burning them. He pushed
back his palmetto hat and wiped his face with his sleeve. By
the sun, it must be nearly ten o'clock. His father had said that
if the sweet potatoes were hoed by noon, he might go in the
afternoon to see Fodder-wing, and get a name for the fawn.

The fawn lay in the hedge-row in the shade of an elderberry
bush. It had been almost a nuisance when he began his work.
It had galloped up and down the sweet potato beds, trampling

193

the vines, and knocking down the edges of the beds. It had come and stood in front of him in the direct path of his hoeing, refusing to move, to force him to play with it. The wide-eyed, wondering expression of its first weeks with him had given way to an alert awareness. It had as wise a look as old Julia. Jody had almost decided that he would have to lead it back and shut it up in the shed, when of its own accord it sought the shade and lay down.

It lay watching him from the corner of one big eye, its head in its favorite position, twisted back against its own shoulder. Its small white tail flicked now and then and its spotted hide rippled, shaking off flies. If it would stay quiet, he could make better time at the hoeing. He liked to work with it near. It gave him a comfortable feeling that he had never had before in the company of a hoe. He attacked the weeds again lustily, and was pleased with himself to see his own progress. The rows fell away behind him. He whistled tunelessly.

He had thought of many names for the fawn, had called it by each in turn, but not one pleased him. All the names by which the dogs of his acquaintance had been called, Joe and Grab, Rover and Rob, on down the line, all were inadequate. It had such a light way of walking, "tippy-toed" as Penny put it, that he would have named it Twinkle-toes and called it "Twink" for short, but that reminded him of Twink Weatherby and spoiled the name. "Tip" itself would not do, because Penny had once had an ugly and vicious bull-dog by the name. Fodder-wing would not fail him. He had a great gift for naming his own pets. He had Racket the raccoon, Push the 'possum, Squeak the squirrel, and Preacher, the lame red-bird, who sang from his perch, "Preacher, preacher, preacher!" Fodder-wing said the other red-birds came to him from the forest to be married, but Jody had heard other red-birds sing the same words. At any rate, it was a good name.

He had done a great deal of work in the two weeks since

Buck had gone home. Penny's strength was returning, but every now and then he became faint and dizzy and his heart pounded. Penny was sure it was the lingering effect of the rattlesnake venom, but Ma Baxter believed it was the fever, and dosed him with lemon-leaf tea. It was good to have him up and about again, with the cold fear gone. Jody tried to remember to spare him. It was so good to have the fawn, to be relieved of the dull lonely ache that had overtaken him so often, that he was filled wth gratitude for his mother's tolerance of its presence. There was no question but that it did require a great deal of milk. It undoubtedly got in her way. It came into the house one day and discovered a pan of cornbread stirred up, ready for baking. It had cleaned the pan. Since then it had eaten—green leaves, cornmeal mixed with water, bits of biscuit, almost anything. It had to be shut in the shed when the Baxters ate. It butted and bleated and knocked dishes out of their hands. When Jody and Penny laughed at it, it tossed its head knowingly. The dogs at first had baited it, but they were now tolerant. Ma Baxter was tolerant, but she was never amused. Jody pointed out its charms.

"Ain't his eyes purty, Ma?"

"They see a pan o' cornbread too fur."

"Well, ain't he got a cute, foolish tail, Ma?"

"All deer's flags looks the same."

"But Ma, ain't it cute and foolish?"

"Hit's foolish, a'right."

The sun crept toward its zenith. The fawn came into the sweet potatoes and nibbled a few tender vines, then returned to the hedge-row and found a new place of shade under a wild cherry tree. Jody checked his work. He had a row and a half yet undone. He would have liked to go to the house for a drink of water, but that would cut down his remaining time too sharply. Perhaps dinner would be late. He pulled the hoe as fast as he dared without cutting the vines. When the sun stood over-head,

he had finished the half-row, and the full row stretched mock-
ingly before him. In a moment now his mother would beat on
the iron ring by the kitchen door and he would have to stop.
Penny had made it plain that there would be no quarter as to
time. If the hoeing was not finished by dinner time, there would
be no visit to Fodder-wing. He heard steps on the other side of
the fence. Penny was standing there, watching him.

"A heap o' taters, ain't it, son?"

"Hit's a mort of 'em."

"Hard to think, this time next year, there'll not be one left.
That baby o' yours there, under the cherry tree, he'll be wantin'
his share of 'em. Remember the time we had, two year gone,
keepin' the deer out?"

"Pa, I cain't make it. I ain't scarcely stopped all mornin', and
I've yet got a row."

"Well now, I tell you. I ain't fixin' to let you off, for I said
I'd not. But I'll strike a bargain. You go fetch fresh water for
your Ma from the sink-hole, and I'll finish the 'taters this
evenin'. Climbin' the walls o' that sink-hole purely beats me.
Now that's a fair deal."

Jody dropped the hoe and started on a run for the house to
get the water-buckets.

Penny called after him, "Don't try to tote 'em plumb full. A
yearling ain't got a buck's strength."

The buckets alone were heavy. They were of hand-hewn
cypress, and the ox-yoke from which they hung was of white
oak. Jody hung the yoke over his shoulders and trotted down
the road. The fawn loped after him. The sink-hole was dark
and still. There was more sunlight in the early morning and at
evening, than at noon, for the thick leaves of the trees cut off
the overhead sun. The birds were still. Around the sandy rim
of the sink-hole they were nooning and dusting themselves. In
late afternoon they would fly down for water. The doves would
come, and the jorees, the red-birds and the bee-martins, the

mocking-birds and the quail. He could not be too hurried to run down the steep slope to the bottom of the great green bowl. The fawn followed and they splashed together across the pool. The fawn bent its head to drink. He had dreamed of this.

He said to it, "Some day I'll build me a house here. And I'll git you a doe, and we'll all live here by the pool."

A frog leaped and the fawn backed away. Jody laughed at it and ran up the slope to the drinking trough. He leaned over it to drink. The fawn, following, drank with him, sucking up the water and moving its mouth up and down the length of the trough. At one moment its head was against Jody's cheek and he sucked in the water with the same sound as the fawn, for the sake of companionship. He lifted his head and shook it and wiped his mouth. The fawn lifted its head, too, and the water dropped from its muzzle.

Jody filled the buckets with the gourd dipper that hung on the rim of the trough. Against his father's warning, he filled them nearly full. He would like to walk into the yard with them. He crouched and bent his shoulders under the yoke. When he straightened, he could not rise against the weight. He dipped out part of the water and was able to stand and pull his way up the remainder of the slope. The wooden yoke cut into his thin shoulders. His back ached. Halfway home, he was obliged to stop and set down the buckets and pour out more of the water. The fawn dipped its nose inquisitively into one of the buckets. Fortunately, his mother need not know. She could not understand how clean the fawn was, and would not admit how sweet it smelled.

They were at dinner when he reached the house. He lifted the buckets to the water shelf and shut up the fawn. He filled the water pitcher from the fresh buckets and took it in to the table. He had worked so hard and was so hot and tired that he was not particularly hungry. He was glad of this and was able to set aside a large portion of his own dinner for the fawn. The meat was a pot-roast from the bear's haunch, pickled in brine for keeping. It was a trifle coarse, with long fibers, but the flavor, he thought, was better than beef and almost as good as venison. He made his meal on the meat, with a helping of collard greens, and saved all his cornpone and his milk for the fawn.

Penny said, "We was mighty lucky 'twas a young bear like this un come scaperin' under our noses. Had it of been a big ol' male, we couldn't of et the meat this time o' year. The bears mates in July, Jody, and allus remember the meat o' the males ain't fitten when they're matin'. Don't never shoot one then unless it's botherin' you."

"Why ain't the meat fitten?"

"Now I don't know. But when they're courtin', they're mean and hateful——"

"Like Lem and Oliver?"

"—like Lem and Oliver. Their gorge rises, or their spleen, and seems like the hatefulness gits right into their flesh."

Ma Baxter said, "A boar hog's the same. Only he's that-a-way the year around."

"Well Pa, do the male bears fight?"

"They'll fight turrible. The female'll stand off and watch the fightin'——"

"Like Twink Weatherby."

"—like Twink Weatherby, and then she'll go off with the one wins the fight. They'll stay in pairs all through July, mebbe into August. Then the males goes off and the cubs is borned in February. And don't you think a male, like ol' Slewfoot, won't eat them cubs do he come on 'em. That's another reason I hate bears. They ain't natural in their affections."

Ma Baxter said to Jody, "You look out, now, walkin' to Forresters' today. A matin' bear's a thing to shun."

Penny said, "Jest keep your eyes open. You're all right as long as you see a creetur first and don't take him by surprise.

Even that rattlesnake that got me, why, I takened him by surprise and he wasn't no more'n lookin' out for hisself."

Ma Baxter said, "You'd stick up for the devil hisself."

"I reckon I would. The devil gits blamed for a heap o' things
is nothin' but human cussedness."

She asked suspiciously, "Jody finish his hoein' like he belonged to?"

Penny said blandly, "He finished his contract."

He winked at Jody and Jody winked back. There was no use
in trying to explain the difference to her. She was outside the
good male understanding.

He said, "Ma, kin I go now?"

"Let's see. I'll need a mite o' wood toted in——"

"Please don't think up nothin' long to do, Ma. You wouldn't
want I should be so late gittin' home tonight the bears'd git me."

"You be later'n dark gittin' home and you'll wish 'twas a bear
had you, 'stid o' me."

He filled the wood-box and was ready to go. His mother
made him change his shirt and comb his hair. He fretted at the
delay.

She said, "I jest want them dirty Forresters to know there's
folks does live decent."

He said, "They ain't dirty. They jest live nice and natural and
enjoy theirselves."

She sniffed. He let out the fawn from the shed, fed it from
his hand, held the pan of milk mixed with water for it to drink,
and the two set off. The fawn ran sometimes behind him,
sometimes ahead, making short forays into the brush, bounding back to him in an alarm that Jody was sure was only pretended. Sometimes it walked beside him, and this was best. He
laid his hand, then, lightly on its neck, and fitted the rhythm
of his two legs to its four. He imagined that he was another
fawn. He bent his legs at the knees, imitating its walk. He
threw his head up, alertly. A rabbit-pea vine was in blossom

beside the road. He pulled a length of it and twined it around the fawn's neck for a halter. The rosy blooms made the fawn so pretty that it seemed to him even his mother would admire it. If it faded before he returned, he would make a fresh halter on the way home.

At the cross-roads near the abandoned clearing, the fawn halted and lifted its nostrils into the wind. It pricked up its ears. It turned its head this way and that, savoring the air. He turned his own nose in the direction on which it seemed to settle. A strong odor came to him, pungent and rank. He felt the hair prickle on the back of his neck. He thought he heard a low rumbling sound and then a snapping that might be of teeth. He was tempted to turn tail and head for home. Yet he would always wonder what the sounds had been. He moved one step at a time around the turn in the road. The fawn stayed motionless behind him. He stopped short.

Two male bears were moving slowly ahead down the road, a hundred yards distant. They were on their hind legs, walking like men, shoulder to shoulder. Their walk seemed almost a dance, as when couples in the square dance moved side by side to do a figure. Suddenly they jostled each other, like wrestlers, and lifted their forepaws, and turned, snarling, each trying for the other's throat. One raked his claws across the other's head and the snarls grew to a roar. The fighting was violent for a few moments, then the pair walked on, boxing, jostling, parrying. The wind was in Jody's favor. They could never smell him. He crept down the road after them, keeping his distance. He could not bear to lose sight of them. He hoped they would fight to a finish, yet he should be terrorized if one should end the fight and turn his way. He decided that they had been fighting for a long time and were exhausted. There was blood in the sand. Each attack seemed less violent than the others. Each shoulder-to-shoulder walking was slower paced. As he stared, a female walked out of the bushes ahead with three males following her. They turned silently into the road and walked on in single file. The fighting pair swung their heads a moment, then fell in behind. Jody stood until the procession passed from sight, solemn and ludicrous and exciting.

He turned and ran back to the cross-roads. The fawn was nowhere to be seen. He called and it emerged from the scrub growth at the side of the road. He took the Forresters' road and ran down it. Now that it was over, he shook at his own boldness. But it was done now, and he would follow again, for all men were not privileged to see the creatures in their private moments.

He thought, "I've seen a thing."

It was good to become old and see the sights and hear the sounds that men saw and heard, like Buck and his father. That was why he liked to lie flat on his belly on the floor, or on the earth before the camp-fire, while men talked. They had seen marvels, and the older they were, the more marvels they had seen. He felt himself moving into a mystic company. He had a tale now of his own to tell on winter evenings.

His father would say, "Jody, tell about the time you seed the two male bears fightin' down the road."

Above all, he could tell Fodder-wing. He ran again, for pleasure in his hurry to tell his friend his story. He would surprise him. He would walk up to Fodder-wing in the woods, or back of the house among his pets, or to his bed, if he were still ailing. The fawn would walk beside him. Fodder-wing's face would shine with its strange brightness. He would hunch his twisted body close and put out his gentle and crooked hand and touch the fawn. He would smile, to know that he, Jody, was content. After a long time Fodder-wing would speak, and what he said would be perhaps peculiar, but it would be beautiful.

Jody reached the Forrester land and hurried under the live oaks into the open yard. The house was somnolent. There was no curl of smoke from the chimney. There were no dogs in sight, but a hound was howling from the dog-pen at the rear. The Forresters were probably all sleeping through the heat of the early afternoon. But when they slept in the day-time, they over-flowed the house, out to the veranda, under the trees. He stopped and called.

"Fodder-wing! Hit's Jody!"

The hound whined. A chair scraped on the board floor inside the house. Buck came to the door. He looked down at Jody and passed his hand over his mouth. His eyes were unseeing. It seemed to Jody that he must be drunk.

Jody faltered, "I come to see Fodder-wing. I come to show him my fawn."

Buck shook his head as though he would shake away a bee that annoyed him, or his thoughts. He wiped his mouth again.

Jody said, "I come special."

Buck said, "He's dead."

The words had no meaning. They were only two brown leaves that blew past him into the air. But a coldness followed their passing, and a numbness took him. He was confused.

He repeated, "I come to see him."

"You come too late. I'd of fotched you, if there'd been time. There wasn't time to fotch ol' Doc. One minute he was breathin'. The next minute he jest wa'n't. Like as if you blowed out a candle."

Jody stared at Buck and Buck stared back at him. The numbness grew into a paralysis. He felt no sorrow, only a coldness and a faintness. Fodder-wing was neither dead nor alive. He was, simply, nowhere at all.

Buck said hoarsely, "You kin come look at him."

First Buck said that Fodder-wing was gone, like candle-light, and then he said that he was here. None of it made sense. Buck turned into the house. He looked back, compelling Jody with his dull eyes. Jody lifted one leg after the other and mounted the steps. He followed Buck into the house. The Forrester men sat all together. There was a oneness about them, sitting so, motionless and heavy. They were pieces of one great dark rock, broken into separate men. Pa Forrester turned his head and looked at Jody as though he were a stranger. Then he turned it away again. Lem and Mill-wheel looked at him. The others did not stir. It seemed to Jody that they saw him from over a wall they had built against him. They were unwilling to hold the sight of him. Buck groped for his hand. He led him toward the large bedroom. He started to speak. His voice broke. He stopped and gripped Jody's shoulder.

He said, "Bear up."

Fodder-wing lay with closed eyes, small and lost in the center of the great bed. He was smaller than when he had lain sleeping on his pallet. He was covered with a sheet, turned back beneath his chin. His arms were outside the sheet, folded across his chest, the palms of the hands falling outward, twisted and clumsy, as in life. Jody was frightened. Ma Forrester sat by the side of the bed. She held her apron over her head and rocked herself back and forth. She flung down the apron.

She said, "I've lost my boy. My pore crookedy boy."

She covered herself again and swayed from side to side.

She moaned, "The Lord's hard. Oh, the Lord's hard."

Jody wanted to run away. The bony face on the pillow terrified him. It was Fodder-wing and it was not Fodder-wing. Buck drew him to the edge of the bed.

"He'll not hear, but speak to him."

Jody's throat worked. No words came. Fodder-wing seemed made of tallow, like a candle. Suddenly he was familiar.

Jody whispered, "Hey."

The paralysis broke, having spoken. His throat tightened as though a rope choked it. Fodder-wing's silence was intolerable. Now he understood. This was death. Death was a silence that

203

gave back no answer. Fodder-wing would never speak to him again. He turned and buried his face against Buck's chest. The big arms gripped him. He stood a long time.

Buck said, "I knowed you'd hate it fearful."

They left the room. Pa Forrester beckoned to him. He went to his side. The old man stroked his arm. He waved at the circle of brooding men.

He said, "Ain't it quare now? We could of spared nigh ary one o' them fellers. The one we cain't spare was the one was takened." He added brightly, "And him a swivveled, no-account thing, too."

He sank back in his rocking chair, pondering the paradox.

Jody bruised them all with his presence. He wandered outside into the yard. He roamed to the back of the house. Fodder-wing's pets were here, caged and forgotten. A five-months' bear cub, brought no doubt to amuse him in his illness, was chained to a stake. It had walked its dusty circle, around and around, until its chain was tangled and it was held tight against the stake. Its water-pan was over-turned and empty. At sight of Jody, it rolled on its back and cried with a sound like a human baby. Squeak the squirrel ran his endless treadle. His cage had neither food nor water. The 'possum was asleep in its box. Preacher the red-bird hopped on his one good leg and pecked at the bare floor of his cage. The raccoon was not in sight.

Jody knew where Fodder-wing kept sacks of peanuts and corn for his creatures. His brothers had made him a little feed-box and kept it filled for him. Jody fed the small things first and watered them. He approached the bear cub cautiously. It was small and roly-poly, but he was not too certain what use it might make of its sharp claws. It whimpered and he reached out one arm to it. It wrapped all four legs around it and clung desperately. It rubbed its black nose against his shoulder. He untangled it and pulled away from it and straightened its chain and brought it a pan of water. It drank again and again, then took the pan from him with its paws like the hands, he thought, of a nigger baby, and turned the last few cool drops on its stomach. He could have laughed aloud if he were not so heavy with sadness. But it relieved him to care for the animals, to give them, for the time, the comfort that their master could never offer them again. He wondered sorrowfully what would become of them.

He played abstractedly with them. The sharp joy that he had once felt when Fodder-wing shared them was muted. When Racket, the raccoon, came in from the forest with its queer, uneven gait, and recognized him, and climbed up his leg to his shoulder, and made its plaintive, chirring cry, and parted his hair with its thin, restless fingers, he longed so painfully for Fodder-wing that he had to lie on his belly and beat his feet in the sand.

The ache turned into a longing for the fawn. He got up and brought a handful of peanuts for the 'coon, to keep it occupied. He went in search of the fawn. He found it behind a myrtle bush, where it had been able to watch unobserved. He thought it might be thirsty, too, and he offered it water in the bear cub's pan. The fawn sniffed and would not drink. He was tempted to feed it a handful of corn from the Forresters' abundance, but decided it would not be honest to do so. Probably its teeth were still too tender to chew the hard kernels in any case. He sat down under a live oak and held the fawn close to him. There was a comfort in it not to be found in the hairy arms of Buck Forrester. He wondered if his pleasure in Fodder-wing's creatures had been dissipated because Fodder-wing was gone, or because the fawn now held all he needed of delight.

He said to it, "I'd not trade you for all of 'em, and the cub to boot."

A gratifying feeling of faithfulness came over him, that the enchantment of the creatures he had so long coveted could not deflect his affections from the fawn.

The afternoon was endless. It came to him that something was unfinished. The Forresters ignored him, yet, somehow, he knew they expected him to stay. Buck would have said good-by to him if he were supposed to go. The sun dropped behind the live oaks. His mother would be angry. Yet he was waiting for something, if only dismissal by a sign. He was bound to Fodder-wing, tallow-white in the bed, and a thing waited that would set him free. At dusk the Forresters filed out of the house and went in silence about their chores. Smoke drifted from the chimney. The smell of fat pine blended with frying meat. He trailed after Buck, driving the cows to water.

He offered, "I done fed and watered the bear cub and the squirrel and them."

Buck touched a switch to a heifer.

He said, "I remembered them oncet today, and then my mind went black agin."

Jody said, "Kin I he'p?"

"They's a plenty of us here, to do. You could wait on Ma like Fodder-wing done. Keep up her fire and sich as that."

He went reluctantly into the house. He avoided the sight of the bedroom door. It was drawn almost closed. Ma Forrester was at the hearth. Her eyes were red. She stopped every few moments to touch them with the corner of her apron. Her straggly hair had been wet and brushed back smooth and neat, as though in honor of a guest.

He said, "I come to he'p."

She turned with a spoon in her hand.

She said, "I been standin' here thinkin' about your Ma. She's burrit as many as I got."

He fed the fire unhappily. He was increasingly uneasy. Yet he could not go. The meal was as meager as the Baxters' own. Ma Forrester set the table indifferently.

She said, "Now I forgot to make coffee. They'd drink coffee when they'd not eat."

She filled the pot and set it on the coals. The Forrester men came one by one to the back porch and washed their hands and faces and combed their hair and beards. There was no talk, no joking and jostling, no noisy stamping. They trooped in to the table like men in a dream. Pa Forrester came in from the bedroom. He looked about him wonderingly.

He said, "Ain't it quare——"

Jody sat down next to Ma Forrester. She served the plates with meat, then began to cry.

She said, "I counted him in, same as always. Oh my Lord, I counted him in."

Buck said, "Well now, Ma, Jody'll eat his portion and mebbe grow up big as me. Eh, boy?"

The family rallied. For a few minutes they ate hungrily. Then a nauseating fullness came over them and they pushed away their plates.

Ma Forrester said, "I got no heart to clean up tonight, nor you neither. Jest stack the plates 'til after tomorrer mornin'."

Release, then, would come in the morning. She looked at Jody's plate.

She said, "You ain't et your biscuit nor drinked your milk, boy. What ailed 'em?"

"That's for my fawn. I allus save him some o' my dinner."

She said, "You pore lamb." She began to cry again. "Wouldn't my boy of loved to seed your fawn. He talked about it and he talked about it. He said, 'Jody's got him a brother.'"

Jody felt the hateful thickening of his throat. He swallowed.

He said, "That's how come me to be here. I came for Fodder-wing to name my fawn."

"Why," she said, "he named it. Last time he talked about it, he give it a name. He said, 'A fawn carries its flag so merry. A fawn's tail's a leetle white merry flag. If I had me a fawn, I'd name him "Flag." "Flag the fawn," is what I'd call him.'"

Jody repeated, "Flag."

He thought he would burst. Fodder-wing had talked of him and had named the fawn. There was happiness tangled with his grief that was both comforting and unbearable.

He said, "I reckon I best go feed him. I best go feed Flag."

He slid from his chair and went outside with the cup of milk and the biscuits. Fodder-wing seemed close and living.

He called, "Here, Flag!"

The fawn came to him and it seemed to him that it knew the name, and had perhaps always known it. He soaked the biscuits in the milk and fed them to it. Its muzzle was soft and wet in his hand. He went back into the house and the fawn followed.

He said, "Kin Flag come in?"

"Bring him right in and welcome."

He sat down stiffly on Fodder-wing's three-legged stool in the corner.

Pa Forrester said, "Hit'd pleasure him, you comin' to set up with him tonight."

That, then, was the thing expected of him.

"And 'twouldn't scarcely be decent, buryin' him in the mornin' without you was here. He didn't have no friend but you."

Jody cast off his anxiety over his mother and father like a too-ragged shirt. It was of no importance, in the face of matters so grave. Ma Forrester went into the bedroom to take the early vigil. The fawn nosed about the room, smelling of one man after the other, then came and lay down beside Jody. Darkness came tangibly into the house, adding its heaviness to theirs. They sat smothered under the thick air of sorrow that only the winds of time could blow away.

At nine o'clock Buck stirred and lit a candle. At ten o'clock a horse and rider clattered into the yard. It was Penny on old Cæsar. He dropped the reins over its head and came into the house. Pa Forrester, as head of the house, rose and greeted him. Penny looked about at the dark faces. The old man pointed to the half-open bedroom door.

Penny said, "The boy?"

Pa Forrester nodded.

"Gone—or goin'?"

"Gone."

"I feared it. Hit come over me, that was what was keepin' Jody away."

He laid one hand on the old man's shoulder.

"I feel for you."

He spoke to one man after the other. He looked directly at Lem.

"Howdy, Lem."

Lem hesitated.

"Howdy, Penny."

Mill-wheel gave him his chair.

Penny asked, "When did it happen?"

"Jest at dawn today."

"Ma goed in to see would he eat a bite o' breakfast."

"He'd been layin' punishin' a day-two, and we'd had ol' Doc, but he seemed to be mendin'."

The talk broke over Penny in a torrent. The relief of words washed and cleansed a hurt that had been in-growing. He listened gravely, nodding his head from time to time. He was a small staunch rock against which their grief might beat. When they finished and fell quiet, he talked of his own losses. It was a reminder that no man was spared. What all had borne, each could bear. He shared their sorrow, and they became a part of his, and the sharing spread their grief a little, by thinning it.

Buck said, "Likely Jody'd like to set up with him alone a whiles."

Jody was in a panic when they took him into the room and turned away to close the door. Something sat in a far dark corner of the room and it was the same thing that had prowled the scrub the night his father had been bitten.

He said, "Would it be all right, did Flag come, too?"

They agreed that it was seemly and the fawn was brought to join him. He sat on the edge of the chair. It was warm from Ma Forrester's body. He crossed his hands in his lap. He looked furtively at the face on the pillow. A candle burned on a table at the head of the bed. When the flame flickered, it seemed that Fodder-wing's eyelids fluttered. A light breeze stirred through the room. The sheet seemed to lift, as though Fodder-wing were breathing. After a time the horror went away and he could sit back in the chair. When he leaned far back, Fodder-wing looked a little familiar. Yet it was not Fodder-wing who lay, pinched of cheek, under the candle-light. Fodder-wing was stumbling about outside in the bushes, with the raccoon at his heels. In a moment he would come into the house with his rocking gait, and Jody would hear his voice. He stole a look at the crossed, crooked hands. Their stillness was implacable. He cried to himself, soundlessly.

The wavering candle was hypnotic. His eyes blurred. He roused himself, but a moment came when his eyes would not open. Death and the silence and his sleep were one.

He awakened at daylight to a heaviness of spirit. He heard a sound of hammering. Some one had laid him across the foot of the bed. He was wide awake instantly. Fodder-wing was gone. He slid from the bed and into the big room. It was empty. He went outside. Penny was nailing a cover on a fresh pine box. The Forresters stood about. Ma Forrester was crying. No one spoke to him. Penny drove the last nail.

He asked, "Ready?"

They nodded. Buck and Mill-wheel and Lem moved forward. Buck said, "I kin tote it alone."

He swung the box to his shoulder. Pa Forrester and Gabby were missing. Buck set out toward the south hammock. Ma

Forrester followed him. Mill-wheel took hold of her arm. The others dropped in behind them. The procession filed slowly to the hammock. Jody remembered that Fodder-wing had a grape-vine swing here, under a live oak. He saw Pa Forrester standing beside it. They had spades in their hands. A raw hole gaped in the earth. The mounded soil beside it was dark with wood-mould. The hammock was light with the dawning, for the sunrise reached out luminous fingers parallel with the earth and covered it with brightness. Buck set down the coffin and eased it into the opening. He stepped back. The Forresters hesitated.

Penny said, "The father first."

Pa Forrester lifted his spade and shovelled earth on the box. He handed the spade to Buck. Buck threw a few clods. The spade passed from one to the other of the brothers. There was a tea-cupful of earth remaining. Jody found the spade in his hands. Numb, he scooped the earth and dropped it on the mound. The Forresters looked at one another.

Pa Forrester said, "Penny, you've had Christian raising. We'd be proud, did you say somethin'."

Penny advanced to the grave and closed his eyes and lifted his face to the sunlight. The Forresters bowed their heads.

"Oh Lord. Almighty God. Hit ain't for us ignorant mortals to say what's right and what's wrong. Was ary one of us to be a-doin' of it, we'd not of brung this pore boy into the world a cripple, and his mind teched. We'd of brung him in straight and tall like his brothers, fitten to live and work and do. But in a way o' speakin', Lord, you done made it up to him. You give him a way with the wild creeturs. You give him a sort o' wisdom, made him knowin' and gentle. The birds come to him, and the varmints moved free about him, and like as not he could o' takened a she wild-cat right in his pore twisted hands.

"Now you've done seed fit to take him where bein' crookedy

in mind or limb don't matter. But Lord, hit pleasures us to think now you've done straightened out them legs and that pore bent back and them hands. Hit pleasures us to think on him, movin' around as easy as ary one. And Lord, give him a few red-birds and mebbe a squirrel and a 'coon and a 'possum to keep him comp'ny, like he had here. All of us is somehow lonesome, and we know he'll not be lonesome, do he have them leetle wild things around him, if it ain't askin' too much to put a few varmints in Heaven. Thy will be done. Amen."

The Forresters murmured "Amen." Sweat stood on their faces. They came to Penny one by one and wrung his hand. The raccoon came running and ran across the fresh-turned earth. It cried and Buck lifted it to his shoulder. The Forresters turned and trooped back to the house. They saddled Cæsar and Penny mounted. He swung Jody up behind him. Jody called the fawn and it came from the bushes. Buck came from the rear of the house. He had a small wire cage in his hand. He handed it up to Jody on the horse's rump. It held Preacher, the lame red-bird.

He said, "I know your Ma wouldn't leave you keep ary o' the creeturs, but this feller'll make out on pure crumbs. Hit's for you to remember him by."

"I thank you. Good-by."

"Good-by."

Cæsar jogged down the road toward home. They did not speak. Cæsar dropped into a walk and Penny did not disturb him. The sun rose high. Jody's arm ached from holding the little cage in the air. The Baxter clearing came into sight. Ma Baxter had heard the horse's hooves and was at the gate.

She called out, "Hit's enough to be fretted about one, then you both go off and stay gone."

Penny dismounted and Jody slid down.

Penny said, "Easy, Ma. We had a duty. Pore leetle ol' Fodder-wing died and we he'ped bury him."

She said, "Well— Pity 'twa'n't that great quarrelin' Lem."

Penny turned Cæsar out to graze and came to the house. Breakfast had been cooked but was now cold.

He said, "Ne' mind. Jest warm the coffee."

He ate abstractedly.

He said, "I never seed a family take a thing so hard."

She said, "Don't tell me them big rough somebodies took on."

He said, "Ory, the day may come when you'll know the human heart is allus the same. Sorrer strikes the same all over. Hit makes a different kind o' mark in different places. Seems to me, times, hit ain't done nothin' to you but sharpen your tongue."

She sat down abruptly.

She said, "Seems like bein' hard is the only way I kin stand it."

He left his breakfast and went to her and stroked her hair.

"I know. Jest be a leetle mite easy on t'other feller."

· 18 ·

AUGUST was merciless in its heat, but it was, mercifully, leisurely. There was little work to be done and no great hurry
about the doing of that little. There had been rains and the
corn had come to maturity. It was drying on the stalks and
could soon be broken for curing. Penny estimated that he
would have a good yield, perhaps as much as ten bushels to
the acre. The sweet potato vines grew lushly. The Kaffir corn
for the chickens was ripening, its long heads like sorghum. The
sunflowers along the fence, also for the chickens, had heads
as big as plates. The cow-peas were abundant. They made the
staple food, with the meat of some game, almost every day.
There would be a fine stand of cow-pea hay for use through
the winter months. The field of pindars was not doing so well,
but because of the killing by old Slewfoot of Betsy the brood

sow, there were not many shoats to fatten. The Baxter hogs had come mysteriously home, and with them a young brood sow. Its mark had been changed from the Forrester mark to the Baxter. Penny accepted it as the peace offering for which it was intended.

The red ribbon cane had made a fair stand. The Baxters looked forward to autumn and the frosts, when sweet potatoes would be dug, hogs butchered, corn ground into meal, and the cane would be ground and the juice boiled into syrup, and plenty would replace the meagerness. There was enough to eat, even now in the leanest season, but there was no variety, no richness, no comfortable feeling of ample reserve stores. They lived from day to day, with meal and flour and fat meat short, dependent on Penny's chance shots at deer and turkey and squirrel. He trapped a fat 'possum in the yard one night, and dug a mess of the new sweet potatoes to roast with it, for a special treat. It was an extravagance, for the potatoes were small and immature.

The sun laid a heavy hand on the scrub and on the clearing. Ma Baxter's bulk suffered with the heat. Penny and Jody, lean and clean-limbed, felt the temperature only in an increasing reluctance to move rapidly, or often. They did the chores together in the morning, milked the cow, fed the horse, chopped wood for cooking, brought water from the sink-hole, and then were through until the evening. Ma Baxter cooked hot dinner at noon, then banked the fire on the hearth with ashes; and supper was cold, consisting of the noon surplus.

Jody was conscious always of Fodder-wing's absence. Living, Fodder-wing had been with him, in the back of his mind, a friendly presence to which he might turn in his thoughts, if not in reality. But Flag grew miraculously, day by day, and that was comfort enough. Jody thought that its spots were beginning to fade, a sign of maturity, but Penny could see little change. It was unquestionably growing in intelligence. Penny said that the bears had the largest brains of any of the scrub animals, and the brain of the deer came next.

Ma Baxter said, "This un's too dad-ratted smart," and Penny said, "Why, Ma, shame on you for cussin'," and winked at Jody.

Flag learned to lift the shoe-string latch on the door and come in the house at any hour of the day or night, when he was not shut up. He butted a feather pillow from Jody's bed and tossed it all over the house until it burst, so that feathers drifted for days in every nook and cranny, and appeared from nowhere in a dish of biscuit pudding. He began to romp with the dogs. Old Julia was too dignified to do much more than wag her tail slowly when he pawed at her, but Rip growled and circled and pretended to pounce, and Flag kicked up his heels and flicked his merry tail and shook his head and finally, with impudence, leaped the slat fence and raced alone down the roadway. He liked best to play with Jody. They tussled and held furious butting matches and raced side by side, until Ma Baxter protested that Jody was growing as lean as a black snake.

In a late afternoon toward the end of August, Jody went with the fawn to the sink-hole for fresh water for supper. The road was bright with flowers. The sumac was in bloom, and the colic root sent up tall stalks of white or orange orchid-like flowers. The French mulberries were beginning to ripen on slim stems. They were lavender in color, close-clustered, like snails' eggs along lily stalks. Butterflies sat on the first purple buds of the fragrant deer-tongue, opening and closing their wings slowly, as though waiting for the buds to open and the nectar to be revealed. The covey call of quail sounded again from the pea-field, clear and sweet and communal. Sunset was coming a little earlier, and at the corner of the fence-row, where the old Spanish trail turned north and passed the sink-hole, the saffron light reached under the low-hanging live oaks and made of the gray pendulous Spanish moss a luminous curtain.

Jody stopped short with his hand on the fawn's head. A horseman with a helmet was riding through the moss. Jody took a step forward, and horse and rider vanished, as though their substance were no thicker than the moss. He stepped back and they appeared again. He drew a long breath. Here, certainly, was Fodder-wing's Spaniard. He was not sure whether he was frightened or no. He was tempted to run back home, telling himself that he had truly seen a spirit. But his father's stuff was in him, and he forced himself to walk forward slowly to the spot in which the apparition had appeared. In a moment the truth was plain. A conjunction of moss and limbs had created the illusion. He could identify the horse, the rider and the helmet. His heart thumped with relief, yet he was disappointed. It would be better not to have known; to have gone away, believing.

He continued on to the sink-hole. The sweet bay was still in bloom, filling the sink-hole with its fragrance. He longed for Fodder-wing. Now he should never know whether the mossy horseman in the sunset was the Spaniard, or whether Fodder-wing had seen yet another, at once more mystic and more true. He set down his buckets and went down the narrow trail that Penny had cut between banks to the floor of the sink-hole, long before he was born.

He forgot his errand and lay down under the lacy shadow of a dogwood tree at the foot of the slope. The fawn nosed about, then lay down beside him. He could see from this spot the whole deep-sunk bowl at once. The rim above caught the glow of the sunset, as though a ring of fires burned invisibly around it. Squirrels, quieted a moment by his coming, began to bark and chatter and swing across the tree-tops, frenzied with the last hour of day, as they were always frenzied with the first. The palm fronds made a loud rattling where they dashed through, but the live oaks gave almost no record of their passing. In the thick sweet gums and hickories they were almost inaudible, always unseen, until they raced up and down the tree trunks or slipped to the edge of a limb to swing into another tree. Birds made sweet sharp sounds in the branches. Far away, a red-bird sang richly, coming closer and closer, until Jody saw him drift to the Baxter drinking trough. A flock of turtle doves whirred in, to drink briefly, then flew away to their roosting places in the adjoining pine forest. Their wings whistled, as though their pointed gray and rosy feathers were thin knives to slash the air.

Jody's eye caught a motion at the edge of the slope. A mother raccoon came down to the limestone troughs, followed by two young ones. She fished the series of troughs carefully, beginning with the drinking trough at the upper level. He had the finest reason now for delaying. He would have to wait until the water had cleared and settled. The mother 'coon found nothing of interest in the troughs. One of the young clambered to the edge of the stock-trough and peered in curiously. She slapped it away, out of danger. She worked her way down the slope. Now she was lost among the tall ferns. Now her black-masked face appeared again between stalks of the Cherokee bean. The two young ones peered out after her, their small faces replicas of her own, their bushy tails ringed almost as decisively.

She reached the seepage pool at the bottom and began to fish in earnest. Her long black fingers groped under fallen twigs and branches. She lay on her side to reach into a crevice for, no doubt, a crayfish. A frog jumped and she made a quick circular pounce and waded back to the edge with it. She sat up on her hind legs and held it a moment, kicking, against her breast, then sunk her teeth in it and shook it, as a dog shakes a rat. She dropped it between her off-spring. They pounced on it and snarled and growled and cracked its bones and finally shared it. She watched dispassionately a moment, then turned back into the pool. Her bushy tail was lifted just above the water level. The young ones waded out after her. Their peaked noses lifted above the water. She turned and saw them and dragged them back to land. She lifted each one in turn and spanked its small furry bottom in so human a way that Jody had to clap his hand over his mouth to keep from shouting. He watched her for a long time, fishing and feeding them. Then she ambled leisurely across the floor of the sink-hole and up the far slope and away over the rim, the young ones following, chirring and grumbling amiably together.

The sink-hole lay all in shadow. Suddenly it seemed to Jody that Fodder-wing had only now gone away with the raccoons. Something of him had been always where the wild creatures fed and played. Something of him would be always near them. Fodder-wing was like the trees. He was of the earth, as they were earthy, with his gnarled, frail roots deep in the sand. He was like the changing clouds and the setting sun and the rising moon. A part of him had been always outside his twisted body. It had come and gone like the wind. It came to Jody that he need not be lonely for his friend again. He could endure his going.

He went to the drinking trough and filled the buckets with as much water as he could carry, and went home. He told at table of the 'coons, and even his mother was interested to hear about the spanking, and no one questioned his delay. After supper, he sat with his father and listened to the hoot-owls and the frogs, and a far wild-cat and still further foxes, and to the north, a wolf that howled and was answered. He tried to tell his father the thing that he had felt that day. Penny listened gravely, and nodded, but Jody could not make the words fit his feeling, and could not quite make his father understand.

· 19 ·

THE first week in September was as parched and dry as old bones. Only the weeds grew. There was a tension in the heat. The dogs were snappish. The snakes were crawling, dog days being past, and their shedding and their blindness ended. Penny killed a rattler under the grape arbor that measured seven feet in length. He had seen the coffee-weed shaking as though an alligator were passing through and had followed. The rattler, he said, was after the quail, to fill his long belly on his way to his winter quarters. He dried the great hide on the smoke-house wall and then hung it on the front-room wall beside the fireplace.

He said, "I like to look at it. I know there's one o' the boogers'll not harm nobody."

The heat was the worst of the whole summer, yet there was a

220

vague change, as though the vegetation sensed the passing of one season and the coming of another. The golden-rod and asters and the deer-tongue thrived on the dryness. The poke-berries ripened and the birds fed on them along the fence-rows. All the creatures, Penny said, were hard put to it for food. The spring and summer berries, the brierberries, the huckleberries, the blueberries and choke-berries and the wild gooseberries, were long since gone. The wild plum and the mayhaw had had no fruit for bird or beast for many a month. The 'coons and foxes had stripped the wild grape-vines.

The fall fruits were not yet ripe, papaw and gallberry and persimmon. The mast of the pines, the acorns of the oaks, the berries of the palmetto, would not be ready until the first frost. The deer were feeding on the tender growth, bud of sweet bay and of myrtle, sprigs of wire-grass, tips of arrow-root in the ponds and prairies, and succulent lily stems and pads. The type of food kept them in the low, wet places, the swamps, the prairies and the bay-heads. They seldom crossed Baxter's Island. They were hard to hunt in the boggy places. In a month, Penny was able only to bring down one yearling buck. Its spike horns were still in the velvet. They felt like a coarse rough wool. Shreds hung, where the yearling had rubbed them against saplings, to ease the itch of growth and hurry their hardening. Ma Baxter ate them boiled, saying they tasted like marrow. Penny and Jody had no taste for them. They could see too plainly the big eyes under the new horns.

The bears, too, were in the low places. They were feeding for the most on palmetto buds, ripping out the hearts ruth-lessly. The palm hammock around Sweetwater Spring looked as though a hurricane had swept through it. The low-growing palmettos were slashed into ribbons, the sweet cream-colored cores eaten below the level of the ground. Even some of the tall palms looked as though struck by lightning, where a less lazy bear or a hungrier one had scaled the trunk and torn out the bud. The palmettos, Penny said, would die. They were like all living things. They could not live with the heart gone. One low palm had been only shredded from the outside. The heart was intact. Penny cut out the smooth cylinder with his hunting knife to carry home to cook. The Baxters liked swamp cabbage as well as the bears.

"But when them scapers runs short o' palmeeters," Penny said, "hit's look out for the shoats. You kin look to see the bears climbin' into the lot most ary night now. And your friend Flag here, you best keep him with you faithful, especial at night. I'll stand up to your Ma, do she quarrel about it."

"Ain't Flag gittin' too big for a bear to bother?"

"A bear'll kill ary creetur cain't out-run him. Why, on the prairie one year, a bear killed my bull, was nigh as big as he was. Hit made him a meal for a week. He come back to it 'til there wasn't nothin' left o' the bull but the beller, and that was gone, too."

Ma Baxter's complaint was at lack of rain. Her rain barrels were empty. All her washing must be done at the sink-hole. The clothes were looking dingy.

She said, "Clothes washes easier, anyways, on a cloudy day. My Ma allus said, 'Soft weather, soft clothes.'"

She needed rain-water, too, to clabber the milk. The milk turned rankly sour in the heat but would not clabber. In hot weather, she always depended on a few drops of rain-water to clabber it, and at every shower would send Jody to a hickory tree to catch some, for rain-water dripped from a hickory was best for the purpose.

The Baxters watched the quartering of the September moon anxiously. Penny called his wife and son when the first quarter appeared. The silver crescent was almost perpendicular. He was jubilant.

"We'll git rain soon, shore," he told them. "If the moon was straight acrost, hit'd push the water out and we'd not git none. But look at it. Hit'll rain to where you kin hang your clothes right on the line and the Lord'll wash 'em."

He was a good prophet. Three days later every sign was of rain. Passing by Juniper Springs from a hunt, he and Jody heard the alligators bellowing. Bats flew in the daytime. Frogs caah-caah-caahed steadily at night. The Dominick rooster crowed in the middle of the day. The jay-birds bunched and flew back and forth together, screaming as one. Ground rattlers crawled across the clearing in the hot sunny afternoon. On the fourth day a flock of white sea-birds flew over. Penny shaded his eyes against the sun and watched after them uneasily.

He said to Jody, "Now them ocean jessies don't belong to be crossin' Floridy. I don't like it. Hit means bad weather, and when I say bad, I mean bad."

Jody felt a lift of spirit like the sea-birds. He loved storm. It swept in magnificently and shut the family inside in a great coziness. Work was impossible and they sat about together and the rain drummed on the hand-hewn shingles. His mother was good-natured and made him syrup candy, and Penny told tales.

He said, "I hope it's a pure hurricane."

Penny turned on him sharply.

"Don't you wish sich as that. A hurricane flattens the crops and drowns the pore sailors and takes the oranges offen the trees. And down south, why, boy, hit tears down houses and cold-out kills people."

Jody said meekly, "I won't wish it agin. But wind and rain is fine."

"All right. Wind and rain. That's another thing."

The sun set strangely that night. The sunset was not red, but green. After the sun was gone, the west turned gray. The east filled with a light the color of young corn. Penny shook his head.

"I don't like it. Hit looks mighty boogerish."

In the night, a gust of wind moved through and slammed both doors. The fawn came to Jody's bed and poked its muzzle against his face. He took it up on the bed with him. The morning, however, was clear, but the east was the color of blood. Penny spent the morning repairing the roof of the smoke-house. He brought drinking water twice from the sink-hole, filling all available buckets. In the late morning, the sky turned gray and remained so. There was no air stirring.

Jody asked, "Is it a hurricane comin'?"

"I don't think. But somethin's comin', ain't natural."

In mid-afternoon the skies turned so black that the chickens went to roost. Jody drove in Trixie and the calf and Penny milked early. He turned old Cæsar into the lot and put a forkful of the last remaining hay in his manger.

Penny said, "Git the eggs outen the nests. I'm goin' to the house. Hurry now, else you'll git ketched."

The hens were not laying and there were only three eggs in the lot nests. Jody climbed into the corn-crib where the old Barred Rock was laying. The left-over husks rustled under his feet. The dry, sweet-scented air was close and thick. He felt stifled. There were two eggs in the nest and he put all five inside his shirt and started for the house. He had not felt the hurry that had infected his father. Suddenly, in the false twilight stillness, he took alarm. A great roaring sounded in the distance. All the bears in the scrub, meeting at the river, might make such a roaring. It was wind. He heard it come closer from the northeast as plainly as though it came on vast webbed feet, brushing the tree-tops in its passing. It seemed to leap the cornfield in one gust. It struck the yard trees with a hissing, and the mulberries bent their boughs to the ground, and the chinaberry creaked in its brittleness. It passed over him with a rustle like the wings of many geese, high-flying. The pines whistled. The rain followed.

The wind had been high overhead. The rain was a solid

wall, from sky to earth. Jody struck it flat, as though he had dived against it from a great height. It hurled him back and threw him off his balance. A second wind seemed now to reach long muscular fingers through the wall of rain and scoop up everything in its path. It reached down his shirt and into his mouth and eyes and ears and tried to strangle him. He dared not drop the eggs in his shirt. He kept one arm cupped under them and put the other over his face and scuttled into the yard. The fawn was waiting, quivering. Its tail hung wet and flat and its ears drooped. It ran to him and tried to find shelter behind him. He ran around the house and to the back door. The fawn bounded close behind him. The kitchen door was latched. The wind and rain blew so hard against it that he could not swing it open. He beat on the thick pine. For a moment he thought he was unheard in the tumult and that he and the fawn would be left outside to drown, like biddies. Then Penny lifted the latch from the inside and pushed the door open into the storm. Jody and the fawn darted inside. Jody stood gasping. He wiped the water from his eyes. The fawn blinked.

Penny said, "Who was it, now, wishin' for sich as this?"

Jody said, "Did I git my wish this quick allus, I'd wish mighty keerful."

Ma Baxter said, "Go change them wet clothes right away now. Couldn't you of shut up that fawn before you come in?"

"There wasn't no time, Ma. He was wet and skeert."

"Well— Long as he don't do no mischief. Now don't put on your good breeches. You got a pair there, full o' holes as a cast-net, but they'll hold together in the house."

Penny said after him, "Don't he look like a wet yearlin' crane. All he needs is tail feathers. My, ain't he growed since spring."

She said, "I think he'll be right nice-lookin', do them freckles fade and that hair ever lay flat and them bones git covered with meat."

"A few more changes," he agreed innocently, "and he'll turn out handsome as the Baxters, thank the Lord."

She looked at him belligerently.

"And mebbe, handsome as the Alverses," he added.

"That makes more sense. You better change your tune."

"I got no idee o' startin' a ruckus, sweetheart, and you and me penned up together by no storm."

She chuckled with him. Jody, overhearing from his bedroom, could not tell whether they were making fun of him, or whether there was indeed hope for his appearance.

He said to Flag, "You think I'm purty, anyways, don't you?"

Flag butted him. He took it for assurance and they ambled back to the kitchen.

Penny said, "Well, hit's a three-day nor'easter. A might early, but I've seed change o' season this early, many a year."

"How kin you tell it'll be three days, Pa?"

"I'd not sign no papers on it, but generally the first September storm be a three-day nor'easter. The whole country changes. I reckon, one way or t'other, the world. I've heered Oliver Hutto tell o' September storm as fur off as China."

Ma Baxter asked, "Why ain't he come to see us this time? Grandma shocks my modesty, but I do like Oliver."

"I reckon mebbe he's had enough o' the Forresters for a whiles and jest ain't travelin' this road."

"They'll not fight without he acts quarrelsome, will they? The fiddle cain't play without the bow."

"I'm feered the Forresters, leastwise Lem, 'll romp on him ary time they come up with him. Until they git the gal business settled."

"Sich doin's! Nobody acted that-a-way when I were a gal."

"No," Penny said, "I was the only one wanted you."

She lifted the broom in pretended threat.

"But sugar," he said, "the rest jest wasn't smart as me."

There was a lull in the fierce beating wind. A pitiful whine sounded at the door. Penny went to it. Rip had found adequate shelter, but old Julia stood drenched and shivering. Or perhaps she had found shelter, too, but longed for a comfort that was more than dryness. Penny let her in.

Ma Baxter said, "Now let in Trixie and old Cæsar, and you'll have things about to suit you."

Penny said to Julia, "Jealous o' leetle ol' Flag, eh? Now you've been a Baxter longer'n Flag. You jest come dry yourself."

She wagged her slow tail and licked his hand. Jody was warmed by his father's inclusion of the fawn in the family. Flag Baxter——

Ma Baxter said, "How you men kin take on over a dumb creetur, I cain't see. Callin' a dog by your own name— And that fawn, sleepin' right in the bed with Jody."

Jody said, "He don't seem like a creetur to me, Ma. He seems jest like another boy."

"Well, it's your bed. Long as he don't bring fleas or lice or ticks or nothin' into it."

He was indignant.

"Look at him, Ma. Lookit that sleekity coat. Smell him, Ma."

"I don't want to smell him."

"But he smells sweet."

"Jest like a rose, I s'pose. Well, to my notion, wet fur's wet fur."

"Now I like the smell o' wet fur," Penny said. "I mind me one time, on a long hunt, I had me no coat and the weather turned cold. It was over about Salt Springs, at the head o' the run. My, it was cold. And we shot a bear, and I dressed out the skin nice, and I slept under it, with the fur side out. And in the night come a cold drizzly rain, and I poked my nose out from under, and I smelt that wet fur. Now the other fellers, Noey Ginright and Bert Harper and Milt Revells, they said I purely stunk, but I puttened my head back under the bear-skin and I was warm as a squirrel in a holler tree, and that wet bear-hide smelt better to me than yellow jessamine."

The rain drummed on the roof. The wind whistled under the eaves. Old Julia stretched out on the floor near the fawn. The storm was as cozy as Jody had hoped for. He made up his mind privately that he would wish for another in a week or two. Now and then Penny peered out of the window into the dark.

"Hit's a toad-strangler of a rain," he said.

Supper was generous. There were cowpeas and smoked venison pie and biscuit pudding. Anything that was remotely an occasion stirred Ma Baxter to extra cooking, as though her imagination could speak only by the use of flour and shortening. She fed Flag a bit of pudding with her own fingers. Jody, with a secret gratitude, helped her wash and wipe the supper dishes. Penny went to bed shortly after, for his strength did not hold out, but not to sleep. A candle burned in the bedroom and Ma Baxter brought her piecing, and Jody lay across the foot of the bed. The rain hissed against the window.

He said, "Pa, tell me a tale."

Penny said, "I've told you all the tales I know."

"No, you ain't. You allus got another."

"Well, the only one comes to me I ain't told, ain't rightly a tale. I ever tell you about the dog I had when I first come to the island? The dog could cold-out study?"

Jody wriggled closer up the counterpane.

"Tell me."

"Well, sir, the dog was part fox-hound and part blood-hound and part jest dog. He had long sorrowful ears, nigh about dragged the ground, and he was so bow-legged he couldn't walk a sweet pertater bed. He had distant kind o' eyes, lookin' off some'eres, and them distracted eyes near about caused me to trade him off. Well, I hunted him a whiles, and it begun to come to me, he didn't act like no other dog I'd ever seed. He'd leave a cat-trail or a fox-trail right in the middle, and go lay down. The first time-two he done it, I figgered I jest didn't have me no dog a-tall.

"Well sir, it begun to come to me, he knowed what he was doin'. Jody boy, go fetch me my pipe."

The interruption was exasperating. Jody tingled. He scrambled for the pipe and tobacco.

"All right now, son. You set on the floor or on a chair and keep offen the bed. Ary time I say 'trail' or 'track' you jiggle the bed to where I think the slats is busted. That's better——

"Well, sir, I was obliged to set down with that dog my own-self, to see what 'twas he was doin'. Now you know how a wild-cat or a fox'll fool most dogs? He'll double back on his own tracks. Yes sir, he'll double back on his own tracks. He'll git a good start on the dogs and he'll light out and put a heap o' distance between 'em. Then what do he do? He turns right back over his own trail. He cuts as far back as he's daresome to do, listenin' all the while for the dogs. Then he cuts off at another angle, so a picture o' his trail'd look like a big V, like the ducks makes flyin'. Well, the dogs follers the trail he made in the first place, extry strong on account of him havin' been over it twicet, and then they come to a place where they jest ain't no more trail. They nose around and they nose around and they complain, and when they jest cain't figger no sense to it, they turns back agin, back-trackin'. 'Course, they picks up then the turn-off where the fox or cat cut off in another direction. But all that time is wasted, and nine to one the cat or fox has made an out of it and got plumb away. Well, what do you figger this lop-eared dog o' mine done?"

"Tell me."

"He figgered it out, that's what he done. He figgered out about when 'twas time for the creetur to double back—and he'd slip back along the trail and lay down and wait. And when Mister Fox or Mister Cat come slippin' back, there was old Dandy waitin' to pop out on him.

"Now sometimes he'd make his cut-off too fur back, and did he hang them long ears when he guessed it wrong! But mostly speakin', he studied it out right, and he ketched me more wild cats and more foxes than ary dog I've had, before or since."

He puffed his pipe. Ma Baxter moved her rocker closer to the candle. It was depressing to have the tale end so soon.

"What else did old Dandy do, Pa?"

"Well, one day he met his match."

"A cat or a fox?"

"Neither one. A big ol' buck, was as smart a deer as he was smart a dog. He was a buck with a twisted antler. Each year it growed in twisted. Now a deer don't generally double back on his tracks. But now and agin this old buck'd do it. And that was jest to this sly ol' dog's likin'. But this is where he wasn't smart enough. The buck'd do jest the opposite to whatever the dog figgered he'd do. One time he'd double back. Next time he'd keep on runnin'. He'd change his ways ever' whip-stitch. That went on, year in, year out, the dog and the buck tryin' to out-smart each other."

"Which was the smartest, Pa. How'd it end?"

"You shore you want the answer?"

He hestitated. He wanted the droopy-eared dog to out-smart the buck, and yet he wanted the buck to get away.

"Yes. I got to know. I got to know the answer."

"Well, hit's got a answer but no endin'. Old Dandy never come up with him."

He sighed with relief. That was a proper tale. When he thought of it again, he could picture the dog trailing the buck perpetually.

He said, "Tell another tale like that un, Pa. A tale has got a answer but no endin'."

"Now boy, they ain't many tales like that in the world. You best be content with that un."

Ma Baxter said, "I ain't much for dogs, but they was a dog oncet I takened a notion to. It was a bitch and she had the purtiest coat. I said to the feller owned her, 'When she finds pups,' says I, 'I'd like one.' He said, 'You're welcome, but 'twon't do, for you got no way o' huntin' it'—I wasn't yit married to your Pa—'and a hound'll die,' he said, 'if it ain't hunted.' 'Is she a hound?' says I, and he said, 'Yessum.' And I said, 'Then I shore don't want one, for a hound'll suck eggs.' "

Jody waited eagerly for the rest of the tale, then understood that was all there was to it. It was like all his mother's tales. They were like hunts where nothing happened. He went back in his thoughts to the dog that could out-smart wild-cats and foxes, but never caught the buck.

He said, "I'll bet Flag'll be smart when he grows up."

Penny said, "What'll you do, do somebody else's dogs take out after him?"

His throat constricted.

"I'll kill ary dog or ary man comes here, huntin' him. Nobody ain't likely to come, is they?"

Penny said gently, "We'll spread the word, so folks'll be keerful. He's not likely to roam far, no-how."

Jody decided to keep his gun always loaded, against marauders. He slept that night with Flag on the bed beside him. The wind shook the windowpanes all night and he slept uneasily, dreaming of clever dogs that ran the fawn mercilessly through the rain.

In the morning he found Penny dressed as for winter, in his heavy coat and with a shawl over his head. He was preparing to go out into the storm to milk Trixie, the only chore that was entirely necessary for the time being. There was no lessening of the torrential downpour.

231

Ma Baxter said, "Now you be peert and git back in here or you'll die o' the pneumony."

Jody said, "Leave me go," but Penny said, "The wind'd blow you away, boy."

It seemed to him, watching the small bones of his father leaning against the tumultuous air, that there was little to choose between them in bulk and sturdiness. Penny came in again, drenched and breathless, the milk in the gourd spotted by the rain.

He said, "Hit's a mercy I toted water yestiddy."

The day continued as stormy as it had begun. The rain fell in sheets and the wind whipped it in under the eaves, so that Ma Baxter set pans and gourds to catch it. The rain barrels outside were overflowing and the rain from the roof gurgled into their fullness. Old Julia and the fawn had to be turned out by force. They were both back at the kitchen door in a brief time, wet and shivering. This time Rip was with them, whining. Ma Baxter protested, but Penny admitted the three. Jody dried them all with the crocus sack rug from in front of the hearth.

Penny said, "We're about due for a lull."

The lull did not come. Now and then there seemed to be a few moments when the wind and rain were less intense and Penny rose hopefully from his chair and peered outside. But he had no sooner decided that he would risk going out to cut wood and see to the chickens, than the deluge came again, as violent as before. In the late afternoon he went again to milk Trixie, to feed and water Cæsar, and to feed the chickens, huddled and frightened and unable to scratch for their living. Ma Baxter made him change his wet clothes immediately. They steamed and dried by the hearth with the sweet, musty smell of wet cloth.

Supper was not so ample. Penny was not inclined to tales. The dogs were allowed to sleep in the house and the family went to bed early. Darkness had come at an unseemly hour and it was impossible to tell the time. Jody awakened at what would ordinarily have been an hour before daylight. The world was dark and the rain was still falling, the wind still blowing.

Penny said, "We'll git a break this mornin'. Hit's a three-day nor'easter a'right, but sich a rain. I'll be proud to see the sun."

The sun did not appear. There was no morning break. In mid-afternoon there came the lull that Penny had expected the day before. But it was a gray lull, the roof dripping, the trees soaked, the earth sodden. The chickens came out from their huddle for a few forlorn moments and scratched half-heartedly.

Penny said, "We'll git a change o' wind now, and all be clare and fine."

The change of wind came. The gray sky turned green. The wind roared in from a distance, as before. When it came, it was not from the northeast but from the southeast, and it brought more rain.

Penny said, "I've never seed sich a thing."

The rain was more torrential than before. It poured down as though Juniper Creek and Silver Glen Run and Lake George and the St. John's River had all emptied over the scrub at once. The wind was no fiercer than before, but it was gusty. And there was no end to it. It blew and rained and blew and rained and blew and rained.

Penny said, "This must be the way the Lord made the blasted ocean."

Ma Baxter said, "Hush. You'll be punished."

"Cain't be no worse punished, woman. The 'taters'll be rotted and the corn flat and the hay ruint, and the cane."

The yard was afloat. Jody looked out of the window and saw two drowned biddies floating about with upturned bellies.

Penny said, "I've seed things in my time, but I've never seed a thing like this."

Jody offered to go to the sinkhole for drinking water.

Penny said, "Hit'll be nothin' but rain-water, and riled to boot."

They drank rain-water from a pan under the northwest corner of the house. It had a faintly woody taste from the cypress shingles. Jody did the evening chores. He went out of the kitchen door with the milk gourd into a strange world. It was a lost and desolate world, like the beginning of time, or the end of it. The vegetation was beaten flat. A river ran down the road, so that a flat-bottomed boat could have gone down it clear to Silver Glen. The familiar pines were like trees at the bottom of the sea, washed across not with mere rain, but with tides and currents. It seemed to him that he might swim to the top of the rain. The water was knee-deep in the lot, which lay at a lower level than the house. Trixie had broken down the bars that separated her from the calf and had taken it with her to a high corner. They stood huddled together. The calf had taken most of the milk and he was able only to draw a quart or so from the drained udders. The passage between the stalls and the corn-crib was a sluiceway. He meant to gather the dry husks for extra feed for Trixie, but the water swept through so discouragingly that he decided to let her make out until morning with the hay from the loft. It was a good thing, he thought, that the new crop of hay would soon be ready. There was little left. He did not know whether to try to separate the over-grown calf from the cow again. There was no place to put it where it would be dry. Yet the Baxters needed the milk as badly. He decided to wait and ask his father, coming back again if necessary. He fought his way outside and plodded to the house. The rain blinded him. The clearing seemed alien and unfriendly. He was glad to push open the door and to be again inside the house. The

kitchen seemed safe and intimate. He made his report on
conditions.

Penny said, "Best leave the calf stay with its mammy, a time
like this. We kin make out without milk 'til mornin'. Hit'll
shorely be clare by then."

Morning brought no abatement. Penny paced up and down
the kitchen.

He said, "My daddy told of a storm in the '50's was mighty
bad, but I don't reckon all Floridy history has had sich a
rain."

The days passed with no change. Ma Baxter usually left the
weather in Penny's hands, but now she cried, and sat rocking
with her hands folded. On the fifth day, Penny and Jody made
a rush to the pea-field to pull enough cow-peas for a meal or
two. The peas were flattened. They pulled up the whole vines
with their backs to the rain and wind. They stopped at the
smoke-house for a piece of pickled meat from the bear Buck
Forrester had shot on his last night with them. Penny remembered that his wife was short of cooking grease. They tipped
the can that held the golden bear grease and filled a stone
crock. They laid the meat over the top to protect it and
rushed for the house.

The cow-peas were already moulding on the outside, but
the peas inside were still firm and good. Supper was again a
feast. There was the wild honey to fall back on, and Ma Baxter
made a pudding sweetened with its rich flavor, tasting faintly
of wood and smoke.

Penny said, "Don't seem possible it'll not clare by mornin',
but if so be 'tain't, Jody, you and me had best git out in it
and pull as many peas as we kin manage."

Ma Baxter said, "But how'll I keep 'em?"

"Cook 'em, woman, and warm 'em ever' day, if need be."

The morning of the sixth day was exactly like the others.
Since they would be drenched in any case, Penny and Jody

stripped to their breeches and went to the field with sacks. They worked until noon in the down-pour, pulling the slippery pods from the bushes. They came in for a hurried dinner and went back again without troubling to change their clothes. They covered most of the field. The hay, Penny said, was a total loss, but they would do what they could to save the peas. Some of the pods were mature. They spent the evening and late into the night shelling the peas, sticky and mouldering. Ma Baxter built up a slow fire on the hearth and spread out the peas close to the heat to dry. Jody was awakened several times in the night by the sound of some one going out to the kitchen to replenish the fire.

The morning of the seventh day might have been the morning of the first. The gusty wind whipped around the house as though it had always blown and always would blow. The sound of the rain on the roof and in the rain-barrels was now so familiar that it was not noticed. At daylight, a limb of the chinaberry crashed to the ground. The Baxters sat silently at breakfast.

Penny said, "Well, Job takened worse punishment than this. Leastways, none of us ain't got risin's."

Ma Baxter snapped, "Find the good in it, that's right."

"They ain't no good in it. Lest it is to remind a man to be humble, for there's nary thing on earth he kin call his own."

After breakfast he took Jody to the cornfield. The corn had been broken on the stalks before the storm. The stalks were beaten to the ground but the ears were unharmed. They gathered them and brought them too into the warm dry refuge of the kitchen.

Ma Baxter said, "I ain't got the peas dried yit. How'll I dry all this?"

Penny did not answer but went to the front room and kindled a fire on the hearth. Jody went outside to bring in more wood. The wood was soaked through, but when the fat-wood was heated a little while it would burn. Penny strewed the ears of corn on the floor.

He said to Jody, "Now your job be to keep changin' it, so's it'll all git a mite o' the heat."

Ma Baxter said, "How's the cane?"

"Hit's flat."

"What you reckon has happened to the 'taters?"

He shook his head. In the late afternoon he went to the sweet potato field and dug enough for supper. They were beginning to rot. By trimming, some were usable. Again, supper seemed lavish, because of the sweet potatoes.

Penny said, "If they ain't no change by mornin', we jest as good to quit fightin' and lay down and die."

Jody had never heard his father speak so disconsolately. It froze him through. Flag was showing the effect of short rations. His ribs and backbone were visible. He bleated often. Penny had given up all attempt to milk the cow, for the sake of the calf.

In the middle of the night Jody awakened and thought he heard his father about. It seemed to him the rain was falling less violently. He was asleep again before he could be certain. He awakened on the morning of the eighth day. Something was different. There was silence instead of tumult. The rain had stopped. The long winds were still. A light the color of pomegranate blossoms sifted through the gray, wet atmosphere. Penny flung all the doors and windows wide open.

" 'Tain't much of a world to go out to," he said, "but let's all go out and be thankful there's a world at all."

The dogs pushed past him and bounded out side by side. Penny smiled.

"Dogged if 'tain't like goin' outen the Ark," he said. "The animals two by two— Ory, come go out with me."

Jody jumped about and leaped down the steps with the fawn.

"We're the two deer," he called.

Ma Baxter looked across the fields and began to cry again. But the air, Jody felt, was cool and sweet and gracious. The fawn shared his feeling and bounded over the yard-gate with swift twinkling heels. The world was devastated with the flood, but it was indeed, as Penny kept reminding his wife, the only world they had.

· 20 ·

THE second day after the storm, Buck and Mill-wheel Forrester came riding to the island to see whether all was well
with the Baxters. They had come straight from their own
work of caring for the stranded stock. Along the main trail
the sights, they said, were new in their generation. The flood
had played havoc with the small animals. It was agreed that
the four of them, Buck and Mill-wheel and Penny and Jody,
should make a tour of exploration for some miles around, so
that they might know what to expect, in the immediate future,
of the movements not only of the game, but of the predatory
creatures. The Forresters had brought two dogs, and an extra
horse, and asked to have Rip and Julia join them. Jody was
excited that he was to be taken.

He asked, "Kin Flag foller along, too?"

Penny turned on him sharply.

"This here is serious," he said. "I'm carryin' you with us to learn you. If you figger on frolickin', you kin stay home, too."

Jody hung his head. He slipped away and shut Flag in the shed. The sand floor was still soaked and the shed smelled musty, but he made a bed of crocus sacks where the fawn might keep dry. He put out water and feed for it in case he should be long away.

"You stay quiet," he said to it, "and I'll tell you all I see when I come home agin."

The Forresters were well stocked, as always, with ammunition. Penny had spent two evenings during the storm in making low-mould shot and in loading his own shells. He had a month's supply filled and capped and ready for use. He filled his shot-bag and polished the barrels of his gun.

He said to the Forresters, "Now I worked a rabbit's-foot on you fellers about that wuthless dog I traded you. Ary time you crave to use this gun, you say so."

Buck said, "Ain't none of us but Lem mean enough to take it back, Penny. I'll swear, he got so mean, cooped up in the storm, I had to dress him down myself."

"Where's he now?"

Buck spat.

"Gone off to the river, fretted about harm comin' to that tormented gal Twink. Figgerin' on makin' it up with her, and layin' for Oliver. He kin fight it out by hisself this time."

It was decided to make a wide circle that would take in both Baxter's and Forresters' Islands, Juniper Springs, Hopkins Prairie, and the good deer territory where the live oak islands that lifted from the marshy saw-grass would certainly have provided refuge for the animals. With the exception of a rolling ridge to the west, toward the Ocklawaha River, the Baxter's Island terrain was the highest in the scrub. But it dropped down all around to low land, and the circle they had mapped out would tell the story. They would try to return to Forresters' Island to sleep, but if that was not practicable they would camp wherever night found them. Penny filled a knapsack carefully. He put in a frying pan, salt, meal, a side of bacon and a twist of tobacco. In a crocus sack he put a handful of lighter'd splinters, a bottle of thin lard, and a bottle of panther oil which he treasured for his rheumatism. The exposure during the days of storm had brought his aches on him with vicious force. He had no meat for the dogs.

Buck said, "We kin shoot somethin' for 'em."

They were ready at last. They swung into the saddles and set off briskly south-east down the road in the direction of Silver Glen and Lake George.

Penny said, "Long as we're this clost, we best go see how ol' Doc Wilson come out. That place o' his is like to be half under water."

Buck said, "And him mebbe too drunk to know it."

The road dipped sharply between Baxter's Island and Silver Glen. The flood had washed down it with such volume and such force that the flat sand road was now a narrow ravine. Rubbish of all sorts was caught in the lower branches of the close-growing scrub pines. Farther down the road the toll of small animal life began to show. Skunks and 'possums seemed the heaviest sufferers. Their bodies lay by dozens on the ground, where the waters, receding, had deposited them, or hung with the trash in the limbs of trees. To the south and east there was a great silence. The scrub was always silent, yet Jody realized now that there had always been an undertone of cry and movement, where the creatures called and stirred, no more discernible than the wind. To the north, where high scrub land was dense with thin pines, there was an unusual rustling and distant chattering. The squirrels had evidently taken up residence here in droves, driven, if not by water, at least by hunger and fear, from the swamps and hammocks below them.

Penny said, "I'll bet that scrub there is purely alive with creeturs."

They hesitated, tempted to go in to the denseness. They agreed that it was best, as first planned, to skirt the low regions and determine the damage, and then to check on the still living creature population. Toward Silver Glen they reined in the horses.

"You see what I see?"

"If you didn't see it, too, I'd not believe it."

Silver Glen had overflowed and backed up, and the flood waters had rushed down to join it and make a greater havoc. Dead animals drifted about in the backwash.

Penny said, "I didn't know there was that many snakes in the world."

The bodies of highland reptiles were as thick as cane-stalks. There were dead rattlesnakes, king snakes, black snakes, coach whips, chicken snakes, garter snakes and coral snakes. At the thin edge of the receding water, cottonmouth moccasins and other water snakes swam about thickly.

Buck said, "I don't understand that. Ary snake kin swim. I've met a rattler in the middle o' the river."

Penny said, "Yes, but the land snakes likely got ketched in their holes."

The flood had reached everywhere, like the searching fingers of a 'coon, and had torn out all the things for whom the solid earth was their only refuge. A fawn lay dead with swelling belly. Jody's heart jumped. Flag might have perished in just this fashion, if he had not become, in time, a Baxter. As they gaped, two rattlers slithered across the ground in front of them. The rattlers ignored them, as though in the face of greater dangers man was of no concern.

Penny said, "Hit'll be all a man's life is wuth, for a while, to cross high land."

Buck said, "I mean."

They could go no farther east and turned north, skirting the low waters. Where there had been swamp, there were ponds. Where there had been hammock, there was swamp. Only the high infertile scrub had turned aside the devastation. Even here, pines were up-rooted, and those that had stood, all leaned to the west, bowed down by the week-long weight of wind and rain.

Penny said, "Hit'll be a long day before them trees stands straight agin."

They became uneasy as they approached the Branch. The water was still high here, well above the level of Lake George. Three and four days ago it must have been much higher. They stopped and stared down at the doctor's land, sloping to the lake. The thick hammock might have been a cypress slough. The giant live oaks, the hickories, the sweet gums, the magnolias, the orange trees, stood deep in a turgid wetness.

Penny said, "Let's try the road."

The road, like the one leading southeast from Baxter's Island, had formed a sluiceway for the waters. It was now a gully, and dry. They rode down it. Doc Wilson's house appeared ahead, dark and shadowy under the great trees.

Buck said, "I'll be blest if I see why ary man would choose a place this dark to live in, even to stay drunk."

Penny said, "If ever'body loved the same places, we'd be right over-crowded."

Water stood ankle-deep around the house. The blocks on which it rested showed that the water had at one time been over the floor. The boards of the broad veranda were warping. They waded to the front steps, eyes open warily for coiled moccasins. A white pillow-slip was tacked across the front door.

A message was printed on it with ink. The ink had run but the letters were plain.

Buck said, "Us Forresters cain't read good. Read it, Penny."

Penny spelled out the liquid words.

"I have gone toward the ocean where this much water ain't so peculiar. I mean to stay drunk until the storm is over. I will be somewhere between here and the ocean. Please don't come after me unless it's a broke neck or a baby. Doc.

P.S. If it's a broke neck no use anyway."

Buck and Mill-wheel and Penny shouted, and Jody laughed because they did.

Buck said, "That Doc, he'd crack him a joke right in the Lord's face."

Penny said, "That's why he's a good doctor."

"How come?"

"Well, he gits to fool the Lord now and agin."

They laughed until they were weak. It was good to be light-hearted, when the world had been gray and heavy so long. They went inside the house and found a tin of crackers and a bottle of whiskey on the table and added them to their stores. They turned back up the road and went north for a mile or so, then west again.

Penny said, "No use goin' to Hopkins Parairie. We kin figger hit's a pure lake."

Buck and Mill-wheel agreed. South of Hopkins Prairie they found the same story. The weaker animals and the ground creatures had been washed down to destruction. At the edge of a bay-head, a bear lumbered across in plain sight.

Penny said, "No use shootin' him. We may need his meat a month from now. Hit's too fur to tote him and we'll git many a shot before night-fall."

The Forresters agreed reluctantly. A shot to them was a

shot, whether or no they could use the game. Penny would shoot nothing for which he could not see a use. He preferred even to kill the enemy bears at a time when their flesh was welcome and usable. They continued west. Here was a long stretch of gallberry flats that in good weather was the favorite haunt of bear and wolf and panther. The ground was always boggy, the vegetation low, and bay-heads to the north and east gave both food and a hiding place. Now the section was a swamp. Water drained off quickly from a sand soil, but where the earth was heavy, it remained as on clay. Islands of scrub oak and live oak, and a few high palm hammocks, lay between the flats and the broad stretch of the scrub itself. They skirted the new-made swamp and made for these.

At first Jody could see nothing. Then when Penny pointed to this tree and that, he was able to make out the forms of animals. They rode close. The creatures seemed unafraid. A fine buck stared at them. The shot was irresistible. Buck brought it down. They rode closer. Wild cats and lynxes peered visibly from the branches of trees. The Forresters urged their killing.

Penny said, "Hit's a pity we should add to their troubles. Seems like there'd ought to be room enough in the world for folks and creeturs, both."

Mill-wheel said, "Trouble with you, Penny, you was raised by a preacher. You look for the lion and the lamb to be layin' down together."

Penny pointed to the high earth ahead of them.

"Well," he said, "the deer and the bob-cat—there you be."

But he was forced to agree that every wild-cat on the loose, every bear, lynx, wolf or panther, meant depredations on hogs, chickens and cattle, and on the milder game, the deer, the 'coons, the squirrels and the 'possums. It seemed to make an endless circle of "Eat or be eaten. Kill or go hungry."

He joined in the attack on the great cats and six fell killed or wounded. Jody brought down a lynx. The recoil of the old muzzle-loader all but knocked him from Cæsar's rump. He dismounted to reload. The Forresters patted him on the back. The men dressed the buck. The meat was lean, showing the week of privation. They flung the carcass over the rump of Buck's horse. They went forward on foot to the oak island. Dim forms scurried at the far side. It was eery, hearing the rustling of creatures, seeing the skulking.

The hides of the wild-cats were poor and not worth saving.

Penny said, "Now them carcasses'd make a fine dinner for the dogs, and easy carried."

The dogs were already chewing on the haunches of the cats. They too had been underfed through the storm. The cat-meat was dressed out and slung over the horses. Mid-afternoon found the exploring party due north and a little west of Forresters' Island. They decided that it was best to continue, and camp out for the night. For an hour or two the sun was strong. A putrid odor began to rise from the wet earth and from the waters. Jody felt a little ill.

Buck said, "I'm proud Fodder-wing ain't here right now. He'd hate it, all these creeturs dead."

Bears began to be seen again. The wolves were not in evidence, nor the panthers. They rode through several miles of scrub. Deer and squirrels were plentiful here. Probably they had never left, feeling secure. They were all bold and plainly hungry. The Forresters, greedy, and anxious as well that both families should surely have meat, shot another buck and slung it over Mill-wheel's horse.

Toward sunset, the scrub dissolved again into live oak islands. Farther south was Juniper Prairie. That would now be flooded. A little to the east lay a stretch of land that was neither scrub nor prairie, neither island nor swamp nor hammock. It was as open as a clearing. It was agreed to camp here for the night, even though an hour or two of daylight remained. No one was of a mind to be caught in the low places, malodorous and crawling with reptiles. They made camp under two giant long-leaf pines. There was not much protection overhead, but the night would be clear, and it was better under such un-natural cicumstances to be in the open.

Mill-wheel said, "When I bed with a panther, I crave for that panther to be dead."

They turned the horses loose with dropped reins to graze before tethering them for the night. Mill-wheel had disap-peared into a patch of scrub oak south of the camp site. The others heard him shout. The dogs had followed him on one of the endless trails that had enchanted them all day. They were moving slowly, tired out from the abundance of scent and track. Old Julia lifted her voice.

Penny said, "That's cat."

Wild-cats had lost their zest. All four dogs were baying, their voices ranging from a high keening to the bass rumble of Rip. Mill-wheel shouted again.

Penny said, "Don't you Forresters ever git a bait o' wild-cats?"

Buck said, "Now he'd not holler that-a-way over no wild-cat."

The dogs' voices lifted into a frenzy. Penny and Jody and Buck became infected with the sound and ran into the thick growth. A scrub oak had grown to considerable size. Half-way up its gray twisted trunk they saw the quarry. It was a female panther with two cubs. She was lean and gaunt but of immense length. The cubs still wore the blue and white spots of panther infancy across their hides. Jody thought they were prettier than any kittens he had ever seen. They were the size of grown house-cats. They lifted back their delicate whiskers in imitation of their mother's snarl. Her appearance was for-midable. Her teeth were bared, her long tail switched back and forth, her claws worked on the oak limb. She seemed

247

about to drop on the first creature, man or dog, to move closer. The dogs were wild.

Jody called out, "I want the cubs! I want the cubs!"

Mill-wheel said, "Let's knock her out and leave the dogs have a go-round."

Penny said, "We'll have four tore-up dogs if you do."

Buck said, "You mighty right. We best drop her and be done with it." He shot.

The dogs were on her the instant she hit the ground. If there was a spark of life, it was at once snuffed out. Buck climbed up the low tree and shook the limb.

Jody called again, "I want the cubs."

He planned, when they dropped, to run to them and pick them up. He was sure they would be gentle. They fell finally under Buck's vigorous shaking. Jody darted in but the dogs were ahead of him. The cubs were dead, and shaken and tossed, before he could approach them. Yet in their dying, he saw that they slashed at the dogs and bit and clawed. He would have had ragged flesh, he realized, to show for his seizing of them. Yet he wished they were still alive.

Penny said, "Sorry, boy. But you'd not have had nothin' you'd of keered to keep. Them scapers learns meanness early."

Jody eyed the small fierce teeth.

"Kin I have the hides for another knapsack?"

"Why, sho'. Here, Buck, he'p me git 'em away from the dogs before they're tore up."

Jody took the limp bodies and cradled them.

"I hate things dyin'," he said.

The men were silent.

Penny said slowly, "Nothin's spared, son, if that be ary comfort to you."

" 'Tain't."

"Well, hit's a stone wall nobody's yit clumb over. You kin

kick it and crack your head agin it and holler, but nobody'll listen and nobody'll answer."

Buck said, "Well, when it come my time, I shore aim to git my money's wuth hollerin'."

They called the dogs away from the dead panther. She measured nine feet from tip of nose to end of long curled tail. She was too lean, however, to dress out for her oil.

Penny said, "I got to either ketch me a fat panther or quit havin' rheumatism."

The hide too was in poor condition. They cut away the heart and liver to roast for the dogs.

Penny said, "No use nussin' them cubs no longer, Jody. Give 'em here and go fetch wood. I'll skin 'em out for you."

He went away. The evening was clear and rosy. The sun was drawing water. Shadowy fingers reached through the luminous sky to the sodden earth. The wet leaves of the scrub oaks, the thin needles of the pines, glittered, and he forgot his distress. There was much to be done to make camp. All wood was wet, but, prowling about, he found a fallen pine whose core was rich with resin. He called, and Buck and Mill-wheel came and dragged it bodily to the camp site. It would make a burning base to dry out the other wood. They chopped it in half and laid the two long pieces side by side. Jody struggled with flint and steel from the tinder horn until Penny took it away from him and kindled a fire between the logs with fat-wood splinters. He piled on small brush that caught fire quickly. Larger limbs and logs were added. They smoked and smoldered but ended by bursting into flame. Now there was a glowing bed on which the wettest logs might dry, and then burn slowly. Jody dragged in all available wood that was not too heavy to handle alone. He had a high pile ready for the night's long burning. Buck and Mill-wheel dragged in logs as big as themselves.

Penny cut out the backstraps from the fattest buck and sliced them for frying for supper. Mill-wheel appeared from a prowl with palmetto fronds to be used as plates, for laying out the food, and other camp means of tidiness. He had as well the hearts of two palms. He pulled away layer after layer of the white cores and came at last to the hearts, crisp and sweet.

He said, "Now I want that fryin' pan, Mr. Penny, please, for my swamp cabbage. Then I'll leave you fry that backstrap when I'm done with the pan."

He sliced the palm-hearts thinly.

"Where's the grease, Penny?"

"In a bottle in the crocus sack."

Jody ambled about, watching the others. His job was to feed the fire with twigs to keep the flame from dying too low. The logs blazed brightly. There were already embers suitable for roasting. Buck whittled forked sticks on which each could roast his meat. Mill-wheel dipped water from a nearby pond for his pan of swamp cabbage, covered it with a section of palm-frond and set it over the coals to cook.

Penny said, "Now I forgot coffee."

Buck said, "Well, with ol' Doc Wilson's whiskey, I'll not miss it."

He brought out the bottle and passed it. Penny was ready for the frying pan for his venison, but the swamp cabbage was not done. He improvised spits on which he hung the wild-cat carcasses. He sliced the wild-cat and panther hearts and livers and stuck them on sticks and propped them over the coals to roast. The smell was enticing. Jody sniffed the air and sniffed again and patted his flat stomach. Penny sliced the deer livers and placed them more carefully on Buck's forked sticks and gave each man his own toasting fork to hold, to cook his meat to his own taste. The flames licked around the dog-meat and the odor brought in the dogs. They came close and lay flat and slapped their tails back and forth and whined. Raw cat-meat was not too much to their fancy. They had gnawed a bit on it by way of proving their victory. The roasted flesh was another thing. They licked their chops.

Jody said, "I'll bet that's good."

"Well, try it." Penny withdrew a portion from the fire and held it out to him. "Look out. It's hotter'n stewed apples."

He hesitated over the strangeness, then touched his finger to the hot savory meat and put his finger in his mouth.

He said, " 'Tis good."

The men laughed, but he ate two slices.

Penny said, "Now some folks'd say hit'd make you fearless, eatin' wild-cat liver. We'll jest see."

Buck said, "Dogged if it don't smell fine. Give a mite here."

He sampled it and agreed that it was as good as any other liver. Mill-wheel ate a portion then but Penny refused.

"If I was to git any braver," he said, "I'd be rompin' on you Forresters and gittin' Hell beat out o' me agin."

They passed the bottle once more. The fire blazed, the meat dripped its juices into the flames, the fragrance eddied up with the smoke. The sun set behind the scrub oaks and Mill-wheel's swamp cabbage was done. Penny emptied it on a clean palm frond and put it over a smoldering log to keep warm. He wiped out the frying pan with a handful of moss and set it back over the coals to heat. He sliced bacon into it. When the bacon was brown and the fat sizzling hot, he fried the thin slices of backstrap crisp and tender. Buck cut scoops from the palm stems and every one dipped, share and share alike, into the swamp cabbage. Penny made hush-puppies of meal and salt and water and fried them in the fat the venison had cooked in.

Buck said, "Now if I knowed they'd feed you this good in Heaven, I'd not holler when I die."

Mill-wheel said, "Rations tastes a heap better in the woods. I'd ruther eat cold bread in the woods than hot puddin' in the house."

"Now you know," Penny said, "the same dog bit me."

The cat-meat was done. They cooled it a little and threw it to the dogs. The dogs bolted it greedily, then went to the pond to drink. They prowled about for a time, excited by the varying scents, then returned to lie by the blazing camp-fire in the increasing chill of the evening. Buck and Mill-wheel and Jody had stuffed. They dropped flat on their backs and stared up into the sky.

Penny said, "Flood or no flood, this is fine. I want you fellers to promise me one thing. When I'm an old man, set me on a stump and leave me listen to the hunt. Don't go off and leave me in the bay."

Stars twinkled, the first in nine days. Penny stirred at last to clean up the debris. He tossed the dogs the left-over cornmeal patties. He put the corncob stopper back in the bottle of fat. He held it up to the firelight. He shook it.

He said, "I'll be blasted. We've et my rubbin' medicine."

He pawed in the crocus sack and brought out the other bottle and opened it. It held unmistakably the lard-oil.

"Mill-wheel, you jay-bird. You opened the panther oil for the swamp cabbage."

There was silence. Jody felt his stomach turn over.

Mill-wheel said, "How'd I know 'twas panther oil?"

Buck swore under his breath. Then he burst into a thunderous laughter.

"I ain't goin' to let my imagination quarrel with what goes in my belly," he said. "I never et better swamp cabbage."

"Nor me," Penny said. "But when my bones gits to achin', I'll wish 'twas back where it come from."

Buck said, "Anyways, we know what to use for grease when we git ketched in the woods."

Jody's stomach quieted. After two slices of wild-cat liver, it would be poor business to be squeamish. But the panther oil did seem different, after having seen Penny rub it on his knees on winter evenings.

Mill-wheel said, "Well, I'll cut ever'body boughs for beds, long as I'm the one's in disgrace."

Penny said, "I'll come with you. If I was to go to sleep and raise up and see you in the bushes, I'd figger 'twas a bear, shore. I'll swear, I don't see how some o' you fellers growed so big."

Mill-wheel said, "Why, hell, we was raised on panther oil."

Every one went in high humor to cut his own bed. Jody broke small pine boughs with the needles on them and gathered moss for a mattress. They laid the pallets close to the fire. The Forresters lay down on their boughs with a crashing sound.

Penny said, "Now I'll bet ol' Slewfoot don't make that much fuss when he lays down."

Buck said, "And I'll bet you kin hear a June bird goin' to bed a heap further'n one o' you Baxters."

Mill-wheel said, "I wisht I had me a sack o' corn shucks now for a mattress."

Penny said, "The best bed I ever had was one made o' the fluff from cat-tail rushes. Hit were like lyin' on a cloud. But it takened a time to gather enough cat-tails."

Buck said, "The best bed in all the world is a feather bed."

Penny said, "Ary one ever tell you fellers about the time your daddy raised pure hell with a feather bed?"

"Tell it."

"Hit were before you were borned. Mebbe two-three of you was back in the house some'eres in cradles. I were jest a leetle ol' young un myself. I come over to your island with my own daddy. Reckon mebbe he come to try to give your Pa salvation. When he was young, your Pa was wilder'n you-all. He could tip a jug o' corn liquor back and drink it down like water. And he done so, in them days, right frequent. Well, we rode up to your door and here was broke dishes and rations all strowed down the walk, and chairs pitched over the gate. And all over the yard, and all along the fence row, was feathers. Looked as if chicken Heaven had done blowed up. Layin' on the stoop was the tickin' o' the feather bed where it had been split open with a knife.

"Your daddy come to the gate. Now I won't say he was drunk, but he shore had done been drunk. He'd tore up ever'-thing had takened his eye. And the last thing he noticed was the feather bed. Now he wa'n't mad nor quarrelin'. He was jest havin' him a big time crackin' things open. He'd got all over it, and was peaceful and happy as could be. Now what your Ma was doin' and sayin' whilst he was at it, you'd know better'n me. But right now she was still, and cold as ice. She was settin' rockin' with her hands folded and her mouth like a steel trap. My daddy had sense, if he was a preacher, and I reckon he figgered another time'd be best for whatever 'twas he'd come to say. So he jest passed the time o' day and set out to ride on agin.

"Well, your Ma come to and remembered her manners and called out to him. 'Stay eat with us, Mr. Baxter,' she said. 'I got nothin' left to offer you but corn-pone and honey. If I kin find a whole plate for you to eat on.'

"Your Pa turned and looked at her, surprised.

" 'Honey,' he said, 'honey, is there any honey in the honey-jug?' "

The Forresters shouted and slapped each other.

Buck said, "Wait 'til I walk in and ask Ma, 'Honey, is there any honey in the honey-jug?' Oh, wait!"

Jody laughed to himself long after the Forresters were quiet. His father made a story so real, he could see the feathers still, blown against the split-rail fence. The dogs, roused by the laughter, stirred and changed their positions. They had edged close for the warmth of the humans and of the fire. Old Julia lay at his father's feet. He wished Flag were with him, to snuggle close with his smooth warm coat. Buck rose and pulled another log on the fire. The men began to talk of the probable movements of the scrub and swamp animals. The wolves were evidently moving in another direction from the rest of the animals. They disliked wet sections even more than the big cats and were no doubt in the heart of the high scrub. Bear had not been as plentiful as expected.

Buck said, "You know where the bears be? South in the scrub around Sellers Bear Hole and Squaw Pond Bear Hole."

Mill-wheel said, "Tollie's Hammock, I'll bet you, toward the river."

Penny said, "They'll not be south. The wind and rain the last days all come from the southeast. They'd put it behind 'em, not go into it."

Jody put his arms under his head and looked up into the sky. It was as thick with stars as a pool of silver minnows. Between the two tall pines over him, the sky was milky, as though Trixie had kicked a great bucket of milk foaming across the heavens. The pines swayed back and forth in a light cool breeze. Their needles were washed with the silver of the starlight. Smoke from the camp-fire eddied up and joined the stars. He watched it drift through the pine tops. His eyelids fluttered. He did not want to go to sleep. He wanted to listen. The hunting talk of men was the finest talk in the world. Chills went along his spine to hear it. The smoke against the stars was a veil drawn back and forth across his eyes. He closed them. For a moment the talk of the men was a deep droning against the snapping of the wet wood. Then it faded into the sound of the breeze in the pines, and was no longer sound, but the voiceless murmur of a dream.

He was awakened in the night by his father, sitting bolt upright. Buck and Mill-wheel were snoring heavily. The fire had died low. The wet wood was sizzling slowly. He sat up beside Penny.

Penny whispered, "Listen."

Far in the night an owl hooted and a panther screamed. There was a closer sound. It sounded like the air dying from a bellows.

"Whoo—oo—. Whoo—oo—oo. Whoo—oo—oo."

It seemed almost at their feet. Jody's flesh crept. It might be Fodder-wing's Spaniard. Were ha'nts susceptible, like mortals, he wondered, to flood and rain? Did they yearn to warm their thin transparent hands at a hunter's camp-fire? Penny eased himself to his feet and fumbled for a pine knot for a torch. He lit it at the fire and started forward cautiously. The sighing sound had ceased. Jody followed close behind him. There was a rustling. Penny swung the torch. A pair of eyes, red as a bull-bat's, caught the light. He shifted the light. He laughed. The visitor was an alligator from the pond.

He said, "He smelt the fresh meat. Now wouldn't I love to drop him on top o' them Forresters."

Jody said, "Was it him, makin' that sighin'?"

"It were him, breathin' and blowin' and raisin' hisself up and down."

"Let's torment Buck and Mill-wheel with him."

Penny hesitated.

"He's a mite big for funnin'. He'll go six feet. If he was to take a chunk outen one of 'em, hit'd be a sorry joke."

"Will we kill him?"

"No use. We'll be gittin' meat for the dogs and to spare. 'Gators is harmless things."

"You goin' to leave him blow around all night?"

"No, for he'd quit blowin' and go to huntin' that meat he smells."

Penny made a rush at the alligator. It lifted its body on its short legs and turned back toward the pond. Penny ran after it, stopping to pick up sand or whatever came under his hand to throw after it. It ran with amazing speed. Penny followed, and Jody behind him, until a splash sounded at some distance.

"There. He's back with his kin folks. Now do he be polite enough to stay there, we'll not bother him."

They turned back to the camp-fire. It glowed comfortingly in the darkness. The midnight was still. The stars were so bright that when they looked away from the fire, they could see the water shining in the ponds. The air was cool. Jody wished that he could camp always like this, with his father. All that he lacked was Flag beside him. Penny moved the torch across the Forresters. Buck threw his arm across his face, but slept on. Mill-wheel was flat on his back. His black beard lifted and fell with his heavy breathing.

"He blows near about as deep as a 'gator," Penny said.

They piled more wood on the fire and returned to their pallets. They did not seem as comfortable as when they had first lain down on them. They shook up the moss and tried to flatten the pine boughs. Jody made a nest for himself in the middle and curled up kitten-wise. He lay a few luxurious moments watching the fresh blaze, then fell into a sleep as deep as the first.

The dogs were the first to awaken at daybreak. A fox had crossed under their noses, leaving its rank taint fresh on the air. Penny jumped up and caught them and tied them.

"We got bigger business today than fox," he told them.

From where he lay, Jody could look straight across into the sunrise. It was strange to see it on a level with his face. At home the thick scrub growth beyond the cleared fields obscured it. Now there was only a morning fog between. The sun did not seem to rise, but to sweep forward through a gray curtain. The curtain began to part its folds for the passing. The light was the thin pale gold of his mother's wedding ring. It grew brighter and brighter until he found himself blinking into the very face of the sun. The light September fog clung tenaciously a little while to the tops of the trees, as though resisting the tearing and destructive fingers of the sun. Then it too was gone and the whole east was the color of ripe guavas.

Penny called, "I need somebody to he'p find the panther oil so I kin cook breakfast."

Buck and Mill-wheel sat up. They were stiff from their heavy sleep.

Penny said, "The 'gators and the foxes has been runnin' right acrost you fellers."

He told of the night's encounter.

Buck said, "You shore 'twasn't one o' them swamp skeeters you seed, after Doc Wilson's liquor?"

"A foot less, and I'd say mebbe. But not scarcely six feet."

"Oh, yes. Why, I went to sleep on a camp like this oncet, and I dreamed I heered a skeeter buzzin', and when I waked up, here was me and my bed both, hangin' up on a snag in a cypress swamp."

Penny called Jody to wash his face and hands at the pond's edge. When they reached the water, the stench turned them back.

Penny said comfortably, "Well, our dirt is nothin' but wood-smoke. Even your Ma wouldn't make you wash in that kind o' water."

Breakfast was the same as supper, except that there was no more swamp cabbage with panther oil. Again the Forresters substituted a draught of whiskey for the missing coffee. Penny refused it. The pond water was not fit to drink and Jody was thirsty. In a world so full of water, it had occurred to no one to carry it.

Penny said, "You watch for a holler log is well off the ground, and has rain water in it. Rain water's allus fitten."

The fried and roasted venison and the hush-puppies did not taste as good as the night before. Penny cleaned up after breakfast. Grazing for the horses had been poor because the grasses were beaten flat. Jody gathered armfuls of moss for them and they ate it with relish. Breaking camp, mounting, turning the heads of the horses south, was the beginning of a fresh journey. Jody looked over his shoulder. The camp site was desolate. The charred logs, the gray ashes, were forlorn. The magic had died out with the flames of the camp-fire. The morning had been cool but the climbing sun began to heat the day. The earth steamed. The stench of the polluted waters was often overpowering.

Penny, in the lead, called back, "I wonder, kin the creeturs' bellies stand this rotten water?"

Buck and Mill-wheel shook their heads. The flood was unprecedented in the scrub. No man could tell what would come of it. The cavalcade continued steadily south.

Penny called to Jody, "Remember where we seed the whoopin' cranes dancin' so purty?"

Jody would not have recognized the prairie. It was a flat body of water, where even a crane might hesitate to wade and wander. Farther south was scrub again, then gallberry flats and bay-heads. But where marsh should be, was a lake. They reined in the horses. It was as though they had camped overnight on some strange borderland and had now come into another country. Fish were leaping in the air from water that a week ago had been land. And here, after all the miles, were the bears— They were fishing with an abandon that made them unaware of, or indifferent to, the approach of horses and riders. Two or three dozen black forms moved through the waters, belly-deep. Fish jumped ahead of them.

Penny called, "Hit's mullet!"

But mullet, Jody thought, lived in the ocean. They lived in Lake George, with its touch of salt, its faint surge of tide. They lived in the tidal rivers, and in a few fresh-water rivers where flowing springs and swift currents pleased them as well as the ocean, and from which they might leap, as they were doing now, in tensile silver arcs.

Penny said, "Hit's plain as day. Lake George backed up Juniper Creek, and the creek backed up, and the spring overflowed onto the parairie. And here's mullet."

Buck said, "We got a new parairie then. Mullet Parairie. And look at them bears——"

Mill-wheel said, "Hit's bear Heaven. Well, men, how many do we want?"

He sighted his rifle experimentally. Jody blinked his eyes. He had never seen so many bears at once in his life, except in dreams.

Penny said, "Don't let's be hogs about it, even if 'tis bears."

Buck said, "Four'll do us for a while."

"One'll do the Baxters. Jody, you want to kill a bear?"

"Yes, sir."

"Well— Now men, if it's agreeable, we'll pick our shots here and spread out a leetle. Somebody'll be obliged to git a second shot. Mebbe three, do Jody miss."

He assigned Jody the closest shot. It was a large fellow, probably a male.

Penny said, "Now Jody, you ride to the left a mite, 'til you git a bead on his cheek. When I give the word, ever'body'll fire. If he's moved by that time, take the best head shot you kin git. And if his head's down, and hid from you, aim for his middle and one of us'll finish him after."

Buck and Mill-wheel indicated their choices and the group spread cautiously in both directions. Penny lifted his hand. They halted. Jody was trembling so violently that when he lifted his gun he could see nothing in front of him but a blur of water. He forced himself to steady his aim. His bear was quartering from him, but he was able to draw a bead on the left cheek from the rear. Penny dropped his hand. Guns barked. There was a second bombardment from Buck and Mill-wheel.

The horses reared a little. Jody could not remember having pulled the trigger. But fifty yards in front of him a black body that had been upright, lay half-sunk in the water.

Penny shouted, "Nice shootin', boy!" and rode forward.

The remaining bears were scrambling across the swamp like paddle boats, churning the water behind them. It would take a long shot now to bring one down. Again Jody was amazed at the speed of the bulky bodies. The first shot of each man had been accurate and deadly. Buck and Mill-wheel had only wounded on their second shots. The dogs, kept at heel, broke into bedlam. They barked in a frenzy and dashed into the water. It was too deep for wading and too thick with growth for swimming. They were forced to retreat, shrill with frustration. The men rode in close on the two wounded animals. They fired again and the game lay still. The unharmed bears were vanishing before their eyes. No game was quicker or cleverer.

Buck said, "Now we never figgered on gittin' these scapers outen the water."

Jody had eyes only for his own kill. He could not believe that he had done it. Here lay food for the Baxter table for a fortnight, and it was of his providing.

Mill-wheel said, "We best go back home and git a yoke o' oxen."

Penny said, "Tell you. You got five to haul and we ain't got but the one. Now I'm satisfied with the hunt, and I'm satisfied we all know for a while where to look for the game. Do it suit you, you he'p me and Jody with this un o' his, and leave me keep this horse a day-two, and we'll jest go on our way and you go yours."

"Suits us."

Penny said, "You'd think men our age would of thought to of throwed in a rope."

"Who'd of guessed the hull blasted scrub was under water?"

Buck called, "Our legs is longer'n you Baxters. You stay in the saddle."

Penny was already on his feet. The water was over his knees. Jody was ashamed to stay on his horse as though he were a child. He too slid off into the water. The bottom was firm. He helped drag his bear to high ground. The Forresters seemed unaware that it was important that he had shot it, for it was his first. Penny touched his shoulder, and that was praise enough. The bear would weigh better than three hundred pounds. They agreed that it was best to halve it lengthwise so that the portions might easily be thrown over the rumps of the two horses. They skinned it and were surprised at its fatness, when deer and panther were so lean. The bears must have fed here through the latter days of the storm.

Old Cæsar jumped and shied when the half of the long frame was thrown across him. The taint of the hide was not to his liking. He had smelled the rank odor too often through alarmed nights at the clearing. Once a bear had climbed into the lot and was in the stall with him before Penny, awakened by his whinnying, had come to him. The Forrester horse was better able to carry the extra load in any case and the bear hide was added to Penny's portion. Buck and Mill-wheel turned their horses' heads toward home.

Penny called, "Turn your hames backward and the oxen kin haul all the load to oncet. Come see us."

"You come."

They lifted their hands and were gone. Penny and Jody jogged after them. They would all use the same trail for some miles, but the Forresters, unburdened, on their fast horses, were already far ahead. To the east, they came out on the trail toward home. The going was slow and troublesome. Old Cæsar would not follow behind the bear hide. But when Penny had Jody ride ahead, the Forrester horse insisted on taking the lead. There was a constant struggle. At last, through Juniper Prairie, Penny touched his heels to the horse and took a long lead. With the bear hide out of sight and smelling, old Cæsar was content to trot along reasonably. At first Jody was uneasy, alone in the new wilderness of water. Then, with his bear meat behind him, he felt bold again, and mature.

He had thought that he wanted to hunt forever. But when the tall trees of Baxter's Island drew in sight, and he passed the path to the sink-hole and came to the split-rail fences of his father's fields, he was glad to be coming home. The fields were desolate from the waste of waters. The yard was swept barren. But he was coming in with meat that he had killed for the family, and Flag was waiting.

· 21 ·

For two weeks Penny concerned himself with the salvaging of crops. The sweet potatoes were not ready, by two months, for digging. But they were rotting and would be a total loss if they were not dug. Jody worked long hours at them. He must be careful to go deeply enough with the potato fork and not go too close to the middle of the beds. Then, by lifting carefully, he brought up a forkful of potatoes unharmed. When they were all dug, Ma Baxter spread them out to dry and cure as best they could on the back porch. They all had to be gone over and more than half discarded. Rotting ends were cut off and with the nubbins set aside for the hogs.

The sugar cane was flattened to the ground. There was nothing to do for the present but leave it, for it was immature. It was already putting out roots along the stalks, but it could be trimmed and salvaged later.

The cow-pea hay was ruined. It had been near maturity and the week's soaking left it on the ground, a mouldy mass. The peas that the Baxters had shelled were the only salvage. Three weeks after the flood, after good days of sun, Penny took his scythe to Mullet Prairie, as he now called it, and cut marsh grass and left it to cure.

"Good fodder in bad times," he said.

The prairie waters had receded and left no trace of the fish except their stench. Even Jody, whom few odors offended, was sickened. The smell of death lay everywhere.

Penny said uneasily, "Somethin's wrong. That stink's due to be done with. Things is yit dyin'."

A month after the flood, in October, he returned with Jody in the wagon beside him to Mullet Prairie to gather the cut and cured hay. Rip and Julia trotted along behind the wagon. Penny allowed Flag, too, to follow, for he had begun to make a great commotion whenever he was shut up and left behind in the shed. He ran, sometimes ahead of old Cæsar, sometimes, when the road was wide enough, beside him. Now and then he dropped back and frolicked with the dogs. He had learned to eat green stuff and he stopped occasionally to nibble a tender bud or sprout.

Jody said, "Look back at him, Pa, pullin' buds like he was growed."

Penny smiled and said, "I tell you, never were sich a fawn."

Suddenly old Julia gave tongue and tore to the right into the bushes. Rip followed and Penny halted the wagon.

"Go see what them fools is after, Jody."

Jody jumped down and went after them. A few yards beyond he was able to identify the trail.

He called back, "Nothin' but cat."

Penny lifted his horn to blow the dogs in when he heard

Julia bay. He dismounted and pushed into the thick growth. The dogs had the cat at bay, but there was no fight. He went to them. Jody stood, puzzled. The wild-cat lay on its side, untouched. Julia and Rip circled, nipping, but with no responding attack. The cat bared its teeth and lashed its tail but did not stir. It was gaunt and weak.

Penny said, "The creetur's dyin'. Leave it be."

He called off the dogs and returned to the wagon.

Jody asked, "What's it dyin' of, Pa?"

"Why, the creeturs dies the same as us. Them as ain't kilt by their enemies. He's likely old and couldn't ketch hisself nothin' to feed on."

"His teeth wasn't wore down, like a old creetur."

Penny looked at him.

"Boy, you gittin' real observin'. Now I like to see that."

There was still no explanation of the wild-cat's feebleness. They reached the prairie and loaded the wagon with hay. Penny estimated that three more trips would be necessary. The marsh hay was coarse and stringy, but when frost had come and the wire grass was dry and harsh, Cæsar and Trixie and the heifer calf would be glad to have it. They drove toward home leisurely. Old Cæsar quickened his gait and even Julia ran on ahead, eager, as all domestic animals, for home. Past the trail to the sink-hole, at the corner of the first fence-row, Julia lifted her nose and bayed.

Penny said, "Now there'd be nothin' there in broad daylight."

Julia was insistent and jumped the fence and stopped, her bay turned to a shrill barking. Rip, clumsy in bull-dog fashion, clambered over the fence that the hound had cleared lightly. He too barked fiercely.

Penny said, "Well, I know better than to question a good dog's sense."

He stopped the wagon and took up his gun and went with

Jody over the fence to the dogs. A buck deer lay in the corner. It shook its head, making a menacing motion with its horns. Penny lifted his gun, then lowered it.

"Now that buck's sick, too."

He approached close and the deer did not move. Its tongue lolled. Julia and Rip were in a frenzy. They could not understand the refusal of live game either to run or to fight.

"No use to waste shot."

He took his knife from its scabbard and went to the deer and slit its throat. It died with the quiet of a thing to whom death is only one short step beyond a present misery. He drove off the dogs and examined it carefully. Its tongue was black and swollen. Its eyes were red and watery. It was as thin as the dying wild-cat.

He said, "This is worse'n I figgered. A plague has hit the wild creeturs. Hit's the black tongue."

Jody had heard of human plagues. The wild animals had always seemed to him to be charmed, and beyond all human ills. A creature died in the chase, or when another creature, more powerful, pounced and destroyed. Death in the scrub was clean and violent, never a slow sickness and lingering. He stared down at the dead deer.

He said, "We'll not eat it, will we?"

Penny shook his head.

" 'Tain't fitten."

The dogs were sniffing farther down the fence row. Julia barked again. Penny looked after her. A pile of carcasses lay in a heap. Two old bucks and a yearling had died together. Jody had seldom seen his father's face so grave. Penny examined the plague-killed deer and turned away without speaking. Death seemed to have appeared wholesale out of the air.

"What done it, Pa? What kilt 'em?"

Again Penny shook his head.

"I've never knowed what give the black tongue. Mebbe hit's the flood water, full o' dead things, has got pizenous."

A fear shot through Jody like a hot knife.

"Pa—Flag. He'll not git it, will he?"

"Son, I've told you all I know."

They returned to the wagon and drove on and into the lot and unloaded the hay. Jody felt weak and sick. Flag bleated. He went to him and clutched him around the neck and held him tightly, until the fawn pulled away for breath.

Jody whispered, "Don't git it. Please don't git it."

At the house, Ma Baxter received the news stolidly. She had shed her tears and wailed her laments when the crops were ruined. As the going of too many of her children had wrung her dry of feeling, now the passing of the game was only another unprotested incident.

She said only, "Best water the stock from the high trough and not let 'em git to the seepage pool."

Jody felt a hope for Flag. He would feed him only what he ate himself, keep him away from the tainted grass, water him from the Baxters' own drinking water. If Flag died, he thought with a mournful satisfaction, they would die together.

He asked, "Do folkses git the black tongue?"

"Only the creeturs."

He tied Flag stoutly in the shed when he made the next trip in the wagon for hay. Penny tied up the dogs as well. Jody asked countless questions. Would the hay be tainted? Would the plague last forever? Would there be any game left? To all, Penny, who knew, he had thought, almost everything, shook his head in ignorance.

"Keep still, boy, for the Lord's sake. A thing's happened has never happened before. How would ary man know the answers?"

His father left him alone to rake hay and load the wagon

while he unhitched Cæsar and rode on to the Forresters for information. Jody felt uneasy and miserable, alone at the edge of the marsh. The world seemed empty. Only over the scrub the buzzards wheeled, profiting. He hurried at his work and had finished it long before his father returned. He climbed to the top of the load of hay and lay flat on his back, staring at the sky. He decided that the world was a very peculiar place to live in. Things happened that had no reason and made no sense and did harm, like the bears and panthers, but without their excuse of hunger. He did not approve.

Against the uncomfortable and alarming things that happened, he balanced Flag. His father, too, of course. But Flag lived in a secret place in his heart that had been long aching and vacant. If Flag were not stricken with the plague, the flood, he decided, would be interesting. If he lived to be as old as Penny, as old as Grandma Hutto and Ma Forrester, he would never forget, he knew, the fright and enchantment of the endless days and nights of storm. He wondered if the quail would die of the black tongue. In another month, his father had told him, he might make a trap of crossed twigs and catch a few for eating. Shot was too valuable to be wasted on such small mouthfuls. But Penny would not allow them to be trapped until the covey was full-grown, and he insisted each year that two or three pairs of cocks and hens be left for seed. And would the turkeys die, and the squirrels, and the wolves and bears and panthers? Speculation absorbed him.

When a muffled sound in the distance became the recognizable beat of old Cæsar's hooves, he had forgotten his discomfort. Penny was as grave as before, but he was relieved and stimulated by his talk with the Forresters. On the trail of game for food, they had discovered the condition two days before. No breed of animals, they said, had been spared. They had found the predatory creatures dead or dying beside their quarry, on an equal footing at last, the weak and the strong brought together to earth, the sharp-toothed and the dull, the clawless and the clawed.

Jody asked, "Will ever'thing die?"

Penny spoke sharply.

"I've told you the last time, don't ask me them questions. Wait like me and see."

· 22 ·

By November, the Baxters and the Forresters knew the extent of the plague and what to expect, both of the game and the predatory animals, during the winter. The deer had been cut down to a fraction of their usual numbers. Where a herd of a dozen had fed across the edge of the clearing, a lone buck or doe leaped the fence into the cow-pea field in search of food that was not there. The deer became bold, nosing in the old sweet potato beds for undiscovered nubbins. The quail appeared in almost their usual numbers, but the wild turkeys were decimated. From that fact, Penny concluded that the damage indeed lay somehow in the polluted swamp waters, for the turkeys fed there and the quail did not.

All the food animals, deer and turkey, squirrel and 'possum, were so scarce that a day's hunt might produce nothing. The unfriendly animals had suffered as heavy losses. At first Penny thought that this would be of advantage. It became plain almost at once that the result was to make the remaining killers hungrier and more desperate because of their own shortened food supply. He became alarmed for the Baxter hogs and built a pen for them inside the lot. All the family went together to the woods and gathered acorns and scrub palmetto berries for the hogs. Penny set aside a measure of the new corn for fattening them. A few days later a stamping and squealing sounded in the lot at midnight. The dogs, aroused, ran barking and Penny and Jody pulled on their breeches and followed with a torch. The fattest barrow was missing. The kill had been made so neatly that there was no sign of struggle. A small trail of blood led across the lot and over the fence. It had required a large animal to kill and carry a heavy hog so handily. Penny took a hasty look at the tracks.

"Bear," he said. "A big un."

Old Julia begged to take the trail and Penny himself was tempted, for the killer might be easily and quickly come up on, gorging. But the night was dark and the risk of an encounter if the bear should be shot and only wounded was, he decided, too great. The trail would still be fresh enough in the morning. They went back to bed, to sleep lightly. At daylight they called the dogs and set out. The track was that of old Slewfoot.

Penny said, "I'd as good to of knowed, him, of all the bears in the scrub, 'd live through a plague."

Slewfoot had fed a short distance away. He had eaten heartily and scratched a covering of trash across the carcass. Then he had gone south and crossed Juniper Creek.

Penny said, "He'll be back agin to feed. A bear'll stay a week with his kill. I've seed 'em fight off the buzzards even when they didn't want to eat, theirselves. If 'twas ary bear but this un, we could set us a trap. But no trap was made will fool him since he lost his toe in one."

"Cain't we come wait for him and ketch him at his feedin'?"

"We'll try."

"Tomorrer?"

"Tomorrer."

They turned back toward home. A light galloping sound came close and closer. Flag had broken loose and joined the hunt. He kicked up his heels and held his small tail erect.

"Ain't he a sight, Pa?"

"He's a sight, son, a'right."

The next day, Penny was down with chills and fever. He was in bed for three days. There was no use in trying to catch old Slewfoot now. Jody begged to go alone and watch for him in ambush, but Penny refused permission. The great bear was too wise and too dangerous, he said, and Jody was too rattle-headed.

Ma Baxter said, "Now I don't crave to feed them shoats to no bear, even if they ain't plumb fat."

When Penny was able to leave the bed, they agreed that it was best to kill the hogs without waiting either for the full moon, or for the animals to be properly fattened. Jody split fat-wood and built a fire under the syrup kettle and brought water from the sink-hole to heat in it. He tilted a barrel on its side and propped it with sand. When the water was exactly right, Ma Baxter ladled it into the barrel. Penny killed the hogs and scalded them one after the other in the barrel, twirling them by the legs with his quick deftness. Ma and Jody had to help him lift them to the cross-trees, for his strength suddenly failed him. All three worked furiously at the scraping, for the hair must come off before it set.

Again Jody marveled at the metamorphosis of live creatures in whom he had felt interest and sympathy, into cold flesh that made acceptable food. He was glad when the killing was over. Now, scraping away on the smooth firm hides, he enjoyed seeing the skin become clean and white. He began to anticipate the smell of sausage frying and of cracklings browning in the fat. Nothing was wasted, not even the entrails. The meat itself was dressed out into hams and shoulders, side-meat and belly-bacon, which would be cured with salt and pepper and brown sugar made from their own cane juice, and then smoked slowly over hickory coals in the smoke-house. There remained the hocks and feet, which would be pickled in brine; the ribs and backbones which would be fried and put down in crocks under a protective layer of lard; the heads and livers and kidneys and hearts which would be made into head-cheese and put down the same way. The trimmings of lean meat would be ground into sausage. The fat would be tried out in the wash-pot and the lard put down in crocks and cans and the brown cracklings laid away for shortening in cornbread. The stomachs and intestines would be scraped and turned and soaked, and then used for casings in which the sausage meat would be stuffed, and the sausages hung in festoons and smoked along with the hams and bacons. Odds and ends would be cooked with cornmeal for the dogs and chickens. Even the tails were dressed. Only one part, like a windpipe, seemed without use and was tossed away.

Jody asked, "What's that, Ma?"

"Why, that's his goozle. What's a goozle? Well, if he didn't have no goozle, he couldn't squeal."

Eight hogs in all were dressed. Only the old boar hog, two young sows, and the brood-sow, peace offering from the Forresters, were left to begin the cycle over again. These must take their chances in the woods. They would be fed the slops, and a little corn at evening, to toll them into their pen to be shut up at night for approximate safety. For the rest, they must root for a living, maintaining life if they could, dying if they must.

Supper that night was a feast, and the table seemed lavish long afterward. There would soon be collards in the garden behind the house, and wild mustard greens all about the clearing. There would be bacon to cook with them, and with the dried shelled cow-peas. Cracklings would hold out for crackling bread for months. The Baxters were in fair shape for the winter. The season was the most abundant of the year. The scarceness of game would not be so serious with the smoke-house full.

The flattened sugar-cane had sent out whiskered roots along the stalks and had to be torn free of the clutching earth. The stalks were like ragged mops. The extraneous roots had to be cut off before the cane could be ground. Jody drove old Cæsar around and around the small cane-mill and Penny fed the thin, fibrous stalks into the revolving gears. The yield was low, and the syrup was thin and acid, but there was again sweetening in the house. Ma Baxter dropped oranges into the last boiling of syrup and the result made a rich preserve.

The corn was not much damaged, even the ears that had stood in the field through the rains. Jody spent hours every day at the millstone. The lower stone had small grooves that waved out from the center like the spirals on a snail shell. The upper stone rested on it, and the pair sat in a wooden frame with four legs. The shelled corn was fed into a hole in the center of the upper millstone, and when the ground meal reached a certain fineness, it sifted out through the waste hole and was collected in a bucket. Swinging the overhead lever in a circle hour after hour was monotonous but not unpleasant. Jody dragged up a high stump and when his back was tired, sat on it by way of rest and variety.

He said to his father, "I do most o' my figgerin' here."

Penny said, "I hope you do a heap of it, for the flood's done you outen a teacher. The Forresters and me had it settled to board a teacher between us for you and Fodder-wing this winter. When Fodder-wing died, I still figgered I'd do some trappin' and git cash money that-a-way. But the creeturs is so scarct now and the hides so pore, hit's no use."

Jody said comfortingly, "That's all right. I know a heap now."

"That jest proves your ignorance, young feller. I do hate for you to grow up and not know nothin'. You'll jest have to make out this year with what leetle I kin learn you."

The prospect was more than acceptable. Penny would start him on his reading lesson, or his sums, and then before either of them knew it, would be off on a tale. Jody went on with his grinding with a light heart. Flag came up and he stopped to let the fawn lick the meal at the waste-hole. He often took a taste himself. The stones became hot from the friction and the meal smelled like popcorn or cornpone. When he was hungry enough, a mouthful was palatable, but it never tasted as good as it smelled. Flag was bored with the inactivity and wandered away. He was becoming bolder and was sometimes gone in the scrub for an hour or so. There was no holding him in the shed. He had learned to kick down the loose board walls. Ma Baxter expressed the belief, only because it was her hope, that the fawn was going wild and would eventually disappear. Jody was no longer even troubled by the remark. He knew that the same restlessness came to the fawn that came to him. Flag merely felt the need of stretching his legs and exploring the world about him. They understood each other perfectly. He knew, too, that when Flag wandered away, he moved in a circle, and was never out of hearing of Jody's call.

That evening Flag got himself in serious disgrace. The sweet potatoes had been cured and heaped in a pile on the back porch. Flag roamed there while every one was occupied and found that by butting the pile, the potatoes would roll. The sound and motion charmed him. He butted the pile until it was strewn over most of the yard. He tramped on the potatoes with his sharp hooves. The odor enticed him and he nibbled one. The taste pleased him and he went from one to another, nibbling. Ma Baxter discovered him too late. Grave damage had been done. She drove him furiously with a palmetto broom. The game was much the one of chase that Jody played with him. When she turned away, he turned as well, and, following, butted her in her ample rear. Jody came in from his grinding to a hullabaloo and a crisis. Even Penny upheld Ma Baxter in the gravity of the matter. Jody could not endure the expression on his father's face. He could not keep back the tears.

He said, "He didn't know what he was doin'."

"I know, Jody, but the harm's as bad to the 'taters as if he done it for meanness. We got scarcely enough rations now to do the year."

"Then I'll not eat no 'taters, and make it up."

"Nobody wants you should do without 'taters. You jest got to keep track o' that scaper. If you keep him, it's your place to see he don't do no damage."

"I couldn't watch him and grind corn, all two."

"Then keep him tied good in the shed when you cain't watch him."

"He hates that ol' dark shed."

"Then pen him."

Jody rose before day the next morning and began work on a pen in the corner of the yard. He studied its position with an eye to using the fence for two corners of the pen, and to having it where he could see Flag from most of his own work-spots, the millstone, the wood-pile and the barn lot in particular. Flag would be content, he knew, if he was in sight of him. He finished the pen in the evening, when his chores were done. The next day he untied Flag from the shed and lifted him into the pen, kicking and struggling. Flag was over the bars and out and at his heels again before he reached the house. Penny found him again in tears.

"Don't git in a swivet, boy. We'll work this out, one way or t'other. Now the 'taters is near about the only thing he'll bother, do you keep him outen the house. They'd ought to be under kiver, anyway. Now you take down that tipply-tumbly pen, and build a coop to kiver the 'taters. Like a chicken coop, with two sides comin' to a peak. I'll start you on it."

Jody wiped his nose on his sleeve.

"I shore am obliged, Pa."

With the potatoes bedded and covered, there was no more serious trouble. Flag had to be kept out of the smoke-house as well as the house, for he had grown so large that by rearing on his hind legs he could reach the hanging sides of bacon and lick the salt.

Ma Baxter said, "I don't want nobody but me lickin' the meat I eat, let alone a nasty creetur."

Flag was annoyingly curious, as well, and butted over a can of lard in the smoke-house to hear the cover fall and see what was inside. The day was cool and the thin loose lard was discovered before it had run out. But such intrusions could be taken care of simply by keeping the doors shut, as was desirable in any case. Jody developed a good memory for such details.

Penny said, "Hit'll do you no harm to learn to be keerful. You got to learn takin' keer o' rations comes first of all—first after gittin' 'em."

· 23 ·

THE first heavy frost came at the end of November. The leaves of the big hickory at the north end of the clearing turned as yellow as butter. The sweet gums were yellow and red and the black-jack thicket across the road from the house flamed with a red as bright as a camp-fire. The grapevines were golden and the sumac was like oak embers. The October blooming of dog-fennel and sea-myrtle had turned to a feathery fluff. The days came in, cool and crisp, warmed to a pleasant slowness, and chilled again. The Baxters sat in the evening in the front room before the first hearth-fire.

Ma Baxter said, "Don't seem possible fire-time's here agin."

Jody lay flat on his belly, staring into the flames. It was here that he was often able to see Fodder-wing's Spaniard. By squinting his eyes and waiting for the blaze to shift just-so up a

crotched log, he could picture, with no trouble at all, a horseman in a red cape, wearing a shining helmet. The picture never
lasted long, for the wood stirred and the logs fell, and the
Spaniard rode away again.

He asked, "Did the Spaniards have red capes?"

Penny said, "I don't know, son. Now you see how handy a
teacher'd be."

Ma Baxter said wonderingly, "Now what put sich a idee as
that in his head?"

He rolled over on his side and stretched one arm across Flag.
The fawn lay asleep, his legs tucked under his stomach, like a
calf. His white tail twitched in his sleep. Ma Baxter did not
mind his being in the house in the evening, after supper. She
even turned an unseeing eye on his sleeping in Jody's bedroom,
for at least then he was into no mischief. She took him for
granted with the critical disinterest she showed the dogs. They
were outside, sleeping under the house. On bitter nights Penny
brought them in too, not that it was necessary, but because he
enjoyed sharing his comfort.

Ma Baxter said, "Throw a stick on the fire. I cain't quite see
to foller my seams."

She had cut down a pair of Penny's winter breeches for Jody.

She said, "Now you take another notion to grow like you
done this spring, and I'll be cuttin' down your breeches to fit
your daddy."

Jody laughed out loud and Penny pretended to be offended.
Then his eyes twinkled in the firelight and his thin shoulders
shook. Ma Baxter rocked complacently. They were all pleased
whenever she made a joke. Her good nature made the same
difference in the house as the hearth-fire had made in the chill
of the evening.

Penny said, "You and me had ought to be gittin' out that
speller, boy."

"Mebbe the roaches has ate it."

Ma Baxter poised her needle in the air. She pointed it at him.

"You best study your grammar, too," she said. "You'd ought to say, 'The roaches has eat it.'"

She rocked again, placidly.

Penny said, "You know, I got a idee we'll not have no great cold this winter."

Jody said, "I like it cold, if 'twa'n't for totin' in wood."

"Yes, sir, hit look like a good winter. We come out a heap better'n I figgered on the crops and meat. Mebbe a feller kin git his breath now."

Ma Baxter said, "About time."

"Yes, sir, ol' Starvation's doin' his huntin' another place."

The evening wore on without further speech. There was no sound but the hearth-fire simmering, the puff of Penny's pipe, and the *creak-pat, creak-pat* of Ma Baxter's rocker on the board floor. Once a great whistling passed over the house, like a sudden wind in the pine trees. Ducks were flying south. Jody looked up at his father. Penny pointed the stem of his pipe upward and nodded. If he were not so comfortable, Jody would have liked to ask what kind they were and where they were going. If he could know such things as his father knew them, he could manage, he thought, without the sums and the spelling. He liked the reading. Most of it was tales, not as good as Penny's—none was—but still, tales.

Penny said, "Well, it's go to sleep here, or find the bed."

He rose and knocked out his pipe on the hearth. As he bent, the dogs began to bark and dashed from under the house. It seemed as though his stirring had awakened them from sleep, and they had plunged after an imaginary enemy. Penny opened the front door and cupped his hand to his ear.

"Now I don't hear a thing but them dogs."

The calf bleated. The cry was at once of terror and pain. There was another that lifted to a scream, then was abruptly muffled. Penny ran to the kitchen for his gun.

"Fetch a light!"

Jody chose to believe that his mother was indicated. He ran after his father with his own gun, which since old Slewfoot's last visit he was allowed to keep loaded. Ma Baxter followed unwillingly with a lighted splinter, feeling her way with slow feet. Jody climbed the lot fence. He was sorry now that he had not brought the torch himself. He could see nothing. He could hear only a tumult of fighting and snarling, a snapping of many teeth, the voices of Rip and old Julia silenced. Above it came the desperate voice of his father.

"Git 'em, Julia! Hold 'em, Rip! My Lord, the light!"

Jody turned back over the fence and ran to his mother and took the torch from her. The thing that was happening was for Penny to handle. He ran back again. He lifted the torch high in his hand. The wolves had invaded the lot and killed the heifer calf. A band of them, three dozen or more, milled about the enclosure. Their eyes caught the light in pairs, like corrupt pools of shining water. They were emaciated and rough-coated. Their fangs glistened as white as gar-fish bones. He heard his mother screaming beyond the fence and became aware that he was screaming, too.

Penny shouted, "Hold that light still!"

He tried to steady it. He saw Penny lift his gun and shoot once, then again. The wolves turned and flowed over the fence in a gray wave. Rip snapped at their heels. Penny ran shouting after them. Jody ran behind him, trying to keep the light on the swift forms. He remembered that he had his own gun in the other hand. He pushed it at his father and Penny took it and shot again. The wolves were gone like a thunderstorm. Rip hesitated, his light hide plain in the darkness, then turned and limped back to his master. Penny stooped and petted him. He, too, turned, and walked back slowly into the lot. The cow was bellowing.

Penny said quietly, "I'll take the light."

He lifted it and swung it about the enclosure. The shredded body of the calf lay in the middle. Near it lay old Julia, her teeth in the throat of a gaunt wolf. The wolf was taking its last breaths. Its eyes glazed. It was tick-ridden and mangy.

Penny said, "All right, gal. Leave go."

Julia released her hold and stood back. Her teeth, worn by age to the flatness of corn kernels, had accounted for the only casualty. Penny looked at the mangled calf, and at the dead wolf. Then, as though he stared into the green eyes of an invisible enemy, he looked off into the night. He seemed small and shrunken.

He said, "Well——"

He handed Jody his gun and retrieved his own from the side of the fence. He leaned and picked up a hoof of the calf and walked decisively toward the house, dragging the carcass. Jody understood, shivering, that his father meant to have it handy if the marauders returned. He was still frightened. A panther or a bear at bay always terrified him. But there the men had always stood with leveled guns. There the dogs had room to dart in and get away. The fierce pack in the lot had made a sight he wanted never to see again. He wished his father had dragged the carcass into the woods. Ma Baxter came to the door and called quaveringly.

"I had to come to the house in the dark. I never been so scairt. Were it bears agin?"

They went into the house and Penny brushed past her to go to the hearth to the swinging kettle for hot water for the dogs' wounds.

"Wolves."

"Oh dear Heaven! Did they kill the calf?"

"They kilt it."

"Oh dear Heaven! And hit a heifer!"

She followed him about while he poured hot water in a basin and bathed the dogs' wounds. They were not serious.

"I wisht I could git the dogs on them beasts one at a time," he said grimly.

In the warm safety of the house, bold now because his mother was afraid, Jody could speak at last.

"Will they be back tonight, Pa? Will we go hunt 'em?"

Penny rubbed boiled pine gum into Rip's one deep wound, a jagged tear on one flank. He was in no mood for answers or talk of any kind. He did not speak until he was done with the dogs and had made them a good bed under the house near his bedroom window. He did not mean to be taken by surprise again. He came in and washed his hands and warmed them by the fire.

"Now this be the kind o' time a man needs a snort," he said. "I shore aim to beg a quart offen the Forresters tomorrer."

"You goin' there tomorrer?"

"I got to have he'p. My dogs is all right, but a big woman and a leetle man and a yearlin' boy is no match for that many hongry wolves huntin' in a pack."

It gave Jody a strange feeling to have his father admit that he could not handle anything alone. But the wolves had never before descended on the clearing in a band. Deer and small animals had been plentiful to feed them. Only a few had come, singly or in pairs, skulking about timorously, running at the first alarm. They had never before been a major menace. Penny took off his breeches and turned his back to the fire.

"Now I was scairt," he said. "My very bottom's cold."

The Baxters went to bed. Jody made sure his window was tight shut. He tried to make Flag lie under the covers with him, but the fawn kicked off the quilt as often as he drew it over him. He was content to sleep on the foot of the bed, and Jody awakened twice in the night and felt down to make sure he was still there. Flag was not as large as the nearly grown calf— His heart thumped in the darkness. The fortress that was the clearing was vulnerable. He drew the quilt over his head and was afraid to go to sleep again. But bed was a comfortable and a sleepy place on the first cold night in autumn——

Penny got an early start for the Forresters' in the morning. The pack had not returned in the night. He hoped that perhaps one or two were wounded. Jody begged to go with him, but his mother refused outright to stay alone.

"Hit's all fun to you," she complained. " 'Kin I go? Kin I go?' No thought o' bein' a man and lookin' out for your Ma."

His pride was touched. He patted her arm.

"Don't fret, Ma. I'll stay and keep off the wolves."

"About time. I git the weak jerks, thinkin' about 'em."

He felt bold after his father's assurance that the pack would not be seen in the daytime, but when Penny rode off on old Cæsar he was uneasy in spite of himself. He tied Flag in his room to a post of the bed and went to the sink-hole for water. On the way back, he was certain he heard sounds that he had never heard before. He looked back frequently, and broke into a trot past the fence-corner. He was not afraid, he told himself, but his mother might be. He chopped wood hurriedly and filled the kitchen wood-box to overflowing and stacked a pile by the hearth, in case his mother thought of it later. He asked if she needed meat from the smoke-house. She did not, but called for a can of cracklings and a bowl of lard.

She said, "Now your Pa went off and never said what to do with the pore calf, bury it or cook it for the dogs or save it for bait. Well, best wait 'til he says."

No further outside work was necessary. He bolted the kitchen door behind him.

"You put that fawn out," she said.

"Ma, don't make me put him out. Why, the smell of him'd jest toll the wolves from all over."

"All right, but you got to clean up after him if he don't mind his manners."

"I will."

He decided to study his speller. His mother fished it out from the trunk that held extra quilts and winter clothes and the deed to the Baxter land. He occupied himself with it all morning.

"I never seed you so content with that book," she said suspiciously.

He scarcely saw the words on the page. He was not afraid, he told himself again. But his ears were strained with listening. He listened all morning for a swift rush of padded feet. He listened for the sweet sound of old Cæsar's hooves in the sand, and his father's voice at the gate.

Penny was back in time for dinner. He had eaten little breakfast and was hungry. He would not talk until he had eaten his fill. He lit his pipe and tilted back his chair. Ma Baxter washed the dishes and brushed out the floor with the palmetto sweep.

"All right," Penny said, "I'll tell you jest how it stand. Hit's like I figgered, the wolves was about the worst destroyed by the plague of ary o' the creeturs. This pack was here last night, is all there is left. Buck and Lem has been to Fort Butler and Volusia and no wolves has been seed nor heered since the plague but these uns. Allus in a bunch. They worked over here from near Fort Gates and has been cleanin' out stock all the way acrost. They ain't got to feed much, for they've been caught at it before they fed, and drove off. They're purely starvin', and night before last they got a heifer and a yearlin' bull o' the Forresters. Toward daylight this mornin' they heered 'em howlin'. After they was here."

Jody now was eager.

"Will we git to hunt with the Forresters?"

"That's it. I had me a good go-round with them jessies. We cain't see it the same way about killin' 'em. I want a couple o' good hunts, and traps around our lot and their corral. But the Forresters is bent on pizenin' 'em. Now I ain't never pizened a creetur and I don't aim to."

Ma Baxter flung her dishcloth at the wall.

"Ezra Baxter, if your heart was to be cut out, hit'd not be meat. Hit'd be purely butter. You're a plague-taked ninny, that's what you be. Leave them wild things kill our stock cold-blooded, and us starve to death. But no, you're too tender to give 'em a belly-ache."

He sighed.

"Do seem foolish, don't it? I jest cain't he'p it. Anyways, innocent things is likely to git the pizen. Dogs and sich."

"Better that, than the wolves clean us out."

"Oh now Ory, they ain't goin' to clean us out. They ain't like to bother Trixie nor Cæsar. I mis-doubt could they git their teeth through their old hides. They shore ain't goin' to mess up with dogs that fights as good as mine. They ain't goin' to climb trees and ketch the chickens. They's nary other thing here to bother, now the calf's gone."

"There's Flag, Pa."

It seemed to Jody that for once his father was wrong.

"Pizen's no worse'n them tearin' up the calf, Pa."

"Tearin' up the calf was nature. They was hongry. Pizen jest someway ain't natural. Tain't fair fightin'."

Ma Baxter said, "Hit takes you to want to fight fair with a wolf, you——"

"Go ahead, Ory. Ease yourself and say it."

"If I was to say it, hit'd take words I don't scarcely know to think, let alone speak."

"Then bust with it, wife. Pizenin's a thing I jest won't be a party to."

He puffed on his pipe.

"If it'll make you feel better," he said, "the Forresters said worse'n you. I knowed they'd mock me in the head when I takened my stand, and they done so. And they're fixin' to go right ahead and set out the pizen."

"I'm proud there's men some'eres around."

Jody glowered at both of them. His father was wrong, he

thought, but his mother was unfair. Something in his father towered over the Forresters. The fact that this time the Forresters would not listen to him, must mean, not that he was not a man, but that he was mistaken. Perhaps, even, he was not wrong.

"You leave my Pa alone. I reckon he's got more sense than the Forresters."

She wheeled on him.

"Now mister impudent big-mouth, you'll git yourself frammed good with a bresh."

Penny rapped on the table with his pipe.

"Leave off! Ain't it enough to have trouble with the animals, without the family quarrelin'? Has a man got to die to find peace?"

Ma Baxter turned back to her work. Jody skulked away to the bedroom and untied Flag and took him outdoors for a run. He was uneasy in the woods and did not go far. He called the fawn in and went and sat with him under the hickory tree and watched the squirrels. He decided to gather hickory nuts before the squirrels finished the crop. Mast was plentiful and the squirrels, because of the plague, were not, but he wished, crossly, not to divide the nuts on his own land. He climbed the tree and shook the limbs. The nuts fell in a shower and he climbed down and gathered a pile. He took off his shirt and made a sack of it and filled it with nuts and took them to the house. He emptied the pile on the ground in the shed and spread them out to dry. When he put on his shirt, he realized that he had stained it past all washing with the juice from the hulls. It was a quite good shirt, with only one small patch on it where he had snagged the sleeve sliding down the roof of the corn-crib. He grunted to himself. It was peculiarly difficult to know ahead of time what would get him into trouble and what would keep him out. However, when his mother was angry at Penny, she seldom noticed anything he did.

She smoothed down through the afternoon. After all, the Forresters would get the job done. Three of them rode in toward sunset. They had come to notify Penny of the exact location of the poison, so that he might keep his dogs away from the trail. They had set it out ingeniously. They had done it entirely from horseback, so that the wolves should not scent the hated taint of man. They had prepared chunks of raw meat from their killed heifer and yearling, handling it with pieces of buckskin over their hands while they inserted the poison. The three had separated and ridden over the trails the pack might be expected to follow. They had dug holes with pointed palmetto stems, leaning from the saddle, and dropped in the poisoned bait, raking leaves over it again with their sticks. They had brought the last trail back toward Penny's lot, in a line from the sink-hole, where the wolves might water or wait for other game. Penny accepted the situation philosophically.

"All right. I'll keep my dogs tied for a week."

They accepted a drink of water and a twist of Penny's tobacco, but refused supper with thanks. They wanted to be home again before night when the pack might return to the corral. They visited with Penny a few minutes and rode away again. The evening passed peacefully. Penny filled more shell-cases, capped them and loaded his gun. He loaded Jody's muzzle-loader as well. Jody took it and propped it carefully by his bed. He was grateful to his father for including him in such preparations. He lay thinking after they were all in bed. He could hear his father talking with his mother.

He heard him say, "I got news for you. Buck told me Oliver Hutto takened a boat from Jacksonville to Boston and figgered on bein' there a while before he shipped agin. He give Twink Weatherby money and she slipped off to Jacksonville and got on a boat and follered him. Lem's rarin'. He says do he meet Twink and Oliver, he'll kill 'em all two."

Jody heard his mother's bulk, turning, creak the bed.

She said, "Now if the gal's honest, why don't Oliver marry her and be done with it? If she's nothin' but one o' them leetle ol' chipperdales, why do he mess up with her?"

"I couldn't rightly say. Been so long sincet I was a young buck, studyin' on courtin', I dis-remember how Oliver mought figger."

"Anyways, he hadn't ought to of let her foller him that-a-way."

Jody agreed with her. He threshed his legs under the covers in fury. He was finished with Oliver. If he ever saw him again, he would tell him what he thought of him. He hoped most to see Twink Weatherby and pull her yellow hair or throw something at her. Because of her, Oliver had gone away without coming to visit them. He had lost him. He was so angry at him that he did not care. He dropped asleep, painting enjoyable pictures of Twink wandering in the scrub and eating the wolf-poison and falling dead in deserved agonies.

· 24 ·

THE Forrester poisoning killed thirty wolves in one week. There was a pack left of a dozen or two that was wary and avoided the poison. Penny agreed to help with their extermination by the legitimate means of trap and gun. The pack ranged wide and never killed twice in the same place. It invaded the Forrester corral one night. The calves bleated and the Forresters poured out. They found the cows holding the wolves at bay. They had formed a ring, with the calves in the center, and were on the defensive with lowered horns. One calf was dying with a torn throat and two had their tails bitten off neatly at the rump. The Forresters brought down six of the pack. The next day they set poison again, but the wolves did not return. Two of their own dogs found the bait and died horribly. The Forresters were willing to track down the rest of the pack in slower fashion.

Buck came one evening at dusk to invite Penny to join them in a hunt the next morning at dawn. The wolves had been heard howling early that day at a water-hole west of Forresters' Island. A long dry spell had followed the flood and the high waters had shrunk away. The swamps, the marshes, the ponds, the creeks, were at nearly their usual level. What game was left, could be counted on to visit various known water-holes. The wolves had made the same discovery. The hunt would serve two purposes. With luck, all the remaining wolves might be killed. Game also could easily be taken. The plague seemed to have run its course. Venison and bear-meat again tempted the imagination. Penny accepted the invitation gratefully. There were enough Forresters to make any hunt without outside help. It was generosity that had sent Buck to Baxter's Island. Jody knew it. He knew, too, that his father's knowledge of the ways of the game was always welcome.

Penny said, "Spend the night, Buck, and we'll git off soon before day."

"No, for do I come up missin' at bed-time, they'll figger they's no hunt and not be ready."

It was agreed that Penny should meet them an hour or so before day, at the intersection of the main trail with their own. Jody tugged at his father's sleeve.

Penny said, "Kin I carry my boy and my dogs?"

"The dogs, we counted on, since Nell and Big Un was pizened. The boy we hadn't figgered on, but if you'll speak for him not to mess up the hunt——"

"I'll speak for him."

Buck rode away. Penny prepared ammunition and oiled the guns. The Baxters went to bed early.

It seemed to Jody that Penny was leaning over him, shaking him awake, before he had even had time to go to sleep. It was still night. Rising was always early, but there was usually at least a thin streak of light across the east. Now the world was as black as tar, and the trees still rustled with the night winds. There was no other sound quite like it. For a moment he regretted his anxiety of the evening before. Then he thought ahead to the hunt and excitement warmed him and he jumped from bed in the cold air. He slid his feet along the snug softness of his deerskin rug as he pulled on his shirt and breeches. He hurried to the kitchen.

A fire was crackling on the kitchen hearth. His mother was placing a pan of biscuits in the Dutch oven. She had an old hunting coat of Penny's over her long flannel nightgown. Her gray hair hung in braids over her shoulders. He went to her and smelled of her and rubbed his nose against her flannel breast. She felt big and warm and soft and he slipped his hands under the back of the coat to warm them. She tolerated him a moment, then pushed him away.

"I never had no hunter act like sich a baby," she said. "You'll be late for the meetin' if breakfast's late."

But her tone was friendly.

Jody sliced bacon for her. She freshened it in hot water then dipped it in flour and put it in an iron skillet to fry to a crisp brown. He had not thought he was hungry, but the sweet nut-like fragrance of it was overwhelming. Flag came from the bedroom and sniffed too.

She said, "You feed that fawn and tie him in the shed before you forget it. I'll not be tormented with him while you're gone."

He led Flag outside. The fawn was frisky and bolted away. He had trouble in following him and catching him in the blackness. He tied him first, then gave him a mash of meal and water.

He said, "You be good and I'll tell you about the wolves when I git home."

Flag bleated after him. If it were only an ordinary hunt, he would almost rather stay home with him. But Penny had said that they meant to kill off the last wolf in the scrub, and he

293

might never see another again as long as he lived. When he went to the house, Penny had come in from milking. The quantity was short because of the early hour. Breakfast was ready. They ate hurriedly. Ma Baxter did not eat but put up a lunch for them. Penny insisted that they would be home again for dinner.

She said, "You've said that before, and then come in after dark with your belly pinchin' you."

Jody said, "Ma, you're shore good."

"Oh, yes. When it's rations."

"Well, I'd a heap ruther you was good about rations and mean about other things."

"Oh, I be mean, be I?"

"Only about jest a very few things," he soothed her.

Penny had saddled Cæsar when he was at the barn. The horse stamped now, hitched at the gate. He knew a hunt as well as the dogs. They came with waving tails, gulped a pan of grits and gravy, and followed after. Penny slung a coil of rope and the saddle-bags over Cæsar's back, mounted into the saddle, and pulled Jody up after him. Ma Baxter handed their guns up to them.

Penny said to Jody, "Now take keer how you swing that thing around. You kill your Pa, and you'll r'aly have to hunt for a livin'."

It seemed surely that day must break. The horse's hooves thumped in the sand. The road gave back the sound, then dropped behind them, as it stretched before, in silence. Strange, he thought, that the night should feel more silent than the day, when most of the creatures stirred then, and did their sleeping when the sun rose. Only a hoot-owl cried, and when its crying ended, they rode forward into a dark emptiness. It was natural to speak in whispers. The air was chill. In his excitement, he had forgotten to put on his ragged jacket. He leaned close against his father's back.

"Boy, you ain't got on your coat. You want mine?"

He was tempted but refused.

"I ain't cold," he said.

Penny's back was thinner than his own. It was his own fault that he had no coat.

"You reckon we'll be too late, Pa?"

"Reckon not. Mebbe day'll hold off 'til we git there."

They were ahead of the Forresters. Jody climbed down and tussled with Rip to warm himself, and because the waiting was intolerable. He began to fear they had missed them. Then a clop-clop of hoofs sounded at what seemed some distance and the Forresters were there. All six had come. They greeted the Baxters briefly. The light wind was favorable, blowing from the southwest. If they did not stumble on a wolf sentry, they might take the pack unawares. It would be long-range shooting at best. Buck and Penny took the lead, side by side. The rest followed in single file.

A grayness that was scarcely light crept through the forest. There was an interval between daylight and sunrise that was an unreal hour. It seemed to Jody that he moved in a dream between night and day, and when the sun rose, he would awaken. The morning would be foggy. The grayness lingered in the fog and seemed unwilling to rise through it. The two merged, joined against the sun that would tear them to tatters. The file of riders came out of the scrub and into an open area of grass and live oak islands. A favorite water-hole of the game lay beyond. It was a clear deep pool and something about the water was to the taste of the creatures. It was protected as well with marsh on two sides, from which danger might be seen approaching, and forest on the other two, into which they might quickly retreat.

The wolves had not yet come, if they were coming. Buck and Lem and Penny dismounted and tied the dogs to trees. A thin strip of color like a yellow ribbon lay low across the east.

The autumn mist hung above it. Figures were visible only a few feet above the ground. At first the water-hole seemed deserted. Then bodies took shape here and there about it, as though the fog itself had solidified, still gray and tenuous. The antlers of a buck deer formed in the distance. Lem lifted his gun instinctively, then lowered it. The wolves were more important for the moment.

Mill-wheel murmured, "I don't remember no stumps around that pond."

As he spoke, the stumps moved. Jody blinked his eyes. The stumps were young bears. There were a good dozen of them. Two larger bears ambled slowly beyond them. They had not seen or winded the buck, or chose to ignore him. The curtain of mist lifted higher. The band of color broadened in the east. Penny pointed. There was movement in the northwest. The forms of the wolves were barely visible, slipping down in single file as the humans had done. The keen nose of old Julia caught a faint taint and she lifted it high and wailed. Penny struck at her to hush her. She dropped flat to the ground.

Penny whispered, "We ain't got a chancet in the world o' gittin' a shot this way. We cain't git clost enough."

Buck's whisper was a growl.

"How about a shot at the buck and mebbe the old bears?"

"Listen to me. One of us kin slip around to the east and south and make a quick dash acrost the south marsh. The wolves'll be too fur down to turn back. They won't go to the marsh. They're obliged to come out to the woods right past where we be now."

Acceptance of the idea was immediate.

"Go ahead."

"Jody kin do it as good as a man. And he's no shot. We'll need all our shots here."

"All right."

"Jody, you ride down jest inside the edge o' the woods

yonder. When you git opposite that tallest pine, you cut right back acrost the marsh towards us here. Jest as you turn, take a pot-shot at the pack. Ne' mind tryin' to hit 'em. Git goin'. Go fast but quiet."

Jody touched Cæsar's rump and trotted away. His heart had jumped from its normal position and was beating somewhere high in his throat. His vision blurred. He was afraid he would never see the tall pine, and cut in too soon or too late and bungle the whole business. He rode unseeing. He straightened his back and slid one hand along the barrel of his gun. A blessed stiffening and clarity came to him. He picked out the pine before he reached it. He swung Cæsar's head sharply to the right, dug his heels into him, slapped his neck with the reins and shot into the open. The marsh water flew under him. He saw the young bears scatter. He was afraid he had not come in far enough behind the wolves. The creeping pack ahead of him hesitated, on the verge of turning back the way they had come. He lifted his gun and shot behind them. They bolted in a mass. He held his breath. He saw them stream toward the scrub. He heard the barking of guns and the sound was music. He had done his part and it was out of his hands. He galloped around the south side of the pond toward the men. The tethered dogs lifted their voices. A single gun spoke now and again. His mind was clear. He wished that he had another shot. He was sure he could take it coolly and accurately.

Penny's ruse had worked to perfection. A dozen of the gray bodies lay about on the earth. An argument was in progress. Lem wanted the dogs turned loose after the rest of the pack. Buck and Penny were opposed.

Penny said, "Lem, you know we ain't got a dog kin run down one o' them streaks o' lightnin'. They won't tree like a cat, they won't turn at bay like a bear. They'll run forever."

Buck said, "He's right, Lem."

Penny turned excitedly.

"Look at what them young bears has done. They've treed. What say we have a go at ketchin' 'em alive? Ain't there a good price on the east coast for live creeturs?"

"That's what they say."

Penny swung up in the saddle and Jody eased back behind him.

"Take it easy, men, slower you work on this, better we'll do."

Three of the spring cubs, motherless, perhaps, long enough to have forgotten discipline, had not even treed. They sat on their haunches, crying like babies. They made no effort to escape. Penny tied the three together and looped the end of the rope around a large pine. Some of the cubs had only climbed saplings. It was a simple matter to shake them out and tie them too. Two others were high in a larger tree. Jody, as the lightest and nimblest, climbed after them. They climbed higher above him, then scrambled out on a limb. He edged along the limb. It was ticklish work to shake it without falling off himself. The limb cracked faintly. Penny shouted to him to wait. An oak limb was cut and trimmed and handed up. Jody slid down the tree until he could reach it and climbed back. He poked it at the cubs. They clung as though they had grown to the limb. At last they dropped. He climbed down.

The old bears and the buck had vanished with the first shot. Two yearling bears showed too much fight to be taken alive. They were sleek and plump and since both houses were in need of fresh meat, they were shot down for food. The take of cubs was ten.

Buck said, "Now wouldn't Fodder-wing of loved to of seed this? Now I wisht he was alive to see it."

Jody said, "If I didn't have me Flag a'ready, I shore would carry one home."

Penny said, "And you and hit both git barred out together."

298

Jody went close and talked to the cubs. They lifted their sharp snouts, scenting him, and stood up on their hind legs.

He said, "Now ain't you-all proud you goin' to git to live?"

He moved closer and reached out a tentative hand to touch one. It raked its sharp claws across his sleeve. He jumped back.

He said, "They ain't grateful, Pa. They ain't a mite grateful we saved 'em from the wolves."

Penny said, "You didn't look at his eyes good. You picked a mean un to pet. I've done told you, where there's twin cubs, one'll be friendly and t'other'll be mean. Now see kin you find one has got a friendly eye."

"I mought not pick good. I'll leave 'em be."

The Forresters laughed. Lem picked up a stick and began to tease one of the cubs. He poked it in the ribs to make it bite the stick. He knocked it over and it squealed in pain.

Penny said, "Now kill the thing, Lem, if you're goin' to torment it."

Lem turned angrily.

"You save your say-so for your young un. I'll do what I please."

"You'll not torment nothin' long as I got breath to interfere."

"You want the breath knocked outen you then, eh?"

Buck said, "Leave off your meanness a little while, Lem."

"You want a fight, too?"

The Forresters took sides among themselves without rhyme or reason, but this time they all sided with Buck and Penny. They were good-natured from the kill and the catch. Lem glowered but put down his fists. It was agreed that Gabby and Mill-wheel should stay and keep an eye on the cubs in case they chewed loose from their bindings, which ranged from Penny's rope to Buck's deer-hide boot laces. The rest would return to Forresters' Island for the wagon to fetch the cubs.

"Now kin we agree on where to carry 'em," Penny said, "me

and Jody jest as good to go on home. I got a leetle huntin' business o' my own on the way."

"You fixin' to go run down that buck?" Lem asked suspiciously.

"If you got to know my business, I'm fixin' to go on to Juniper Spring and shoot me a 'gator. I need grease for my boots and I want to smoke me the tail for meat for my dogs. Now you satisfied?"

Lem did not answer. Penny turned to Buck.

"Don't you reckon St. Augustine's the best place to sell them cubs?"

"Well, if the price ain't right, hit'd be wuth a try to go on to Jacksonville."

"Jacksonville," Lem said. "I got some business there myself."

"I got a gal in Jacksonville," Mill-wheel said, "but I got no business there."

"If she's the one got married," Buck said, "you shore as the devil got no business there."

Penny said patiently, "Hit's Jacksonville, then. Now who's goin'?"

The Forresters looked at one another.

Penny said, "Buck's the only one o' you kin trade without quarrelin'."

Lem said, "The wagon don't go without me."

"That's Buck and Lem, then. Now you want I should go? Ain't room for but three on the seat."

They were silent.

Mill-wheel said at last, "You got high shares in the cubs, Penny, but I shore do crave to go. Come to think on it, I got a barrel o' somethin' else I'd love to carry and trade."

Penny said, "Well, I got no cravin' a-tall to go. Buck, I'll be beholden to you to look out for my share and do my tradin' for me. When'll you go? Tomorrer? All right, if you'll stop by tomorrer, me and Ma'll have it figgered what-all we want you to trade for."

"I'll not fail you, you know that."

"I know."

The party separated. The Forresters went north and the Baxters south.

Penny said, "Love nor money wouldn't git me to the east coast with them jay-birds. There'll be broke jugs and broke heads all the way along their track."

"You reckon Buck'll do us right?"

"He'll do right. Buck's the only one o' the litter was wuth raisin'. Him and pore Fodder-wing."

Jody said, "Pa, I feel peculiar."

Penny halted Cæsar and looked around. Jody was white.

"Why, boy, you jest had too much excitement. Now it's over, you've give out."

He got down and lifted Jody in his arms. He was limp. Penny propped him against a sapling.

"You've done a growed man's work today. Now set easy and I'll fetch you a bite to eat."

He fumbled in the saddle-bags and brought out a cold baked sweet potato and peeled it.

"This'll freshen you up. When we git to the spring, you take a good drink o' water."

At first Jody could not swallow. Then the taste of the sweet potato touched his palate. He sat up and ate it in small mouthfuls. He felt better immediately.

"You're jest like I was when I were a boy," Penny said. "You take ever'thing hard and hit leaves you faintified."

Jody grinned. With any one but his father, he would have been ashamed. He clambered to his feet. Penny laid a hand on his shoulder.

"I didn't keer to praise you in front o' the men, but you done noble."

The words were as strengthening as the sweet potato.

"I'm all right now, Pa."

They mounted and rode on. The morning haze had thinned and vanished. The November air was crisp. The sun was a warm arm across their shoulders. The black-jacks flamed, the scrub oaks glistened. The fragrance of the purple deer-tongue filled the road. Scrub jays flew across the road. Their solid blue feathered coats, Jody thought, were prettier than the bluebirds', because there was more of it. The strong smell of the yearling bear over old Cæsar's rump behind him blended not unpleasantly with the sweat of the horse, the rich smell of the saddle, the deer-tongue and the lingering odor of the sweet potato. He would have a great deal, he thought, to tell Flag when he got home. The finest part about talking to Flag was that he could think most of the talk and not have to try to say it. He preferred talking to his father, but he could never find the words in which to make things clear. When he tried to say a thing that he had thought, the idea vanished while he was still floundering. It was like his efforts to shoot doves in a tree. He saw them, he cocked his gun, he crept close. Then they were gone before he could pull the trigger.

With Flag, he could say, "There come the wolves, slippin' in to the pond," and he could sit and see the whole thing, and feel the feelings again, the fears and the sharp ecstasies. Flag would nuzzle him and look at him with his soft liquid eyes, and he could feel that he was understood.

He came to himself with a start. They had picked up the old Spanish trail through the hammock to Juniper Spring. The spring was at its normal level. Debris from the flood was thick about its banks. The spring itself bubbled clear and blue from a bottomless cavern. A fallen tree lay across it. They hitched Cæsar to a magnolia and skirted the spring for 'gator sign. There was none. An old female alligator who was almost tame inhabited the spring. She raised a swarm of young every second year, and she would swim to the bank when called and take meat thrown to her. She was perhaps down in her cave with the year's young. Because she was so tame and had been there so long, no one ever disturbed her. Penny was afraid that some day a stranger would come and kill her, finding her easy prey. They worked down the bank of the run. A shipoke flew.

Penny put out a hand behind him to halt Jody. On the opposite bank was a fresh 'gator wallow. The mud had been packed smooth where they turned and rolled their hard bodies. Penny dropped to his haunches behind a buttonwood bush. Jody dropped behind him. Penny had reloaded his gun. There was shortly a commotion in the waters of the swift-running creek. What seemed a log lifted not quite to the surface. There were two bumps at one end. The log was an eight-foot alligator. The bumps were its heavy-lidded eyes. It submerged again, then raised clear and lifted its fore-quarters to the bank. It crawled slowly to the wallow, heaved its bulk up and down on its short legs, flipped its tail and lay quietly. Penny drew a bead more carefully than Jody had ever seen him do on bear or deer. He fired. The long tail thrashed wildly, but the body sank instantly to the mud. Penny ran up-stream, around the head of the spring with Jody at his heels, and down-stream on the other side of the wallow. The broad flat jaws were opening and closing automatically. Penny held them shut with one hand and gripped a fore-leg with the other. The dogs barked excitedly. Jody took hold and they dragged the body to firm ground. Penny stood up and wiped his forehead with his sleeve.

"That's light totin' for a little bit," he said.

They rested, then bent to the work of slicing out the tail meat, which, smoked, would make convenient hunting rations for the dogs. Penny turned back the hide and sliced out the layers of fat.

"The 'gators is one thing got fat on the flood," he said.

Jody sat back on his heels with his knife in his hand.

"And likely the moccasins and the turtles," he said.

"And the birds now," Penny said. "All excusin' the turkeys, the birds ain't suffered pertickler."

Jody pondered the strangeness of it. The creatures of the water and the creatures of the air had survived. Only the things whose home was the solid land itself, had perished, trapped between the alien elements of wind and water. The thought was one of those that stirred him, and that he could never bring to earth to share with his father. It moved now across his mind like a remnant of the morning's haze. He returned to the fat of the alligator.

The dogs were not tempted by the 'gator flesh, just as frogs were not to their taste, or coots, or ducks that fed on fishy matters. But when the tail meat, pink as veal, was smoked, the foreign taste and odor would disappear and they would eat it when no better meat was at hand. Penny emptied the lunch from the saddlebags and filled them with the strips of meat and of fat. He looked at the package of food.

"Kin you eat now, boy?"

"I kin near about eat ary time."

"Then we'll eat it jest to be done with it."

They washed their hands in the running creek and went to the head of the spring for drinking water. They lay flat on their bellies and drank deeply. They opened the lunch and divided it evenly into two portions. Penny left a biscuit filled with mayhaw jelly and a square of cassava pudding. Jody accepted them gratefully. Penny looked at the small protruding belly.

"Where you put it all, I cain't see. But I'm proud I got it to give to you. There was times when I were a boy, they was sich a passel of us, my own belly lay mighty flat."

They lay comfortably on their backs. Jody stared up into the magnolia tree over him. The under-sides of the thick leaves were like the copper of the pot that had belonged to his mother's grandmother. The red cones of the magnolia were beginning to spill their seeds. Jody gathered a handful and dropped them idly on his chest. Penny rose lazily and fed the dogs the scraps. He led Cæsar to the spring to drink. They mounted and turned north toward Baxter's Island.

West of Sweetwater Spring, Julia began to work a trail. Penny leaned down to look at it.

"Now that's a mighty fresh buck track she's got there," he said. "I've a notion to leave her foller it."

Her tail was in constant motion. Her nose was glued to the ground. She moved ahead rapidly. She lifted her nose high and began to trot with a gaited motion, scenting only by the wind.

"He must o' cut in right ahead of us here," Penny said.

The trail kept to the road for several hundred yards, then turned to the right. Julia gave a high thin cry.

Penny said, "Now he's clost. I'll bet he's layin' up right in the thick."

He rode into the thicket after the dog. She bayed and a buck swayed to its knees and leaped to its feet. The buck was in full antlers. Instead of rushing away in flight, he charged headlong at the dog. The reason was instantly plain. A doe lifted her smooth unhorned head beyond him. Because of the interruption of the flood, the deer were late with their mating. The buck was courting and ready for fight. Penny held his fire, as he did often when a thing was strange. Old Julia and Rip were as amazed as he. They were fearless with bear and panther and wild-cat, but here, they had expected the game to run. They retreated. The buck pawed the earth like a bull and shook his antlers. Julia gathered her wits and jumped for his throat. He caught her on his horns and tossed her into the bushes. Jody saw the doe wheel and bolt away. Julia was unhurt and came back for action. Rip was at the buck's heels. The buck charged again, then stood at bay with lowered antlers.

Penny said, "I'm shore sorry, ol' feller," and fired.

The buck dropped, kicked a moment and lay still. Julia lifted her hound's voice in a howl of triumph.

Penny said, "Now I hated to do that."

The buck was large and fine, well fattened on acorn mast and palmetto berries. His red coat of summer, however, was already shabby. It had turned to the winter's grayness, the color of the Spanish moss, or the lichens that grew on the north side of the pine trees.

"A month from now," Penny said, "what with runnin' all over the scrub courtin', he'd of been pore and his meat stringy."

He stood beaming.

"Now ain't this our day, boy? Ain't this jest our day?"

They dressed the buck.

Penny said, "I mistrust kin old Cæsar tote all we got."

"I'll walk, Pa. Do the buck weigh more'n me?"

"As many stone agin. We'd both best walk."

Cæsar accepted his load patiently. He seemed to have no fear of the yearling bear, as he had had of the large one. Penny walked ahead, leading him. Jody felt as fresh as though the day were only beginning. He ran in front. The dogs trailed behind. It was not much after noon when they reached the clearing. Ma Baxter was not expecting them so soon. She heard them and came to the gate to meet them. She shaded her eyes against the sun. Her heavy face lightened at sight of the game.

"I don't mind stayin' alone when you-all come home with sich as that," she called.

Jody broke into a babble of talk. His mother only half-listened, concerned with the quality of the meat of buck and bear. He left her and slipped into the shed to Flag. There was not time to sit and talk. He let Flag smell his hands and shirt and breeches.

"That's bear smell," he told him. "You run like lightnin' do you ever smell it clost. And that's wolf. Since the flood, they're wusser'n the bear, but we shore cleaned 'em out this mornin'. There's three-four left, and you run from them. Now t'other smell is your kin-folks." He added with a horrified fascination, "Mebbe your daddy. No need to run from them. Yes, they is, too. A ol' buck'll kill a fawn or a yearlin', Pa says, times, in ruttin' season. You jest run from ever'thing."

Flag switched his white tail and stamped his feet and tossed his head.

"Don't you say 'No' to me. You listen to what I tell you."

He untied him and took him outside. Penny was calling him to help with the carrying of the game to the back of the house. Flag bolted at scent of the bear, then returned to sniff cautiously from a distance, craning his slim neck. The skinning and cutting up of the meat took the rest of the afternoon. Dinner had not been cooked. They were not hungry and Ma Baxter waited and cooked the big hot meal an hour ahead of the usual supper time. Penny and Jody ate ravenously at first, but were suddenly so tired that appetite left them when they were half through. Jody left the table to go to Flag. The sun was only now setting. His back ached and his eyes grew heavy. He whistled Flag in. He had wanted to listen to his mother's and father's talk about the trading, and to decide what he wanted from Jacksonville for his special portion. But his eyes would not stay open. He stumbled into bed and was instantly asleep.

Penny and Ma Baxter spent the evening discussing their most urgent needs for the winter. Ma Baxter drew up at last a list, carefully written in pencil on ruled paper.

A bolt good wool for huntin jeans for Mr. B & Jody
A haf bolt perty blue and wite check gingham for Mrs. B
    now a real perty blue
A bolt domestick
A sack cofee beans

307

A barrl flowr
A ax hed
Sack salt 2 lb sody
2 stiks lead for shot
Buckshot 4 lb
Some more shel casis Mr. B's gun
1 lb powder for shels
Homespun 6 yd
Hickory shirtin 4 yd
Osnaburg 6 yd
Brogan shoes, Jody
½ quire paper
1 box buttons, pantaloon
1 paper shirt buttons
1 bottle caster oil 50¢
1 box worm candy
1 box liver pills
1 pain curer
1 vial laudnum
1 do camphire
1 do Paragorick
1 do lemon
1 do pepermint
Now if enuf money left 2 yd black alpacy

The Forresters stopped the next morning on their way. Jody ran out to meet them and Penny and Ma Baxter followed. Buck and Mill-wheel and Lem were crowded together on the wagon seat. The wagon body behind them was filled with a quarreling, wrestling, whining tangle of shiny black fur, shot through with flashes of small teeth and claws and pairs of bright beady black eyes. Their individual ropes and chains were hopelessly tangled. A barrel of moonshine whiskey stood in the middle. One cub with a longer chain had climbed to its top and sat loftily above the tumult. Jody jumped up on a wagon wheel to peer in. A clawed paw went past his face and he dropped back to the ground. The wagon-load was bedlam.

Penny called, "Don't be surprised do all Jacksonville take out and foller you."

Mill-wheel said, "Mebbe hit'd raise the price."

Buck said to Jody, "I cain't git over how Fodder-wing would of loved to of seed 'em."

If Fodder-wing had been alive, Jody thought wistfully, the two of them might have been taken along to Jacksonville. He looked longingly at the cramped space on the floor-boards under the men's feet. He and Fodder-wing could have sat there comfortably, and so have seen the world.

Buck took the Baxters' list.

He said, "This look like a heap o' things wrote out here. If we don't git a good price and the money don't hold out, what must I skip?"

"The gingham and the domestick," Ma Baxter said.

Penny said, "No, Buck, you git Ma's gingham, whatever come. Git the gingham and the ax head and the shell cases and lead. And the hickory shirtin', that's Jody's portion."

"Blue and white," Jody called. "All mingledy, Buck, like a joint snake."

Buck shouted, "Well, if they ain't money enough, we'll stop and ketch some more bears."

He slapped the reins over the backs of the horses.

Ma Baxter shrilled after him, "The wool cloth's the worst needed."

Lem said, "Stop this wagon. You see what I see?"

He jerked his thumb at the deer-hide stretched on the smoke-house wall. He jumped down from the wagon-seat and opened the gate and walked with long rangy strides to the smoke-house. He turned aside, searching. He discovered the antlers, drying on a nail. He walked deliberately to Penny and knocked him against the smoke-house wall. Penny went white. Buck and Mill-wheel came hurrying. Ma Baxter turned and ran into the house for Penny's gun.

Lem said, "That'll learn you to lie to me and slip off that-a-way. Wasn't goin' after the buck, eh?"

Penny said, "I'd ought to kill you for that, Lem, but you're too sorry to kill. Gittin' that buck was pure happen-so."

"You're lyin'."

Penny turned to Buck, ignoring Lem.

He said, "Buck, no man's never knowed me to lie. If you-all had remembered that, you'd not of got beat in the dog-trade."

Buck said, "That's right. Don't pay him no mind, Penny."

Lem turned and stalked back to the wagon and climbed into the seat.

Buck said in a low voice, "I'm powerful sorry, Penny. He's mean, at best. He's been this-a-way ever since Oliver takened his gal away from him. He's got ugly as a buck-deer that cain't find his doe."

Penny said, "I was aimin' to give you-all a quarter o' the venison on your way back. I'll swear, Buck, this be hard to forgive."

"I'd not blame you. Well, don't fret about your share in the cubs, or the tradin'. Me and Mill-wheel kin tie Lem in knots ary time he need it."

They returned to the wagon. Buck lifted the reins and turned the horses around. He would pick up the north road past the sink-hole. It would take them through Hopkins Prairie, past Salt Springs, and so north to Palatka, where they would cross the river and perhaps spend the night before proceeding. Jody and Penny watched after the wagon and Ma Baxter, peering from the door, set down the gun. Penny went into the house and sat down.

Ma Baxter said, "Why'd you take it from him?"

"When one man's on-reasonable, t'other has got to keep his

head. I ain't big enough to fight him jest-so. All I could of done was to of takened the gun and shot him. When I kill a man, hit'll be for somethin' more serious than a ignorant man's meanness."

He was plainly unhappy.

"Now I would love to live peaceable," he said.

To Jody's surprise, his mother said, "I reckon you done the right thing. Don't set studyin' about it no more."

He could not quite understand either of them. He was filled with resentment at Lem, and with disappointment that his father had let him go unpunished. He was confused by his own feelings. Just as he had changed his allegiance from Oliver to the Forresters, Lem betrayed his father. He finally solved it in his mind by deciding to hate Lem, but to continue to like the others, especially Buck. The hate and the friendliness were of equal satisfaction.

There was nothing in particular to be done in the way of work, and he spent the morning helping his mother peel pomegranates and string the peelings to dry. They were the best remedy, she said, for dysentery. He ate so many pomegranates that she was afraid he would need the remedy before it was ready. He liked to bite the transparent crispness from around the seeds.

· 25 ·

NOVEMBER slid into December with no more sign than the high, sad cry of the wood ducks flying. They left their hammock nests and moved from lake to pond and back again. Jody wondered why some birds cried in flight while others were silent. The whooping cranes gave their rusty call only in motion. Hawks screamed from the air but sat still and frozen in the tree. Sapsuckers were noisy on the wing but gave themselves to the bark of trees with no further sound than the tat-tat of their pecking. Quail spoke only from the ground, and soldier blackbirds shrilled from the rushes. Mocking birds sang and chattered day or night, on the wing, or perched along the fences or in the poke-berry bushes.

The curlews were coming south. They came every winter from Georgia. The old ones were white with long curved bills.

The young ones, from the spring hatching, were gray-brown in color. The young curlews made fine eating. When fresh meat was scarce, or the Baxters were tired of squirrel, Penny and Jody rode old Cæsar to Mullet Prairie and shot half a dozen. Ma Baxter roasted them like turkey and Penny swore the flavor was even sweeter.

Buck Forrester had traded the bear cubs in Jacksonville for a good price. He had brought the Baxters all the articles on Ma's list and a small sack of silver and copper in change, to boot. Relations between the Forresters and the Baxters were strained since Lem's attack on Penny and after the settlement the big dark men rode by without stopping.

Penny said, "Likely Lem persuaded the rest I raly meant to cheat about the deer. We'll git it all straight one day."

Ma Baxter said, "Hit suits me jest as good to have nothin' to do with 'em."

"Now Ma, don't fergit how Buck lit in when I was snake-bit."

"I ain't fergot. But that Lem's like a snake hisself. Turn and strike at you jest 'cause he hears the leaves rustle."

Buck stopped one day, however, to announce that he believed they had accounted for all the wolves. They had shot one at the corral, had trapped three more and had seen no sign of one since. The bears were giving them constant trouble. The most troublesome was old Slewfoot, whose maraudings were taking him, Buck said, from the river on the east to Lake Jumper on the west. His favorite stopping place was the Forrester corral. He watched the wind and eluded both dogs and traps, slipped into the corral and made off with a calf whenever it pleased him to do so. The nights the Forresters sat up and waited for him, he did not appear.

Buck said, "Hit'll not do you much good to look out for him, but I thought I'd pass the word."

Penny said, "My lot lays so clost to the house, mebbe I kin

ketch him at his tricks. I thank you. Buck, I been wantin' to say somethin'. I hope you ain't mixed up in your mind about that buck Lem got so ornery about."

Buck said evasively, "That's all right. What's one deer? Well, so long."

Penny shook his head and went back to his work. It disturbed him not to be on friendly terms with his only neighbors in his small scrub-world.

Work was light and Jody spent long hours with Flag. The fawn was growing fast. His legs were long and spindling. Jody discovered one day that his light spots, the emblem of deer infancy, had disappeared. He examined the smooth hard head at once for signs of horns. Penny saw him at it and was obliged to laugh at him.

"You shore expect wonders, boy. He'll be butt-headed 'till summer. He'll not have no horns 'til he's a yearlin'. Then they'll be leetle ol' spiky ones."

Jody knew a content that filled him with a warm and lazy wonder. Even Oliver Hutto's desertion and the Forresters' withdrawal were distant ills that scarcely concerned him. Almost every day he took his gun and shot-bag and went to the woods with Flag. The black-jack oaks were no longer red but a rich brown. There was frost every morning. It made the scrub glitter like a forest full of Christmas trees. It reminded him that Christmas was not far away.

Penny said, "We'll flunk around 'til Christmas, and we'll go to the Christmas doin's at Volusia. Then after that we'll git down to work agin."

Jody found a patch of Cherokee beans in the pine woods beyond the sink-hole. He gathered his pockets full of the bright red seeds. They were as hard as flint. He stole a large needle and a length of stout cotton thread from his mother's sewing basket and took them with him when he went prowling. He sat down in the warmth of the sun with his back against a tree and strung them laboriously, a few each day, to make a necklace for his mother. The seeds were strung unevenly but the effect pleased him. He carried the completed necklace in his pocket so that he might look at it often, until it began to have a sticky appearance from crumbled biscuits and squirrel tails and other such articles. He washed the necklace at the sink-hole and hid it on a rafter of his bedroom.

There had been nothing special for Christmas the year before except a wild turkey for dinner because there had been no money. This year there was the money left from the sale of the bear cubs. Penny set aside a portion for cotton-seed and said the rest might be spent for Christmas.

Ma Baxter said, "Now if we goin' to the doin's, I want to go tradin' to Volusia 'fore then. I want me four yards o' alpacy so I kin have Christmas decent."

Penny said, "Wife, your figger's no secret. I ain't quarrelin', for you're plumb welcome to all I got. But seems to me four yards won't no more'n make you a pair o' drawers."

"If you got to know, I aim to fix over my weddin' dress. Hit's long enough, for I ain't growed up nor down. I done my growin' sideways, and I aim to set in a piece down the front so's it'll meet around me."

Penny patted her broad back.

"Now don't take on. A good wife like you deserves a piece o' goods to set down the front of her weddin' dress."

She said, mollified, "You jest tootlin' me. I don't never ask for nothin' and you git so you don't expect me to ask for nothin'."

"I know. Hit frets me, you makin' out with so leetle. I'd love to fetch you a bolt o' silk, and do the Lord spare me, one day you'll have a well o' water at the house, and not have to wash no more at the sink-hole."

She said, "I want to go to Volusia tomorrer."

He said, "Now give Jody and me a day-two to hunt some,

and mebbe we kin carry some meat and hides to the store and you kin trade to your heart's content."

The first day's hunt brought nothing.

"When you ain't lookin' for deer," Penny said, "they're all over the place. When you hunt 'em, you'd think you was in a tormented city."

A puzzling incident occurred. South of the island Penny tried to put the dogs on the track of what appeared to be a small yearling or a well-grown fawn. The dogs refused to take the trail. Penny did a thing he had not done in years. He broke a switch and thrashed old Julia for her stubbornness. She yelped and whined, but still refused. The mystery became clear at the end of the day. Flag showed up, as he had made a habit of doing, in the middle of the hunt. Penny exclaimed sharply, then knelt to the ground to compare his tracks with those the dogs had refused to follow. They were the same. Old Julia, wiser than he, had recognized either the track or the scent of the newest Baxter.

He said, "That makes me feel right humble. A dog knowin' what you mought call kin-folks."

Jody was elated. He felt a deep gratitude to the old hound. He should have hated having Flag frightened by their pursuit.

The second day's hunt was more profitable. They found deer feeding in the swamp. Penny shot a large buck. He trailed still another, a smaller, and jumped it in a bay-head. He gave Jody a shot, and as he missed, shot it down. They had come on foot, for slow-trailing was the only chance these days of getting game, except by accident. Jody tried to carry the smaller deer, but its weight knocked him almost to the earth. He stayed with the kill while Penny went back for the horse and wagon. Flag was with them when they returned.

Penny called, "This pet o' yours loves a hunt as good as the dogs."

On the way home, Penny pointed out where the bears were feeding. They were eating the berries of the saw palmetto.

"Hit cleans 'em out and tonics 'em. They go into their winter beds fat as butter. The bears is like to be our salvation for fresh this year."

"What else eats the berries, Pa?"

"The deer loves 'em. And leave me tell you, do you fill a demi-john with 'em and pour Cuby rum over 'em and leave 'em stand five months, you've got a drink would make even your Ma shout Hallelujah, could you oncet git it down her."

Where the palmettos began to grow on higher land and merge into black-jack, Penny pointed out narrow trails leading into the gopher holes. The rattlesnakes had denned up for the winter but on warm bright days they came out for a few hours and sunned themselves near the holes. It seemed to Jody that all the invisible creatures of the scrub walked in plain sight before Penny's eyes.

At the house, Jody helped him skin the deer and dress out the hides and the hindquarters, which would be the only salable portions. Ma Baxter fried the meat from the forequarters and put it down for keeping in its own fat. The bones and scraps were boiled in the wash-pot for the dogs. The family feasted that night on the hearts and livers. There was not much wasted on Baxter's Island.

In the morning, Penny said, "We got to agree now, will we stay with Grandma Hutto tonight or come home. Do we spend the night, Jody's got to stay here to milk and feed the dogs and chickens."

Jody said, "Trixie's near about dry, Pa. And we kin leave feed. Leave me go, but please let's stay with Grandma Hutto."

Penny said to his wife, "You want to stay there tonight?"

"No, I don't. Her and me don't never swop much honey."

"Then we'll not stay. Jody, you kin go, but no teasin' to stay after we git there."

"What must I do with Flag? Cain't he foller along so Grandma kin see him?"

Ma Baxter burst out, "That blasted fawn! They ain't never been such a nuisance on the place, even countin' you."

He said with hurt pride, "I reckon I'll jest stay here with him."

Penny said, "Now boy, tie up the creetur and fergit him. He ain't a dog, he ain't a young un, though you've near about made one outen him. You cain't carry him places like a gal would a play-dolly."

He tied Flag reluctantly in the shed and changed into clean clothes to go to Volusia. Penny was dressed in his broadcloth suit with the shrunken sleeves, with his black felt hat on top of his head. The roaches had eaten a hole in the brim, but it was after all a hat. He had no other except his wool hunting cap and his palmetto field hat. Jody was in his best, brogan shoes, homespun breeches, big wire-grass hat and a new black alpaca coat bound with red tape. Ma Baxter was clean and crisp in a new dress made of the blue and white checked gingham from Jacksonville. It was a darker blue than she wanted, but the check was pretty. She wore her blue sun-bonnet but carried her black frilled bonnet to put on when she should approach the village.

It was pleasant, jogging down the sand road in the wagon. Jody sat on the floor of the wagon body with his back against the seat. It was interesting to see the scrub drop away behind him as he watched it. The sense of progressing was more acute than when he faced forward. The wagon jolted and his thin rump felt bruised by the time they reached the river. He had nothing much to think about and he gave himself over to thoughts of Grandma Hutto. She would be surprised to know that he was angry with Oliver. He pictured her face with satisfaction. Then he felt uncomfortable. He felt toward her exactly as he had always felt, except that through the summer he had actually forgotten her. Perhaps he would not tell her that he was through with Oliver. He saw himself being kind to her and maintaining a noble silence. The imagined scene pleased him. He made up his mind definitely to inquire politely after Oliver's health.

Penny had the deer meat in two pokes. The hides were in crocus sacks. Ma Baxter had a basket of eggs and a small pat of butter to trade at the store, and another basket containing gifts for Grandma Hutto: a quart of new syrup, a peck of sweet potatoes, and a shoulder of the Baxters' sugar-cured ham. She would not have gone empty-handed even to the house of an enemy.

Penny hallooed on the west side of the river to call the ferry from the east. The sound echoed down the river. A boy appeared on the opposite bank. He came leisurely. For an instant it seemed to Jody that the boy had an enviable life, pulling the ferry back and forth across the river. Then it occurred to him that such a life was quite without freedom. There would be for such a boy no hunts, no jaunts into the scrub, no Flag. He was glad he was not the ferry-man's son. He said "Hey" to him with condescension. The boy was ugly and bashful. He helped lead the Baxters' horse on the ferry with lowered head. Jody was filled with curiosity about his life.

He asked, "You got a gun?"

The boy jerked his head sideways in a negative and fastened his eyes on the east shore of the river. Jody recalled Fodder-wing longingly. From the minute he used to come in sight, Fodder-wing had talked to him. He gave up the new boy as a bad job. Ma Baxter was anxious to do her trading before she went visiting. They drove the wagon the short distance to the store and laid their articles of exchange on the counter. Storekeeper Boyles was in no hurry to trade. He wanted news of the scrub. The Forresters had given an incredible account of conditions after the flood. A few hunters from the Volusia territory had been there and had reported game almost impossible to find. The bears were troubling stock along the river, which they had not done in years. He wanted Penny's verification of the tales.

"Hit's ever' word true," Penny said.

He leaned over the counter and settled himself for talk.

Ma Baxter said, "You know I cain't stand on my feet too long. If you men'll agree on your trade, I'll do my buyin' and go on to Mis' Hutto's. Then you kin talk here all day."

Boyles weighed out the meat promptly. With venison scarce, he could find a ready sale for it at a good price. The river steamer would take a haunch or two by way of novelty to the English and Yankee travelers. He examined the hides carefully, and at last expressed his satisfaction with their condition. He had an order and could pay five dollars each. The rate was higher than the Baxters had hoped for. Ma turned to the dry goods counter with a complacent air. She was high-handed and would have only the best. He was out of brown alpaca. He could send for it by the next boat, he said. She shook her head. It was too far to send back for it from the Island.

He said, "Now why don't you take a dress length of this black alpaca and start new?"

She fingered it.

"Shore is purty. How much did you say? Oh——"

She turned away. She retreated into her pride.

"I said 'brown' and I meant 'brown,'" she said coldly.

She bought spices and raisins for a Christmas cake.

She said, "Jody, go look and see has old Cæsar broke loose."

The request was so absurd that he gaped at her. Penny winked at him. He wheeled quickly so that she could not see him smile. She meant to buy something to surprise him for Christmas. Penny would have thought of a better excuse to get him out of the way. He went outside and stared at the boy who tended the ferry. The boy sat and studied his own knees. Jody picked up bits of limestone and aimed them at the trunk of a live oak up the road. The boy watched him furtively, then came behind him without speaking and picked up bits, too, and hurled them at the tree. The contest continued wordlessly. After a time Jody thought his mother would have finished and he ran back into the store.

His mother said, "You comin' with me or stayin' with your Pa?"

He stood hesitant. Grandma Hutto would bring out cake or cookies the moment he was in her house. On the other hand, he could never get enough of hearing his father talk with other men. The matter was settled for him by the storekeeper's handing him a licorice stick for himself. It would keep body and soul together for the time being.

He said loftily, "Me and Pa'll foller."

She went out. Penny watched after her. He frowned. Boyles was stroking the fur of the deer hides with approval.

Penny said, "I'd figgered on takin' cash for them hides. But if you'd as soon trade me a dress length o' that black alpacy, why, I don't much keer."

Boyles said reluctantly, "I'd not do it for anybody else. But you've traded here a long time. All right."

"Best cut it up and wrap it before I change my mind."

Boyles said wryly, "You mean before I change mine."

The scissors snipped crisply across the alpaca.

"Now gimme silk thread to match and a card o' them glass buttons."

"That's not in the bargain."

"I got money for it. And put the alpacy in a box, do it rain this evenin'."

Boyles said good-naturedly, "Now you've cheated me, tell me where a man can go to shoot him a wild turkey for Christmas dinner."

"I cain't no more'n tell you where I'm fixin' to hunt one myself. They're mighty scarce. The plague got 'em bad. But you cross the river about where Seven-Mile Branch flows into it. You know that cypress swamp with two-three good big cedars in it, jest southwest o' the run? You work through there——"

The good male talk was beginning. Jody sat down on a cracker box to listen. There were no other customers and Boyles came out from behind the counter and pulled up a straight chair and an old cowhide rocker beside the thumper stove for himself and Penny. They got out their pipes and Penny shaved Boyles a pipeful of his own tobacco.

"Nothing like home-raised tobaccy for satisfaction," Boyles said. "You plant a patch for me this spring. I'll pay as high as anybody. Now go on— Southwest o' the run——?"

Jody chewed on his licorice stick. The rich black juice filled his mouth and the talk filled another hunger, back of his palate, that was seldom satisfied. Penny told of the flood in the scrub. It had been bad along the river, too, Boyles interrupted to say, but the river had carried most of the water away as fast as it fell. The banks had been flooded, and Easy Ozell's shack had swayed back and forth in the wind and finally capsized.

"He's living in Grandma's shed," Boyles said, "and happy as a pine borer in a fresh log."

Penny recounted the wolf hunt and the bear hunt; told of the rattler's strike, which the Forresters had not thought to mention. Jody lived the summer over again, and it was better than when it happened, the way Penny told it. Boyles was as fascinated, and sat leaning forward, forgetting to smoke. A customer came in and he left the stove grudgingly.

Penny said, "Your Ma's been gone a hour-two, boy. You best run on to Grandma's. Tell 'em I'll be along directly."

The licorice had long been swallowed. It was getting on toward noon and he was famished.

"Will we eat dinner at Grandma's?"

"Why, yes. If we wasn't invited, your Ma'd of been back by

now. You go on now. And carry that forequarter to her your-self."

He went, a little drugged with Penny's tale-telling.

Grandma's tidy yard was recovering from the effect of the high water. The river had been over its bank here and her fall flower garden had been washed away. There was unaccustomed debris here and there. The second planting was thriving, but there was no bloom, except of shrubs close beside the house. The blooms of the indigo had fruited into small black seed-pods, curved like scythe blades. Grandma was inside the house with his mother. He heard their voices and as he stepped up on the porch and looked through the window, he saw the flickering of flames on the hearth. She saw him and came to the door.

Her embrace was friendly, but it lacked something of enthusiasm. The two Baxter men were more welcome without Ma. There was no plate of cookies anywhere in sight. The smell of cooking, however, came from the kitchen. Otherwise he could scarcely have endured his disappointment. Grandma Hutto sat down again to talk with his mother with a tight-lipped patience. His mother was behaving no better. She looked critically at Grandma's frilled white apron.

She said, "No matter where I be, I like to dress plain in the mornin'."

Grandma Hutto said tartly, "I wouldn't be caught dead without a frill on me. Men-folks like a woman dressed pretty."

"I was raised to call it indecent, to dress to please the men. Well, some of us plain folks has had to go pore on this earth, 'll git our frills in Heaven."

Grandma Hutto rocked rapidly.

"Now I don't want to go to Heaven," she announced.

Ma Baxter said, "Reckon there's no danger."

Grandma's black eyes snapped.

"Why wouldn't you want to go, Grandma?" Jody asked.

"One thing, the company I'd have to keep."

Ma Baxter ignored this.

"Another thing's the music. There's nothin' played there, they claim, but harps. Now the only music I like is a flute and a bass viol and an octave harp. Unless one o' your preachers'll guarantee that, I'll jest refuse the trip with thanks."

Ma Baxter's face was stormy.

"Another thing's the food. Even the Lord likes the incense of roasted meat before him. But accordin' to the preachers, folks in Heaven live on milk and honey. I despise milk and honey makes me sick to my stummick." She smoothed her apron complacently. "I figger Heaven's only folks' longin' for what they ain't had on earth. Well, I've had near about ever'-thing a woman could want. Mebbe that's why I've got no interest."

Ma Baxter said, "Includin' Oliver runnin' off with a yaller-headed chipperdale, I reckon."

Grandma's rocker beat a tune on the floor.

"Oliver's up-standin' and fine-lookin' and women has allus follered him and allus will. Take Twink, now. She's not to blame. She'd never had a fine thing in her life and then Oliver takened a notion to her. Why wouldn't she foller him? The pore child's an orphan." She shook out her frills. "Left an orphan at the mercy of the Christians."

Jody fidgeted in his chair. The coziness of Grandma's house was chilled, as though the doors were open. It was more woman-business, he decided. Women were all right when they cooked good things to eat. The rest of the time they did nothing but make trouble. Penny's step sounded on the porch. Jody was relieved. Perhaps his father could straighten them out. Penny came into the room. He rubbed his hands together by the open fire.

He said, "Now ain't this fine? The two women I love the most in all the world, waitin' for me by the hearth-fire."

Grandma said, "If the two women loved each other as good, Ezra, all'd be well."

"I know you two don't git on," he said. "You want to know the reason? You're jealous, Grandma, 'cause I'm livin' with Ory. And Ory, you're jealous 'cause you ain't as handsome as Grandma. Now hit takes a bit of age to make a woman handsome—I don't say purty—and time Ory's got a bit of age on her, mebbe she'll be handsome, too."

It was impossible to quarrel around his good-nature. The two women laughed and bridled.

Penny said, "What I want to know, is the Baxters invited to eat o' the fat o' the land, or be they obliged to turn around and go home to cold cornpone?"

"Now you know you're welcome, day or night. And I do thank you for the deer meat. I only wish Oliver was here to eat it with us."

"What's the news from him? We was right hurt he didn't come to visit us before he put to sea."

"It was a long time before he got over his beatin'. Then he had word there was a boat in Boston wanted him for mate."

"I reckon there was a gal in Floridy wanted him for the same thing, eh?"

They laughed together and Jody laughed with them for relief. Grandma's house was warm again.

She said, "Dinner's ready, and if you scrub creeturs don't eat hearty, my feelin's'll be mighty hurt."

Dinner was not as lavish as when Penny and Jody came alone. Yet there were furbelows to impress Ma Baxter that were very tasty. The meal was friendly.

Ma Baxter said, "Well, we made up our minds to come to the Christmas doin's. We couldn't come last year for we'd not come empty-handed. You figger a fruit cake and a bait o' syrup candy'll be welcome for my share?"

"Nothin' better. How about you-all spendin' the night and havin' Christmas with me?"

Penny said, "That'll be fine. And you kin depend on me for meat. I'll git a turkey if I have to hatch one."

Ma Baxter said, "What about the cow and dogs and chickens? We cain't all come off and leave 'em, Christmas or no Christmas."

"We kin leave enough for the dogs and chickens. They'll not starve in a day. And I got a idee Trixie'll be fresh and we kin leave the calf to nuss her."

"And lose the calf to a blasted bear or panther."

"I kin fix a corral inside the barn where nothin' won't bother 'em. Now if you want to stay home and keep off the creeturs, you stay, but I mean to have Christmas."

"And me," Jody said.

Ma Baxter said to Grandma, "I got no more chancet agin 'em than a rabbit agin a pair o' wild-cats."

Penny said, "Now allus seemed to me 'twas Jody and me was two rabbits agin one wild-cat."

"You make a mighty good race of it," she said, but she had to laugh.

It was settled that they would come for Grandma to go to the doings, returning to her house to spend the night and the next day. Jody was elated. Then the thought of Flag came over him like a dark cloud in a sunny sky.

He burst out, "Now I jest cain't come. I got to stay home."

Penny said, "Why, what ails you, boy?"

Ma Baxter turned to Grandma Hutto.

"Hit's that tormented fawn o' hissen. He cain't bear it out of his sight. I never knowed a young un so crazy for a live thing to mess with. He'll go hongry to feed it, he sleeps with it, he talks to it like it was a person—oh, I've heered you, out in that shed— he don't think of nary thing else but that troublesome fawn."

Penny said gently, "Don't make the boy feel like he has the small-pox, Ory."

Grandma said, "Why can't he bring it along?"

He threw his arms around her.

"You'll love Flag, Grandma. He's so smart, you kin learn him like a dog."

" 'Course I'll love him. Will he git along with Fluff?"

"He likes dogs. He plays with ourn. When they go on a hunt, he slips off another way and meets up with 'em. He loves a bear hunt good as the dogs."

Praise of the fawn tumbled from him. Penny stopped him, laughing.

"You tell her all them things, you'll leave nothin' good for her to find out about him. Then she mought find out some o' the bad."

"They's nothin' bad about him," he said passionately.

"Only jumpin' on the table and knockin' the tops off the lard cans and buttin' over the 'taters, and into ever'thing worse'n ten young uns," Ma Baxter said.

She went into the garden to look at the flowers. Penny took Grandma aside.

"I been worryin' about Oliver," he said. "Them big bullies ain't drove him off 'fore he was ready to go, have they?"

"It was me drove him off. I got tired o' him traipsin' off on the sly to see that gal. I said to him, 'Oliver,' I said, 'you jest as good go on back to sea, for you ain't a mite o' good to me nor a mite o' comfort.' He said, 'I ain't a mite o' good to myself. The sea's the place for me.' I never figgered the gal'd foller him."

"You know Lem Forrester's rarin', don't you? Do he ever come here drunk, remember he ain't human when he gits to sullin'. Ease him off the best you kin."

"Now I shore as the devil won't waste no time tootlin' him. You know me better'n that. You know I'm made outen whalebone and hell."

"Ain't the whalebone gittin' a mite limber?"

" 'Tis, but the hell's hot as ever."

327

"I'd depend on you to back most men down, but Lem's different."

Jody was all ears. Now that he was at Grandma's again, Oliver seemed real once more. It was satisfying, however, to find that she had lost patience with Oliver, too. He would show his displeasure when he saw him again, but he would forgive him. He would never forgive Twink.

The Baxters gathered up their baskets and bags and purchases. Jody tried to guess which sack contained his Christmas surprise, but they all looked alike. The distressing thought came to him that perhaps his mother had really wanted him to see if old Cæsar had broken loose and had bought nothing for him at all. All the way home he sounded her out on the subject.

"You jest as good ask questions o' that wagon-wheel," she said.

He took her evasion as a sure sign that she did have something for him.

· 26 ·

THE cow freshened the week before Christmas. The calf was a heifer and there was rejoicing on Baxter's Island. It would take the place of the one the wolves had killed. Trixie was no longer young and it was necessary to raise a heifer soon to replace her. There was little talk at the house except of the coming Christmas. Now that the calf was born, the whole family would be able to be away for over-night on Christmas Eve, for the nursling would take care of the milking.

Ma Baxter baked a fruit-cake in the largest Dutch oven. Jody helped her pick out hickory nut meats for it. It took all day to bake it. For three days, the cake was all there was of life; a day for preparing it, a day for baking it, and the day after for admiring it. Jody had never seen a cake so huge. His mother bulged with her pride.

329

She said, "I don't go to the doin's often, and when I do go, I aim not to go scarce."

Penny presented her with the black alpaca the evening the cake was done. She looked at him and at the material. She burst into tears. She dropped into a chair and threw her apron over her head and swayed back and forth with every appearance of grief. Jody was alarmed. She must be disappointed. Penny went to her and laid his hand on her hair.

He said, " 'Tain't the lack o' will I don't do sich as that for you all the time."

Jody understood then that she was pleased. She wiped her eyes and gathered the alpaca in her lap and sat holding it for a long time, now and then stroking it lengthwise.

She said, "Now I got to move quick as a black snake to git this made in time."

She worked day and night for three days, her eyes bright and contented. She was forced to call on Penny for help in the fitting. He knelt humbly, his mouth full of pins, and took up and let out as she directed. Jody and Flag watched, fascinated. The dress was done and hung under a sheet for clean keeping.

Four days before Christmas, Buck Forrester stopped by. He was good-humored and Penny decided that he had imagined any mistrust. Old Slewfoot had visited Forresters' Island again and had killed a two hundred and fifty pound blue male hog in the nearby hammock. The kill had been in battle and not for food. The hog had put up a mighty fight, he reported. The ground was torn up for yards around. One of the boar's tusks was broken off and the other was wrapped with old Slewfoot's black fur.

"Hit's a good time to come up with him," Buck said, "for he belongs to be hurt."

They themselves had not discovered the kill until the day after it had happened. It had been too late to follow. Penny thanked him for the information.

"I reckon I'll set a trap inside the lot, jest to scare him," he said. "We-all are fixin' to go to the river for the doin's." He hesitated. "You fellers comin'?"

Buck too hesitated.

"I reckon not. We don't fool much with them Volusia jessies. No fun goin' if we wasn't drunk, and Lem'd likely pick a fight with some of Oliver's friends. No, reckon we'll git Christmas-drunk to home. Or mebbe Fort Gates."

Penny was relieved. He could imagine the distress of the river folk if the Forresters had rolled into the prim and Christian gathering.

He oiled his largest bear-trap. It was six feet in width and weighed, he said, nearly six stone. The chain alone weighed two. He planned to shut the cow and calf together inside the stable, barricade the door and set the trap just outside. If old Slewfoot came to make Christmas dinner of the new heifer while they were all away, he would have to take the trap first. The day passed busily. Jody polished again the necklace of Cherokee beans. He hoped his mother would wear them with the black alpaca. He had nothing for a gift for Penny. He worried and puzzled and in the afternoon went to a low place where pipe-elders grew. He cut a reed and made a pipe stem, and cut a bowl from a corn-cob and fitted it. The Indians who had once been here had made pipe-stems of the reeds, Penny had told him, and he had always meant to make one for himself. He could think of nothing for Flag. He admitted to himself that the fawn would be satisfied with an extra piece of cornbread. He would make him a halter of mistletoe and holly.

That night Penny stayed up after Jody had gone to bed. He occupied himself with a mysterious pounding and slapping and scraping that had something to do, no doubt, with Christmas. The three days left seemed like a month.

No one, not even the dogs, heard any sound in the night. When Penny went to the lot in the morning to milk Trixie, and then to the calf's stall to turn it in to the mother to nurse, the calf was gone. He thought it had broken down its bars. They were intact. He went into the soft sand of the lot and studied it for tracks. In a straight line across the criss-cross of cow and horse and human trails, the track of old Slewfoot stretched inexorably. Penny came to the house with the news. He was white with anger and frustration.

"I've had a bait of it," he said. "I mean to track that creetur down if I foller him clare to Jacksonville. This time, hit's me or him."

He went immediately at the business of oiling his gun and preparing shells. He worked rapidly, his manner grim.

"Put me some bread and 'taters in a bag, Ory."

Jody asked timidly, "Kin I go, Pa?"

"If you kin keep the pace with me and not holler quits. If you give out, you got to lay where you fall or come on back alone. I ain't stoppin' before night-fall."

"Must I shut up Flag or leave him foller?"

"I don't give a blasted rap who follers. Jest don't nobody look to me for mercy do the goin' git rough."

He went to the smoke-house and cut strips of 'gator tail for the dogs. He was ready. He trudged through the yard to the lot to take up the trail. He whistled for the dogs and put Julia on the track. She bayed and was off. Jody looked after him in a panic. His gun was not loaded, he had on no shoes, and he could not remember where he had left his jacket. He knew from the set of Penny's back that it was useless to beg him to wait. He scrambled about, gathering up his belongings. He shouted to his mother to put bread and potatoes in his shot-bag, too.

She said, "You're like to be in for it. Your Pa's locked horns with that bear. I know him."

He called to Flag and tore madly after his father and the dogs. Their pace was swift. He was out of breath by the time he caught up to them. Old Julia was jubilant on the fresh trail. Her voice, her merry tail, her easy lope, showed plainly that this was the thing above all others she wished to be doing. Flag kicked up his heels and ran beside her.

"He'll not be so frisky," Penny said ominously, "do old Slewfoot raise up in front of him."

A mile to the west they found the remains of the calf. The old bear, kept perhaps by his injuries inflicted by the Forresters' boar, from recent hunting, had eaten heavily. The carcass was well covered with trash.

Penny said, "He's due to lay up not too fur away, figgerin' on comin' back."

But the animal followed no rules. The trail continued. It led nearly to Forresters' Island, swung north and west and skirted Hopkins Prairie to the north. The wind was strong from the southwest and Penny said that it was almost certain old Slewfoot was not far ahead of them, but had winded them.

The pace was so rapid and the distance so long that in the late morning even Penny was obliged to stop for a rest. The dogs were willing to continue, but their heaving sides and hanging tongues showed that they too were weary. Penny stopped on a high live oak island by a clear pond on the prairie for the dogs to drink. He threw himself on the ground in the sunlight. He lay on his back without speaking. His eyes were closed. Jody lay down beside him. The dogs dropped flat on their bellies. Flag was unwearied and pranced about the island. Jody watched his father. They had never come so hard and so fast. Here was not the joy of the chase, the careless pitting of man's brain against creature speed and cunning. This was hate and revenge and there was no happiness in it.

Penny opened his eyes and rolled over on his side and opened his shot-bag and took out his lunch. Jody took out his own. They ate without speaking. The biscuits and cold baked sweet potato seemed almost savorless. Penny threw a few strips of the 'gator meat to the dogs. They gnawed contentedly. It was all one to them whether Penny hunted casually or with a desperate intent. The game was the same, the strong sweet trail, and the good fight at the end. Penny sat upright and swung to his feet.

"All right. Time to git goin'."

The siesta had been brief. Jody's shoes were heavy on his feet. The trail led into scrub, then out again, back to Hopkins Prairie. Old Slewfoot was trying to shake the dogs. Their scent still came to him. Penny was obliged to stop twice in the afternoon to rest. He was furious.

"Dog take it, time was I didn't have to stop," he said.

Yet each time that he set out again his walk was so fast that Jody was tired out from following him. He dared not say so. Only Flag frisked and frolicked. The long trek was a casual jaunt for his long legs. The trail led almost to Lake George, cut back sharply south, and again, to the east, lost itself in the dusk of the swamp. The sun was setting and visibility was low in the shadows.

Penny said, "Uh-huh. He's fixin' to come back and feed on that calf agin. We'll go home and fool him."

The distance back to Baxter's Island was not great, but it seemed to Jody that he could never make it. On any other hunt, he could have said so and Penny would have waited for him patiently. His father moved toward home as doggedly and relentlessly as he had left it. It was dark when they reached it, but Penny at once loaded the great bear trap on the slide, hitched Cæsar to it and dragged it to the site of the kill. He allowed Jody to ride on the slide. He himself walked beside Cæsar, leading him. Jody stretched out his aching legs with relief. Flag had lost interest and hung around the kitchen door.

Jody called, "Ain't you tired, Pa?"

"I don't git tired when I be this mad."

Jody held a fatwood torch for him while he lifted the ragged carcass with sticks, in order to leave no human taint, baited the trap and set it, and scratched leaves and rubbish over it with a pine bough. Penny squatted on the slide for the ride home, dropping the reins and allowing old Cæsar to pick his own way. He put up the horse and found gratefully that Ma Baxter had done the milking. They went to the house. Hot supper was on the table and he ate quickly and lightly, then went directly to his bed.

"Ory, what'd you take to rub my back with panther oil?"

She came and worked on him with big strong hands. He groaned with the comfort of it. Jody stood watching. Penny rolled over and dropped his head on the pillow with a sigh.

"How you makin' it, boy? Had enough?"

"I feel good sincet I ate."

"Uh. A boy's strength rise and fall on his belly. Ory."

"What?"

"I want breakfast before crack o' day."

He closed his eyes and was asleep. Jody went to bed and lay a moment aching, then he too passed beyond hearing of Ma Baxter clattering in the kitchen, laying out materials for the early breakfast.

He slept through the first sounds in the morning. He awakened, still drowsy. He stretched. He was stiff. He heard his father's voice in the kitchen. Evidently Penny was in the same grim mood as yesterday and had not even thought to call him. He got out of bed and pulled on his shirt and breeches and went sleepily to the kitchen with his shoes in his hand. His hair was shaggy in his eyes.

Penny said, "Mornin', feller. You ready for more?"

He nodded.

"That's the spirit."

He was too sleepy to eat much. He rubbed his eyes and dallied with his food.

He said, "Ain't it too soon to see?"

"Time we git there it'll jest be soon enough. I aim to creep up on him, do he be suspicious and jest sniffin' around."

Penny rose and leaned a moment on the table. He grinned wryly.

"I'd feel right good," he said, "if my back wasn't broke smack in two."

The black morning was bitter cold. Ma Baxter had made up the wool from Jacksonville into hunting jackets and jeans for both of them. They seemed too fine to wear, but walking slowly through the pine woods they wished they had put them on. The dogs were still sleepy and tired and were willing to follow silently at heel. Penny put his finger in his mouth and lifted it to test any imperceptible stirring of air. There seemed to be none and he went in a direct line toward the baited trap. It was in a place that was comparatively open and he halted a hundred yards away. Day was breaking in the east behind them. He slapped the dogs lightly and they dropped to the ground. Jody grew numb with the cold. Penny was shivering in his thin clothes and ragged jacket. Jody saw old Slewfoot in every stump and behind every tree. Interminably slow, the sun rose.

Penny whispered, "If he's ketched, he's dead, for I've heered nothin'."

They crept forward with lifted guns. The trap was exactly as they had left it the night before. There was not light enough to make certain of the tracks, to determine whether the wary creature had come and been suspicious and gone away. They rested their guns against a tree and swung their arms and stamped their feet to warm themselves.

"If he's been here," Penny said, "he ain't fur away. Ol' Julia'll jump him right quick."

The light was without warmth but it spread through the forest. Penny walked forward, bent low to the ground. Julia was snuffing, silently.

Penny said, "I be dogged. I jest be dogged."

Even Jody could see that the only tracks were the day-old ones.

"He ain't been anywhere near," Penny said. "He wouldn't foller a rule to save him."

He straightened and called in the dogs and turned back for home.

"Anyways," he said, "we know where he left off yestiddy."

He did not speak again until they reached the house. He went to his room and pulled on his new wool hunting clothes over the old thin ones.

He called to the kitchen, "Ma, put me up meal and bacon and salt and coffee and all the cooked rations you got. Put 'em in the knapsack. And scorch me some more rags for my tinder-horn."

Jody tagged after him.

"Must I put on my new things, too?"

Ma Baxter came to the door of the room with the knapsack. Penny paused in his dressing.

"Now boy, you're plumb welcome to go. But git this in your head and git it good. This is nary pleasure hunt. Hit's cold weather and hit'll mebbe be hard goin' and cold campin'. I jest ain't comin' home agin until I git that bear. Now you still want to go?"

"Yes."

"Then git ready."

Ma Baxter glanced at the sheet over the black alpaca dress. "You'll be gone tonight?"

"More'n likely. He's got a night's start on me. Mebbe to-morrer night, too. Mebbe a week."

She swallowed.

She said weakly, "Ezra—tomorrer's Christmas Eve."

"Cain't he'p it. I got a right fresh trail to foller and I'm takin' it."

He stood up and fastened his braces. His eye caught the look of misery on his wife's face. He pursed his mouth.

"Tomorrer's Christmas Eve, eh? Ma, you'd not be afeered to drive the horse and wagon to the river in daylight, would you?"

"No, not in daylight."

"Then if we ain't back tomorrer by time to make it, you hitch up and go on. And if they's a chancet in the world, we'll come on to the doin's. You milk before you go, and if we don't make it in, you'll be obliged to come on back next mornin' and milk. Now that's the best I kin do."

Her eyes were moist but she went without comment and filled the knapsack. Jody waited his chance when she went to the smoke-house for meat for Penny. He pilfered a quart of meal from the barrel and hid it, for Flag, in his own new knapsack made of the hides of the panther kittens. It was the first time he had carried it. He stroked it. It was not as soft as the albino, coonskin knapsack he had given Doc Wilson, but the blue and white spots were almost as pretty. Ma Baxter returned with Penny's meat and finished the packing. Jody stood hesitant. He had anticipated eagerly the Christmas doings at the river. Now he would miss them. His mother would be glad to have him stay with her, and he would be considered honorable and even unselfish for doing so. Penny slung his knapsack over his shoulder and picked up his gun. Suddenly Jody would not be left behind for all the festivities in the world. They were out to kill old Slewfoot. He swung his little knapsack over his own warm wool shoulder and picked up his gun and followed his father with a light heart.

They cut directly north to pick up the trail where it had ended the evening before. Flag made a sortie into the brush. Jody whistled shrilly.

"Huntin's a man's business, ain't it, Pa, even on a Christmas?"

"Hit's a man's business."

The track was still fresh enough for old Julia to keep it without pause or difficulty. It led east only a short distance beyond the point where they had left it, then turned sharply north.

"Jest as good we didn't foller it last night," Penny said. "He was makin' for other counties."

The trail swung west again toward Hopkins Prairie and ran into wet marsh. It was difficult to follow. Old Julia splashed through the water. Now and then she lapped it, tasting, it seemed, the very scent of it. Again she laid her long nose against the rushes and stared vacantly, deciding for herself on which side the rank fur had brushed them. Then she was off again. She lost the scent entirely at times. Then Penny cut back to firm land and followed the line of the marsh to watch for the great nubbed track where it came out. If he found it before she struck, he called her with the hunting horn and put her on it.

"Here he goes, gal! Here he goes! Git him!"

Rip with his short legs followed Penny. Flag was everywhere. Jody asked anxiously, "Flag ain't no hindrance, is he, Pa?"

"Not a bit in the world. Did a bear wind him, he'd pay him no mind, lessen it was to turn around and come to him."

In spite of Penny's grimness the hunt began to take on the old delight. The day was crisp and bright. Penny slapped Jody on the back.

"This is better'n Christmas play-dollies, ain't it?"

"I mean."

The cold food at noon tasted better than most hot dinners. They sat and ate and rested under the good strong sun. They loosened their jackets. When they rose to go on, the knapsacks seemed heavy for a time, then they became once more accustomed to them. It seemed for a time that old Slewfoot meant either to make a wide circle back to Forresters' or Baxter's

Island, or to continue straight across the scrub to new feeding grounds on the Ocklawaha.

"If Forresters' hog hurt him," Penny said, "he shore don't give a tinker's dam."

Irrationally, in mid-afternoon, the great tracks turned back into the swamp toward the east. The going was rough.

"Minds me o' the time last spring you and me tracked him through Juniper swamp," Penny said.

In the late afternoon they were not far, he said, from the lower reaches of Salt Springs Run. Suddenly old Julia gave tongue.

"He would bed up in sich a place!"

Julia dashed forward. Penny began to run.

"She's jumped him!"

There was a crashing ahead as though a storm broke through the denseness.

"Git him, gal! Hold him! Yippee! Git him! Yippee!"

The bear moved with incredible speed. He crashed through thickets that slowed the dogs. He was like a steamboat on the river, and the dense tangle of briers and thorny vines and fallen logs was no more than a fluid current under him. Penny and Jody were sweating. Julia gave tongue with a new note of desperation. She could not gain. The swamp became so wet and so dense that they sank in muck to their boot-tops and must pull out inch by inch, with no more support perhaps than a bull-brier vine. Cypress grew here, and the sharp knees were slippery and treacherous. Jody bogged down to his hips. Penny turned back to give him a hand. Flag had made a circle to the left, seeking higher ground. Penny stopped to get his wind. He was breathing heavily.

He panted, "He's like to give us the slip."

When his breath came more easily, he set out again. Jody dropped behind, but across a patch of low hammock found better going and was able to catch up. The growth was of bay and ash and palmetto. Hummocks of land could be used for stepping stones. The water between was clear and brown. Ahead, Julia bayed on a high long note.

"Hold him, gal! Hold him!"

The growth dissolved ahead into grasses. Through the opening old Slewfoot loomed into sight. He was going like a black whirlwind. Julia flashed into sight, a yard behind him. The bright swift waters of Salt Springs Run shone beyond. The bear splashed into the current and struck out for the far bank. Penny lifted his gun and shot twice. Julia slid to a stop. She sat on her haunches and lifted her nose high in the air. She wailed dismally, in misery and frustration. Slewfoot was clambering out on the opposite shore. Penny and Jody broke through to the low wet bank. The black rounded rump was all that was visible. Penny seized Jody's muzzle-loader and fired after it. The bear gave a leap.

Penny shouted, "I teched him!"

Slewfoot continued on his way. There was a moment's crashing as he broke a path through the thicket, then even the sound of him was gone. Penny urged the dogs desperately. They refused flatly to cross the wide creek. He threw up his hands in despair and dropped down on his haunches in the wetness and shook his head. Old Julia rose and snuffed the foot-prints at the edge of the bank, then sat down and took up her lament where she had left it. Jody's flesh quivered. He supposed the hunt was done with. Old Slewfoot had given them the slip again.

He was astonished when Penny rose, wiped the sweat from his face, reloaded both guns and set off northwest along the open edge of the run. He decided that his father knew a less tangled way of returning home. Yet Penny kept to the creek even when open pine woods showed to their left. He dared not question him. Flag had disappeared and he was in a panic for him. It was part of his bargain not to whimper, either for himself or the fawn. Penny's narrow back was stooped with weariness and discouragement, but it was a back of stone. Jody could only follow with sore feet and aching legs. The old muzzle-loader was heavy across his shoulder. Penny spoke, but rather to himself than to his son.

"Now I seem to remember her house yonder——"

The edge of the creek began to lift to high ground. Oaks and pines towered against the sunset. They came to a tall bluff overlooking the run. There was a cabin at the top of it and a cleared field below. Penny climbed the winding path and walked up on the stoop. The door was shut and no smoke came from the chimney. The cabin had no windows. Wooden shutters over square openings served the purpose. These were drawn closed. Penny walked around to the back of the cabin. A shutter here was ajar. He looked in.

"She ain't here, but we'll go in all the same."

Jody asked hopefully, "Will we go home from here to-night?"

Penny turned and eyed him.

"Go home? Tonight? I tol' you, I'm goin' to git that bear. You kin go home——"

He had never seen his father so cold and implacable. He followed after him meekly. The dogs had lain down in the sand by the house, panting. Penny went to the wood-pile and chopped wood. He gathered an armful and dropped it through the shutter opening. He climbed through after it and unbarred the kitchen door from the inside. Jody went back to the wood-pile and split off a handful of fatwood splinters and brought them in and laid them on the floor. A Dutch oven and iron kettles stood or hung on cranes at an open hearth.

Penny kindled a fire and hung a shallow kettle over it. He opened his knapsack on the floor and took out the slab of bacon and cut slices of it into the kettle. It began to sizzle slowly. He went outside to an open well and drew up a bucket of water on the windlass. He took a stained coffee-pot from a shelf in the kitchen and made coffee and set it close to the growing blaze. He stirred up a cornpone in a borrowed pan. He laid two cold baked sweet potatoes near the fire to warm through. When the bacon had fried, he scraped the cornmeal batter into the grease, turned it in a solid cake when it was brown and turned the crane away from the blaze to finish the baking. The coffee boiled. He set it aside. He took cups and plates from the rickety safe and set them on the bare deal table.

"Draw up," he said. "Hit's ready."

He ate quickly and hungrily and took what cornpone seemed likely to be left and gave it to the dogs outside, with two more strips each of 'gator meat. Jody was cold with more than the evening's bitterness. He hated having his father so silent. It was like eating with a stranger. Penny heated water in the kettle he had cooked in and washed the cups and plates and put them back in the safe. There was coffee left and he set the pot aside on the hearth. He swept the floor. He went outside and gathered armfuls of moss from a live oak and made a bed under a sheltered corner of the house for the dogs. The night was settling down, very still and bitter cold. He brought in logs from the woods and pushed the ends of two of them into the fire, to be pushed forward from time to time, nigger-fashion. He filled his pipe and lit it and lay down on the floor by the fire with his rolled knapsack for a pillow.

He said kindly, "You best do the same, boy. We'll be settin' out soon in the mornin'."

He seemed more himself and Jody dared now to question him.

"You figger ol' Slewfoot'll come back by here, Pa?"

"Not him. Not for longer'n I keer to wait. I'm right certain he's wounded. I'm goin' up to Salt Springs and cross over above the head o' the run. Then down t'other side to where he lit into the thicket this evenin'."

"That's a heap o' distance, ain't it?"

"Hit's a fur piece."

"Pa——"

"Well?"

"You reckon Flag ain't come to no harm?"

"You ain't forgot what I tol' you, about lettin' him foller?"

"I ain't forgot. I——"

Penny relented.

"He ain't lost, if that's frettin' you. You couldn't lose no deer in the woods. He'll turn up, if he ain't takened the notion to go wild."

"He'll not go wild, Pa. Never."

"Not so young, anyways. He's likely tormentin' your Ma this minute. Go to sleep."

"Whose house is this, Pa?"

"Used to belong to a widder woman. I ain't been here in a long whiles."

"Will she keer, us comin' in?"

"If it's the woman used to be here, she'll not keer. I come all around courtin' her, 'fore I married your Ma. Go to sleep."

"Pa——"

"Now you got one more question comin' to you 'fore I take a bresh to you. And if 'tain't a question with sense to it, I will anyway."

He hesitated. The question was whether Penny thought they could possibly reach the Christmas doings the next night. He decided that the query was not sensible. Following old Slewfoot was probably a life-time job. He brought his thoughts back to Flag. He pictured him lost and hungry and followed by a panther. He was lonely without him. He wondered if his mother had ever been so concerned about him, her only son, and doubted it. He went with some mournfulness to sleep.

He was awakened in the morning by the sound of wagon

wheels in the yard. He heard the dogs bark and a strange dog answer. He sat up. Penny was on his feet, shaking his head to clear it. They had overslept. The sunrise lay rosy about the cabin. The fire had burned to embers and the charred ends of two logs still extended over the hearth. The air was like ice. Their breaths hung in frosty clouds. They were chilled to the bone. Penny went to the kitchen door and pulled it open. A step sounded and a middle-aged woman came into the room, followed by a youth.

She said, "For the Lord's sake."

Penny said, "Well, Nellie. Looks like you cain't git rid o' me."

"Ezra Baxter. Now you could wait to be invited."

He grinned at her.

"Meet my boy, Jody."

She glanced at Jody quickly. She was a pretty woman, plump and rosy.

"He favors you a mite. This here's my nephew, Asa Revells."

"Not Matt Revells' boy? I'll swear. Why, boy, I knowed you when you was no bigger'n a dirt-dauber."

They shook hands. The youth looked sheepish.

The woman said, "Now you're so mannerly and all, Mr. Baxter, you could tell me how come you're makin' free o' my house."

Her tone was jovial. Jody liked her. Women ran in breeds, like dogs, he thought. She was of Grandma Hutto's breed, that made men easy. And two women could say the same words and the meaning would not be the same, as the bark of two dogs, one menacing and the other friendly.

Penny said, "Lemme git us a fire goin'. My breath's too froze to talk."

He knelt by the hearth and Asa went outside for wood. Jody followed to help. Julia and Rip were moving with stiff tails around the strange dog.

Asa said, "Your dogs like to scared Aunt Nellie and me to death."

Jody could think of no suitable response and hurried into the house with wood.

Penny was saying, "If you never been a angel from Heaven, Nellie, you was one last night. Jody and me and the dogs has been trailin' a big nub-footed bear two days steady. He's kilt my stock one time too many."

She interrupted, "A bear with one toe gone off his front foot? Why, he's cleaned me out o' hogs, the past year."

"Well, we trailed him clear from home and jumped him in the swamp south o' the lower end o' the run. Iffen I'd had ten more yards on him, I'd o' had him. I shot after him three times, but he was too fur. The last time I stung him. He swum the creek and the dogs wouldn't take the water. Well, Nellie, I never been so near give out since the time you told me Fred wanted to keep steady comp'ny with you."

She laughed, "Oh, go on with you. You never wanted me."

"Hit's too late to commit myself— Well, I knowed if you hadn't married agin and moved off, your place was up here some'eres. And I knowed you'd not begrudge me your floor and hearth. And when I laid down to sleep last night, I said, 'God bless leetle Nellie Ginright.'"

She laughed out loud.

"Well, I don't know nobody is more welcome. But next time, I'd not have sich a start did I know ahead o' time. A widder woman ain't used to strange dogs in the yard and a man by the hearth. What you fixin' to do now?"

"Soon as I eat a bite o' breakfast, I'm fixin' to cross the run above the head o' the spring and take up the trail on t'other side where we last seed him."

She knitted her forehead.

"Now Ezra, no need to do that. I got a old dug-out right

above here, is mighty sorry and season-cracked, but hit'd carry you acrost the creek. Take it and welcome and save the miles."

"Hi-yippee! You hear that, Jody? Now I got to say agin, 'God bless leetle Nellie Ginright.'"

"Not so leetle as when you knowed me."

"No, but you're a heap better lookin' now. You was allus purty, but you was too thin. You had legs like a buck-rubbed saplin'."

They laughed together. She took off her bonnet and bustled about the kitchen. Penny seemed now in no great hurry. The distance saved by the use of the dug-out to cross the creek gave them time for a leisurely breakfast. He donated the rest of the bacon. She cooked grits and made fresh coffee and biscuits. There was syrup for the biscuits, but no butter or milk.

"I cain't keep stock here," she said. "The 'gators gits what the bears and panthers don't." She sighed. "A widder woman's hard put to it, times."

"Asa, here, don't live with you?"

"No. He jest come back with me from Fort Gates, and he's goin' to the doin's at the river with me tonight."

"We was aimin' to go, too, but I reckon we jest as good fergit it." A thought struck him. "But now my wife'll be there. You tell her you met up with us, so she'll not be fretted."

"You're jest the kind, Ezra, would worry was his wife fretted. You never asked me, but I often figger I made a sorry out of it, not encouragin' you."

"And I reckon my wife figgers she made a sorry out of it, doin' so."

"None of us don't never know what we want 'til it's mebbe too late to git it."

Penny was judiciously silent.

Breakfast was a feast. Nellie Ginright fed the dogs generously and insisted on putting up a lunch for the Baxters. They left reluctantly, warmed in body and spirit.

"The dug-out's less'n a quarter up the run," she called after them.

There was ice everywhere. The switch grass was coated with it. The old canoe was embedded in it. They broke it loose and launched it. It had been out of water a long time. It leaked so fast behind their efforts that they gave up bailing and got in to make a dash for it. The dogs were suspicious of the boat and as fast as Penny lifted them into it, they jumped out. In the wasted minutes, the canoe acquired several inches of icy water. They bailed again. Jody climbed into the middle and squatted. Penny handed him the two dogs by the scruff of their necks. He clasped them tightly around their middles and held on desperately against their struggles. Penny poled out from shore with an oak limb. Once out from the fringes of ice, the current ran swiftly. It caught the dug-out and swung it down-stream. The water seeped in to Jody's ankles. Penny sculled madly. The water gushed in from a crack at the bow. The dogs stood quiet now, trembling with fear at the strangeness. Jody crouched and paddled with his hands.

The creeks all seemed friendly in summer. When he was dressed in a thin ragged shirt and as ragged breeches, a spill meant only a quick cool swim to either shore. The heavy wool jeans and jackets would be poor friends in the freezing water. The canoe was sluggish and unmanageable with its weight of water. Penny made the far bank just as it settled obstinately to the creek bottom. The water sloshed over their boot tops and numbed their feet. But they were on land, on the same side of the run as old Slewfoot, and they had saved hours of heavy going. The dogs shivered with the cold and looked to Penny for orders. He gave none, but set out immediately southwest along the creek bank. In places it was so low and marshy that they were forced to cut back into the swamp or even higher into the woods. The area lay between an arm of Lake George and the continued northward reach of the St. John's River. It was boggy and treacherous going.

Penny halted to take his bearings. He could depend on old Julia to pick up the trail when they crossed it, but he dared not push her too rapidly. He had an uncanny feeling for distance. He identified a dead cypress across the run as one they had passed shortly after losing the bear. He slowed his pace to a walk and went cautiously, studying the frozen earth. He pretended to find a track.

He said to Julia "Here he goes. Git him. Here he goes——"

She stirred from her cold lethargy, swayed her long tail and began to snuff noisily. After a few yards she gave a small thin cry.

"There 'tis. She's got it."

The great tracks were imprinted solidly in the muck. They could be followed easily with the eye. Bushes were broken in the thicket where Slewfoot had crashed through. Penny was close behind the dogs. The bear had bedded as soon as he was certain he was no longer followed. A scant four hundred yards beyond the creek bank, Julia jumped him. He was invisible in the thicket. His ponderous leap sounded. Penny could not shoot without a sight, for the dogs were close on the leathery heels. Jody expected his father to break into as much of a run as was possible in the dense swamp growth.

Penny said, "We cain't ketch him ourselves, no-way. Leave him to the dogs. I got a idee slow time'll prove the fastest."

They pushed through steadily.

Penny said, "We got this much satisfaction, he's wore out, too."

He underestimated his enemy. The chase continued.

Penny said, "Looks like he's got a ticket to Jacksonville."

Bear and dogs were out of sight and hearing. The trail was still plain to Penny's eyes. A broken bough, a bent clump of grasses, unrolled a map before him even where the ground was hard and showed no foot-prints. In late morning they were winded and had to stop to rest. Penny cupped his ear into the light icy wind that had risen.

"Now I think I hear old Julia," he said. "At the bay."

The impetus sent them forward again. At high noon they came up with the quarry. He had decided, at long last, to stop and fight it out. The dogs had him at bay. He swayed sideways on his thick short legs, growling and baring his teeth. His ears were laid flat in his fury. When he turned his back for further retreat, Julia nipped at his flanks and Rip rounded him to spring for his shaggy throat. He slashed at them with great curved claws. He backed away. Rip swung behind him and sunk his teeth in a leg. Slewfoot squealed shrilly. He wheeled with the swiftness of a hawk and raked the bulldog to him. He caught him up in his fore-paws. Rip yelped in pain, then fought gamely to keep the jaws above him from closing on his backbone. The two heads tossed back and forth, snarling and snapping, each trying for the other's throat while protecting his own. Penny lifted his gun. He took steady aim and fired. With Rip hugged to his breast, old Slewfoot dropped. His killing days were done.

It seemed so easy now that it was over. They had followed him. Penny had shot him. There he lay——

They looked wonderingly at each other. They approached the prone carcass. Jody was weak in the knees. Penny's walk was unsteady. Jody felt a clear lightness fill him, as though he were a balloon.

Penny said, "I declare, I believe I'm surprised."

He slapped Jody on the back and cut a buck-and-wing.

He screeched, "Yippee!"

The sound echoed through the swamp. A jay-bird screeched after him and flew away. Jody took up his excitement and shrilled "Yippee!" Old Julia crouched and barked with them. Rip, licking his wounds, wagged his stumpy tail.

Penny shouted tunelessly,

> "My name is Sam.
> I don't give a damn.
> I'd ruther be a nigger
> Than a pore white man."

He pounded Jody again.

"Who's a pore white man?"

Jody shouted, "We ain't pore. We got ol' Slewfoot."

They capered together and shouted and yipped until their throats were hoarse and the squirrels were chattering all about them. They were at last relieved. Penny laughed breathlessly.

"I ain't whooped and hollered that-a-way, I don't know when. I'll swear, it done me good."

Jody's exuberance was still on him and he whooped again. Penny sobered and leaned to examine the bear. He would weigh five hundred pounds. His hide was magnificent. Penny lifted up the huge front paw with its missing toe.

He said, "Well, old fellow, you was a mighty mean enemy, but you got my respect."

He sat down victoriously on the stout ribs. Jody touched the thick fur.

Penny said, "Now we got to do a piece o' studyin'. Here we be in the middle o' nowhere, with a thing bigger'n you and me and your Ma put together, and the cow throwed in."

He took out his pipe and filled and lighted it leisurely.

"Jest as good to study comfortable," he said.

He was in such high spirits that the problem which seemed insoluble to Jody, was no more to him than a pleasant challenge. He began to figure, half to himself.

"Let's see, now. We'd ought to be jest about between Bear

Spring and the river. The Fort Gates road to the west—the river to the east. Now kin we git the black gentleman here to Horse Landin'—there's boats passin' all the time— Well, we'll git him gutted and figger some more."

It was like turning a wagon-load of sacks of meal all at once, to turn him over on his back. The thick layers of fat under the hide made him roly-poly and flabby. He would not stay firmly when held.

"Jest as ornery dead as alive," Penny said.

He disemboweled the carcass neatly. Old Slewfoot was as trim and harmless as a whole beef hanging in a butcher shop. Jody tingled, holding out the heavy legs so that Penny could get at his work. He had never thought to see the day when he would hold the huge paws in his small ones. He had had no share in the hunt except to follow his father's small inexorable back, but now he felt strong and mighty.

Penny said, "Now we'll see be we men enough to budge him."

Each took a fore-paw and strained ahead. The effort needed to move the dead weight was prodigious. By heaving and jerking it was possible to pull it a foot at a time.

"We'll not git to the river by spring, this-a-way," Penny said, "and starve to death on the way to boot."

The inability to keep a firm grip on the smooth-haired paws was the greatest bar to their progress. Penny sat on his heels and pondered.

He said at last "We kin walk on to Fort Gates and git he'p. That'll cost us a good share o' the meat but hit'll spare our own gizzards. Or else we kin rig up a kind of a pullin' harness and fight it out to the river. And mebbe tear our very hearts out. Or we kin make it on in home and git the wagon."

"But the wagon'll not be there, Pa. Ma'll be done gone to the doin's."

"Now you know I plumb forgot 'twas Christmas Eve day."

Penny pushed back his cap and scratched his head.

"Well, come on, boy."

"Where we goin'?"

"Fort Gates."

The road leading to the small settlement on the river was a scant two miles to the west, as Penny had been certain. It was good to turn from the swamp and the scrub to the open sandy road. A cold wind blew down it but the sun was beneficent. Penny found a patch of cancer-weed by the road-side and broke the stems and let the healing sap drip on Rip's wounds. He was talkative, and as they walked on he brought out from his half-forgotten lore tales of other bear hunts, long ago.

Penny said, "When I were about your size, my uncle Miles come visitin' from Georgia. And a cold day about like this he takened me in the very swamp we come through today. We was moseyin' along, not lookin' for nothin' in pertickler, and on beyond us we seed what looked like a buzzard settin' on a stump, peckin' at somethin'. Well, we got there and what do you suppose 'twas?"

" 'Twasn't no buzzard?"

" 'Twasn't no buzzard a-tall. 'Twas a bear cub cuffin' play-ful-like at his twin on the ground below him.

"My uncle Miles said, 'Now we'll jest ketch us a bear cub.' They was right gentle and he goes up to the one on the stump and ketched it. Well, when he'd ketched it, he didn't have nary thing to tote it in. And them scaper's'll gnaw on you if they ain't in a sack. Well, them up-country folks wears under-wear in the winter. He takened off his breeches and he takened off his long drawers and he tied knots in the legs of 'em and he made him a sack. He puttened the cub in it and about the time he reached for his breeches to put 'em back on agin, here come a crashin' and a woofin' and a stompin' in the bresh, and the old she-bear come outen the thick right at him. Well, he takened out through the swamp and dropped the cub and the mammy gathered it up, drawers and all. But she were so clost behind him she stepped on a vine and it tripped him and throwed him flat amongst the thorns and brambles. And aunt Moll was a muddle-minded kind o' woman and she couldn't never make it out how he come home without his drawers on a cold day, and his bottom scratched. But uncle Miles allus said that wasn't nothin' to the puzzlin' the mammy bear must o' done over them drawers on her young un."

Jody laughed until he could laugh no more.

He complained, "Pa, you got all them tales in your mind and you don't tell 'em."

"Well, it takes a thing like bein' in the swamp where it happened, to call it back to me. Now in that same swamp, one very cold March, I remember comin' on another pair o' bear cubs. They was whimperin' with the cold. New-borned cubs is no bigger'n rats and plumb naked, and these uns hadn't yit growed much fur. They was huddled up in a red bay thicket and cryin' like human babies. Listen!"

The sound of hoof beats was unmistakable along the road behind them.

"Now wouldn't it be fine not to have to go clare to Fort Gates for he'p?"

The sounds came closer. They stepped to the side of the road. The riders were the Forresters.

Penny said, "Looks like I mis-called myself."

Buck led the cavalcade. They streamed down the road. They were drunk as lords. They reined in.

"Now look at this! Ol' Penny Baxter and his he-cub! Hey, Penny! What the devil you doin' up here?"

Penny said, "I been on a hunt. And this un was deliberate. Me and Jody takened out after ol' Slewfoot."

"Whoops! On foot? Listen to that, boys! That's better'n a pair o' biddies rompin' on a hawk."

"And we got him," Penny said.

Buck shook himself. The whole array seemed to sober.

"Don't tell me none o' them tales. Where's he at?"

" 'Bout two mile to the east, between Bear Spring and the river."

"Reckon he is. He fools around there a good bit."

"He's dead. How I know he's dead, I gutted him. Me and Jody's walkin' to Fort Gates for he'p in totin' him outen the swamp."

Buck stiffened in a drunken dignity.

"You goin' to Fort Gates for he'p gittin' out ol' Slewfoot? And the best slew-footers in the county right here beside you?"

Lem called, "What'll you give us, do we go tote him out?"

"Half the meat. I figgered on givin' it to you anyways, account of him tormentin' you so, and Buck comin' to warn me."

Buck said, "You and me's friends, Penny Baxter. I warn you and you warn me. Git up here behind me and point the way."

Mill-wheel said, "I don't know as I crave goin' into no swamp today, and clare back to Baxter's Island. I got my mind set on a frolic."

Buck said, "You ain't got no mind. Penny Baxter!"

"What you want?"

"You still figgerin' on goin' to them doin's at Volusia?"

"Could we git the bear out in time to make it, we figgered on it. We're runnin' mighty late."

"Git up here behind me and point the way. Boys, we'll git out the bear and we'll go to the doin's at Volusia. If they don't want us, they kin throw us out—if they kin."

Penny hesitated. Help of any sort from Fort Gates, especially Christmas Eve day, would be hard to obtain. But the Forresters at the respectable gathering would scarcely be welcome. He decided to let them help him with the big carcass and then trust to luck to send them on their way again. He swung up behind Buck. Mill-wheel held down a hand for Jody to clamber up behind him.

Penny said "Who's big-hearted enough to tote my bulldog? He's not bad hurt, but he's done a heap o' runnin' and fightin'."

Gabby picked up Rip and carried him in the saddle in front of him.

Penny said, "Likely the way we come out is as good as any. You kin about see where we come."

The walk that had seemed so long was as nothing on the Forresters' horses. The Baxters remembered that they had not eaten since breakfast. They fished in their knapsacks and munched on Nellie Ginright's bread and meat. Penny in his light-heartedness fell into the spirit of the Forresters' drunkenness.

He shouted back, "Spent the night with an old gal o' mine."

They whooped noisily in applause.

"Only she wasn't there!"

They whooped again.

Jody, at leisure, remembered the jovial air of Nellie Ginright.

He said to Mill-wheel's back, "Mill-wheel, if my Ma had been somebody else, would I be me, or would I be somebody else, too?"

Mill-wheel shouted ahead, "Hey! Jody wants a new Ma!"

He thumped on Mill-wheel's back.

"I do not either. I jest want to know."

The question was beyond Mill-wheel, sober. It was only a source of ribald comment, drunk.

Penny said, "Now jest past that stretch o' low hammock, there's our bear."

They dismounted. Lem spat in disgust.

"You lucky son of a preacher——"

"Ary man could of come up with him that was willin' to stay with him," Penny said. "Or got mad enough, the way I done, to foller."

There was disagreement as to how to cut up the meat. Buck wanted to take it in whole for effect. Penny struggled to convince him of the impossibility. They talked him as last into agreeing to quarter it as was usually done with a bear of so great a size. Each dressed quarter would weigh a hundred pounds. They skinned and quartered it. The hide was left intact, with the great head and clawed feet.

Buck said, "I got to have it that-a-way. I got a idee for some fun."

They had a round of drinks from their bottles. They set back for the road with a bear quarter over each of four horses and the hide over a fifth. It needed a family as big as the Forresters' to provide transportation for old Slewfoot and both Baxters, too. The procession was boisterous. They shouted back and forth to one another.

They reached Baxter's Island after dark. The house was barred and shuttered. There was no light, no curl of smoke from the chimney. Ma Baxter had gone on to the river with the horse and wagon. Flag was not about. The Forresters dismounted and drank again and called for water. Penny suggested cooking supper, but their minds were fixed on Volusia. They hung the bear-meat in the smoke-house. Buck clung stubbornly to the hide.

Jody found it strange to go around his own closed house in the dark, as though other people lived there and not the Baxters. He went to the back and called, "Flag! Here, feller!" There was no answering thump of small sharp hooves. He called again, fearfully. He turned back to the road. Flag came galloping to him from the forest. Jody clutched him so hard that he broke loose in impatience. The Forresters were shouting to him to hurry. He longed to have Flag follow along with them, but he could not endure it if he should run away again. He led him into the shed and tied him safely and barred the door against marauders. He ran back and opened it and spread out the meal he had been carrying for him in his knapsack. The Forresters thundered at him. He barred the door again and ran and climbed up behind Mill-wheel with a full heart. He could depend on Flag to come home to him.

When the Forresters burst into harsh-voiced song, like a flock of crows strung out along a fence-row, he sang with them.

Buck sang:

> "I went to see my Susan.
> She met me at the door.
> She told me that I needn't to come
> To see her any more."

Mill-wheel called, "Whoopee! How 'bout it, Lem?"
Buck went on:

> "She'd fallen in love with Rufus
> Of Andrew Jackson fame.
> I looked her in the face and said,
> 'Good-bye, Miss Susan Jane!'"

"Whoopee!"
Gabby sang a plaintive lament of matrimony, each stanza ending with the refrain:

> "I married another,
> The devil's grandmother.
> I wish I was single again."

The scrub echoed with their shouting.
They reached the river at nine o'clock and bellowed for the ferry. Across the river, they rode on to the church. It was

lighted. Horses and wagons and oxen and carts were tethered to the trees in the yard.

Penny said, "Now we're all right rough-lookin' for church doin's. How about Jody goin' in and fetchin' us out rations?"

But the Forresters had passed beyond persuasion or interference.

Buck said, "Now you-all he'p me git fixed. I'm aimin' to scare the devil right outen that church buildin'."

Lem and Mill-wheel draped the bear-skin over him. He got down on all fours. He could not get an effect realistic enough to suit him, for the hide, split down the belly, allowed the great heavy head to slide forward. Penny was impatient to be inside and to reassure Ma Baxter, but the Forresters were in no hurry. They donated two or three pairs of boot laces and laced the hide together across Buck's chest. The result was all he could ask for. His bulky back and shoulders filled out the hide almost as completely as the original owner. He gave a trial growl. They crept up the steps of the chuch. Lem swung the door open to let Buck pass inside, then pulled it back, leaving a crack wide enough for the rest to watch through. It was a moment or two before the visitor was noticed. Buck swayed forward with so true an imitation of a bear's rolling gait that Jody felt the hair crawl on the back of his neck. Buck growled. The assembled company turned. Buck halted. There was an instant of paralysis, then the church emptied through the windows as though a gale of wind had blown a pile of oak leaves.

The Forresters entered through the door, bellowing with laughter. Penny and Jody followed. Suddenly Penny leaped for Buck and pulled the bear's head away so that the human face was exposed.

"Git outen that thing, Buck. You want to git kilt?"

His eye had caught the glint of a gun-barrel at one of the windows. Buck stood up and the hide slipped to the floor. The frolickers crowded in again. Outside, a woman screaming could not be quieted and two or three children wailed in fear. The first reaction of the gathering was one of anger.

One man called, "This be a purty way to come celebratin' Christmas Eve. Scarin' young uns outen their wits."

But the holiday spirit was strong, and the drunken joviality of the Forresters was infectious. Interest centered in the great bear hide. Here and there a man guffawed and at last the crowd was laughing, and agreeing that Buck had looked more like a bear than old Slewfoot himself. The big bear had done damage for several years. His reputation was known to all.

Penny was surrounded by most of the men and boys. His wife greeted him and bustled away to bring him a plate of food. He sat on the edge of one of the church benches, pushed back against the plain bare walls, and tried to eat. He swallowed a few mouthfuls. Then the men's eager questions enmeshed him and he was away on the flowing stream of his tale of the hunt. The food sat in his lap, uneaten.

Jody looked shyly about in the unaccustomed color and brightness. The small church was decorated with holly and mistletoe and donations of house plants; sultanas and geraniums, aspidistras and coleas. Kerosene lamps shone from brackets along the walls. The ceiling was half hidden with suspended ropes of colored paper, green and red and yellow. At the front, where the rostrum stood for services, a Christmas tree was hung with tinsel and strings of popcorn, figures cut from paper, and a few shining balls that had been a present from the captain of the *Mary Draper*. Gifts had been exchanged and the wrappings were strewn under the tree. Little girls moved trance-like with new rag dolls clutched to their flat gingham breasts. The boys too young to be engrossed with Penny, played on the floor.

The food was on long plank tables near the Christmas tree. Grandma Hutto and his mother bore down on him to lead him to it. He found that glory hung about him, too, in a sweet aroma. Women crowded around him and pressed food on him. They too asked questions about the hunt. At first he was struck dumb and could not answer. He felt hot and cold and spilled salad from the plate in one hand. The other hand held three varieties of cake.

Grandma Hutto said, "Now leave him be."

He was suddenly afraid he would not have a chance to answer the questions and would miss the shining triumph of the hour.

He said quickly, "We follered him near about three days. We jumped him twice. We got into mud Pa said would bog a buzzard's shadow, and we wrangled out of it——"

They listened with flattering attention. He was filled with enthusiasm. He began at the beginning and tried to tell it as he thought Penny would do. Half-way through, he looked down at the cake. He lost interest in the account.

"Then Pa shot him," he ended abruptly.

He crammed a chunk of pound cake in his mouth. The clustered women turned to bring him more sweets.

Ma Baxter said, "Now you begin on cake, you'll not be able to hold nothin' else."

"I don't want nothin' else."

Grandma Hutto said, "Leave him be, Ory. He kin eat corn-bread the rest o' the year."

"I'll eat it tomorrer," he promised. "I know you got to have cornbread to grow on."

He went from one kind of cake to another and back again.

He asked, "Ma, did Flag come in 'fore you left?"

"He come in yestiddy at dark. I declare, hit worried me, him comin' in without you. Then Nellie Ginright was here a while tonight and reported you."

He looked at her with approval. She was really handsome, he thought, in the black alpaca. Her gray hair was combed smoothly and her cheeks were flushed with her contentment and her pride. The other women addressed her respectfully. It was a great thing, he thought, to be kin to Penny Baxter.

He said, "I got somethin' purty for you, home."

"Have? 'Twouldn't be red and shiny, would it?"

"You found it!"

"I got to clean house now and agin."

"You like it?"

"Purty as kin be. I'd of wore it, but I figgered you'd want to give it to me. You want to know what I got hid for you, or no?"

"Tell me."

"I got a sack o' pep'mint candy. And your Pa made you a deer-leg scabbard for the knife Oliver give you. And he made a buckskin collar for your fawn."

"How'd he do it without me knowin'?"

"When you're oncet asleep, he could put a new roof over you, and you'd not know it."

He sighed with repletion of soul and body. He looked at the remnants of cake in his hands. He thrust them at his mother.

"I don't like it," he said.

"About time."

He looked about at the company and was again stabbed with shyness. Eulalie Boyles was doing a hop-skip-and-jump in a corner with the wordless boy who sometimes ran the ferry. Jody stared from a distance. He would scarcely have known her. She had on a white dress with blue ruffles and blue bows of ribbon swung at the ends of her pig-tails. He was swept with resentment, not of her, but of the ferry-boy. Eulalie in a remote fashion belonged to him, Jody, to do with as he pleased, if only to throw potatoes at her.

The Forresters had formed a group of their own at the end of the church near the door. The bolder of the women had taken them plates of food. To look twice at a Forrester was to invite scandal. The more roistering of the men were with them, and the bottles were going around again. The Forrester voices boomed above the hum of the festivities. The fiddlers went outside and brought in their instruments and began to tune and scrape. A square dance was formed and called. Buck and Mill-wheel and Gabby induced giggling girls to be their partners. Lem frowned from the outskirts. The Forresters made a violent and noisy affair of the dance. Grandma Hutto retired to a far bench. Her black eyes snapped.

"You'd never of got me here, did I know them black devils was comin'."

"Nor me," Ma Baxter said.

They sat stonily side by side, for once in agreement and harmony. Jody was half-drunk himself with the noise and music, the cake and the excitement. The outside world was cold, but the inside of the church was hot and stuffy with the roaring wood-stove and the heat of the packed and sweating bodies.

A man, a newcomer, entered the door. A cold gust of air followed him, so that every one looked up to see what had brought it. A few noticed that Lem Forrester spoke to him, and the man answered, and Lem said something to his brothers. In a moment the Forresters went out together. The group around Penny had been filled and satisfied with his story of the hunt and was now supplementing it with tales of their own. The square dance continued with a reduced number. Some of the women went to the group of hunters, protesting their absorption. The newcomer was brought to the still-loaded tables for food. He was a traveller who had disembarked from a steamer that had stopped for wood at the river landing.

He said, "I was tellin' the men, ladies, there was other passengers got off here. I reckon you know 'em. Mr. Oliver Hutto and a young lady."

Grandma Hutto stood up.

"You sure o' that name?"

"Why, yes, Ma'am. He said his home was here."

Penny was pushing his way toward her. He took her aside. He said, "I see you've done had the news. I'm feered the Forresters has gone to your house. I'm fixin' to go there to try to ward off trouble. You want to go? Could be, they'd behave theirselves better was you there to shame 'em."

She bustled about for her shawl and bonnet.

Ma Baxter said, "Now I'll jest go with you. I'd as soon give them varmints a piece o' my own mind."

Jody trailed behind them. They piled in the Baxter wagon and turned back toward the river. The sky was strangely bright.

Penny said, "Must be a woods fire some'eres. Oh, my God."

The position of the fire was unmistakable. Around the bend of the road, down the lane of oleanders, flames were shooting high into the air. Grandma Hutto's house was burning. They turned into the yard. The house was a bonfire. The flames showed details of the rooms within. Fluff ran to them, his tail between his legs. They jumped down from the wagon.

Grandma called, "Oliver! Oliver!"

It was impossible to approach within yards. Grandma ran toward the blaze. Penny pulled her back.

He shouted above the roaring and crackling, "You want to git burnt to death?"

"Oliver's there! Oliver! Oliver!"

"He cain't be. He'd of got out."

"They've shot him! He's in there! Oliver!"

He struggled with her. In the bright light the earth was plain. It was cut and trampled with the hooves of horses. But the Forresters and their mounts were gone.

Ma Baxter said, "There's jest nothin' them black buzzards won't do."

Grandma Hutto fought to break free.

Penny said, "Jody, for the Lord's sake, drive back to Boyles' store and see kin you find somebody seed where Oliver headed when he left the boat. If there's nobody there, go on to the doin's and find out from the stranger."

Jody clambered to the wagon seat and turned Cæsar back up the lane. His hands seemed wooden and he fumbled with the reins. He was panicked and could not remember whether his father had told him to go first to the doings or first to the store. If Oliver was alive, he would never be unfaithful to him, even in his mind, again. He turned into the road. The winter night was bright with stars. Cæsar snorted. A man and woman were walking down the road toward the river. He heard the man laugh.

He cried, "Oliver!" and jumped from the moving wagon.

Oliver called, "Now look who's drivin' around by hisself. Hey, Jody."

The woman was Twink Weatherby.

Jody said, "Git in the wagon, quick, Oliver."

"What's the hurry? Where's your manners? Speak to the lady."

"Oliver, Grandma's house is a-fire. The Forresters done it."

Oliver tossed his bags into the wagon. He lifted Twink and swung her to the seat, then vaulted the wheel and took the reins. Jody scrambled up beside him. Oliver groped with one hand inside his shirt and laid his revolver on the seat.

"The Forresters is gone," Jody said.

Oliver whipped the horse to a trot and turned down the lane. The frame of the house stood revealed around the flames, as though a box enclosed them. Oliver caught his breath.

"Ma wasn't in it?"

"She's yonder."

Oliver stopped the wagon and they climbed down.

He called, "Ma!"

Grandma threw her arms in the air and ran to her son.

He said, "Easy, there, old lady. Quit tremblin' now. Easy."

365

Penny joined them.

He said, "No man's voice was never more welcome, Oliver."

Oliver pushed Grandma aside and stared at the house. The roof crashed and a fresh blaze leaped to the moss in the live oaks.

He said, "Which-a-way has the Forresters gone?"

Jody heard Grandma murmur, "Oh God."

She braced herself.

She said loudly, "Now what in tarnation you want o' the Forresters?"

Oliver wheeled.

"Jody said they done it."

"Jody, you fool young un. The idees a boy'll git. I left a lamp burnin' by a open window. The curtain must of blowed and ketched. Hit worried me all through the evenin' at the doin's. Jody, you must want a ruckus mighty bad."

Jody gaped at her. His mother's mouth was open.

Ma Baxter said, "Why, you know——"

Jody saw his father grip her arm.

Penny said, "Yes, son, you got no business thinkin' sich things of innocent men is miles away."

Oliver let out his breath slowly.

He said, "I'm shore proud 'twasn't their doin'. I'd not of left one alive." He turned and drew Twink close to him. "Folks, meet my wife."

Grandma Hutto wavered, then walked to the girl and kissed her cheek.

"Now I'm glad you got it settled," she said. "Mebbe Oliver'll take time to visit with me now and again."

Oliver took Twink by the hand and went to circle the house. Grandma turned fiercely on the Baxters.

"If you dast to let it out— You think I aim to have two counties strowed with Forrester blood and my boy's bones, for a burnt-up house?"

Penny laid his hands on her shoulders.

"Ol' lady," he said. "Ol' lady— Did I have the sense you got——"

She was quivering. Penny held her and she quieted. Oliver and Twink returned.

Oliver said, "Don't take it too hard, Ma. We'll build you the best house on the river."

She gathered her strength.

"I don't want it. I'm too old. I want to live in Boston."

Jody looked at his father. Penny's face was drawn.

She said defiantly, "I want to go in the mornin'."

Oliver said, "Why, Ma— Leave here?"

His face lightened.

He said slowly, "I always ship out of Boston. Ma, I'd love it. But do I turn you loose amongst them Yankees, I'm feered you'll start another war between the states."

· 27 ·

THE Baxters stood at the river landing in the cold dawn, saying good-by to Grandma and Oliver and Twink and Fluff. Around the bend to the south, the north-bound steamboat whistled for the landing. Grandma and Ma Baxter embraced. Grandma caught Jody to her and held him tight.

"You learn to write, so you kin write to Grandma in Boston."

Oliver shook hands with Penny.

Penny said, "Jody and me'll miss you fearful."

Oliver put out his hand to Jody.

"I thank you for stickin' by me," he said. "I'll not forget you. Not even in the China Sea."

Grandma's chin was a flint arrowhead. Her mouth was tight.

Penny said, "If you folks ever change your minds and want

to come back, there's a welcome at the Island day or night."

The steamboat rounded the bend and warped in to the landing. It carried a few lights, for the river between its banks was still dark.

Twink said, "We 'bout to fergit what we got for Jody."

Oliver fished in his pocket and handed her a round parcel. She said, "This is for you, Jody, 'cause you he'ped fight for Oliver."

He was numb with the happenings of the day. He took it and stared stupidly. She leaned forward and kissed him on the forehead. Her touch was strangely agreeable. Her lips were soft and her yellow hair was fragrant.

The gang-plank was thrown down. A bundle of freight was tossed to the dock. Grandma stooped and gathered Fluff in her arms. Penny took her soft wrinkled face between his hands and laid his cheek against hers.

He said, "I got a real love for you. I—" His voice broke.

The Huttos filed up the gang-plank. The paddle-wheels thrashed the water, the current sucked at the boat. It swung out into mid-stream. Grandma and Oliver stood at the rail and waved to them. The boat whistle blew again and the steamer moved down the river. Jody stirred in his numbness and waved violently.

"Good-by, Grandma! Good-by, Oliver! Good-by, Twink!"

"Good-by, Jody——"

Their voices trailed away. It seemed to Jody that they were moving away from him into another world. It was as though he saw them die. There were rosy streaks across the east but the daylight seemed even colder than the night had been. The ashes of the Hutto house glowed faintly.

The Baxters drove home toward the scrub. Penny was wracked with sorrow for his friends. His face was strained. Jody was swept with so contradictory a tumult of thoughts that he gave up trying to sort them and snuggled down on the wagon-seat between the warmth of his mother and father. He opened the package Twink had given him. It was a small pewter canister for his gunpowder. He hugged it to him. He remembered that Easy Ozell was on the east coast, and wondered if he would follow Grandma Hutto to Boston when he found her gone. The wagon jogged on to the clearing. The day would be cold but brilliant.

Ma Baxter said, "Now if 'twas me, I'd not of left without havin' the law on them baboons."

Penny said, "Nobody couldn't prove a thing. Them horse tracks? Why, the Forresters'd only say they seed the fire and come to watch it. They could say the county was full o' horses and 'twasn't even them had been there."

"Then I'd of let Oliver know the truth."

"Yes, and what'd he of done then? Lit in and killed two-three of 'em. Oliver's hot-headed and why wouldn't he be? Most ary man'd take out after fellers did sich as that to him. All right. Kill him a few Forresters and mebbe hang for it. Or else have the rest of 'em pitch in and kill the bunch of 'em, him and his Ma and his purty leetle wife."

"Purty leetle wife!" she snorted. "Chipperdale!"

Jody felt a new loyalty surge up in him.

"She do be mighty purty, Ma," he said.

"Men is all alike," she said conclusively.

Baxter's Island was at hand. A sense of safety, of well-being, came over Jody. Other people had catastrophe, but the clearing was beyond it. The cabin waited for him, and the smoke-house full of good meat, with old Slewfoot's carcass added to it, and Flag. Above all, Flag. He could scarcely contain himself until he reached the shed. He had a tale to tell him.

· 28 ·

The January weather was mild. Now and then the sun would set in a cold red stillness, quilts would be inadequate through the night, and morning would show a thin film of ice on the water buckets. Then in a day or two it would be so warm that Ma Baxter could sit on the porch in the sun in the afternoon and work at her mending and patching, and Jody could run through the woods without his wool jacket.

The Baxter life had quieted along with the weather. The river folk were no doubt in a swivet, Penny said, over the burning of the Hutto house and the migration of the sharp-tongued mother, never understood, the sailor son, almost like a foreigner, and their own golden-headed Twink. Belief must be general that the drunken Forresters had set fire to the place on receipt of the word that Oliver had returned with the girl. But the river was a long way off, and news filtered slowly to Bax-

ter's Island. Penny and Ma and Jody sat by the hearth-fire evening after evening, reliving the night through which they had
stood with the Huttos and watched the house char into embers;
had waited with them, warmed by its heat, for the morning
boat that nothing could dissuade Grandma from taking.

"To my notion," Penny said, "if that stranger that come in
to the doin's had knowed it was Oliver's wife, and not jest said
it were a gal with him, not even Lem'd of bothered 'em. They'd
of figgered 'twas time to call quits, oncet she was married."

"Wife or no wife, hit's low-down varmints'll burn a house
down, figgerin' somebody's in it."

Penny sighed and was forced to agree. The Forresters must
be doing their trading at Fort Gates. They never passed. They
had not picked up their share of the bear meat on their return.
Their avoidance of Penny made their guilt incontrovertible. It
saddened him. His hard-won peace lay shattered about him. A
stone thrown at some distance, and meant for some one else,
had struck him. He was bruised and troubled.

Jody was concerned, but it was the anxiety he felt for char-
acters in a tale. Grandma and Oliver and Fluff and Twink had
steamed away down the river as people in a book might steam.
Oliver became one with the stories he had told of distant places.
Now, in the stories, there were Grandma and Twink and
Fluff. Oliver had said, "I'll not forget you, not even in the China
sea." And it was in the China sea, for the most part, that he
pictured him, infinitely remote and abused by people as ficti-
tious as he.

The end of January brought continued warmth. There would
be frost, even, perhaps, a freeze again, before spring truly came.
But the balmy days were a harbinger. Penny plowed the fields
that would have early crops. He turned the new ground
that Buck had cleared for him during his illness from the
rattler's striking. He had decided to try a little cotton for a
money crop. The low ground near the north hammock would

go into tobacco. He prepared his seed-beds between the house and the grape-arbor. With the stock reduced to old Cæsar and Trixie, he decided to plant cow-peas more sparingly and to put the extra land in corn. There seemed never to be enough. The chickens went short of feed, the hogs were not properly fattened, the Baxters themselves gave out of meal at the end of summer, all for lack of enough corn. Nothing on the clearing was more important. Jody helped him carry the winter's compost from the lot and scatter it over the sandy acres. He planned to have the ground in good condition, bedded up and ready to plant in early March, by the time the first whip-poor-will should call.

Ma Baxter complained bitterly that she had always wanted a ginger bed. Every one else had one. The storekeeper's wife at the river had promised her roots any time she was ready for them. Penny and Jody prepared the bed. They dug down four feet deep at the side of the house and laid down cypress slats. They hauled clay from the southwest and filled it in. The first time he went trading to the river, Penny promised to bring back the roots, knobby and peaked, like antlers.

The hunting was poor. The bears were feeding over a wide range, preparing themselves to go in February into hibernation. Their dens were under up-turned hurricane stumps, or where two large logs lay crossed, affording protection. Sometimes they dragged in oak and palmetto limbs and piled them in a hollow tree to make a rough nest. Wherever the bed, it was hollowed out in a trench, over the edge of which the bear would rest his forequarters. Jody thought that it was strange that they did not go into their winter beds in December, when the first really cold weather came, and then come out earlier, in March instead of April.

"I reckon they know their own business," Penny said.

The deer were distressingly scarce, both because of the plague and the increased voracity of the remaining killers. The bucks were in poor condition, the meat lean, their coats moss-gray and shabby. They wandered usually alone. The does traveled alone or in pairs. An old doe traveled with a maiden doe, or with her male yearling. Many of the does were already heavy with fawn.

The principal work once the land was turned was hauling in wood and chopping and splitting it for both fire-places. Wood at least was more easily gotten than ever before, for the storm had brought down large numbers of trees, and the weakening of their roots from the long days of rain and steady wind, had toppled still more. Timber had died by the acre in the low places. The effect was as though fire, not flood, had passed through such sections, for the dead trees stood gray and naked.

Penny said, "Now I'm proud I live in a high place. Hit'd fret me, havin' to look at all that bleakness."

Jody loved the morning jaunts for wood as well as a hunt. They were leisurely. Penny would hitch old Cæsar to the wagon on a cool sparkling morning after breakfast, and they would jog one way or another along the road as their fancy took them. The dogs would trot under the wagon and Flag would gallop ahead or to the side. He looked peculiarly wise in his buckskin collar. They would turn off into a clear place in the woods and prowl on foot for a suitable fallen tree, water oak or yellow pine by preference. There was abundant fat pine. This made the hottest and brightest hearth-fire and made fine kindling, but it smoked and smuttied the pots and kettles. They would take turns chopping, or use the cross-cut saw together. Jody liked the rhythmic swing of the saw, the singing hum as it ate into the wood, the sweet smell of the sawdust sifting to the ground.

The dogs nosed nearby in the bushes or ran rabbits. Flag nibbled at the leaf-buds or found a succulent sprig of grass that had escaped the frost. Penny always carried his shotgun. Sometimes Julia ran a rabbit within range, or a fox squirrel whisked injudiciously up a nearby pine, and there was pilau for supper. One day a pure white fox squirrel peered boldly at them and Penny would not shoot. It was a curiosity, he said, like the albino 'coon. The meat of old Slewfoot had been coarse and stringy with age and it took long cooking to tender it. The Baxters had been glad when the last of it was gone. Most of it had been smoked for the dogs, and while it would have been edible in necessity, no one was ever tempted to ask for it. His fat, however, tried out, filled a large wooden bucket. It was as clear and golden as early honey and was fine for all cooking. The cracklings were as flavory as those from a prime hog. There was a double satisfaction whenever any of the Baxters snapped them between their teeth.

Ma Baxter spent long hours at her quilting. Penny held Jody to his lessons. The evenings were spent by the hearth-fire, blazing brightly to supply light as well as heat. The wind howled cozily around the house. On still nights of moonlight, the foxes could be heard barking in the hammock. Then the lesson stopped and Penny nodded to Jody and they listened together. The foxes seldom came to raid the Baxter hen-roost.

"They know ever' hair o' Julia's head," Penny chuckled. "They ain't temptin' Providence."

One cold bright night at the end of January, Penny and Ma Baxter had gone to bed while Jody lingered with Flag by the fire. He heard a sound outside in the yard, as though the dogs were scuffling. The commotion was livelier than the pair usually made. He went to the front window and pressed his face to the cold pane. A strange dog was romping with Rip in play. Julia watched tolerantly. He caught his breath. It was not a dog. It was a gray wolf, lean and lame. He turned to run and call his father, then, irresistibly drawn, went back to watch again. Wolf and dog had plainly played together before. They were not strangers. They played silently, as though the dogs kept the secret. Jody went to the door of the bedroom and called softly. Penny came.

"What's the matter, son?"

Jody tiptoed to the window, beckoning. Penny followed on bare feet and looked out where Jody pointed. He whistled under his breath. He made no move for his gun. They watched silently. In the bright moonlight the motions of the animals were plain. The visitor was crippled in one hip. Its movements were clumsy.

Penny whispered, "Someway piteeful, ain't it?"

"Reckon it's one o' them we rounded up that day at the ponds?"

Penny nodded.

"Hit's almost certain the last one. Pore thing, hurt and lonesome— Come visitin' its nighest kin to pick a play."

Perhaps the sibilance of their whispers reached beyond the closed window or their scent drifted to its nose. Soundlessly, it turned and left the dogs and clambered with difficulty over the fence and was gone into the night.

Jody asked, "Will it do harm here?"

Penny stretched out his feet to the embers on the hearth.

"I mis-doubt it's in shape to ketch itself a square meal. I'd not dream o' botherin' it. A bear'll finish it, or a panther. Leave it live out the rest of its life."

They squatted together by the hearth, caught up in the sadness and the strangeness. It was a harsh thing, even for a wolf, to be so alone that it must turn to the yard of its enemy for companionship. Jody laid an arm across Flag. He wished Flag could understand that he had been spared desolation in the forest. As for himself, Flag had eased a loneliness that had harassed him in the very heart of his family.

He saw the lone wolf once again on the waning moon. It never came again. By tacit consent, its visits were not revealed to Ma Baxter. She would have demanded its death, whether or no. Penny believed that the dogs had made its acquaintance on one of their hunts, or perhaps when they were cutting wood, and the dogs had wandered away on their own business.

· 29 ·

In February, Penny became badly crippled for a time with his rheumatism. It had bothered him for several years in cold or wet weather. He was careless always about exposure, doing whatever he wished to do, or what seemed necessary, regardless of the weather and unsparing of himself. It was as good a time as any, Ma Baxter said, for him to be laid up, but he was uneasy for fear he would not be ready for his spring planting.

"Then let Jody do it," she said impatiently.

"He's never done nothin' but foller me at it. There's so many things a boy kin do wrong at sich work as that.'

"Yes, and whose fault is it he don't know more about it? You've spared him too long. When you was nearly thirteen, wasn't you plowin' like a man?"

"Yes, and that's jest why I don't crave for him to do it 'til he's got his growth and his strength."

"Old butter-hearted," she muttered. "Plowin' never hurt nobody."

She pounded poke-root and boiled it and made poultices for him, and made him a tonic of prickly ash and poke-root and potassium. He accepted her ministrations gratefully, but was no better. He went back to his panther oil, and rubbed his knees patiently with it, an hour at a time, and said it helped him more than the other remedies.

While his father was idle, Jody did the light chores and kept up with the wood. He had an incentive to hurry at his work, for when it was done, he was free to wander away with Flag. Penny even permitted him to take the shotgun with him. He missed his father's company, yet he liked to hunt alone. He and Flag were free together. They liked best going to the sink-hole. They had stumbled on a game there one day when Flag had gone with him when he went to fetch drinking water. The game was a mad one of tag, up and down the steep slopes of the great green bowl. Flag was unbeatable at it, for he was up and down one side half a dozen times while Jody was making one climb to the top. Finding that he could not be caught, he alternated between a teasing business of wearing Jody out, and a more satisfying and ingratiating trick of deliberately allowing himself to be captured.

On a warm sunny day in mid-February, Jody looked up from the bottom of the sink-hole. Flag stood in silhouette at the top. For a startled moment, it seemed to him that it was another deer. Flag was so big— He had not seen how fast he was growing. Many a young yearling shot for food was no bigger than he. He went home to Penny in excitement. Penny sat by the kitchen hearth, wrapped in quilts, though the day was mild.

Jody burst out, "Pa, you reckon Flag's near about a yearlin'?"

Penny looked at him quizzically.

"I been thinkin' that myself lately. Give him a month more, I'd say he was a yearlin'."

"How'll he be different?"

"Well, he'll stay off in the woods longer. He'll grow a good bit bigger. He'll be betwixt and between. He'll be like a person standin' on the state line. He'll be leavin' one and turnin' into t'other. Behind him's the fawn. Before him's the buck."

Jody stared into vacancy.

"Will he have horns?"

"He'll likely not show no horns before July. The bucks is sheddin' their horns right now. They'll be butt-headed all through the spring. Then along in the summer the spikes'll show and by ruttin' season they'll have full sets agin."

Jody examined Flag's head carefully. He felt the hard edge of his forehead. Ma Baxter passed by with a pan in her hand.

"Hey, Ma, Flag'll soon be a yearlin'. Won't he be purty, Ma, with leetle ol' horns? Won't his horns be purty?"

"He'd not look purty to me did he have a crown on. And angel's wings."

He followed her to cajole her. She sat down to look over the dried cow-peas in the pan. He rubbed his nose over the down of her cheek. He liked the furry feel of it.

"Ma, you smell like a roastin' ear. A roastin' ear in the sun."

"Oh git along. I been mixin' cornbread."

"'Tain't that. Listen, Ma, you don't keer do Flag have horns or no. Do you?"

"Hit'll be that much more to butt and bother."

He did not press the point. Flag was in increasing disgrace, at best. He had learned to slip free from the halter about his neck. When it was tightened so that he could not get out of it, he used the same tactics that a calf used against restraint. He strained against it until his eyes bulged and his breathing choked, and to save his perverse life, it was necessary to release him. Then when he was free, he raised havoc. There was no holding him in the shed. He would have razed it to the ground. He was wild and impudent. He was allowed in the house only when Jody was on hand to keep up with him. But the closed door seemed to make him possessed to enter. If it was not barred, he butted it open. He watched his chance and slipped in to cause some minor damage whenever Ma Baxter's back was turned.

She set the dish of shelled dried peas on the table and went to the hearth. Jody went to his room to look for a piece of rawhide. There was a clatter and commotion and then Ma Baxter's storm of fury. Flag had leaped onto the table, seized a mouthful of the peas and sent the pan sprawling, the peas scattered from one end of the kitchen to the other. Jody came running. His mother threw the door open and drove Flag out with the broom. He seemed to enjoy the fracas. He kicked up his heels, flicked his white flag of a tail, shook his head as though threatening to attack with imaginary antlers, sailed over the fence and galloped away to the woods.

Jody said, "That were my fault, Ma. I shouldn't of left him. He were hongry, Ma. The pore feller didn't git enough for breakfast. You should of beat me, Ma, not him."

"I'll tear down all two of you. Now git down and pick up ever' one o' them peas and wash 'em off."

He was only too glad to do so. He crawled under the table and reached behind the kitchen safe and under the inside water-shelf and in every corner, to retrieve them. He washed them carefully and went to the sink-hole for extra water, to replace what he had used, and more. He felt entirely righteous.

"Now see, Ma," he said, "they's no harm done. Ary leetle harm Flag do, you kin depend on me to take keer of it."

Flag did not return until sunset. Jody fed him outside and waited to smuggle him into his bedroom after Penny and Ma were in bed. Flag had lost his fawn's willingness to sleep long hours and had been increasingly restless at night. Ma Baxter had complained that she had heard him tripping about in Jody's room or the front room several times. Jody had invented a plausible tale of rats on the roof, but his mother was sceptical. Perhaps Flag had had a sleep that afternoon in the woods, for this night he left his moss pallet and pushed open the rickety door of Jody's bedroom and wandered about the house. Jody was aroused by a piercing shriek from his mother. Flag had awakened her from a sound sleep by pushing his wet muzzle against her face. Jody slipped the fawn out by the front door before she should do a more thorough job of it.

"Now that ends it," she raged. "The creetur gives me no peace day or night. Now he cain't come in this house, no time, never no more."

Penny had kept apart from the controversy. Now he spoke from his bed.

"Your Ma's right, boy. He's got too big and restless to be in the house."

Jody went back to bed and lay wakeful, wondering if Flag were cold. He thought it was unreasonable of his mother to object to the clean soft nose against her own. He could never get enough of fondling the delicate muzzle, himself. She was a mean, hard woman and did not care if he was lonely. His resentment eased him and he went to sleep, clutching his pillow and pretending that it was Flag. The fawn snorted and stamped around the house most of the night.

In the morning Penny felt well enough to dress and hobble around the clearing, leaning on a stick. He made the rounds. He returned to the rear of the house. His face was grave. He called Jody to him. Flag had trampled back and forth across the tobacco seed-bed. The young plants were almost ready to set out. He had destroyed nearly half of them. There would be enough for the usual patch for Penny's own use. There would be no money crop, as he had planned, for storekeeper Boyles at Volusia.

"I don't figger Flag done it malicious," he said. "He were jest racin' back and forth and it were somethin' to jump on, was all. Now you go set up stakes all through the bed amongst the plants and all around the bed, to keep him offen the rest of 'em. I should of done it before, I reckon, but I never studied on him rompin' in that pertickler place."

Penny's reasonableness and kindness depressed Jody as his mother's rage had not done. He turned away disconsolately to do the job.

Penny said, "Now it jest bein' accidental-like, we'll not say nothin' to your Ma. Hit'd be a pore time for her to know it."

As Jody worked, he tried to think of a way to keep Flag out of mischief. Most of his tricks he considered only clever, but the destruction of the seed-bed was serious. He was sure that such a thing would never happen again.

· 30 ·

MARCH came in with a cool and sunny splendor. The yellow jessamine bloomed late and covered the fences and filled the clearing with its sweetness. The peach trees blossomed, and the wild plums. The red birds sang all day, and when they had done with their song in the evening, the mocking birds continued. The ground doves nested and cooed one to another and walked about the sand of the clearing like shadows bobbing.

Penny said, "If I was dead, I'd set up and take notice, a day like this un."

There had been a light shower during the night and the hazy substance of the sunrise indicated there would be another before night. But the morning itself was luminous.

"Jest right for corn," Penny said. "Jest right for cotton. Jest right for 'baccy."

"I take it you're pleased with the day," Ma Baxter said.

He grinned and finished his breakfast.

"Now jest 'cause you feel better," she warned him, "don't git in the field and kill yourself."

"I feel so good," he said, "I'll kill ary thing keeps me from plantin'. All day. I'm fixin' to plant all day. Today. Tomorrer. The next day. Plantin'. Corn. Cotton. 'Baccy."

"I heered you," she said.

He stood up and thumped her on the back.

"Cow-peas! 'Taters! Greens!"

She had to laugh at him, and Jody laughed too.

"Hear you tell it," she said, "you're fixin' to plant the world."

"I'd purely love it." He threw out his arms. "A day like this un, I'd love to plant rows from here to Boston and back agin to Texas. Then when I come to Texas, I'd turn around and go back to Boston to see had the seeds come up yit."

"I see where Jody gits his fairy-tales," she said.

He pounded Jody on the back.

"You got a sweet job, boy. You kin set out the 'baccy plants. If my back didn't near about kill me when I stoop, I'd take it from you, for I love settin' plants. Leetle ol' young green things— Givin' 'em a chancet to grow."

He went whistling to his work. Jody gulped his breakfast and followed him. Penny was at the tobacco seed-bed, lifting out the tender plants.

"You belong to handle 'em like they was new-borned babies," he said.

He set out a dozen plants by way of lesson, then watched and corrected Jody while he went on with the row. He brought old Cæsar and the scooter plow and turned in to the field, laid off and bedded up ready for the corn, to open the furrows for the planting. Jody hunched along on his heels, or dropped to his knees when his legs grew tired. He worked leisurely, for Penny said there was no hurry, and that the job must be done well. The March sun grew strong in mid-morning, but a fresh breeze blew. The tobacco plants wilted behind him, but the night's dark coolness would bring them upright again. He watered them as he went and had to go twice to the sink-hole for water. Flag had disappeared after breakfast and was not in sight. Jody missed him, but he was relieved that the fawn had chosen the particular morning to stay away. If he joined him, and gamboled about as usual, he would destroy the plants faster than Jody could set them out. He finished the task by dinner time. The tobacco patch filled only a portion of the ground that Penny had prepared for it according to the original size of the seed-bed. When Penny went with him after dinner to look it over, his father's exuberance ebbed.

"You ain't left no plants in the bed, boy? You got 'em all?"

"Ever' one. I even set them leetle ol' spindly ones."

"Well— I'll put in somethin' else to fill out."

Jody offered eagerly, "I kin he'p you with t'other plantin' now. Or tote water for you."

"No need to water. Hit looks more prosperous for a shower ever' minute. You kin he'p plant."

Penny had the furrows open for the corn. Now he went ahead, drilling his holes with a pointed stick down the long rows. Jody followed, dropping two kernels to the hole. He was anxious to please, to have his father forget the shrunken tobacco patch.

He called, "Goes fast, two workin', don't it, Pa?"

Penny did not answer. Yet as the early spring day clouded and the light wind shifted into the southeast and it was plain that a shower would come on the planting, insuring the quick sprouting of the corn, his spirits lifted again. The rain caught them in the late afternoon, but they continued to work and finished the field. It rolled gently, well-tilled and tawny, its soft bosom receptive to the rain. Leaving it, Penny rested on the split-rail fence and looked back over it with satisfaction.

There was a wistful look in his eyes as well, as though he were obliged now to leave his handiwork to forces he could only trust blindly not to betray him.

Flag came bounding out of the rain from the south. He came to Jody to be scratched behind the ears. He leaped back and forth in a zig-zag across the fence, then stopped under a mulberry tree and reached up to catch the tip of a bough. Jody sat on the fence beside his father. He turned to call Penny's attention to the slim neck of the fawn stretched up to the new green leaves of the mulberry. His father was studying the young deer with an unfathomable expression. His eyes were narrowed and speculative. He seemed, as when he had set out after old Slewfoot, a stranger. A chill passed over the boy that was not of the dampness of the rain.

He said, "Pa——"

Penny turned to him, startled from his thoughts. He looked down, as though to hide a thing in his eyes.

He said carelessly, "That fawn o' yourn shore growed up in a hurry. He ain't the baby you toted home in your arms all the way that black night— He's a yearlin' now, for shore."

The words gave Jody little pleasure. Somehow, he sensed they were not quite what his father had been thinking. Penny laid his hand an instant on his son's knee.

"You're a pair o' yearlin's," he said. "Hit grieves me."

They slid from the fence and went to the lot to do the chores, then to the house to dry out by the fire. The rain beat lightly on the shingled roof. Flag bleated outside to be allowed to come in. Jody looked appealingly at his mother but she was deaf and blind. Penny felt stiff and sat with his back close to the heat, rubbing his knees. Jody begged some stale cornbread and went outside. He made a fresh bed in the shed and enticed Flag inside with the bread. He sat down and the deer finally doubled his long legs under him and lay down beside him. Jody took hold of the two pointed ears and rubbed his nose against the wet muzzle.

"You a yearlin' now," he said. "You hear me? You growed up. Now you listen to me. You got to be good, now you're growed. You cain't go gallivantin' acrost no t'baccy. Don't you git Pa down on you. You listenin'?"

Flag chewed ruminatively.

"All right, then. Now soon as we git done with the plantin', I kin go off with you agin. You wait for me. You was gone too long today. Don't you go wild, jest 'cause I told you you was a yearlin'."

He left Flag and had the satisfaction of seeing him remain contentedly in the shed. Ma Baxter and Penny had begun supper when he went into the kitchen. They made no comment on his lateness. They ate in silence. Penny went to bed at once. Jody was suddenly tired out and dropped into bed without washing his dusty feet. When his mother came to his door to remind him of it, he was asleep with one arm thrown back over the pillow. She stood looking at him, then turned away without arousing him.

In the morning, Penny was blithe again.

"Today's cotton day," he said.

The soft rain had stopped in the night. The morning was dewy. The fields were rosy, dipping into lavender at the far misty edges. The mocking-birds made a musical din along the fence-rows.

"They tryin' to hurry the mulberries," Penny said.

The cotton was sowed free in drills. Later it would be chopped out to a stand, a foot apart, with the hoe. Jody followed his father as before, dropping the small shining seeds. He was curious about the new Baxter crop and asked endless questions. Flag had disappeared shortly after breakfast, but came trotting to the planters in mid-morning. Again Penny watched him. His sharp hooves cut deeply into the soft moist earth, but the seeds were planted deeply enough so that no harm was possible.

"He do take out after you when he misses you," Penny said.

"He's like a dog that-a-way, ain't he, Pa? He wants to tag me jest like Julia tags you."

"You think a heap of him, don't you, boy?"

"Why, shore."

He stared at his father.

Penny said, "Well, we'll wait and see."

The remark made no particular sense and Jody ignored it.

The planting continued all week. Cow-peas followed the corn and cotton. Sweet potatoes followed the cow-peas. The vegetable garden back of the house was planted to onions and turnips, for the moon was dark, and root crops must be planted then. Penny had been forced by his rheumatism to let pass the fourteenth of February, the date on which collards should be planted, so as not to go to seed. He was tempted to put them in now, but since the leafy crops did best when planted on an increasing moon, he decided to wait a week or so.

He was up early each day and finished late. He drove himself mercilessly. The planting itself was done, but he was not content. He was in a fever over the spring work, for weather conditions were favorable and the year's living depended on the immediate results. He carried the two heavy buckets full of water from the sink-hole again and again to water the tobacco plants and the garden.

A stump that Buck Forrester had left to rot out in the new ground where the cotton was planted, annoyed him. He dug and chopped around it, then hooked trace chains to it and put old Cæsar at pulling on it. The old horse tugged and strained, his sides heaving. Penny lashed a rope about the stump, said "Gee-up!" to Cæsar and pulled with him. Jody saw his father's face turn white. Penny clutched at his groin and sank to his knees. Jody ran to him.

"Hit's all right. I'll be all right in a minute— Reckon I strained myself——"

He dropped to the ground and stirred in agony.

He murmured, "I'll be all right— Go put Cæsar up— Wait— Take a-holt o' my hand— I'll ride him in."

He was bent double and could not straighten, for pain. Jody helped him to the stump. From there he managed to clamber on Cæsar's back. He leaned forward, resting his head on Cæsar's neck, gripping the mane. Jody unhitched the trace chains and led the horse out of the field and through the gate into the yard. Penny made no move to get down. Jody brought a chair for him to stand on, to break the descent. Penny slid to it and to the ground and crept into the house. Ma Baxter turned from her work at the kitchen table. She dropped a pan with a clatter.

"I knowed it! You've hurted yourself. You don't never know to quit."

He shuffled to his bed and threw himself face down on it. She followed and turned him over and put a pillow under his head. She pulled off his shoes and laid a light quilt over him. He stretched out his legs with relief. He closed his eyes.

"That's good— Oh Ory, that's good— I'll be all right in a minute. Must o' strained myself——"

· 31 ·

PENNY did not recover. He lay suffering without complaint. Ma Baxter wanted Jody to ride for Doc Wilson, but Penny would not allow it.

"I owe him a'ready," he said. "I'll git easement direckly."

"You're likely ruptured."

"Even so— Hit'll clare up."

Ma Baxter lamented, "If you had a mite o' sense— But you'll try to do like as if you was big as a Forrester."

"My uncle Miles were a big man and he were ruptured. He got around all right. Please to hush, Ory."

"I'll not hush. I want you should learn your lesson and learn it good."

"I've done learned it. Please hush."

Jody was disturbed. Yet Penny was always having minor

accidents, trying, with his small stout physique, to do the work of ten. Jody could remember dimly when a tree that Penny was felling had caught him, crushing one shoulder. His father had carried his arm in a sling for long months, but he had recovered and been as strong as ever. Nothing could harm Penny for long. Not even a rattlesnake, he thought comfortingly, could kill him. Penny was inviolable, as the earth was inviolable. Only Ma Baxter fretted and fumed, but she would have done so if it were only a little finger that had been strained.

Shortly after Penny was laid up, Jody came in to report that the corn was up. The stand was perfect.

"Now ain't that fine!"

The pale face on the pillow was bright.

"Now if it so happen I ain't outen the bed, you're jest the feller to plow it out." He frowned. "Boy, you know as good as I do, you got to keep that yearlin' outen the fields."

"I'll keep him out. He ain't bothered nary thing."

"That's fine. That's jest fine. But you keep him out, religious."

Jody spent most of the next day on a hunt with Flag. They went nearly to Juniper Spring and returned with four squirrels.

Penny said, "Now that's what I call a son. Come in with rations for his old man."

Ma Baxter made a pilau of the squirrels for supper.

"They do eat good," she said.

"Why, the meat's so tender," Penny said, "you could kiss it off the bones."

Jody, and Flag with him, was in high favor.

A light rain fell in the night. In the morning he went to the cornfield at Penny's request to see whether the rain had pushed the corn and whether there was any sign of cutworms. He leaped the split-rail fence and set out across the field. He had gone some yards when it occurred to him that he should be seeing the pale green shoots of the corn. There were none. He was bewildered. He went farther. There was no corn visible. It was not until he reached the far end of the field that the delicate sprouts appeared. He walked back along the rows. Flag's sharp tracks were plain. He had pulled up the corn in the early morning as neatly as though it had been pulled by hand.

Jody was frightened. He dawdled about the field, hoping to have a miracle happen and the corn appear again when his back was turned. Perhaps he was having a nightmare in which Flag had eaten the corn crop, and when he awakened he would go out and find it growing, green and tender. He pushed a stick into one arm to make sure. The dull misery he felt was that of a bad dream, but the pain in his arm was as real as the destruction of the corn. He dragged back to the house with slow and heavy feet. He sat down in the kitchen and did not go to his father. Penny called him. He went to the bedroom.

"Well, boy? How's the crops?"

"The cotton's up. Hit looks like okry, don't it?" His enthusiasm was spurious. "The cow-peas is breakin' the ground."

He spread the toes of his bare feet and wriggled them. He was absorbed in them, as though they had developed an interesting new function.

"And the corn, Jody?"

His heart beat as fast as a humming-bird's wings. He swallowed and took the plunge.

"Somethin's et off most of it."

Penny lay silent. His silence was a nightmare, too. At last he spoke.

"Couldn't you tell what 'twas, done it?"

He looked at his father. His eyes were desperate and beseeching.

Penny said, "Ne' mind. I'll git your Ma to go look. She kin tell."

"Don't send Ma!"

"She's obliged to know."

"Don't send her!"

"Hit were Flag done it, wa'n't it?"

Jody's lips trembled.

"I reckon— Yes, sir."

Penny looked at him pityingly.

"I'm sorry, boy. I more'n half looked for him to do it. You go play a while. Tell your Ma to come here."

"Don't tell her, Pa. Please don't tell her."

"She's got to know, Jody. Now go on. I aim to do the best I kin for you."

He stumbled to the kitchen.

"Pa wants you, Ma."

He went out of the house. He called Flag, quaveringly. The deer came to him from the black-jack. Jody walked down the road with his arm across his back. He loved him more than ever, in his sin. Flag kicked up his heels and invited him to romp. He had no heart for play. He walked slowly as far as the sink-hole. It was lovely as a spring flower garden. The dogwood had not finished blooming. The last blossoms were white against the pale green of the sweet gums and the hickories. He was not even tempted to walk around it. He turned back to the house and went inside. His mother and father were still talking. Penny called to him to come in beside the bed. Ma Baxter's face was flushed. She was hot with defeat. Her mouth was a tight line.

Penny said quietly, "We've come to a agreement, Jody. What's happened is powerful bad, but we'll have a try at a remedy. I take it you're willin' to work extry hard to fix things."

"I'll jest do ary thing, Pa. I'll keep Flag shut up 'til the crops is made——"

"We got no earthly place to shut up a wild thing like that.

Now listen to me. You go now and git corn from the crib. Pick the best ears. Your Ma'll he'p you shell it. You go then and plant it jest like we done before, right where the fust lot was put. Drill your holes like I done, and go back over and drop the seed and kiver it."

"I know jest how."

"Then time you git that done, likely along tomorrer mornin', you hitch Cæsar to the wagon and go yonder to the old clearin' on the way to the Forresters, where the road turns off. You tear down that old rail fence there and load the rails on the wagon. Not too heavy a load, for Cæsar cain't pull too much on that piece of up-grade. You make as many trips as you need to. Pile the rails here and yon along our fence. Dump your first loads along the south side o' the cornfield and along the east side, borderin' the house yard. Then you build up that fence—workin' first on them two sides—jest as high as you got the rails to do it. I been noticin' your yearlin' allus takes the fence on this end. If you kin keep him out up here, he'll mebbe stay out 'til you kin build up the rest."

It seemed to Jody that he had been shut up in a small black box and now the lid was off, and the sun and light and air came in across him, and he was free.

Penny said, "Now when you git your fence higher'n you kin reach, if I ain't on my feet by then, your Ma'll he'p you with the riders."

Jody turned joyously to embrace his mother. She was patting one foot ominously on the floor. She stared straight ahead and did not speak. He decided that it was probably best not to touch her. Nothing could alter his relief. He ran outside. Flag was feeding along the road near the gate. Jody threw his arms around him.

"Pa's fixed it," he told him. "Ma's pattin' her foot, but Pa's fixed it."

Flag's mind was on the tender sprigs of grass and he shook

free. Jody went whistling to the crib and sorted over the corn for the ears with the largest kernels. It would take a good many ears of the remaining corn for seed for the second planting. He carried it in a sack to the back door and sat down on the stoop and began the shelling. His mother came and sat beside him. Her face was a frigid mask. She picked up an ear and went to work.

"Huh!" she snorted.

Penny had forbidden her outright to scold Jody. He had not forbidden her to talk to herself.

" 'Spare his feelin's!' Huh! And who's to spare our bellies this winter? Huh!"

Jody swung around so that his back was partly turned on her. He hummed under his breath, ignoring her.

"Hush that racket."

He left off his humming. It was no moment to be impudent or to argue. His fingers flew. The corn popped from the cobs. He wanted to be away from her and at his planting as quickly as possible. He gathered up the sack of seed and slung it over his shoulder and went to the field. It was nearly dinner time, but he could get in an hour's work. In the open field he was free to sing and whistle. A mocking-bird in the hammock sang, whether in competition or harmony, he could not tell. The March day was blue and gold. The feel of the corn in his fingers, the feel of the earth that reached out to enclose the corn, was good. Flag discovered him and joined him.

He said, "You do your rompin' right now, ol' feller. You goin' to git barred out."

He bolted his dinner at noon and hurried back to the planting. He worked so fast that a couple of hours would finish it the next morning. He sat at Penny's bedside after supper, chattering like a squirrel. Penny listened gravely, as always, but his responses were sometimes detached and vacant, and his thoughts were elsewhere. Ma Baxter kept stonily to herself.

Dinner and supper had both been meager and indifferently cooked, as though she took her revenge from behind her own citadel, the cook-pot. Jody paused for breath. In the hammock, a whip-poor-will called. Penny's face brightened.

" 'When the first whip-poor-will calls, the corn had ought to be in the ground.' We still not too late, boy."

"Ever' last bit'll be in tomorrer mornin'."

"That's good."

He closed his eyes. Relief from acute agony had come, as long as he lay quiet. When he moved, the pain was excruciating. He was wracked constantly with his rheumatism.

He said, "You go on to bed now and git your rest."

Jody left him and washed his feet without being told. He went to bed, peaceful of mind and tired of body, and was asleep in an instant. He awakened before dawn with a feeling of responsibility. He got out of bed and dressed immediately.

Ma Baxter said, "Pity hit take a thing like this to make you put out."

In standing between her and Flag during the past months, he had learned the value of his father's trick of an unarguing silence. It annoyed his mother more for the moment, but she stopped scolding sooner. He ate heartily but hurriedly, slipped a handful of biscuits inside his shirt for Flag, and went at once to his work. He could scarcely see, at first, to plant. He watched the sun rise beyond the grape arbor. In the thin golden light the young leaves and tendrils of the Scuppernong were like Twink Weatherby's hair. He decided that sunrise and sunset both gave him a pleasantly sad feeling. The sunrise brought a wild, free sadness; the sunset, a lonely yet a comforting one. He indulged his agreeable melancholy until the earth under him turned from gray to lavender and then to the color of dried corn husks. He went at his work vigorously. Flag came to him from the woods where he had evidently spent the night. He fed him the biscuits and let him nose inside his shirt bosom for the crumbs. He tingled with the sensation of the soft wet nose against his bare flesh.

When the planting of the corn was finished in the early morning, he bounded back to the lot. Old Cæsar was pasturing south of it. He lifted his grizzled head from the grass with a mild astonishment. Jody had seldom had the harnessing of him. He behaved meekly for the hitching and stepped backward politely between the shafts of the wagon. It gave Jody an agreeable sense of authority. He made his voice as deep as possible and gave unnecessary orders. Cæsar obeyed humbly. Jody took his seat alone, slapped the reins and set off to the abandoned clearing to the west. Flag was pleased with the business and trotted ahead. Now and then he stopped dead in the middle of the road, for mischievousness, and Jody had to stop the horse and cajole the deer into moving.

"You mighty biggety now you're a yearlin'," he called to him.

He flicked the reins and made Cæsar jog-trot, then remembered that he would have many trips to make, and allowed the old animal to slow down to his usual walk. At the clearing, it was no job at all to pull the old split-rail fence apart. The stakes and riders collapsed conveniently. The loading seemed easy for a time, then his back and arms began to ache and he had to stop and rest. There was no danger of over-loading, because it was too difficult to pile the rails past a certain height. He tried to coax Flag to jump up on the seat beside him. The yearling eyed the narrow space and turned away and could not be induced. Jody tried to lift him in, but he was astonishingly heavy and he could no more than get his front legs over the wagon wheel. He gave it up and turned around and drove home. Flag went into a sprint and was waiting ahead of him when he reached there. He decided to begin dumping his piles at the fence corner near the house and working in both directions, alternately. In that way, when the rails gave out, he would have built up the fence highest across Flag's favorite crossing places.

The hauling and unloading took longer than he dreamed of. Midway, it seemed an endless and a hopeless task. The corn would be up before he had begun the fencing. The weather was dry and the corn was slow in germinating. Each morning he looked fearfully for the pale shoots. Each morning he found with relief that they were not yet showing. He was up each day in the dark before dawn and either ate a cold breakfast without disturbing his mother, or hauled a load before he came to the table. He worked at night until the sun had set, and the red and orange faded through the pines, and the split rails merged with the color of the earth. He had dark circles under his eyes for lack of enough sleep. Penny had not had time to cut his hair, and it hung shaggily in his eyes. He made no complaint when, his eyelids drooping after supper, his mother asked him to fetch in wood that she could easily have brought in herself during the day. Penny watched him with a pain keener than the rupture in his groin. He called him to the bed one night.

"I'm proud to see you workin' so hard, boy, but even the yearlin', much as you think of him, ain't wuth killin' yourself over."

Jody said doggedly, "I ain't killin' myself. Feel my muscle. I'm gittin' powerful strong."

Penny felt of the thin hard arm. It was true. The regular and heavy lifting and heaving of the rails were developing his arms and back and shoulders.

Penny said, "I'd give a year o' my life to be to where I could he'p you with this."

"I'll git it done."

On the fourth morning he decided to begin building up the fence at the end Flag had been using. Then if the corn was up before he had finished, Flag would not take him unaware. He would even tie him by the legs to a tree, day and night, and let him kick and flounder, if necessary, until the fence was done. He found to his relief that the work went rapidly. In two days, he had raised the south and east fence lines to a height of five feet. Ma Baxter, seeing the impossible materialize, softened. On the morning of the sixth day, she said, "I got nothin' to do today. I'll he'p you git another foot on that fence."

"Oh, Ma. You good ol' Ma——"

"Now ne' mind squeezin' the life outen me. I never figgered you had it in you to work this-a-way."

She gave out of breath easily, but the work itself, while arduous, was not heavy with a pair of hands at each end of the light rails. The swing of it was rhythmic, like the swing of the cross-cut saw. She grew red in the face and panted and sweat, but she laughed and stayed with him most of the day and part of the next. There were enough rails piled at the corner to go even higher, and they built it well over the six feet that Penny had said would be high enough to keep out the yearling.

"If 'twas a full-growed buck now," he said, "he could clear eight feet easy."

That night Jody discovered the corn breaking the ground. In the morning he tried to put a hobble on Flag. He tied a rope from one hind shin to the other, with a foot of play between. Flag bucked and kicked and threw himself on the ground in a frenzy. He stumbled to his knees and fought so wildly that it was plain he would break a leg if he were not released. Jody cut the rope and let him go. He galloped away to the woods and was gone all day. Jody worked furiously at the west fence line, for that would be the yearling's most logical line of attack on the field when the south and east ends turned him. Ma Baxter gave him two or three hours of help in the afternoon. He used up all the rails he had dumped to the west and north.

Two showers of rain pushed the corn. It was more than an inch high. On the morning that Jody was ready to return to the old clearing for more rails, he went to the new high fence and climbed to the top to look over the field. His eye caught sight of Flag, feeding on the corn near the north hammock. He jumped down and called his mother.

"Ma, will you go he'p me haul rails? I got to hurry. Flag's done come in the north end."

She hurried outside with him and climbed part-way up the fence until she could peer over.

"North end nothin'," she said. "He takened the fence right here at the highest corner."

He looked down where she pointed. The sharp tracks led to the fence and appeared again on the other side, inside the cornfield.

"And he's got this crop, too," she said.

Jody stared. Again, the shoots had been pulled up by the roots. The rows were bare. The yearling's tracks led regularly up and down between them.

"He ain't gone fur, Ma. Look, the corn's still there, yonder. He ain't et but a leetle ways."

"Yes, and what's to keep him from finishin' it?"

She dropped back to the ground and walked stolidly back into the house.

"This settles it," she said. "I was a fool to give in before."

Jody clung to the fence. He was numb. He could neither feel nor think. Flag scented him, lifted his head and came bounding to him. Jody climbed down into the yard. He did not want to see him. As he stood, Flag cleared, as lightly as a mockingbird in flight, the high fence on which he had labored. Jody turned his back on him and went into the house. He went to his room and threw himself on his bed and buried his face in his pillow.

He was prepared for his father to call him. The talk between

Penny and Ma Baxter this time had not taken long. He was prepared for trouble. He was prepared for something ominous that had dogged him for days. He was not prepared for the impossible. He was not prepared for his father's words.

Penny said, "Jody, all's been done was possible. I'm sorry. I cain't never tell you, how sorry. But we cain't have our year's crops destroyed. We cain't all go hongry. Take the yearlin' out in the woods and tie him and shoot him."

· 32 ·

Jody wandered west with Flag beside him. He carried Penny's shotgun over his shoulder. His heart beat and stopped and beat again.

He said under his breath, "I'll not do it. I'll jest not."

He stopped in the road.

He said out loud, "They cain't make me do it."

Flag looked at him with big eyes, then bent his head to a wisp of grass by the roadside. Jody walked on again slowly.

"I'll not. I'll not. I'll jest not. They kin beat me. They kin kill me. I'll not."

He held imaginary conversations with his mother and father. He told them both that he hated them. His mother stormed and Penny was quiet. His mother whipped him with a hickory switch until he felt the blood run down his legs. He bit her hand and she whipped him again. He kicked her in the ankles and she whipped him once more and threw him in a corner.

He lifted his head from the floor and said, "You cain't make me. I'll not do it."

He fought them in his mind until he was exhausted. He stopped at the abandoned clearing. A short length of fence was left that he had not yet torn down. He threw himself in the grass under an old chinaberry tree and sobbed until he could sob no more. Flag nuzzled him and he clutched him. He lay panting.

He said, "I'll not. I'll jest not."

He was dizzy when he stood up. He leaned against the rough trunk of the chinaberry. It was in bloom. The bees buzzed in it and the fragrance was sweet across the spring air. He was ashamed of himself for having taken time to cry. It was no time to cry. He would have to think. He would have to study his way out of it, as Penny did out of things that threatened him. At first he conjectured wildly. He would build a pen for Flag. A pen ten feet tall. He would gather acorns and grass and berries and feed him there. But it would take all his time to gather feed for a penned animal— Penny was on his back in the bed— The crops would have to be worked— There was no one but himself to do it.

He thought of Oliver Hutto. Oliver would have come and helped him work the crops until Penny was better. But Oliver had gone to Boston and the China Sea, away from the treachery that had swooped down on him. He thought of the Forresters. He regretted bitterly that they were now the Baxters' enemies. Buck would have helped him. Even now— But what could Buck do? A thought struck him sharply. It seemed to him that he could endure to be parted from Flag if he knew that somewhere in the world the yearling was alive. He could think of him, alive and mischievous, carrying his flag-like tail high and merry. He would go to Buck and throw himself on his mercy. He would remind Buck of Fodder-wing, talk of Fodder-wing until Buck's throat choked. Then he would ask him to take Flag in the wagon, as he had taken the bear cubs, to Jacksonville. Flag would be taken to a broad park where people came to look at the animals. He would bound about and be given plenty of feed, and a doe, and every one would admire him. He, Jody, would raise money crops of his own, and once a year he would go and visit Flag. He would save his money and he would get a place of his own, and he would buy Flag back, and they would live together.

He was flooded with excitement. He turned from the clearing up the road to the Forresters', trotting. His throat was dry and his eyes were swollen and smarting. His hope refreshed him and in a little while, when he swung up the Forresters' trail under the live oaks, he felt all right again. He ran to the house and up the steps. He rapped at the open door and stepped inside. There was no one in the room but Pa and Ma Forrester. They sat immobile in their chairs.

He said breathlessly, "Howdy. Where's Buck?"

Pa Forrester turned his head slowly on his withered neck, like a turtle.

"Been a long time since you was here," he said.

"Where's Buck, please, sir?"

"Buck? Why, Buck and the hull passel of 'em has rode off to Kentucky, hoss-tradin'."

"In plantin' time?"

"Plantin' time be tradin' time. They'd ruther trade than plow. They figgered they'd make enough, tradin', to buy our rations." The old man spat. "And likely, they will."

"They're all gone?"

"Ever' one of 'em. Pack and Gabby'll be back in April."

Ma Forrester said, "Heap o' good it do a woman to birth a

mess o' young uns and raise 'em and then have 'em all go off to oncet. I will say, they left rations and stacked wood. We won't need nothin' 'til some of 'em's back in April."

"April——"

He turned dully from the door.

"Come set with us, boy. I'd be proud to cook dinner for you. Raisin' puddin', eh? You and Fodder-wing allus loved my raisin' puddin'."

"I got to go," he said. "I thank you."

He turned back.

He burst out desperately, "What would you do, did you have a yearlin' et up the corn and you couldn't keep it out no-way and your Pa told you to go shoot it?"

They blinked at him. Ma Forrester cackled.

Pa Forrester said, "Why, I'd go shoot it."

He realized that he had not made the matter clear.

He said, "Supposin' it was a yearlin' you loved like you-all loved Fodder-wing?"

Pa Forrester said, "Why, love's got nothin' to do with corn. You cain't have a thing eatin' the crops. Lessen you got boys like mine, has got other ways o' makin' a livin'."

Ma Forrester asked, "Hit that fawn you carried here last summer for Fodder-wing to put a name to?"

"That's him. Flag," he said. "Cain't you-all take him? Fodder-wing would of takened him."

"Why, we got no better way'n you o' keepin' him. He'd not stay here, no-how. What's four mile to a yearlin' deer?"

They too were a stone wall.

He said, "Well, good-by," and went away.

The Forrester clearing was desolate without the big men and their horses. They had taken most of the dogs with them. Only a mangy pair remained, chained at the side of the house, scratching themselves mournfully. He was glad to get away again.

He would walk to Jacksonville with Flag himself. He looked about for something to make a halter by which to lead him, so that he would not turn and run home, as he had done on the Christmas hunt. He hacked laboriously at a grapevine with his pocket knife. He looped a length of it around Flag's neck and set off to the northeast. The trail came out somewhere near Hopkins Prairie, he knew, on the Fort Gates road on which he and Penny had intercepted the Forresters. Flag was docile for a time under the leash, then grew impatient of the restraint and tugged against it.

Jody said, "How come you to grow up so unlawful?"

It wore him out, trying to coax the yearling into going willingly. At last he gave it up and took off the grapevine halter. Flag was then perversely content to keep in sight. In the afternoon, Jody found himself tired with a fatigue born of hunger. He had left the house without breakfast. He had wanted only to get away. He looked along the road for berries to eat, but it was too early and there were none. The blackberries had not yet finished blooming. He chewed some leaves, as Flag was doing, but they made him feel emptier than before. His feet dragged. He lay down by the road in the sun for a rest and induced Flag to lie beside him. He was drugged with hunger and misery and the strong March sun on his head. He fell asleep. When he awakened, Flag had gone. He followed his tracks. They led in and out of the scrub, then turned back to the road and continued evenly toward home.

There was nothing to do but follow. He was too weary to think further. He reached Baxter's Island after dark. A candle burned in the kitchen. The dogs came to him. He patted them to quiet them. He crept close silently and peered in. Supper was over. His mother sat in the candle-light, sewing her endless patchwork pieces. He was trying to make up his mind whether to go in or not, when Flag galloped across the yard. He saw his mother lift her head and listen.

He slipped hurriedly beyond the smoke-house and called Flag in a low voice. The yearling came to him. He crouched at the corner. His mother came to the kitchen door and threw it open. A bar of light lay across the sand. The door closed. He waited a long time until the light went out in the kitchen. He allowed time for her to go to bed and to sleep. He prowled inside the smoke-house and found the remainder of the smoked bear-meat. He hacked off a strip. It was hard and dry, but he chewed on it. He supposed Flag had fed on buds in the woods, but he could not bear to think of him hungry. He went to the corn-crib and took two ears of corn and shelled them and fed the kernels to him. He chewed some kernels himself. He thought longingly of the cold cooked food that must be in the kitchen safe but he dared not go in after it. He felt like a stranger and a thief. This was the way the wolves felt, he thought, and the wild-cats and the panthers and all the var-mints, looking in at the clearing with big eyes and empty bellies. He made a bed in a stall at the lot with an armful of the scant remaining marsh-grass hay. He slept there with Flag beside him, not quite warm enough through the chill March night.

He awakened after sunrise, stiff and miserable. Flag was gone. He went reluctantly but compelled to the house. At the gate he heard his mother's voice raised in a storm of anger. She had discovered the shotgun where he had leaned it against the smoke-house wall. She had discovered Flag. She had discov-ered, too, that the yearling had made the most of the early hours and had fed, not only across the sprouting corn, but across a wide section of the cow-peas. He went helplessly to her to meet her wrath. He stood with his head down while she flailed him with her tongue.

She said finally, "Git to your Pa. For oncet, he's with me."

He went into the bedroom. His father's face was drawn.

Penny said gently, "How come you not to do what I told you?"

"Pa, I jest couldn't. I cain't do it."

Penny leaned his head back against the pillow.

"Come here clost to me, boy. Jody, you know I've done all I could to keep your leetle deer for you."

"Yes, sir."

"You know we depend on our crops to live."

"Yes, sir."

"You know they ain't a way in the world to keep that wild yearlin' from destroyin' 'em."

"Yes, sir."

"Then why don't you do what's got to be done?"

"I cain't."

Penny lay silent.

"Tell your Ma to come here. Go to your room and shut the door."

"Yes, sir."

There was a relief in following simple orders.

"Pa says to go to him."

He went to his room and closed the door. He sat on the side of the bed, twisting his hands. He heard low voices. He heard steps. He heard a shot. He ran from the room to the open kitchen door. His mother stood on the stoop with the shotgun smoking in her hands. Flag lay floundering beside the fence.

She said, "I didn't want to hurt the creetur. I cain't shoot straight. You know I cain't."

Jody ran to Flag. The yearling heaved to his three good legs and stumbled away, as though the boy himself were his enemy. He was bleeding from a torn left forequarter. Penny dragged himself from his bed. He sank on one knee in the doorway, clutching it for support.

He called, "I'd do it if I could. I jest cain't stand up— Go finish him, Jody. You got to put him outen his torment."

409

Jody ran back and snatched the gun from his mother.

He screamed, "You done it o' purpose. You allus hated him."

He turned on his father.

"You went back on me. You told her to do it."

He screeched so that his throat felt torn.

"I hate you. I hope you die. I hope I never see you agin."

He ran after Flag, whimpering as he ran.

Penny called, "He'p me, Ory. I cain't git up——"

Flag ran on three legs in pain and terror. Twice he fell and Jody caught up to him.

He shrieked, "Hit's me! Hit's me! Flag!"

Flag thrashed to his feet and was off again. Blood flowed in a steady stream. The yearling made the edge of the sink-hole. He wavered an instant and toppled. He rolled down the side. Jody ran after him. Flag lay beside the pool. He opened great liquid eyes and turned them on the boy with a glazed look of wonder. Jody pressed the muzzle of the gun barrel at the back of the smooth neck and pulled the trigger. Flag quivered a moment and then lay still.

Jody threw the gun aside and dropped flat on his stomach. He retched and vomited and retched again. He clawed into the earth with his finger-nails. He beat it with his fists. The sink-hole rocked around him. A far roaring became a thin humming. He sank into blackness as into a dark pool.

· 33 ·

Jody walked north up the Fort Gates road. His gait was wooden, as though nothing of him were alive except his legs. He had left the dead yearling without daring to look at him. Nothing mattered but getting away. There was no place to go. That did not matter, either. Above Fort Gates he would cross the river on the ferry. His plans became clear. He was headed for Jacksonville. He was going to Boston. He would find Oliver Hutto in Boston and go to sea with him, leaving his betrayal behind him, as Oliver had done.

The best way to get to Jacksonville and Boston was by boat. He had better get on the river itself at once. He needed a boat. He remembered Nellie Ginright's discarded dug-out, in which he and Penny had crossed Salt Springs Run on the hunt for old Slewfoot. At thought of his father, a sharp knife struck his cold numbness, then the wound froze over again. He would tear his shirt in strips and stuff the cracks of the dug-out and pole down the creek to Lake George, then north down the big river. Somewhere along it he would hail a passing steamer and go to Boston. Oliver would pay his fare when he got there. If he could not find him, they would put him in jail. That did not matter, either.

He turned in at Salt Springs. He was thirsty and waded out in the shallow water and bent and drank from the bubbling spring. Mullet jumped nearby and blue crabs scuttled sideways. Below the spring a fisherman was setting out. Jody walked along the bank and called to him.

"Kin I go down with you a piece to my boat?"

"I reckon."

The fisherman swung in to shore and he stepped in.

The man asked, "You live around here?"

He shook his head.

"Where's your boat at?"

"Down past Mis' Nellie Ginright's."

"You kin to her?"

He shook his head. Questions from a stranger were probes in his wounds. The man looked at him curiously, then gave himself to his rowing. The rough boat moved smoothly down the swift current. The run was broad at its upper reaches. The water was blue and the March sky over it was blue. A light wind stirred the white clouds. It was the kind of day he had always liked particularly. The banks were of a rosy red, for the swamp maple and the red-bud were in full spring color Swamp laurel was in bloom and its sweetness filled the creek. An ache choked him, so that he wanted to put his hand to his throat and tear it out. The beauty of the late March day held only pain to hurt him. He did not want to look at the new-needled cypresses. He watched the water and the garfish and the turtles and did not lift his eyes again.

The fisherman said, "Here's Mis' Nellie's place. You want to stop?"

He shook his head.

"My boat's on yonder."

As they passed the bluff, he saw Mis' Nellie standing in front of her house. The fisherman lifted his hand to her and she waved. Jody did not stir. He remembered the night in her house and the morning when she had cooked breakfast and had joked with Penny, and sent them on their way feeling warm and strong and friendly. He pushed the memory aside. The run narrowed. The banks came close and there were swamp and cat-tails.

He said, "Yonder's my boat."

"Why, boy, hit's half-sunk."

"I aim to fix it."

"You got ary one comin' to he'p you? You got oars?"

He shook his head.

"Here's a piece of a paddle. Shore don't look like much of a boat to me. Well, so long."

The man pushed out into the current and waved to the boy. He took a biscuit and a piece of meat from a box under the board seat and began cramming them in his mouth as he moved away. The odor of the food came to Jody. It reminded him that he had had nothing to eat in two days except the few mouthfuls of smoked bear meat and the few kernels of dried corn. That did not matter. He was not hungry.

He pulled the dug-out on land and bailed it. Long immersion had swelled it, and the bottom was tight. There were cracks in the bow that let in water. He tore the sleeves from his shirt and ripped them in strips and caulked the cracks. He went to a pine and scraped resin with his pocket knife and worked it in on the outside.

He pushed the dug-out into the stream and picked up the broken paddle and began to paddle downstream. He was clumsy at it and the current took him from one bank to the other. He landed in sawgrass and cut his hands trying to push through it. The dug-out swung sideways and stuck in the soft muck along the south bank. He pushed free. The trick of it began to come to him, but he felt weak and faint. He wished that he had asked the fisherman to wait for him. There was nothing living in sight except a buzzard, wheeling in the blue sky. The buzzards would find Flag by the pool in the sinkhole. He began to be sick again and let the boat drift among the cat-tails. He rested his head on his knees until the nausea passed.

He stiffened and began paddling. He was on his way to Boston. His mouth was tight. His eyes were narrowed. The sun was well down in the sky when he came to the end of the run. The creek emptied at once into a broad bay of big Lake George. A spit of dry land extended a little distance to the south. On the opposite side there was only swamp. He turned the dug-out and swung up to the land, stepped out and pulled the boat high. He sat down under a live oak and leaned against the trunk and stared out to the open waters. He had hoped that he might encounter a river boat at the end of the run. He saw one passing south, but it was far out in the lake. He realized that the end of the creek must join only an arm or bay.

It was no more than an hour or two until sunset. He was afraid to let dark find him on the open lake waters in the unsteady canoe. He decided to wait on the point of land for a passing boat. If none came, he would sleep under the live oak and paddle farther in the morning. Numbness had held off his thoughts all day. Now they poured in on him, as the wolves had poured in to the calf-pen. They tore him, so that it seemed to him that he must, invisibly, be bleeding, as Flag had bled. Flag was dead. He would never run to him again. He tortured himself with saying the words.

"Flag's dead."

They were as bitter as alum-root tea.

He had not yet probed the deepest pain.

He said aloud, "Pa went back on me."

It was a sharper horror than if Penny had died of the snake-bite. He rubbed his knuckles over his forehead. Death could be borne. Fodder-wing had died and he was able to bear it. Betrayal was intolerable. If Flag had died, if bear or wolf or panther had slipped in on him, he would have grieved with a great grief, but he could have endured it. He would have turned to his father, and his father would have comforted him. Without Penny, there was no comfort anywhere. The solid earth had dissolved under him. His bitterness absorbed his sorrow, and they were one.

The sun dropped below the tree-tops. He gave up hope of hailing any vessel before night. He gathered moss and made a bed for himself at the base of the oak tree. A bittern cried rustily in the swamp across the run, and as the sun set, the frogs began to croak and sing. He had always liked the sound of their music, coming from the sink-hole at home. The cry they were making now was mournful. He hated it. They seemed to be grieving. Thousands of them were crying out in an endless and unappeasable sorrow. A wood-duck called, and its cry, too, was sad.

The lake was rosy, but shadows had taken over the land. It would be supper-time at home. In spite of his nausea, he thought now of food. His stomach began to ache as though there was too much in it, instead of nothing. He remembered the smell of the fisherman's meat and biscuit. His mouth watered. He ate some stalks of grass. He ripped the joints with his teeth, as animals ripped flesh. Instantly he saw creatures creeping in to Flag's carcass. He vomited the grass.

Darkness filled both land and water. A hoot owl cried in the thicket near him. He shivered. The night wind stirred and was chill. He heard a rustling that might be leaves moving ahead of the wind, or small creatures passing. He was not afraid. It seemed to him that if a bear came, or a panther, he might touch it and stroke it and it would understand his grief. Yet the night sounds about him made his flesh creep. It would be good to have a camp-fire. Penny could start a fire even without his tinder-horn, in the way the Indians did, but he had never been able to do it. If Penny were here, there would be a blazing fire, and warmth and food and comfort. He was not afraid. He was only desolate. He pulled the moss over him and cried himself to sleep.

The sun awakened him, and the red-winged blackbirds chattering in the reeds. He stood up and pulled the long strands of moss from his hair and clothing. He was weak and dizzy. Now that he was rested, he knew that he was hungry. The thought of food was torture. Cramps struck like small hot knives across his stomach. He thought of paddling back up the run to Mis' Nellie Ginright and asking her to feed him. But she would ask him questions. She would ask him why he was here alone, and there was no answer, except that his father had betrayed him, and in the betrayal, Flag was dead. It would be better to go on, as he had planned.

A fresh wave of loneliness swept over him. He had lost Flag and he had lost his father, too. The gaunt little man he had last seen crouched in pain in the kitchen doorway, calling for help to stand, was a stranger. He pushed out his dug-out and took up his paddle and headed for the open waters. He was out in the world, and it seemed to him that he was alien here, and alone, and that he was being carried away into a void. He paddled for the location where he had seen the steamer pass. Living was no longer the grief behind him, but the anxiety ahead. Leaving the mouth of the creek behind him, he found the wind freshening. Out from the shelter of the land a brisk breeze was blowing. He ignored the gnawing in his belly and paddled desperately. The wind caught the dug-out and slewed it around. He could not keep it headed. The waves were mounting. Their soft lapping changed to a hissing. They began to break over the bow of the canoe. When it swung sideways, they washed in and it tipped and rolled. There was an inch of water across the bottom. There was no vessel of any sort in sight.

He looked back. The shore had receded alarmingly. Ahead of him, the open water seemed to stretch without an end. He turned about in a panic and paddled madly for the shore. It would be best, after all, to go back up the creek and get help from Mis' Nellie Ginright. It might be better even to walk to Fort Gates and make his way from there. The wind behind him helped him, and it seemed to him that he could feel the north-bound current of the great river. He headed for an opening that must be the end of the Salt Springs run. When he reached it, it was a blind opening in the shore that led only into swamp. The mouth of the run was nowhere to be found.

He was trembling from his exertion and from his fear. He told himself that he was not lost, for the river ran north out of Lake George and came at the end to Jacksonville, and he had only to follow it. But it was so wide, and the shore line was so confusing— He rested a long time, then began to paddle slowly north, close to the thick-cypressed land, following the endless curves and bays and indentations. The gnawing in his stomach was an acute pain. He began to have a feverish vision of the usual Baxter table. He saw slices of ham steaming, brown and dripping in their own juice. He smelled the sweet savor. He saw tawny biscuits and dark-crusted cornbread and swimming bowls of cow-peas, with squares of white bacon floating among them. He smelled fried squirrel so definitely that the saliva ran in his mouth. He tasted the warm foam of Trixie's milk. He could have fought with the dogs for their pan of cold grits and gravy.

This, then, was hunger. This was what his mother had meant when she had said, "We'll all go hongry." He had laughed, for he had thought he had known hunger, and it was faintly pleasant. He knew now that it had been only appetite. This was another thing. The thing was terrifying. It had a great maw to envelop him and claws that raked across his vitals. He fought off a new panic. He would soon reach a cabin or a fisherman's camp, he told himself. He would beg food shamelessly before continuing. No man refused another rations.

He worked his way north along the shore line all day. In the late afternoon he was sick at his stomach from the heat of the sun, but there was nothing to vomit but the river water he had drunk. A cabin showed ahead among trees and he pulled in to it hopefully. It was deserted. He prowled inside, like a hungry 'coon or 'possum. There were cans on a dusty shelf, but all were empty. In a jar he found a cupful of musty flour. He mixed it with water and ate the paste. It was flavorless, even in his hunger, but it stopped the pain in his stomach. There were birds and squirrels in the trees and he tried to hit them with stones, but he only drove them all away. He was feverish and exhausted and the flour in his belly made him sleepy. The cabin offered shelter, and he made a pallet of some rags, from which the roaches scurried. He slept a drugged, nightmare-ridden sleep.

In the morning he was again conscious of acute hunger, and the cramps were sharp-nailed fingers that twisted his entrails. He found some last year's acorns that the squirrels had buried and ate them so ravenously that the hard, unchewed pieces were fresh knives in his contracting stomach. A lethargy settled on him, and he could scarcely force himself to take up his paddle. If the current had not been with him, he decided he could have gone no farther. He covered only a short distance during the morning. In the afternoon, three boats passed in mid-stream. He stood up and waved his arms and shouted.

They paid no attention to his cries. When they had passed from sight, he was torn unwillingly with sobbing. He decided to cut out away from the shore to intercept the next vessel. The wind had died. The water was calm. The glare from it burned his face and neck and bare arms. The sun was scalding. His head throbbed. Black spots alternated before his eyes with bobbing golden balls. A thin humming whined in his ears. The humming snapped.

All that he knew when he opened his eyes was that it was dark and he was being lifted up.

A man's voice said, "He ain't drunk. It's a boy."

Another said, "Lay him in the bunk there. He's sick. Tie his dug-out on behind."

Jody looked up. He lay in a bunk on what must be the mail-boat. A lamp flickered on the wall. A man leaned over him.

"What's the matter, young un? We near about run you down in the dark."

He tried to answer but his lips were swollen.

A voice called from above, "Try him on somethin' to eat."

"You hungry, boy?"

He nodded. The boat was now in motion. The man in the cabin clattered at the galley-stove. Jody saw a thick cup thrust in front of him. He lifted his head and clutched at it. The cup held cold soup, thick and greasy. For a mouthful or two it had no taste at all. Then the saliva ran in his mouth and his whole being reached out for it, and he bolted it so ravenously that he choked on bits of meat and potato.

The man said curiously, "How long since you et?"

"I don't know."

"Hey, Cap, the young un don't even know when he et last."

"Give him plenty but feed him slow. Don't give him too much or he'll puke in my bunk."

The cup came back again, and biscuits with it. He tried to control himself, but he trembled when the man waited too long between feedings. The third cupful tasted infinitely better than the first, then further food was refused him.

The man said, "Where'd you come from?"

A languor crept over him. He breathed deeply. The swinging lamp drew his eyes back and forth. He closed them. He dropped into a sleep as deep as the river.

He was awakened by the stopping of the small steamer. He thought for a moment that he was in the dug-out, drifting with the current. He got to his feet and rubbed his eyes. He looked at the galley-stove and remembered the soup and biscuits. The ache in his stomach was gone. He climbed the few steps to the open deck. Day was breaking. The mail sack was being lowered to a landing. He recognized Volusia. The captain turned to him.

"You had a close call, young feller. Now what did you say your name was, and where do you think you're goin'?"

"I was headin' for Boston," he said.

"You know where Boston lies? So far north it'd take you the rest of your life to get there, the way you was travelin'."

Jody stared.

"Hurry up, now. This is a gov'ment boat. I can't wait on you all day. Where you live?"

"Baxter's Island."

"Never heard of no Baxter's Island in this river."

The mate spoke up.

" 'Tain't a real island, Cap. It's a place off in the scrub. 'Bout fifteen miles up the road from here."

"Then you want to get off here, boy. Boston? Hell. You got folks?"

Jody nodded.

"They know where you was goin'?"

He shook his head.

"Runnin' away, eh? Well, if I was a scrawny little bigeyed booger like you, I'd stay home. Nobody but your folks'll bother with a little ol' shirt-tail boy like you. Swing him down to the dock, Joe."

Brawny arms lifted him down.

"Turn his dug-out a-loose. Catch it, boy. Let's go."

The whistle blew. The side-wheels churned. The mail-boat chugged up-stream. The wake boiled after her. A stranger lifted the mail sack and slung it over his shoulder. Jody crouched on his heels, holding the bow of the dug-out. The stranger glanced at him and walked away toward Volusia with the mail. The first rays of the sun lay on the river. Alligator lilies on the far bank caught them like white cups. The current tugged at the dug-out. His arm was tired, holding it. The stranger's footsteps faded up the road. There was no place left to go, but Baxter's Island.

He dropped into the canoe and took up his paddle. He paddled across to the west shore. He tethered the dug-out to a stake. He looked back across the river. The rising sun lay on the charred ruins of the Hutto house. His throat tightened. The world had discarded him. He turned and walked slowly up the road. He was weak, and conscious again of hunger, but the night's food had renewed him. The nausea was gone, and the pain.

He walked west without plan. There was no other direction in which to go. Baxter's Island drew him like a magnet. There was no reality but the clearing. He trudged on. He wondered if he dared go home. Probably they would not want him. He had caused them a great deal of trouble. Perhaps if he walked into the kitchen, his mother would drive him out as she had driven Flag. He was no good to anybody. He had prowled and played and eaten recklessly. They had put up with his impudence and his appetite. And Flag had destroyed the better part of the year's living. Almost certainly, they would feel they were better off without him, and he would not be welcome.

He loitered along the road. The sun was strong. The winter

was over. He thought hazily that it must now be April. Spring had taken over the scrub, and the birds were mating and singing in the bushes. Only he, in all the world, was homeless. He had been out in the world, and the world was a troubled dream, fluid and desolate, flanked by swamps and cypresses. He stopped to rest in mid-morning at the intersection of the main road and the north road. The low vegetation here was open to the heat of the sun. His head began to ache and he got to his feet and headed north toward Silver Glen. He told himself that he did not mean to go home. He would only go to the spring, and go down between the cool dark banks, and lie a little while in the running water. The north road dipped and rose and dipped again. The sand was scalding under his bare feet. The sweat ran down the grime of his face. At the top of a rise, he could look down and see Lake George far below him to the east. It was pitilessly blue. Thin white lines were the implacable choppy waves that had turned him back to the unfriendly shore. He trudged on.

To the east, the vegetation became luxuriant. There was water near. He turned down the trail to Silver Glen. The steep bank dropped to the ribbon of creek that ran south of the great spring itself, and had a kindred source. He ached in all his bones. He was so thirsty that his tongue seemed glued to the roof of his mouth. He stumbled down the bank and fell flat beside the cool shallow water and drank. The water bubbled over his lips and nose. He drank until his belly was swollen. He felt sickened and rolled over on his back and closed his eyes. The nausea passed and he was drowsy. He lay in a stupor of weariness. He hung suspended in a timeless space. He could go neither forward nor back. Something was ended. Nothing was begun.

In the late afternoon, he roused. He sat up. An early magnolia blossom was wax-white over him.

He thought, " 'Tis April."

A memory stirred him. He had come here a year ago, on a bland and tender day. He had splashed in the creek water and lain, as now, among the ferns and grasses. Something had been fine and lovely. He had built himself a flutter-mill. He rose and moved with a quickening of his pulse to the location. It seemed to him that if he found it, he would discover with it all the other things that had vanished. The flutter-mill was gone. The flood had washed it away, and all its merry turning.

He thought stubbornly, "I'll build me another."

He cut twigs for the supports, and the roller to turn across them, from the wild cherry tree. He whittled feverishly. He cut strips from a palmetto frond and made his paddles. He sunk the up-rights in the stream bed and set the paddles turning. Up, over, down. Up, over, down. The flutter-mill was turning. The silver water dripped. But it was only palmetto strips brushing the water. There was no magic in the motion. The flutter-mill had lost its comfort.

He said, "Play-dolly——"

He kicked it apart with one foot. The broken bits floated down the creek. He threw himself on the ground and sobbed bitterly. There was no comfort anywhere.

There was Penny. A wave of homesickness washed over him so that it was suddenly intolerable not to see him. The sound of his father's voice was a necessity. He longed for the sight of his stooped shoulders as he had never, in the sharpest of his hunger, longed for food. He clambered to his feet and up the bank and began to run down the road to the clearing, crying as he ran. His father might not be there. He might be dead. With the crops ruined, and his son gone, he might have packed up in despair and moved away and he would never find him.

He sobbed, "Pa— Wait for me."

The sun was setting. He was in a panic that he would not reach the clearing before dark. He exhausted himself, and was obliged to slow down to a walk. His flesh quivered. His heart pounded. He had to stop entirely and rest. Darkness overtook him half a mile from home. Even in the dusk, landmarks were familiar. The tall pines of the clearing were recognizable, blacker than the creeping night. He came to the slat fence. He felt his way along it. He opened the gate and went into the yard. He passed around the side of the house to the kitchen stoop and stepped up on it. He crept to the window on bare silent feet and peered in.

A fire burned low on the hearth. Penny sat hunched beside it, wrapped in quilts. One hand covered his eyes. Jody went to the door and unlatched it and stepped inside. Penny lifted his head.

"Ory?"

"Hit's me."

He thought his father had not heard him.

"Hit's Jody."

Penny turned his head and looked at him wonderingly, as though the gaunt ragged boy with sweat and tear-streaks down the grime, with hollow eyes under matted hair, were some stranger of whom he expected that he state his business.

He said, "Jody."

Jody dropped his eyes.

"Come close."

He went to his father and stood beside him. Penny reached out for his hand and took it and turned it over and rubbed it slowly between his own. Jody felt drops on his hand like a warm rain.

"Boy— I near about give you out."

Penny felt along his arm. He looked up at him.

"You all right?"

He nodded.

"You all right— You ain't dead nor gone. You all right." A light filled his face. "Glory be."

It was unbelievable, Jody thought. He was wanted.

He said, "I had to come home."

"Why, shore you did."

"I ain't meant what I said. Hatin' you——"

The light broke into the familiar smile.

"Why, shore you ain't. 'When I was a child, I spake as a child.'"

Penny stirred in his chair.

"They's rations in the safe. In the kittle there. You hongry?"

"I ain't et but oncet. Last night."

"Not but oncet? Then now you know. Ol' Starvation—" His eyes shone in the firelight as Jody had pictured them. "Ol' Starvation—he's got a face meaner'n ol' Slewfoot, ain't he?"

"Hit's fearful."

"There's biscuits there. Open the honey. There's due to be milk in the gourd."

Jody fumbled among the dishes. He ate standing, wolfing down the food. He dipped into a dish of cooked cow-peas with his fingers, scooping them into his mouth. Penny stared at him.

He said, "I'm sorry you had to learn it that-a-way."

"Where's Ma?"

"She's drove the wagon to the Forresters to trade for seed-corn. She figgered she'd try to plant a part of a crop agin. She carried the chickens, to trade. It hurted her pride turrible, but she was obliged to go."

Jody closed the door of the cabinet.

He said, "I should of washed. I'm awful dirty."

"There's warm water on the hearth."

Jody poured water in the basin and scrubbed his face and arms and hands. The water was too dark even for his feet. He threw it out of the door and poured more, and sat on the floor and washed his feet.

Penny said, "I'd be proud to know where you been."

"I been on the river. I aimed to go to Boston."

"I see."

He looked small and shrunken inside the quilts.

Jody said, "How you makin' it, Pa? You better?"

Penny looked a long time into the embers on the hearth.

He said, "You jest as good to know the truth. I ain't scarcely wuth shootin'."

Jody said, "When I git the work done, you got to leave me go fetch ol' Doc to you."

Penny studied him.

He said, "You've done come back different. You've takened a punishment. You ain't a yearlin' no longer. Jody——"

"Yes, sir."

"I'm goin' to talk to you, man to man. You figgered I went back on you. Now there's a thing ever' man has got to know. Mebbe you know it a'ready. 'Twa'n't only me. 'Twa'n't only your yearlin' deer havin' to be destroyed. Boy, life goes back on you."

Jody looked at his father. He nodded.

Penny said, "You've seed how things goes in the world o' men. You've knowed men to be low-down and mean. You've seed ol' Death at his tricks. You've messed around with ol' Starvation. Ever' man wants life to be a fine thing, and a easy. 'Tis fine, boy, powerful fine, but 'tain't easy. Life knocks a man down and he gits up and it knocks him down agin. I've been uneasy all my life."

His hands worked at the folds of the quilt.

"I've wanted life to be easy for you. Easier'n 'twas for me. A man's heart aches, seein' his young uns face the world. Knowin' they got to git their guts tore out, the way his was tore. I wanted to spare you, long as I could. I wanted you to frolic with your yearlin'. I knowed the lonesomeness he eased for you. But ever' man's lonesome. What's he to do then? What's he to do when he gits knocked down? Why, take it for his share and go on."

Jody said, "I'm 'shamed I runned off."

Penny sat upright.

He said, "You're near enough growed to do your choosin'. Could be you'd crave to go to sea, like Oliver. There's men seems made for the land, and men seems made for the sea. But I'd be proud did you choose to live here and farm the clearin'. I'd be proud to see the day when you got a well dug, so's no woman here'd be obliged to do her washin' on a seepage hillside. You willin'?"

"I'm willin'."

"Shake hands."

He closed his eyes. The fire on the hearth had burned to embers. Jody banked them with the ashes, to assure live coals in the morning.

Penny said, "Now I'll need some he'p, gittin' to the bed. Looks like your Ma's spendin' the night."

Jody put his shoulder under him and Penny leaned heavily on it. He hobbled to his bed. Jody drew the quilt over him.

"Hit's food and drink to have you home, boy. Git to bed and git your rest. 'Night."

The words warmed him through.

" 'Night, Pa."

He went to his room and closed the door. He took off his tattered shirt and breeches and climbed in under the warm quilts. His bed was soft and yielding. He lay luxuriously, stretching his legs. He must be up early in the morning, to milk the cow and bring in wood and work the crops. When he worked them, Flag would not be there to play about with him. His father would no longer take the heavy part of the burden. It did not matter. He could manage alone.

He found himself listening for something. It was the sound of the yearling for which he listened, running around the house or stirring on his moss pallet in the corner of the bedroom. He would never hear him again. He wondered if his mother had thrown dirt over Flag's carcass, or if the buzzards had cleaned it. Flag— He did not believe he should ever again love anything, man or woman or his own child, as he had loved the yearling. He would be lonely all his life. But a man took it for his share and went on.

In the beginning of his sleep, he cried out, "Flag!"

It was not his own voice that called. It was a boy's voice. Somewhere beyond the sink-hole, past the magnolia, under the live oaks, a boy and a yearling ran side by side, and were gone forever.